THE LESOTHO DIAMOND

AN AFRICAN HISTORICAL ROMANTIC SUSPENSE

A WINGS OVER AFRICA NOVEL
BOOK TWO

B. G. NETTELTON

MAP OF SOUTH AFRICA AND LESOTHO

This story is set in the early 1960s, a time of profound change for the British Crown Colony of **Basutoland**. While this was the formal name used on maps and by colonial authorities, the Basotho people, along with those in the growing independence movement, referred to their nation by its true Sesotho name: **Lesotho** (pronounced *Le-soo-too*). The choice of which name a character uses—the colonial 'Basutoland' or the nationalist 'Lesotho'—often reflects their identity during this pivotal time.

This transition from colony to kingdom was not just a matter of politics; for my family, it was written into our very names. I was born just days after the country's first General Elections in April 1965 and was given the Sesotho name **'Malikhetho**, meaning *Mother of Elections*. My sister's birth was similarly tied to the nation's destiny. She arrived a few days after the Independence celebrations of October 4, 1966, and was named **'Maboipuso**, or *Mother of Independence*.

It was a fitting tribute, as my father, Spencer "Ted" Nettelton, was the man responsible for organising those very celebrations.

CHAPTER
ONE

CAPE TOWN, 1961

6PM!

Where was Matthew?

Philippa, still dressed only in her cream silk slip, craned her head out of the top-floor dormitory window, leaning into the cool evening air. Far below, the red terracotta roofs of Fuller Hall's lower wings spread out, catching the last rays of sun as she scanned the long, curved driveway that led up to Cape Town University's women's residence.

Taking a deep breath to quell the familiar flutter in her heart that always preceded large social gatherings, she managed a smile for her roommate, Susan, who joined her at the window.

"Be honest now—are you in love with Matthew or just that sports car of his?" Susan's voice carried a hint of mockery as they both shielded their eyes from the late afternoon sun, now glinting off the sleek green MG that had finally appeared at the entrance to the avenue.

Against the grandeur of Table Mountain's backdrop, the sports car appeared diminutive, but Philippa Tremain had grown up amid even more impressive peaks in neighbouring Basutoland. The view from their window, sweeping over the manicured lawns of the university and across the suburbs to the shimmering ocean, was more of a novelty. She hoped that after Angela's party that night, Matthew might propose a visit to the beautiful... romantic... beach.

"The sports car, silly!" Philippa pretended to play along as she turned, reaching for the burnt-orange, full-skirted evening dress draped over her desk chair. "Promise you won't tell Matthew, though. Now, won't you help me into this? I should have been ready ages ago."

"The orange is so daring, but it contrasts beautifully with your dark hair. Honestly, Matthew doesn't deserve you." Susan sighed as she followed Philippa to the small mirror near the door. "And he's always late," she added as she zipped up Philippa's dress, her tone no longer light-hearted. "You know, it wouldn't hurt to make him wait now and then."

Ignoring her, Philippa pulled on her elbow-length gloves and smoothed her sleek chignon before twirling around. "How do I look?" Her confidence was wavering, wracked with sudden nerves.

"Not bad." Susan grinned as she turned to focus on her own reflection in the little mirror above the basin, helping herself to Philippa's new Revlon mascara. "But you know that."

"Come on, Susan, what do you really think?" Philippa's heart fluttered dangerously, and for a moment, she thought she might be ill. Matthew's approval mattered more than she cared to admit to Susan, who always expressed such disdain for her new boyfriend.

Surely Philippa could call him that after five weeks of exclusive dating?

Susan darkened her sandy lashes before turning back to Philippa with another sigh. "Are you asking me if Matthew will approve? Of course he will. You're stunning—and this year's Rag Queen!" she said, and Philippa wondered if that was jealousy she detected.

Poor Susan was not a beauty, it was generally acknowledged, with her sandy hair more frizzy than curly and her freckled face. But the two girls had been friends for as long as Philippa could remember—neighbours and schoolmates —both of them travelling the thousand miles from Mokhotlong in the African mountain kingdom of Basutoland where they'd grown up, to begin university in the exciting, cosmopolitan city of Cape Town on South Africa's southern tip, where the Atlantic and Indian Oceans met in a swirl of currents beneath the watchful gaze of Table Mountain.

Susan continued applying her makeup before glancing out of the window, saying in that faux-surprise tone that generally irked Philippa, "Well, the young man is ready to escort you to the party at last, you'll be happy to know, though it seems Eliza has captured his attention. He hasn't even got out of his car. Maybe I will be ready in time to go with both of you to the party." She hesitated, adding, "Except—I forgot!—there's only room for two in his MG."

Philippa, who'd been ready to dash out the door to greet her beloved, hesitated as she put her hand on the door handle, remembering Susan's words from last week:

Matthew Myburgh is rich and entitled. He'll play with your heart and then trample on it.

Was Susan really jealous? Did she truly feel Philippa had prioritised her budding relationship with Matthew at the expense of their friendship?

Hesitating, she spun around on her elegant new kitten heels. "Oh, Susan, I completely forgot!" she said, dashing over to the chest of drawers at the foot of her bed. "I meant to give you this to wear with your blue chiffon dress."

Susan frowned at the white silk scarf Philippa held out. "I might spill something on it," she said, her tone more churlish than grateful.

"That wouldn't matter since I'm giving it to you." Philippa tried not to let Susan's tone rankle. Susan hadn't always been the most gracious of playmates since their days of playing with dolls. But it was thanks to Philippa's beautiful, kind late mother that Philippa now saw this as reflective of Susan's own perceived inadequacies rather than ingratitude.

"All right then. If you think my blue chiffon needs something extra," Susan said, reaching for the scarf while Philippa, anxious to be gone, nervously smoothed the lovely burnt-orange creation her talented mother had made for her nineteenth birthday nearly two years before. She turned the doorknob and smiled at Susan. "See you at the party, then."

Susan nodded as she stroked the white silk scarf she'd openly admired when Philippa had received it from her father for her last birthday. "Just make sure Matthew takes you to Angela's and doesn't whisk you off to see the whales instead," she said to Philippa's departing back. "You know how unpredictable Matthew is, and you know how much I hate parties when you're not there to help me talk to people."

"MATTHEW!" Philippa greeted him with a smile, forcing herself to slow her pace as she descended the last few wide stone steps of the residence entrance; forcing herself to remember the poise drilled into her at finishing school while she curved her lips the way her mother, a celebrated English beauty, had shown her for such situations: welcoming, but not overenthusiastic.

Matthew Myburgh might be rich, but Philippa's mother had been one of the Richmond sisters, featured in magazines throughout the thirties and forties, famed for their ivory skin, lustrous dark hair, and violet eyes.

And their propensity for marrying into the aristocracy.

Except for Eleanor Richmond, Philippa's mother. The black sheep of the family. Arguably the most beautiful of the three girls, and certainly the most wilful, Eleanor had been disowned when she'd eloped with a Colonial to live in the tiny mountainous kingdom of Basutoland just six months before Philippa had been born.

The scandal had been enormous. The sacrifice, greater still. Eleanor had given up wealth, position, and family for love—a choice Philippa had never fully understood, having grown up craving the glamorous life her mother had abandoned.

Still, Philippa's family could hold their own, she reminded herself as she assessed Matthew's handsome tousled head and muscled torso from the other side of his sports car as he chatted with his rugby mate, Hugh, and Hugh's girlfriend, Eliza.

Square-jawed, blue-eyed and fair-haired, Matthew had the Adonis good looks that made the girls either tongue-tied in his presence, or over-talkative. Philippa fell into the latter category, though she'd worked hard lately to emulate those sultry, dark-haired beauties of the screen who made more impact by being silent and enigmatic.

"Philippa! Sorry I'm late!" Matthew looked up from his conversation as Hugh farewelled him with a salute and a 'good luck' for their rugby match the following day.

His white teeth gleamed as he came round from the driver's side to greet her.

Why did his smile always make her knees feel weak? Literally, weak. And why did it also stir something uneasy in her chest—a quiet voice that whispered this was too easy, too perfect?

Because, really, the last five weeks with Matthew lavishing her with his company had been more than she could have dreamed of.

Except that, right now, this was not acceptable—

Interpreting her frown, Matthew gave a sheepish glance at his filthy rugby jersey and mud-stained shorts. "I got caught up at rugby practice."

"Philippa! Your father's on the phone!" Susan's voice floated down from an open window above the portico.

Philippa ignored her. "But, Matthew... the party starts in ten minutes."

"Philippa! It's long distance!"

"And it'll only take me ten minutes to get changed." Matthew's tone was soothing.

No, it won't. Philippa didn't need to put that into words. She managed a shaky smile, though she felt like stamping her foot or crying as she stepped back from his approach.

"Come on, darling, don't give me that cross look," he said, attempting to kiss her.

"I'll kiss you when you won't get mud on my dress," grumbled Philippa, remembering all the disdainful things

Susan had said about him. As usual, Matthew expected Philippa to forgive him.

Yet the things Susan said were true. Many of them, anyway. Matthew was always late. And he did always expect her to forgive him.

Should she stop making so many allowances if he was to respect her?

"Tell Daddy I'm coming now!" she shouted back to Susan. Turning on her heel, she said in clipped tones over her shoulder to Matthew, now lounging against the spotless green paintwork of his car, "I'll see you at the party, later. Daddy's probably waited an hour to get put through. I wouldn't dream of keeping *him* waiting."

No doubt the irony was wasted on Matthew, she thought, as she marched back up the grand steps, past the heavy oak doors, ignoring Susan's enquiring look and settling herself on a chair in the corridor by the communal telephone. The scent of floor polish and old wood filled the hallway.

"Sorry I took so long, Daddy," she said, picking up the receiver Susan had left hanging by its cord, and trying to sound cheerful. "Everyone's in a mad rush here. We're off to Angela Myers's twenty-first birthday. How are things in the mountains?"

Philippa's father's role as District Commissioner in Mokhotlong—known also as the British Empire's remotest outpost at 10,000 feet amidst the rocky peaks—required a broad repertoire of skills. Philippa never knew whether he was currently investigating illegal diamond trading or culturally sanctioned 'medicine' murder, whereby a local chief shored up his power by inducing fear amongst their villagers using the flesh of some unfortunate victim.

Using the crackling down the phone line to give her

time to calm her anger and disappointment over Matthew's behaviour, she waited for her father's response. She had done the right thing, hadn't she? Susan would be proud of her for standing up for herself and making it clear to Matthew that she wouldn't be treated with such cavalier disregard. Susan's phrase.

"... another murder last week in the Qthing district. I doubt you'd have read about it yet, but it's in the Cape Times."

Her father's voice was suddenly clear enough to understand, and Philippa drew in a quick breath. "Again? I thought the evidence was sufficient to convict. Do you think—?" She wasn't sure whether she should ask. Now that her focus was on her father's troubles, and how she could help, even by being just a sounding board, she had to tread carefully. Her father's disappointment that there'd been no justice for those responsible for the mutilation and murder of a young boy the previous year tended to make him irritable. "Do you think the same chief is responsible for this one, too?"

"It doesn't matter what I believe. Let's see what evidence turns up this time, eh?"

The line crackled once more before her father's voice returned, crisp and businesslike. "Now... I wondered if you'd thought about coming home for half term."

Philippa hesitated, reluctant to say no. Her father had been so lonely since her mother died.

"There's room on the Saturday flight from Maseru to Mokhotlong."

She cringed. Her father sounded so hopeful.

"Diana from Drakensberg Air said Mrs Vermoed just cancelled as she's staying in Durban another week. Of course, it's a long journey to make from Cape Town, but I thought I'd put it to you, nonetheless."

Philippa breathed out slowly. Mrs Myburgh was hosting a tennis party the following Saturday, and Philippa desperately hoped Matthew would invite her to the family home, a sprawling mansion in Kenilworth. Even though she was angry with him right now. She knew five weeks was early days, but such an invitation would surely be a sign that Matthew intended their relationship to be more... permanent?

"I'm so sorry, but I can't, Daddy," she said in a rush. "There are quite a few things on and... Matthew's introducing me to his parents," she lied, hating herself for the deception but knowing it was the only excuse her father would readily accept.

"Of course, of course." Her father sounded understanding, which was a relief. "And is this boy worthy of you, my darling? Mrs Lehmann asked if she'll be hearing wedding bells soon."

Philippa tried for a light-hearted laugh. "We've only been seeing each other for a few weeks. I can't wait for you to meet him, though. Oh, and, Daddy! He said he'd love to go on trek if you had something interesting that coincides with the end of term." Another half-truth—Matthew had expressed vague interest when she'd mentioned her father's work, but nothing committal.

"I'm sure that could be arranged. As long as he can stay on a Basuto pony for six hours at a time and isn't afraid of heights." With few roads traversing the treacherous terrain this was a requirement. Her father sounded more relaxed now. "Why don't you bring him home with you at Christmas? I'd like to reassure your dear mother that I've done my due diligence when it's my time to meet her at the pearly gates." He paused. "It's been two years, my girl. My, but you've grown up in that time. She'd be so proud."

Philippa shifted, feeling uncomfortable. She hadn't exactly distinguished herself in her academic career to date. And her mother would have considered that more important than the fact that Philippa had been chosen Cape Town University's Rag Queen and was going out with the only son of the famous Myburgh diamond dynasty.

A niggling kernel of doubt made her squirm as she went on, "Mummy would definitely have approved of not just Matthew but of Mrs Myburgh, too. Or at least, her dress sense." She laughed to diffuse the tension. "Mrs Myburgh was in the social columns of Saturday's Argus and this month's Fair Lady Magazine."

There was more crackling before their connection resumed.

Then Philippa heard, "Well, good for her. Now, if you've got a party to go to, I won't keep you talking."

"It's all right. Matthew—" She hesitated. "Matthew was held up after rugby, so I'll see him at the party later. Tell me more about the investigation. What you're allowed to, anyway." Despite her focus on Cape Town society, Philippa couldn't deny the pull of her father's world—the mysteries and challenges of colonial administration that had formed the backdrop of her childhood.

"You have your mother's tact," her father remarked. "Well, for one thing, it means long days for me. And for the police troopers. They're doing an excellent job, as they did last time. Don't envy the poor fellows. The resident commissioner wants the preliminary report on his desk by next week. And then Stuart's flying me up to Letseng-la-Terai tomorrow. The miners were snowed in last week."

"Stuart, the pilot? I thought he went back to England." Philippa felt a quickening of interest despite herself.

"For his mother's funeral. He returned to Maseru on the first of this month." He chuckled. "I wondered if you'd ask. You had quite the schoolgirl crush on him, if I recall. I have no doubt the Lehmanns and Oosthuysen were all involved in making sure he was rostered to fly you out to St Anne's each term."

"Oh, Daddy, that was when I was sixteen!" Philippa felt her cheeks burn at the memory of the taciturn English pilot with his angular jaw, rock star good looks, and piercing eyes who'd treated her with amused indulgence. "Didn't those gossips have anything better to do?" She turned at the sound of heels clicking down the stairs.

Josie, holding the arm of her latest boyfriend Frank, who played left wing with Matthew, stopped in the corridor to silently mouth an offer of a lift to the party as she pointed to Frank's car keys.

Philippa nodded vigorously.

Let Matthew go to the party on his own. She wasn't always going to be at his beck and call.

"Daddy, I have to go now." She stood up to finish the conversation. "My friends are waiting. Have a good weekend!"

"Don't you two look a sight for sore eyes?" remarked Frank gallantly as Philippa replaced the handset. "Susan got a lift with Barney," he added, offering Philippa his free arm to lead the girls down the steps towards his car.

"And Matthew's gone back to his digs to get changed. He'll meet us at Angela's." Philippa hoped she didn't sound disappointed. "That's if he doesn't fall asleep instead."

Frank flicked a wry glance at Josie. "I'd do the same if I could get away with it. I'm hardly going to be rested for tomorrow's match, am I, Josie, my girl?" He pinched her ear playfully. "Wouldn't you rather hang off the arm of a top South African rugger bugger than—?"

"You boys have never let a good party get in the way of anything," Josie interrupted as he opened the car door. "You drink yourselves stupid the night before and think you can play the hero on the rugby field the day after. And mostly you do, though don't think you can get away with it forever," she grumbled, running one hand through her pixie cut and the other down her emerald green slim-line dress.

"It's called sowing our wild oats. We can't change what nature intended. Why hurry into dull domesticity before we have to?"

Philippa decided to ignore Frank's feigned solemnity as she climbed into the car, shivering in the evening breeze.

Her shiver was from anticipation, too.

Domesticity wasn't dull if one was successful in one's career.

Mr and Mrs Myburgh were successful, and they'd got married when they were younger than Matthew and Philippa. Success was a big house with a swimming pool, parties, clothes and frequent mentions in the press.

That had been Philippa's mother's world back in England, and Philippa was sure her mother would be proud if Philippa regained what had been lost.

Not that Philippa was ashamed of how she'd been brought up, but wouldn't it be wonderful to win back the love and acceptance of her mother's estranged family? To restore the Richmond name to its former glory?

Philippa was every bit Matthew's equal, she reminded herself fiercely. And he was ready to settle down.

Even if he didn't yet know it.

FRANK TURNED onto the jacaranda-lined avenue in front of the cottage where Angela and her two university girlfriends had digs. Music spilled out onto the street and, excitedly, the girls tugged at their gloves and bit colour into their lips as they climbed out of the car.

Matthew was unlikely to have arrived, Philippa surmised, so she was happy to be waylaid by a group of admirers in the passageway where she still had a good view of the front door.

"Hey, Philippa, when are you going to go out with Tommy and put him out of his misery?" asked John, the resident clown, handing her a glass of fizz, which she downed in one go for Dutch courage.

Tommy, who was going to be a nuclear physicist, sent her a panicked look through coke-bottle horn-rimmed glasses as he flushed to the roots of his oily dark hair and disappeared into the crowd.

John roared with laughter. Brains didn't count for much in their circles. John was popular because he made people laugh, while Matthew enjoyed star billing because not only was he Adonis-handsome, and the heir to a diamond dynasty, he was their best rugby hope. Philippa knew the reason she had any sort of cachet was because she'd been Cape Town University's Rag Queen earlier that year.

And because she was Matthew's girlfriend.

"Tommy is a darling, but I can't risk breaking Matthew's heart!" Philippa responded with mock regret as John peered owlishly at her, brandishing the champagne bottle once more.

"I don't understand why you insist..." he pointed an accusing finger at her, "on going out with no-hoper

Matthew Myburgh when you could have me!" He grinned as he carelessly emptied champagne into the various upturned glasses held out towards him, unperturbed by the shrieks of those whose feet got wet in the process.

"Talking of no-hoper Matthew Myburgh, he's certainly taking his time in getting here," Philippa remarked with a pointed look at the door.

Some time later, she was shocked to hear the clock strike ten. How long had she been talking? "Matthew was only going home to change. I knew he'd fall asleep!"

"Matthew? He got here ages ago," said Tommy, re-emerging from the direction of the kitchen.

"He did?" Philippa looked about her but could see no sign of him in the press of bodies.

A few couples were jitterbugging on the Chinese rug that occupied a tiny rectangle of space amongst the party-goers and the furniture that had been pushed against the walls.

"I saw him upstairs a little while ago." He stabbed a finger in that general direction.

"Philippa... your hair! You look just like Audrey Hepburn!" came an enthusiastic voice after Philippa excused herself to weave through the throng. "And I love your dress!" Marcia Didcott, lounging upon the arm of a comfortable chair as she ruffled the curls of a young man who appeared to be asleep, raked her with an admiring look. "Where did you get it?"

"My mother made it," Philippa didn't mind confessing. Despite her father's position in the Colonial Service, there wasn't a lot of money to splash around, but her mother, who'd always liked to cut a dash, had sewed most of their evening wear. "You haven't seen Matthew, have you?"

Marcia pointed to the ceiling. "He was up there half an hour ago."

Half an hour ago?

Philippa pushed through the crowded sitting room as she made for the stairs. On the first floor, a couple with their arms wrapped about each other swayed to the mellifluous tones of a scratched Bobby Darin record someone had put on for the third time.

It was quieter up here. Philippa leaned against the wall and closed her eyes. She wished she hadn't drunk so much. The walls seemed to throb with sound, and her head spun.

"Somewhere Beyond the Sea" was the song playing.

Philippa swayed to the lyrics and felt the same longing for reunion as sung by her favourite rock 'n roll artist.

Where was Matthew? She missed him. How could he not have come looking for her? Was he punishing her for not letting him kiss her and for being cross when he was late?

Oh, why had she let Susan get into her ear? Matthew needed gentle nurturing if he was to properly appreciate Philippa and consider her for the role she so desperately wanted. She needed to remember what she was working toward—a place in society that would make her mother's family regret having cast them aside.

That's what her grandmother had said in the letter Philippa had seen in her mother's desk drawer: that Eleanor shouldn't be surprised at being cast aside by her family if she insisted on being so selfish by marrying a nobody and living like a gypsy.

A gypsy! Even two years after reading that old letter, Philippa still burned with indignation.

When the song ended, she returned to the present and opened her eyes. It was time to resume her search, the

Persian runner muting her kitten-heeled pumps as she trailed from room to room.

The first door she tried was locked.

The second bedroom was unoccupied.

Frustrated, she retraced her footsteps. Surely Matthew wouldn't have left the party without her?

Outside, a car hooted its horn. Looking towards the window behind her, Philippa noticed an alcove that hid the door to another room. The cottage was like a rabbit warren, bigger than it looked from the outside.

She knocked.

No answer. Perhaps he'd gone to sleep in here. The poor darling must be exhausted after rugby practice. Philippa shouldn't have insisted he come to the party.

"Hello?" she whispered, pushing open the door.

The room was in darkness, but the half-open curtains let in enough light from the street for her to make out movement on the bed.

"Matthew?"

There was a muffled shriek and, in the dim light, some furtive scrambling and smoothing of skirts.

It wasn't Matthew. "Sorry!" Hot with embarrassment, Philippa began to back out of the room. She was just closing the door when a familiar defensive feminine wail, "It's not what you think, Philippa!" made her flick the light switch by the door.

"Susan?"

The guilty lovers on the bed blinked owlishly, Susan smoothing her passion-spoiled chignon and straightening her blue chiffon skirts; Matthew, straightening his tie and adjusting his trousers, his gaze sliding guiltily away from Philippa's shocked face as he slid off the bed and came towards her.

"We weren't doing anything," Susan gabbled. "Really!"

"It's not what it looks like, Philippa—"

Philippa jerked her arm back as Matthew reached forward, his aftershave enveloping her like a cloud of betrayal. Tears stung the back of her eyes as she wrenched open the door behind her once more, trying to make sense of the scene.

Susan? Her best friend?

And Matthew? Her boyfriend?

"It's not what you think." Matthew pleaded innocence now, but in the harsh light, there was no mistaking the lipstick on his shirt collar and around his mouth, nor the guilt on both of their faces.

Without waiting to hear another word, Philippa spun round and ran from the room. Her careful plans, her dreams of a life with Matthew, her path back to her mother's world —all of it crumbling around her as she fled.

CHAPTER

TWO

Circling vultures had led the two herd boys to the body at the base of the ravine. Petreous, one of the oldest of the miners, regaled the crowd with the grisly news from the top of a boulder, shivering in the icy wind that howled through the diamond diggings, his cheeks growing pinker and his gestures more extravagant as his ragged listeners gasped at every detail.

Stuart gathered the victim was an albino, his ears and testicles cut away, familiar hallmarks of medicine murder or *diretlo*. After four years in Basutoland, he had a smattering of Sesotho but was having trouble understanding Petreous, whose responses reflected the fast and furious questioning of the men jostling each other on the barren ground.

He leant across to Samuel, the young police trooper he'd just flown from the lowlands into Letseng-la-Terai and who was also straining to catch the main points of Petreous's theatrical account.

"Where did they find the body? Buthe Buthe? That's the second in three weeks." As a white man, Stuart knew he was in no danger of becoming the next victim. Medicine murder was a chief's way of instilling fear into his villagers. But the administration took a dim view of what some regarded as a cultural matter outside the preserve of the Westminster justice system and Stuart knew Charles Tremain would direct his police troopers in the mountains to leave no stone unturned in their search for evidence to condemn the perpetrators.

"Quthing district," Samuel confirmed, rubbing his eyes as a handful of gritty snow swept across the barren landscape. "Tell the DC you heard it from me, *Rra*." He hoisted the box of provisions he'd brought for his two-week rotation at the diamond diggings onto his shoulder. "Ah, but it is a very bad business."

A second murder was very bad business indeed. Only that morning, Stuart had picked up Charles Tremain's preliminary report on the previous murder to deliver to the Resident Commissioner in Maseru.

"I'll make sure he knows," Stuart muttered as he squinted into the wind to look for the two passengers he was dropping off at Mokhotlong.

Not that he'd planned to break his downward journey in view of the bad weather. However, Charles had made a special request when Stuart had picked up the investigation dossier that morning. Apparently, Charles's daughter had been unwell, and her father preferred that she fly rather than take the jolting, four-hour journey by land rover down the Sani Pass.

Or perhaps it had been Philippa's idea.

Stuart hadn't seen her in years but, remembering the occasions he'd flown her to Maseru or Bloemfontein to make a rail connection to her posh boarding school, she had been what his ma would have termed 'a little madam.'

All gangly limbs and entitled attitude, with a way of looking down her nose that suggested her boarding school education had taught her to regard working-class men like him as little more than servants.

"Moeketsi!" he shouted, catching sight of the grizzle-headed miner who'd jumped at the chance to take a flight down the mountain rather than walk. It was another way to show off his new wealth following his recent celebrated find at the diggings. "We're going now, now!"

Moeketsi was cackling with a group of miners around the rocky detritus of his diamond lease. Like many, the old miner wore the traditional colourful Basuto blanket to keep out the cold.

"Eh, *Rra*!" he called back before continuing his conversation.

"Moeketsi!" Stuart shouted again as he raised his collar against the biting cold and waded through the thick snow to untie the plane. "Where's Philemon? Last call for Mokhotlong! We're leaving now!"

Obviously, there would be wild speculation amongst the miners regarding the murders, but weather waited for no one. Dark storm clouds were gathering with the speed of vultures to fresh carrion, and Stuart couldn't afford to miss this window of opportunity to be airborne if he was to make it to the Maseru Country Club at six for a drink before dinner with Lizzie Cameron.

Finally, Moeketsi left the huddle of miners and ambled across the barren landscape, grinning his gap-toothed grin. The snow had partially melted but whatever the weather, Letseng-la-Terai was a forbidding place to carve out a living.

At more than eleven thousand feet, and accessible only by a bridle path—and a dangerously short east-west runway used only sporadically—it was considered by the diamond consortiums too remote and logistically difficult for large-scale mining. In the past few years, it had become a free-for all for the local Basotho. But there'd been mixed returns for those brave and intrepid enough to register their nine-foot by four-foot leases and toil away in such spartan conditions.

Moeketsi had been there a good year, living in a makeshift tent with some tin to help keep out the cold, finding nothing until the sieving equipment for which he'd traded a dozen sheep had thrown up the sparkle that would make him a rich man.

Though whether he'd profit long-term was not a topic Stuart cared to dwell on, knowing how little financial expertise this handful of lucky miners could call upon. He'd seen it too often—fortunes won and lost within months, with nothing but regret to show for the brief prosperity.

"I think the captain must be in a big hurry," Moeketsi replied slyly as he clambered into the plane and Stuart helped him with his seat belt. "Perhaps to see a pretty lady, eh, *Rra?*"

Stuart rolled his eyes, stamping his feet to keep warm while he waited for Philemon to strap himself in.

All being well, Stuart would soon be gazing into Lizzie's cornflower blue eyes, chinking wine glasses as they listened to a blues pianist at the Maseru Country Club.

What would happen after dinner was anyone's guess.

Lizzie was contemplating a nursing position that had come up at Grey's Hospital in Pietermaritzburg, but Stuart knew he only had to ask her to stay and it would be tantamount to a marriage proposal.

A bit of warmth and companionship after his bachelor years had its appeal.

Lizzie wasn't really his type, but she was sweet and kind-hearted. And he suspected she was lonely, too. Their relationship was comfortable—perhaps too comfortable. They'd drifted into it without passion, without that spark he'd always hoped would ignite when he met the right woman. But at twenty-six, Stuart was beginning to wonder if such women existed outside film posters.

If dinner went really well and if Stuart had too much wine, he'd probably pop the question—or, at least, tell Lizzie not to take up the nursing position in South Africa, which would just about be the same thing and, he supposed, buy him a little time to save for an engagement ring. There'd been precious few marriageable young women crossing his orbit during his four years in this remote Colonial outpost.

By THE TIME he took off, the wind was still in Stuart's favour.

But his normally garrulous passengers were silent.

On the ground, the miners had passed the time of day making jokes and telling stories as if they hadn't a care in the world.

Now, Moeketsi and Philemon were tongue-tied until they levelled off. The rocky, treeless ground was far beneath them before the pair began to chatter among themselves.

With Stuart's concentration focused on the size of the storm cell he had to fly around in order to pick up the DC's daughter, he only pricked up his ears when he heard the Sesotho word for diamond—*taemane*—repeated a number of times.

Adjusting the mixture so the engine ran more smoothly,

he shouted over his shoulder, "How big was this diamond, Moeketsi?"

"Eh, *Rra*, it was a very big one!" The grizzled miner's lips parted in an almost toothless grin. "Better than gold. Diamonds are much better than gold."

Stuart presumed Moeketsi had, like so many Basotho, spent his youth working in the gold mines around Johannesburg, sending his wages back to his family.

"How big is big?"

If Moeketsi had struck it rich, then good luck to him. It was a hellish existence that not even the possibility of a diamond the size of a duck's egg could entice Stuart to swap for a fair wage, doing the flying he enjoyed. Stuart had seen enough of poverty growing up to know that no amount of money was worth sacrificing your freedom, your health, and perhaps your life.

"Big enough to make me a rich man, *Rra*!"

"So, what will you do now that you're a rich man, Moeketsi?"

Moeketsi laughed. "I will buy peacocks instead of goats to make my wife happy, and we will live in a very fine brick house."

"Look, *Rra*!" Philemon tapped on his window and pointed excitedly to a swathe of dense white precipitation in the distance. "That belongs to a very big plane, *Morena*." He was obviously familiar with the jet contrail of the BOAC 707 that sometimes tracked off course from Johannesburg on its way to London.

"But this plane can go more places," Stuart countered as he stared out at the barren ravines far below and the jagged peaks around him. It was impressive and majestic scenery, but he couldn't deny feeling envy. For four years he'd been trying to build his twin-engine time for a shot at the airlines.

Four years of flying into these remote mountain strips, battling unpredictable weather, eking out a living on the fringes. Four years of watching other pilots with less experience but more connections move on to bigger planes, better routes, proper careers. All while Stuart remained stuck in place, his dream of the airlines growing more distant with each passing season.

His friend Lawrence had reminded Stuart that he had connections, and it was true.

But Stuart was damned if he was going to swallow his pride and use them.

"Big is better," Philemon remarked sagely.

"Big is better," Moeketsi agreed, warming to his theme. "Peacocks are better than goats, says my wife. Only rich men can afford peacocks, and everyone admires a rich man. Do you have peacocks, Captain?"

Stuart snorted. "Tell your wife that peacocks are vain and difficult creatures, Moeketsi." He had to raise his voice even more above the hum of the engine, which had started to run rough. "If I had money, I'd spend it on wiser investments than pretty things to please my wife."

"I think that pleasing my wife is a very wise investment."

Stuart joined in the laughter. "I'll have to learn from that piece of wisdom."

"Why do you not have a wife, Captain?"

"I have to find myself a diamond as big as the one you found before I can afford a wife." Buying dinner for Lizzie tonight was going to make a dent in his meagre savings. Buying her an engagement ring was going to require a loan. Stuart had never owed money in his life.

Unlike his dad, he reflected with a grimace. His father had been a master at borrowing—from friends, from neighbours, from loan sharks with broken noses and scarred knuckles who would appear at their door demanding payment with interest. Stuart had sworn he'd never put himself in that position.

No, unlike his dad, he would never owe anyone anything.

"You do not need to find a big diamond, Captain. You just need to fly the big plane." Moeketsi said with a wheezy laugh. "Then you'll be rich and you can buy your wife peacocks because even if you don't want them, she will, and I am thinking that when you are married, you will learn how important it is to please your wife."

"You sound like a very wise man, Moeketsi. And if I could only fly the big plane, believe me, I would."

"The man who flies the biggest plane can afford the fattest wife, eh *Morena*?" Philemon said with a boyish giggle. "It is why my sister cannot find a husband. Too many bones. But when you fly the big plane, you can choose the biggest wife in all of Basutoland, Captain Price, and all the men will envy you."

A sudden image flashed uncomfortably into Stuart's consciousness of Rubenesque Magda Kloppings, the wife of one of the Afrikaans mining contractors. The curvaceous beauty had taken the raw, twenty-one-year-old Stuart under her wing during his first year in the country and her pillowy bosoms and syrupy koeksisters—a sweet South African delicacy—had been a buffer against the loneliness of his first six months.

"Are you looking for a wife, *Morena*? A big, beautiful wife?" Philemon asked boldly.

Magda marched into his consciousness once again.

He'd not been prepared for the sexual advances of a woman so much older than himself, but after she'd overcome Stuart's shy reluctance, she'd been a patient and diligent instructor.

But Stuart wasn't looking for a wife like Magda.

"The wife of my choice will be tall and graceful with long glossy dark hair, high cheekbones and sparkling eyes," he said, inspired by the poster plastered on his bedroom wall throughout most of his teenage years. "Unfortunately, she lives in another country, and I don't think I'd persuade her to come and live here."

"*Ach*, shame, Captain! And who might your first choice have been?" Moeketsi enquired politely.

"Audrey Hepburn."

"Then Miss Hepburn has made a great mistake if she does not wish to live in Basutoland with you, but perhaps that is not a bad thing because a big woman makes the best wife, Captain," Moeketsi said, adding with conviction, "After you are flying the big plane I am thinking you will persuade Miss Hepburn to marry you as Wife Number Two. For when she sees what a great country the new Lesotho is, she will never want to leave."

"Cold as charity, eh?" Charles Tremain called in greeting as Stuart cut the engine and leapt to the ground.

Smoking his pipe, the District Commissioner leaned on the gate that opened from the DC Residence's garden onto the airfield while, behind him, the tiny community of Mokhotlong looked like it was taking shelter against a backdrop of black mountains in anticipation of the oncoming storm.

"I never did understand that expression," Stuart remarked as he strode over the yellow grass to shake hands, tempering his impatience to get going for he'd expected to pick up the DC's daughter earlier that morning when he'd collected the documents from Charles having stopped at Mokhotlong on his way up from Maseru in the lowlands en route to the diamond diggings further up the mountain.

"Never really thought much about it." Charles shrugged, tapping out his pipe with focused concentration before raising his candid gaze to Stuart's face. As usual, he looked dapper in a carefully pressed though well-worn hounds tooth sports jacket, which made Stuart feel shabby by comparison, for his shirt was frayed around the collar, and it most certainly wasn't from Savile Row like the DC's. "I suppose the poor aren't used to warmth in general and there's more pleasure in dishing out charity than receiving it."

Stuart felt the truth of that as he glanced at the team of prisoners, in their distinctive red and white horizontal striped jerseys, tending the lush green lawns and colourful flower beds of the DC's garden behind the gate that sepa-rated it from the airfield. There hadn't been much warmth in his world with parents waging an unrelenting war against each other, which became physically violent when-ever his father came home from gaol.

Childhood memories like this had taught him to stand alone—never depend on others, never let anyone depend too much on him. It was safer that way.

"Is Philippa ready?" He blew on his hands, glancing over the DC's shoulder at the storm clouds.

"She won't be long, I'm sure. You know what women are like?"

The DC said it indulgently, which startled Stuart,

though it shouldn't have. He changed the subject. "This must be her final year at school."

"Good lord, no!" Charles choked on a laugh. "My little girl's all grown up. Second year at Cape Town University, but she decided to come home here to her poor old dad in Mokhotlong for the holidays early. Not quite sure what happened, but she's not at all her usual bright self." He removed the pipe from his mouth and tamped in a fresh wad of tobacco. "Philippa was supposed to go down the Sani Pass yesterday with the Lehmanns. She's staying with an old friend, Elizabeth, in Maseru before heading to Bloemfontein to take the train to Cape Town tomorrow. But I thought my girl would be more comfortable hitching a ride with you. The Lehmanns will be waiting for her in Bloemfontein. They're taking the same train."

"Stuart! I haven't seen you in years!"

Stuart turned at the welcome and wondered if his eyes were deceiving him. The gangly schoolgirl he used to fly to and from Bloemfontein to make her connection to her boarding school in Durban was nothing like the gorgeous, long-legged brunette smiling at him as she slipped her hand through the crook of her father's arm.

"Philippa?" Stuart clarified. He blinked, and she laughed, clearly delighted by the surprise in his tone.

"I've changed since you saw me last, haven't I? But you're just the same."

Stuart couldn't put his observations into words: that she was the most stunning woman he'd ever laid eyes on. So stunning that for a moment he forgot his manners. The awkward, entitled schoolgirl had transformed into someone who looked remarkably like his description of the perfect woman—the one he'd jokingly told Moeketsi and

Philemon about just moments ago. The coincidence was unsettling.

Taking Philippa's suitcase from the housemaid, who was bringing up the rear, he said awkwardly, "Sorry to hear you weren't well."

Philippa's lips curved, her dark blue, almost violet, eyes twinkling. She twirled a lock of hair around her finger, then tapped her chest. With an effort, Stuart concentrated on her mouth as she replied, "The cough's gone and I'm fine now. Just glad you had room to take me as I wasn't looking forward to seven hours in a land rover sitting next to Mrs Lehmann, who never stops talking."

Mrs Lehmann was well known for her garrulity. Stuart smiled before a smattering of rain made him say abruptly, "We must go before we're weathered in."

He waited as Philippa hugged first her father, then the weeping housemaid. Francina, he recalled, had been the girl's nanny since Philippa had been born.

"Don't you hate goodbyes?" Philippa asked as he helped her climb into the plane before reaching across to buckle her seat belt. "They're so hard and never get easier."

Stuart managed a grunt, which she could take however she wanted, he thought, as he jumped into the left seat and prepared to go through his checklist. Goodbyes were not a subject he intended to be drawn on; not even when she laughed and added, "Typical male. Haven't you ever felt a pang at saying goodbye?"

Stuart didn't answer. Goodbyes were goodbyes. The only person he'd ever felt sad to say goodbye to was his sister, and he wasn't going to talk to Miss Philippa Tremain about that. That was safely locked away under lock and key.

Once they'd reached the end of the short dirt strip and

were airborne, he slid his glance sideways and found her gaze trained on him.

Did she expect a response? he wondered.

Conversation was difficult with the rushing of the wind so loud in the cockpit, but Philippa seemed determined to pursue her line of questioning once they were airborne.

"Men hate admitting to matters of the heart. Of course, you English are the worst, aren't you? So buttoned up. Not that your accent is very English."

She raised her eyebrows enquiringly, while Stuart focused his attention on the mountains through the windshield and chose his words carefully. "My sister and I were evacuees in South Africa for five years during the war." He was not about to admit to being a slum kid from London's East End. "I guess the accent from my Pretoria family rubbed off on me."

Now that the plane had levelled off, it was easier to hear.

"Yes, I remember now! Daddy said you'd done well, considering—"

She stopped herself, then, clearly to change the subject out of embarrassment, bent down to retrieve something at her feet. "Poor Daddy, I hope he didn't see that!" she said, brandishing a newspaper with the headline emblazoned across the front page: Diamonds Stolen in Brazen Heist.

Stuart had no doubt that if Charles hadn't, he soon would, for the Bloemfontein newspaper, The Friend, was mandatory reading for everyone in the small community. "Hardly your father's fault," he remarked. "Besides, he's got bigger worries."

"Hasn't he just?" Philippa agreed absently as she scanned the news story before folding it up and tucking it away. "But this doesn't reflect well on the administration. Brazen, it certainly was! You've read the story?"

Stuart nodded.

"And they got away with it!" Philippa sounded as admiring as outraged. "At least it didn't happen in Mokhotlong, though I'm sure Daddy would have preferred to prosecute illegal diamond buying than medicine murder. He's got no sympathy for people who come into the country and try to cheat the locals, but he says that while he doesn't condone murder, he understands the cultural side of it." She shrugged. "Still, murder is murder, and what's done to these poor albino or crippled people is horrible!"

Stuart nodded. "He suspects it's the same chief, doesn't he?"

"Of course. But it's not so easy to prove. He was on trek most of last week and although it's the police troopers who do most of the questioning and take the witness statements, getting anyone to speak up against their chief is almost impossible. Even if the whole village knows who ordered his minions to carry out the killings to get strong *muti* for his medicine horn, which shores up his power."

"Your dad hopes that with this one being so soon after the last, someone will finally speak up and provide evidence for a conviction."

Instead of responding to his remark, Philippa changed the subject. "So, do you enjoy mountain flying?" Her look was assessing. "You've been doing it for more than four years. You must like this place."

Four years. Had it really been that long? Four years of his life spent in this remote corner of Africa, while his dreams of flying bigger planes and seeing more of the world remained tantalisingly out of reach. He'd only managed a little over half of the required 500 hours of twin time needed for him to get a shot at the airlines.

"Yes, I enjoy mountain flying." He had to admit the truth of it. The bleak, treeless mountain ranges and plunging ravines were balm to the soul, while bustling crowds were less and less to his taste. "It's a beautiful country but—" He hesitated, feeling vulnerable articulating his long-held dream. His only dream, really.

"But what?"

He glanced at her and, seeing that she was opening her mouth to ask the next question, quickly turned the tables. "I believe congratulations are in order. Your dad says you're engaged. Or… almost."

He was surprised at the fierceness of her response.

The speculative smile was replaced by flashing eyes and the sharp retort: "I no longer have a boyfriend, which is why I came home for the half term. Telling Daddy I was sick was an excuse. The truth is, I was…" Blinking rapidly, she wiped her eyes with the back of her hand. "I was betrayed."

"Sorry."

Acknowledging his apology with the faintest inclination of her head, she sniffed and continued to stare straight ahead.

Although she'd been so frank with him, Stuart gathered this was a topic she had no wish to pursue. He sought in vain for a mundane remark to break the silence.

"I was the one who ended it," she said firmly, as if he'd asked. "You don't have to feel sorry for me." She looked combative as she pressed her pretty pink lips together, her eyes widening as the engine sputtered.

Stuart was about to reassure her. A bit of engine sputtering was normal when he adjusted the air-to-fuel ratio. But he hesitated, his hand on the red knob in front of him.

Philippa surely wouldn't want him to quiz her about her failed romance. He, in turn, could do without answering her inevitable questions if they turned to his miserable family. It would only be a matter of time before she delved into the meat of why Stuart had even come back to Southern Africa.

His grip tightened around the red knob. If he twisted it just a little more, he'd cut the supply of fuel to the single engine. While this would turn the Cessna into a glider, there would be no danger.

However, it would be the perfect means of putting an end to the Spanish Inquisition, and he'd be doing them both a favour. She'd be so disconcerted by the silence, he could change the subject and talk planes instead of personal stuff.

Of course, after a minute or so, Stuart would simply twist the knob back to restore the fuel supply, and they'd resume their flight to Maseru.

It was the perfect solution for both of them.

"So, Stuart, how did you get your pilot's licence?"

She stopped mid-sentence as she registered the change from sputtering to silence and looked at him questioningly. "Stuart?"

He noticed her whitened knuckles as an eerie silence filled the cockpit, broken only by the whistling wind rattling the fuselage. Below them, a thick white cloud canopy stretched in all directions, punctuated by a mountain range in the distance. Stuart knew the area like the back of his hand, though only a fool would risk descending through cloud.

"Stuart!"

He sent her a reassuring glance, ready to restart the

engine in a second or two. Ready for the moment they both could laugh at the joke.

But as his mouth curved into a conspiratorial grin, the precursor to his intended confession, Philippa lunged across the cabin.

"Oh God, the engine's died!" Her pink-tipped fingers dug into his arm, surprisingly strong through his leather jacket. "What are we going to do?" Her panic-filled eyes searched his face, her breath staccato gasps.

As he opened his mouth to confess the truth, ashamed for having frightened her, a waft of Chanel No. 5 caught him off guard.

And suddenly he was undone.

A beautiful woman was placing all her faith and trust in him to get her out of danger. The knowledge was like an aphrodisiac, and although he knew it was wrong, he wanted to milk the unprecedented situation for all it was worth: a good sixty seconds' worth because he supposed any more than that would make him a lying bastard.

"Just a blockage in the fuel line." He tried to combine reassurance with measured capability. He squeezed her seeking hand briefly as he leant forward, appearing busy with the various switches and knobs on the dashboard.

They were in no danger. They could soar for some time while he looked for a hole in the canopy, then he'd 'fix' the blockage, they'd dip beneath the clouds and he'd land on schedule in about fifteen minutes.

"All sorted!" He grinned as the engine sputtered back to life and he nosed the plane down through the clouds and into the lowlands. "Maseru will soon be in sight."

"Thank God for that." Philippa slumped back in her seat while Stuart descended over the yellow plains, wondering whether she'd laugh or be furious when he confessed. It would be nice to do that over a companionable glass of wine.

Remembering Lizzie with a guilty jolt, he glanced at his watch. Damn. He was due at Lancers Inn in a bit over an hour, while Philippa, of course, was headed for Bloemfontein in the morning to catch her train to Cape Town.

However, all thoughts of what the evening held for both of them were swept away by the poor weather in the lowlands.

An intense storm cell hung just over Maseru, and the air was electric with activity. It was as if they'd entered a different universe; a world that was black and grim, while fierce winds buffeted the small aircraft like a Coke can.

Stuart did a quick reconnaissance. Dark thunderclouds sandwiched the fields in the distance, while the eye of the storm was just where he'd intended to land.

Gripping the controls tightly, he made a half-hearted attempt to maintain course while he sent a worried glance at the fuel gauge. He'd known that an unscheduled pickup in Mokhotlong would leave little margin for error, but he'd not expected weather as bad as this.

He should have, of course. The afternoon storms were unpredictable.

Outside, rain sliced through the sky like silver lances. Inside, the airspeed indicator bounced violently because of the wind currents whipped up by the mountain ranges and the heavy cell of cumulonimbus clouds, which refused to budge.

Philippa, whose equilibrium had returned the moment the engine choked back to life, sent him a nervous glance as she tucked her dark hair behind her ear. "Is everything all right?"

And Stuart wished, more than he'd wished for anything

in his life, that he could tell her it was. But though his little prank had used little fuel, they now faced a genuine danger that his carelessness had created. A danger from which there might be no simple escape.

CHAPTER
THREE

Relief washed over Philippa. Just briefly, she'd thought Stuart seemed concerned. Not when the engine had stopped but after they'd descended through the clouds and encountered the full force of the storm.

Now Stuart was smiling at her, and she had to resist the urge to squeeze his hand in silent thanks that he'd got them through the worst of it. His smile transformed his face, softening the hard angles of his jaw and making tiny crinkles appear at the corners of his eyes. It was reassuring in a way that Matthew's easy charm had never been.

She glanced at his hands gripping the controls and wondered if they'd be the rough and calloused hands of a man used to outdoors physical work—the working man from a working-class background as she knew him to be— or soft and tender like a professional's. Except that tender was not a description she'd use for Matthew's hands, now she thought about it. Matthew's hands roamed a bit too freely when he got passionate. Not that he'd ever crossed the line. Respect was a word he'd used the last time they'd ended up on top of each other in the armchair in his dorm room. She was not supposed to have been there, but his roommate was away and, well, one thing had led to the other and before she knew it, Matthew's hand was up her skirt and a strange curdling feeling of desire was making her want things she didn't know how to articulate.

Until she'd stood up abruptly, saying in an almost strangled tone, "I think I should go, Matthew," to which he'd responded, "Yes... and, of course, I respect you too much—"

Clearly, he hadn't respected Philippa enough to keep his hands off Susan, though, she reflected bitterly. Nor had he respected Susan either, though Susan had encouraged it, it would seem. After her initial shame and embarrassment when Philippa had caught them, Susan had taken a more combative approach after she'd returned from the party and slunk into their dorm room while Philippa had muffled her sobs into the pillow.

"Keep up with the times, Philippa," Susan had whispered as she'd climbed into bed. "It's 1961. We're not all shrinking violets like you."

By shrinking violet, she'd insinuated a virgin, Philippa supposed. Then Susan had said that if Philippa really wanted 'this thing' with Matthew to go anywhere, she should stop pretending to the boys that she was more sophisticated than she really was and start making the most of her assets.

Making the most of her assets? Like Susan?

Philippa's throat swelled, and tears stung the back of her lids. The humiliation burned anew, made worse by the realisation that perhaps Susan was right. Everyone was changing with the times—the music, the fashions, the morals—while Philippa clung to the values her mother had instilled in her. Values from another era, perhaps. Values that had left her naïve and unprepared for a world where girls like Susan seemed to know exactly how to navigate the complex terrain of modern relationships.

She sucked in a breath, opening her eyes suddenly when Stuart grasped her hand.

"Please don't cry." He sounded tense. "We'll make it down safely, I promise. But be ready to brace if I tell you!"

What was he talking about?

Now Stuart was telling her to brace? Oh God, they *were* going to die.

Before Philippa made everything right with Matthew?

The thought surprised her. Was that really what she wanted? To reconcile with someone who had betrayed her so easily? The old Philippa would have plotted and schemed to reclaim her prize, but sitting here, facing mortality, she wondered if Matthew was worth fighting for at all.

Of course, she would not close her eyes if these were her last minutes alive. She fixed her gaze on Stuart and took a deep breath.

If she could put everything out of her mind—the fear of the storm, the anguish over Matthew's disloyalty, her confusion over what Matthew expected of her—and just concentrate on Stuart and what he was doing, then she could concede that it was rather impressive the way he was managing matters. His jaw was clenched, and there was a determined, fierce look in his eyes, but his movements inspired confidence.

Between assessing the eerie storm-filled world outside and the knobs and buttons on the dashboard, he seemed competent and in control.

Philippa leaned back in her seat and let out her breath slowly. If anyone was going to get them out of danger, it would be Stuart, she decided. Unlike Matthew, who thrived on the admiration of an audience, Stuart seemed to find his confidence from within.

She glanced down, relieved at how close the ground looked. And how flat.

By the time she'd returned her attention to Stuart's dark blonde hair with its too-long fringe, her fear had completely evaporated.

Well, compared with Matthew's clean-cut image, Stuart's hair was too long, but if he got them on the ground safely, that floppy dark blonde hair would definitely be worthy of further investigation.

Or would that court more rejection?

Philippa felt a niggle of self-doubt. She'd never in a million years have imagined Matthew would favour Susan over her. But then, Susan had never made Matthew wait. The thought caused a flush of heat to rise to her cheeks. Had her upbringing made her a prude?

"Weather's turning sour over Bloemfontein." Stuart indicated a dark mass of cloud ahead with a nod. "Ladybrand's the closest strip, and it looks like they've still got blue sky. For now."

Philippa was jerked back to the present. "Ladybrand? But what about my train from Bloemfontein tomorrow?"

He shrugged a little too casually. "Fine by me. We can press on. I've never tried landing on a proper runway without being able to see it. Could be an experience."

"Of course I don't care about my train if you put it like that!" She clenched her teeth.

Great. So now Stuart thought she was a spoiled brat. The kind of privileged, cosseted product of the administration who cared more about social engagements than survival. Yet another person with a poor opinion of her, just when she was already feeling so low.

"Sorry." His voice was tight, his eyes fixed on the churning grey wall of cloud that now blocked their path. "That front is moving faster than I thought. We can't push through to Bloemfontein. Ladybrand is our only shot." He glanced at her, his expression softening slightly. "It's not far. You'll still make your train tomorrow."

"It's all right." She nodded, her charitable feelings for him returning. He was trying to save her life, after all. And he was very good-looking. Not in the polished, golden-boy way of Matthew, but in a rugged, authentic way that she found herself increasingly drawn to.

A simple diversion it was not. By the time Stuart had the grass strip at Ladybrand in sight, the front had caught them. Fierce rain lashed the windscreen, and a keening wind tossed the aircraft like a leaf. Lightning bleached the sky white, illuminating a world that seemed a black, unwelcoming funnel with no sanctuary to offer. How had she missed the escalation of danger? It was not going to be all right. Once again, she had trustingly put herself in denial.

Just as she'd done with Matthew, a voice in her head whispered. *Ignoring the signs, believing what you wanted to believe.*

"We can't land in that!" Philippa shouted over the roar of the engine, following Stuart's tense gaze to the fuel gauge. The needle flickered deep in the red. "What are we going to do?"

He didn't answer, his jaw set. With a sharp bank that pressed her into her seat, he turned the Cessna northwest, flying parallel to the storm's leading edge. He was searching, she realised, not for sunshine, but for a break. A seam in the clouds.

Then they found it. A dark curtain of rain seemed to part right in front of them, and in the distance, a ribbon of gold beckoned. A road.

Philippa pointed excitedly. "There! We can land there!" But even she could see they were coming upon it too fast and that the road curved sharply. "What about that field?" Hope, not common sense, motivated the question. Philippa knew the dangers of landing on what looked from a distance to be a flat surface. It took only a fallen log or termite mound concealed by tall waving grass or ripe mealies to spell instant death.

"Brace yourself!"

One moment Philippa was staring over the dashboard, the next she was nearly flattened as Stuart flung out his right arm to press her back into her seat. With her heart knocking against her ribs and her mouth parched with fear, she watched Stuart try to sideslip the little plane onto the road. Before, they'd seemed to be barely moving, the wind was so strong, but suddenly the ground was coming up like a mountain range filling the windscreen.

Philippa blinked at the ribbon of dirt dancing before them as the plane battled the eddying gusts to level out.

So, this was it. They'd either go up in a ball of flame, though the way her heart was thundering so fiercely in her chest, she'd pass out before then.

The road was like a twisting waterway, tantalisingly accessible, then gone again. They flew low over the mealie field, the tall green fronds brushing the undercarriage. Now the flat, gravelled surface was ahead of them, but they were racing towards it too fast, for the mealie field was beyond the curve. She forced her eyes open, her breathing fast and shallow, her nails digging into her palms as she waited for the inevitable.

Nearly. They were nearly down or nearly dead, but at the last moment she couldn't bring herself to look.

Shielding her face with her folded arms, she bit her lip, tasting the metal tang of blood as the impact jolted her. The Cessna bounced high, once, twice, its pace barely slowing as it careened over the road's gravel surface.

They'd made the road.

Surely, now they'd touched down on solid earth, everything would be all right?

But while the plane had felt under control in the air, it was suddenly like an out-of-control can with wings and wheels as it sped over the slippery surface.

Or was that the wind buffeting them like a plaything?

Opening her eyes, Philippa reared back at the field of mealies rushing towards them, tall green corn fronds waving in the wind.

Curling into a foetal position, her echoing scream competed with the sound of thick, dense stalks scraping and scratching the fuselage as the plane left the road and ploughed through the grain crop.

Never had she felt such a loss of control.

Not with Matthew's betrayal, not with her mother's death, not with any of the carefully managed crises of her sheltered life. This raw, elemental danger stripped away pretense and left her with nothing but the primal will to survive.

When the plane finally slowed, bumping almost nonchalantly over the last few yards of rutted ground before a deep corrugation in the earth brought them up short, Philippa still had her hands over her face.

She dropped them into her lap.

The contrasting silence that followed was almost deafening. No keening wind, no booming thunder.

No ghastly explosion.

Only her heavy breathing.

Tentatively, Philippa straightened and stared ahead through the still-intact windshield, dazed and shocked. A beetle was navigating the tall, long-leaved frond pressed against the glass in front of her. She watched its busy progress, its back glossy in the sunlight.

Sunlight? She tried to think why the observation jarred. After all, they'd been through, this small creature continued its journey, oblivious to the human drama that had nearly ended in tragedy. Life in all its stubborn resilience continued.

Then she turned at the sound of her name and stared into the handsome face of the pilot who'd just saved her life.

Stuart.

She blinked, opened her mouth to speak, but no sound came.

He squeezed her hand, casually leaned across her to unbuckle her seat belt as if they'd just returned from a pleasure jaunt, and asked, "That wasn't so bad, was it?"

And in that moment, with her heart still racing and her body trembling from the shock, Philippa realised that perhaps Matthew and Susan had done her a favour. Without their betrayal, she would never have been on this plane. She would never have experienced this terror or this triumph. She would never have discovered what it felt like to put her life in the hands of someone truly capable, rather than someone merely confident.

She would never have met the real Stuart Price.

CHAPTER

FOUR

Stuart wasn't sure what to do.

He'd been feeling pretty pleased with himself. He'd landed in sub-optimal conditions, and they weren't dead. The late afternoon sun had broken through the storm clouds, casting long golden shadows across the mealie field and turning the scattered stalks around the plane into something almost beautiful.

He wouldn't think just yet about how he'd explain this to Dan, though he was sure he could spin it just right. It wasn't as if he was the only pilot who'd crash-landed a plane in rough weather after navigating mountain thermals during a storm.

But now Philippa had rewarded him like some conquering hero, and the scent of Chanel No. 5 as her arms went round him was a potent and arousing combination.

Not one he really deserved, though he couldn't remember the last time he'd felt so good.

Awkwardly, he patted her shoulder as he fought the impulse to hold her close while his brain whirred through

45

the many practicalities arising from this unexpected situation.

The plane had ploughed through the field of green mealies, leaving the orange dirt road several hundred yards away. And while Stuart was reasonably confident the hard landing had not caused too much damage, it would take a few shoulders to the pump to get the plane back onto the road in order to take off again.

But first he'd need fuel.

And the evening was closing in, though all that seemed suddenly insignificant because a gorgeous woman was clinging to him, and that hadn't happened in years. The warmth of her body against his chest awakened something he'd almost forgotten existed—a hunger for connection that went beyond his careful, measured relationship with Lizzie.

Guiltily, he remembered Lizzie. Would she already be waiting for him at Lancer's Inn? He'd momentarily lost track of time.

"I'm sorry." Philippa wiped her eyes with the back of her hand and sent him a watery smile. "I knew someone who died in a plane crash, and I thought I was going the same way. But then you—"

She choked on the words, and Stuart was relieved at the excuse to discard his reserve and enfold her in his arms so that she cried even harder against his chest.

In the strange stillness of the afternoon heat, every sound was amplified: her breathing. His. The sound of birds calling across the vast landscape, and the rustlings of the bush. The air smelled of dust and crushed corn stalks, over-laid with the sweetness of Philippa's perfume.

"Morena?"

They jerked their heads up at the tentative voice. A

small group of African children had materialised from the tall grass bordering the field. With wide white smiles and curious eyes, they peered into the plane, chattering excitedly as the tall, serious-looking boy who'd spoken stepped forward. His bare feet were dusty, his khaki shorts patched but clean, and he was definitely the leader.

"*Het jy hulp nodig?*" the boy asked, tapping the wing.

Stuart looked at Philippa, who was self-consciously dabbing at her eyes. "What did he say?" he asked.

She sent an uncertain glance at the ragged children, who were running their hands over the hull as if it were some rare and exotic creature. "My Afrikaans is terrible, but I think he asked if we needed help."

"Can you reply? In your terrible Afrikaans?"

"My Sesotho is better. What should I say?"

Stuart leant back and watched as she spoke to the boy, smiling as she explained they needed fuel, and did he know of a farmhouse nearby.

In her chic blue wool pencil skirt and paler blue cashmere sweater, her elegance was a startling contrast to the bleak landscape. Against the endless expanse of the high veld, with its golden grass stretching to purple mountains on the horizon, she looked impossibly refined.

Suddenly the contrast between them seemed infinite.

Philippa, with her exotic plumage, raven hair, violet eyes and expensive clothes, was a bird of paradise.

Stuart was a bird of prey. He would do well to remember that.

"He says the nearest farmhouse is a good half an hour's walk away. It'll be dark soon. What should we do?" She smoothed her skirt over her hips, smiling as her eyes met his, her hair cascading down one shoulder like a tumble of dark molten toffee. Now that she'd recovered from her shock, she was back in top form; a vision of loveliness transporting him back to his earliest days in Basutoland. Back to Magda's sitting room where he remembered his gauche young self scoffing at the incongruous image of an elegant, gazelle-like magazine model on a location shot in the heart of Africa gazing at him from the pages of the glossy fashion magazine Magda had open on her coffee table. Magda had laughed and said Stuart had no imagination.

He certainly did now. But there were more important matters to worry about.

"Ask the boy if he can deliver a note asking for help," Stuart said, digging in his pocket for some coins. "I need to check on the plane." He also needed a few moments alone to think and to confirm that the plane was still flyable.

He'd felt optimistic after a cursory glance over it, but now that the shock had abated, he felt sick at the thought of telling his boss what had happened. That's if he could get to a telephone.

And Charles Tremain would be beside himself when they failed to make their ETA.

He reached into the cockpit to retrieve paper and a stubby pencil and quickly scratched a few lines, conscious of the children's bright eyes watching his every movement with fascination.

By the time he'd walked back to the road—his boots crunching on the scattered gravel and corn husks—Philippa was surrounded by children and pointing to a plume of dust in the distance. "See, Stuart! Someone's coming! And look!" She pointed to a wedge-tailed eagle circling gracefully above them in the vastness of the African sky. "That might have been a vulture if we'd had a less fortunate landing."

She laughed at their lucky escape, and Stuart thought of the unfortunate medicine murder victim who had been found at the bottom of the ravine. He wondered if Tremain's investigation would uncover on whose orders he'd died.

Though his thoughts took a different turn when Philippa put her hand in his and whispered shyly, "Thank you, Stuart."

He nearly dropped the pencil, freezing as he struggled to read her intention. There was a look in her eye that Stuart had seen in Lizzie's when she'd waited hopefully for some sign that he returned her feelings.

Lizzie. Guilt flicked him in the gut like a pebble. There was no skirting around the fact that his last date with the pretty Australian nurse had laid the groundwork. Not very long from now, he should be sitting across the dining table from Lizzie, saying the words she expected of him: "Don't take that nursing job in Pietermaritzburg, Lizzie. Stay here."

But he couldn't be there for dinner with her tonight. Of course, she'd understand the drama with the weather and that he'd not intentionally stood her up. Lizzie's ability to forgive was her greatest virtue.

But the closer he got to being forced to honourably declare himself, the less sure Stuart was that he wanted to spend the rest of his life with Lizzie. The safe choice. The sensible choice. The choice that would never set his heart racing the way it was racing now.

When he didn't answer, Philippa pulled back her hand and followed the tall Mosotho boy while the rest of the children gathered about. She looked over her shoulder at him, her gaze clear and direct as she said, "Anyway, I just want you to know that I appreciate what you did just then."

Stuart felt like an idiot. Why hadn't he made the most of the opportunity she'd offered?

He took a couple of strides to catch up with her, raising his head to look at the plume of dust that shimmered in the now still air. The car that had inspired such hope had disappeared out of sight around a bend in the road.

Stuart ran a grimy hand across his face, dropped his gaze, and then impulsively snatched Philippa's wrist. He hadn't meant to pull her off balance, but she stumbled, falling into his arms. Shocking him to find her there until he realised by the look in her eye that it had been her intention.

Her face, tilted up to his, was so close he could define each dark lash. Could see the way the golden light caught the violet depths of her eyes.

She didn't speak or move.

Nor did Stuart. He was too aroused by the rapid beat of her heart against his chest and her warm, sweet breath on his cheek.

And by the tiny beauty spot by her beautifully shaped mouth.

He wasn't expecting it, but he was more than ready when Philippa twined her arms around his neck and planted a short, fierce kiss on his lips.

Some of the children had turned around and were giggling. Stuart ignored them, conscious of his hand supporting the curve of her slender waist and of the feel of her chest and soft cheek fused to his.

She sighed gently after she'd withdrawn, her face only inches from his while Stuart battled his doubts as to whether it would be appropriate to take this as a prelude to something more.

"*'Wat maak julle twee verliefdes so ver van die huis af?*"

The cheerful voice jerked him back into reality, and they both turned to see a freckle-faced lad grinning at them through the window of the brown sedan that had drawn up, its engine ticking in the late afternoon heat.

Philippa gathered her equilibrium faster than Stuart. "Tell that to the ignorant Englishman in a language he can understand," she said, leaning into the car with the confidence of someone born to charm strangers. "Except he's got an excuse because he really is from England, whereas I just speak terrible Afrikaans."

Knowing that Stuart had not understood the boy's remark, she translated in an undertone, "What are you lovebirds doing so far from home?" She pointed in the plane's direction, just a speck near the edge of the distant field. "We're a long way from anywhere, it seems, though we were headed for our honeymoon in the Cape before Captain Darling here ditched us in a mealie field."

Stuart jerked his head around to stare at her, shocked that she could sound so flippant in the telling of such a blatant lie, while the young man squinted in the direction she indicated.

"That yours? *Nei*, man." The lad's eyes widened, and he gave a low whistle. "Had problems, then?" He spoke with a slow, easy-going country Afrikaans drawl. "Get in and I'll take you to my house. Honeymooners! Wait 'til I tell Ma. It'll break her heart." The grin, which seemed a permanent feature, remained in place as he opened the door and climbed out, introducing himself as Jacobus van Wyk, the youngest son of the family who owned all the fields for more than a hundred miles about.

Jacobus reminded Stuart of a gangly, cheeky comic strip character. His sweat-darkened fringe was plastered to his brow after what must have been an energetic tennis match judging by his sweat-soaked whites, and his light skin was full of freckles.

"Ma'll have dinner ready, but there's always plenty. Climb in."

After Philippa had thanked the chief's son and Jacobus had waved the children on their way, ushering Philippa and Stuart into the car, he hopped into the driver's seat.

"Maybe you can show me how your aeroplane works if I help you get it out of the field," he suggested cheerfully as he released the clutch and the car lurched over the gravelled road, kicking up small clouds of red dust.

"Thanks. A bit of help would be appreciated." Stuart tried to keep the worry from his tone. Far from tempering Philippa's high spirits, this setback seemed to have fired her up with some kind of devilry. The 'Captain Darling' remark had been amply followed up by signs of affection a newlywed might show, and her head now rested on Stuart's shoulder.

Maybe the sharp jolt had unhinged her, but if she wanted him to play her game, he couldn't. He'd spent his childhood being forced to act as a decoy so his father could profit from a shed full of items that had fallen off the back of a truck or that had come into his possession through other dubious means. The memory of those days still left a sour taste in his mouth—the fear, the shame, the constant worry about being caught.

"What a gorgeous diamond, darling." Philippa held out her left hand, which suddenly sported a small glittering stone on her ring finger. "When do you think we'll get to Cape Town?" She reached up to cup Stuart's cheek with fingers that smelled faintly of her perfume. "Though I'm not complaining. This is rather an adventure."

What was she doing?

He swallowed, his throat dry but his hands clammy. When he was seven years old and his father had forced him to nick stuff from shops, he'd put on the tearful act if he got caught, like his father had taught him. Usually, he got off with a warning. Sometimes he just ran, though he'd been caught a couple of times and been dealt rough justice rather than being handed over to the police. No shopkeeper had ever whipped him more thoroughly than his father had, though.

Now he was in Africa, a world away from his father and that whole murky world.

He didn't need Philippa making the same demands his pa had that he be complicit in someone else's lies. She was playacting, and every instinct honed by years of avoiding his father's schemes told him to distance himself from her charade.

Yet the feel of her body pressed against his was almost more than he could bear.

If her little charade had actually meant something, he'd have joined in. Instead, he ignored her and stared out of the window at the endless expanse of golden grassland dotted with thorn trees.

After about ten minutes, they turned onto a farm track, which wound through acres of cultivated land—neat rows of maize and wheat. Clearly a prosperous and carefully managed farm. At the end of a twisting avenue of golden ash trees, their leaves rustling in the evening breeze, Jacobus brought the sedan to a halt outside a large white farmhouse surrounded by emerald lawn and heavy-laden fruit trees.

The house was quintessentially South African Cape Dutch—thick walls designed to keep out the heat, a wide stoep with elegant pillars, and green-painted shutters that could be closed against the fierce summer sun. Yellow roses climbed the walls, their sweet scent carried on the evening air.

Still grinning, Jacobus slid off the seat, stepped out, and then put his head back into the cab. "Just give me a minute while I tell Ma," he said before disappearing up the red-polished steps to the veranda and through the heavy wooden front door.

"Behave yourself, Philippa," Stuart cautioned, reaching out to study her hand. "Where did you get that ring?"

"It's Granny's. I sometimes wear it on my other hand. Anyway, don't worry, they'll be more accommodating if they think we're newlyweds," Philippa whispered back. "Besides, don't you think it's fun pretending to be something you're not—and getting away with it? My friend Susan and I used to play this game all the time." She frowned when she saw he didn't share her amusement. "It's only a game to make them be good to us."

"Well... you and Susan are not children anymore."

Philippa pressed her lips together, but she didn't look chastened. More as if she were trying not to laugh and Stuart forced himself not to let his gaze linger on her long legs as she finally unfolded herself from the car. She straightened in that graceful, sensuous manner that was peculiarly hers, then gripped his hand and kissed the back of it.

Above, the sky darkened from gold to deep orange, and the wind picked up a little, carrying the scents of the farmyard—hay, animals, and the wholesome smell of bread baking.

Stuart withdrew from the contact and ran his finger round the inside of his collar. The lady of the house would emerge from the front door any minute.

More important than anything, though, was the need to get to a telephone so he could let Dan know the plane had landed and all passengers were safe.

"I didn't know you were so serious, Stuart Price. Susan and I thought you were anything but. We'd heard whispers, of course." Philippa gave him a knowing look, and Stuart felt heat burn his cheeks. He wondered if she was referring to Magda.

Airily she added, as they waited on the gravel, "You must know you're the most handsome man in the whole of Basutoland. Even the married women have crushes on you."

"Shh," said Stuart. "Someone's coming."

Philippa looked suitably demure as the door opened and a broad-girthed woman in a floral dress with tightly permed greying hair and an enormous smile emerged. For a moment, she stared at them from the wide veranda, then hurriedly took the stairs at an angle, beckoning them forward with hands still dusted with flour.

"Welcome to Groot Plaas. Jacobus tells me you're newlyweds! Goodness, but what excitement you've had! I'm Jacobus's mother, Betty van Wyk. You will, of course, stay with us until you can get your plane out of our field tomorrow." Her progress in her high heels was impressive across the uneven ground. "My word, what a terrible thing to happen!" she went on. "But you're safe and alive, thank the Lord. Come in!" After greeting them warmly, she led the way into the house.

The interior was cool and welcoming, with polished yellowwood floors covered in Persian rugs and heavy, carved furniture. The whitewashed walls were adorned with a variety of sombre religious scenes and prints of the

Dutch masters, while family photographs in silver frames clustered on side tables.

Mrs van Wyk's Afrikaans accent reminded Stuart of Magda, but instead of Magda's smouldering sexuality, she exuded a motherliness that reminded him with a pang of his South African foster mother, Mrs Franklin. The same warm hospitality, the same unconscious assumption that all young people needed feeding and caring for.

Mrs van Wyk patted Philippa's cheek as she passed through the door that was being held open by a thin black servant in a starched white and apple green uniform. "We were waiting for Jacobus, but now Dolly is laying two extra places and there's plenty of food to go round. How lovely to have guests this evening."

Philippa accepted the hospitality graciously, while Stuart felt constricted by the fear of exposure. If he'd been with any other female in the whole of Basutoland, it would have been fine but this was the DC's unmarried daughter and until Stuart delivered her to Mr and Mrs Lehmann who were waiting to put her on the train to Bloemfontein, he was also custodian of her reputation.

They were led into a dark sitting room where the rest of the family were seated, waiting—they were told—for Jacobus to change. The room smelled of beeswax polish and pipe tobacco, with heavy curtains drawn against the evening chill and a fire crackling in the stone hearth.

From the kitchen, wafts of rich, wholesome food made Stuart's stomach clench with longing. He hadn't eaten since the bully beef sandwich he'd had at Letseng-la-Terai.

Hovering upon the threshold, Stuart politely greeted short, wiry Mr van Wyk and nodded at the bent and gnarled ancient grandmother, whose rheumy eyes assessed him with sharp intelligence despite her age. There were also the two other sons of the house: Isaac the eldest who smiled shyly up at them in welcome and whose skin was tanned from working the family land all day, and a pale, wary looking middle lad called Piet, who told them in a surly tone that he was a mechanic in town. He was nothing like his brothers, with his oily black hair slicked back, unsettling grey-eyed gaze and thin lips. Stuart judged him to be in his mid-twenties, perhaps a year or two older than himself.

After Dolly had brought in the bobotie—a traditional South African dish of curried mince with egg topping that filled the room with the warm spices of the Cape—the family bent their heads in prayer.

Stuart was surprised to see Philippa blink before following his lead as he clasped his hands and intoned a few words of divine appreciation after Mr van Wyk's prelude in Afrikaans, though the family otherwise had switched to English for their guests.

Because of the extra two places laid at the polished stinkwood table, Philippa sat close to Stuart. Once, she put her hand on his thigh, causing him to jump in surprise, as she chatted to her hostess, embellishing her answers as Mrs van Wyk quizzed her about the journey and then...

The wedding.

"Mummy made the cake. It was three-tiered with pink sugar flowers," she said happily, bending to tickle the van Wyk family dog between the ears before Piet dispatched it with a fierce "*Voetsek!*"

"Lily of the Valley in a trailing bouquet and so beauti-ful!" Philippa went on, her voice taking on a dreamy quality that almost convinced Stuart she was reliving real memo-ries. "Mummy always carries off first prize at the Agricul-tural Show for flower decorating and at the cake stall and she helped me design the dress though it was made by Madame Latoufe, her French designer in Pretoria, with imported lace and the widest skirts with layers of stiffened petticoats. I wish I had a photograph to show you."

Stuart stared. Had the hard landing really unhinged her? He could only nod dumbly when Philippa turned to him occasionally for endorsement, her eyes sparkling with mischief that only he could see.

With the meal at an end, they stood up, scraping back their chairs on the polished floor, neatly curling their napkins into their silver rings and setting them by their dirty plates, which Dolly had begun to tidy.

Retiring to the sitting room, Mr van Wyk turned on the wireless for the evening news—the familiar voice of the SABC announcer filling the room—and the two older women pulled out their knitting, needles clicking rhythmically in the lamplight.

Stuart asked to borrow the telephone and then followed Isaac into the hallway, his palms clammy. The telephone sat on a small table beneath a portrait of a stern Voortrekker ancestor.

Fortunately, the operator connected him with Maseru almost immediately and, after reassuring his boss that he and Philippa and the plane were fine, and then asking Dan to pass on the message to the DC that Stuart would get Philippa to Bloemfontein in the morning so she could catch the train to Cape Town, he returned to find the others listening to Philippa's account of their emergency landing. He wished he'd heard the start of her clearly dramatic re-enactment.

"This is the first time we've had a pilot in the house. And you were en route for... where?" Piet addressed Stuart directly for the first time, and all eyes turned on him as he settled himself in the only available place to sit: the small, floral sofa next to Philippa.

Stuart forced himself to meet the young man's intense look. "I hadn't expected the weather front we encountered when we dropped beneath the cloud canopy, but I'm sure we'll have no problem getting Philippa to Bloemfontein to make her connection tomorrow to Cape Town." That was where Philippa had said they were headed, wasn't it? He felt sick speaking the lie when he'd vowed never again to be caught up in someone else's falsehoods.

"And the Cessna is yours?" There was both longing and admiration in Piet's tone, though something calculating flickered behind his eyes.

"It is." Philippa responded before Stuart, though he supposed that was better than the truth. With Philippa's little game pushing the boundaries, he was sure the elder van Wyks would not approve of a dalliance between the daughter of a District Commissioner and someone like Stuart, a lowly pilot employed to fly her out of the mountains.

Jacobus leapt into the conversation, running his hand over his tow-headed scalp and shifting in his seat like he had ants in his pants.

"Stuart's going to show me around the cockpit tomorrow, aren't you, Stuart? I'm going to help him push the plane out. What's it like being a pilot, Captain?"

It was a relief not having to pretend now that Stuart was in familiar territory. He felt himself relax for the first time all day. "I never wanted to do anything else. It's great." But then he remembered this morning's bitter disappointment as Dan had told him of a further two-week delay before Stuart could continue accumulating the twin-engine time he needed to further his career.

Would his unfortunate forced landing jeopardise his chance to fly the Dornier when it returned from Johannesburg for its hundred-hour overhaul?

Surely not? Many other pilots in Drakensberg Air's three-plane fleet had nearly come to grief, yet they dined out on their stories with no embarrassment.

He glanced at Philippa, and her smile was like the sun breaking through the clouds. She looked like the adoring fiancée of any man's dreams, and he wished he could tell her and the van Wyks that he was on track to becoming a jet pilot, flying a Boeing 707 within a few short months.

The sad reality was that he needed a few hundred hours of twin time on the Dornier before he could even think of applying to South African Airways.

With the way things were going, it would be another two years before he'd be even close to meeting the minimum requirement.

Everyone turned as old Mrs Van Wyk muttered something in Afrikaans and the men rose as Jacobus's mother helped her to her feet, bending down to gather up her workbasket before leading her to the door.

"*Ouma* is very tired, but I will come back after I have put her to bed," she said. "It is very special to welcome newlyweds into our household." She leant over and put her hand briefly on Philippa's head, then smiled warmly at Stuart.

And although Stuart felt guilty and uncomfortable about Philippa's charade, and although the van Wyk Afrikaans household was so different from his old home in Pretoria—for there was nothing homely about the London squalor in which he'd grown up—he felt encompassed by the same warmth and hospitality the Franklins had extended towards him during those precious five years he'd lived with them as a boy, and he was flooded with memories of the happiest times of his life.

For a brief moment, sitting in this warm, lamplight-filled room with Philippa beside him and the van Wyks treating them like family, Stuart could almost believe that the pretence was real. That he was worthy of such acceptance, such easy inclusion in their world.

It was a dangerous thought—one that made his carefully guarded heart skip with possibility even as his mind reminded him that it was all a lie.

CHAPTER

FIVE

Stuart had drifted in and out of the conversation since Mr and Mrs van Wyk had switched to Afrikaans, but a meaningful pause caught his attention.

Their hostess had returned, obviously with something to say to her husband after she'd settled her mother-in-law.

Now Mr van Wyk was frowning, nodding his head, before responding in the measured tones of a man making an important decision.

It must have been profound because Stuart caught Philippa's look, her eyes wide. She turned to Stuart as if to say something before clearly deciding against it. Then she, too, nodded, smiling her gratitude with the gracious acceptance of someone born to receive hospitality. Stuart gathered they'd been offered accommodation for the night, so thought it best he take his cue from Philippa and offer a similar level of enthusiasm.

After a few minutes' conversation, Stuart noticed the maid enter and converse discreetly with her mistress before Mrs Van Wyk stood up.

"Let me take you to your room," she said, holding up a

hurricane lamp to light the way as they crunched down a narrow gravel path bordered by lavender bushes whose sweet scent hung heavy in the cool night air. In the gloom, Stuart heard the warmth in her voice, but something in her tone made his stomach tighten with apprehension. "I have no daughters, but I was a bride once, and although it won't be the same as having your wedding night in a smart hotel, you will be comfortable and have your privacy."

The vague uneasiness that had clawed its way up Stuart's gullet as she began her speech had turned to full-blown panic by the time Mrs van Wyk halted a few yards away by the door of what was clearly the guest rondavel. The traditional round building sat nestled beneath ancient blue gum trees, its whitewashed walls glowing pale in the lamplight, thatched roof dark against the star-studded sky.

As the wind played in the leaves of the large, over-hanging Monkey Puzzle tree, creating an otherworldly whisper in the darkness, Stuart swung round to elicit Philippa's aid in dispersing the woman's delusions but to his horror Philippa was already talking—gushing—about how thoughtful Mrs van Wyk was; how kind and that what had started out as the most unfortunate of incidents to blight any bride's enthusiasm had now turned out for the best: adventure topped by the kindness of strangers. Philippa really was going to town while Mrs van Wyk continued beaming, patting Philippa's shoulder as if she were the most charming creature.

Stuart stared, horrified.

Philippa was playing games for the childish fun of it. He tried to remind himself that that was what she was: a child. If he blinked, he could conjure up the sixteen-year-old girl he remembered from his early flying days—gangly, awkward, and trying so hard to be more sophisticated than she was. Though when he looked properly at her now, all he could see was a beautiful, sophisticated young woman who had, for reasons entirely unworthy, made him her hero for a day.

The moment Mrs van Wyk excused herself after throwing open the door—releasing the scent of lavender and beeswax from within—saying she'd leave Stuart to carry Philippa over the threshold, Stuart shook his head.

"We can't!" he hissed.

"Why not?"

Why not?

Philippa was a sexy, gorgeous woman smouldering with desire and the fact she wanted Stuart to carry her over the threshold as if they truly were newlyweds was placing far too much trust in Stuart's ability to reign in his impulses. The small rondavel beckoned like a secret world, intimate and private, far from the watchful eyes of proper society.

"Come on, Stuart," she urged, her eyes excited in the glow of the lantern, which had been hung up on a nail over the lintel. "Just in case they're watching. It's too late to tell the truth now, anyway."

The touch of her fingertips sent desire charging through him, but it was only because he felt trapped in the charade that he scooped her up in his arms. The perfume she was wearing mingling with the fragrance of her hair was the final ingredient in a potent cocktail of desire that was fast banishing every good intention he'd ever had. She felt impossibly light in his arms, yet substantial enough to remind him that this was real—dangerously, intoxicatingly real.

"Hey, man!"

Guiltily, he swung around, setting Philippa to her feet

as Jacobus hailed them. The lad had materialised from behind a large bougainvillea, whose purple bracts rustled in the evening breeze. Carrying an old record player and wearing a grin ripe enough to burst a watermelon, Stuart realised Jacobus was only going to complicate matters.

"Got it yesterday!' he said, tossing back his fringe and brandishing a vinyl LP with youthful enthusiasm. " 'Yellow Polka Dot Bikini.' " Ma won't let me play it in the house. Thought you'd like it." His grin broadened as he held it out, whispering loudly, "You'll want some music and it's top of the charts."

For a moment, there was silence. The night sounds of the high veld filled the space—the distant call of a nightjar, the rustle of small creatures in the undergrowth, the soft sigh of wind through grass. Philippa's gorgeous smile was trained on him as if she were just waiting for Stuart to crack and throw himself into the spirit of fun she'd orchestrated. Fabricated.

He couldn't.

Undeterred, she then laughed and snaked an arm around Jacobus's waist. "Who'd have believed it? It's Stu's and my favourite, isn't it? Don't you think Stuart looks just like Bryan Hyland? I don't think he sings as well, though. You are a clever boy, Jacobus."

Jacobus blushed fiercely when she kissed him on the cheek, then asked shyly if she'd like him to put it on for them. Hanging back, Stuart was still struggling for something to say when the crunch of gravel heralded Piet coming around the corner with a bottle in his hand, his pale face ghostlike in the lamplight.

The young man's narrow gaze roamed over each of them, and Stuart had the uncomfortable feeling he was being thoroughly assessed, catalogued, perhaps even judged wanting. "Pa won't have liquor in the house. I was saving this, but..." He shrugged, his voice carrying an undertone Stuart couldn't quite place. "Thought it would make a good wedding present.'

"That's very kind!" Philippa took the bottle with another of her radiant smiles. "My word, what a lovely family you are and how lucky we've been to find ourselves here."

Piet muttered something as he scuffed his boots on the gravel. Then he looked up, his grey eyes unreadable in the shadows. "You might need more help to push your plane onto the road than Jacobus can give you when you take off tomorrow. Just give me a shout."

Stuart thanked him, and Piet looked away as if embarrassed, saying over his shoulder as he retreated into the darkness, "I won't disturb you, so just let me know in the morning when you're ready."

He was barely out of hearing and Stuart was still gazing at Piet's back, wondering where things would go from here, when Philippa pushed him over the threshold and into the gloomy, suddenly noisy rondavel.

"Come on, Stuart! Let's have some fun!" she cried as Jacobus, in the far corner, set his hurricane lamp on the dark wood dresser and turned up the volume of 'Yellow Polka Dot Bikini'. The low eaves and dark thatching of the roof lent the space an unsettling intimacy, the circular walls seeming to embrace them while the lamplight created dancing shadows that transformed the simple room into something magical and secretive.

Philippa danced over to join the lad who'd started nodding his head and rolling his shoulders to the beat of the music while Stuart stood awkwardly near the door, feeling more out of his depth than he could remember. It was impossible not to admire Philippa's lithe, youthful body as she wiggled her hips in time to the music and waved her arms, her pert breasts seeming to have a life of their own beneath the soft cashmere. It was quite another to think what would happen when Jacobus left them.

He glanced at the double bed with its brown and gold woollen bedspread—clearly Mrs van Wyk's best guest linens—and a wave of disbelief mixed with pure lust swept through him. This was a game Philippa could not possibly intend carrying through. He had to tell himself this in order to temper the lascivious thoughts that were fast turning him from the gentleman Mrs Franklin had created out of the urchin he'd once been, into the greatest Neanderthal ever.

"Good night, Jacobus, you've been a real sweetheart." Raising the bottle he'd opened for her, Philippa winked, then kissed the lad's cheek.

"Smile!" The lad whipped up his camera and snapped a photograph.

"And now it's time for you to go," Philippa added, as she gently pushed him out of the room.

When Stuart turned back from closing the door—the solid wood barrier suddenly seeming inadequate protection from the world outside—his hastily rehearsed call for reason was cut short by the glass Philippa thrust into his hand.

She didn't stop as she danced past him. She was caught up in the music and perhaps the novelty of the occasion, but Stuart's survival instincts had been differently formed. Necessity had forced him from a young age to practise self-control, and this was no occasion to let it desert him now, just because a willing and desirable young woman had cast sense to the wind.

He'd never be able to look Charles Tremain in the face again.

"You're a hero, Captain Price!" Philippa hooked her arm through his and rubbed her body against his side, her warmth penetrating the cotton of his shirt. "You saved my life today." She tipped back her head, taking a deep draught of the sweet, bubbly wine, and indicated Stuart should do the same.

After hesitating, he complied, and although he thought the wine was terrible, the sweet alcohol seemed to instantly lighten his mood, softening the edges of his anxiety.

Philippa smiled wickedly. She really was lovely, and her youthful glee was endearing in a way that made his chest tighten with unfamiliar emotion. She stood on tiptoe and put her lips to his ear, her breath warm against his skin. "And I'm going to reward you."

Stuart stepped back and gently disengaged her arms. His mood might be less sombre than it had been, but it was his responsibility to nip Philippa's foolishness in the bud. "I'm not quite sure what you mean by that, but if you mean what I think you do, then this has gone quite far enough."

Stuart's words echoed in his head as if they were uttered by someone at least a generation older than his twenty-six years. How could any sane man with an ounce of red blood turn down an offer like this? Philippa was the incarnation of his fantasies; a Hollywood starlet playing to her audience, her pouting lips revealing pretty, pearl-like teeth, her eyes dark with promise. She was somewhere between Elizabeth Taylor and Audrey Hepburn, and she was looking at Stuart as if he were the incarnation of her dreams.

The music ended abruptly, and Philippa threw herself onto her stomach across the bed, the springs creaking under her weight, and rested her chin in her hands as she looked at him. "Come on, Stuart, you're not very fun company."

"I can't. This is madness, Philippa. Dangerous!"

She didn't look chastened in the least. Bouncing onto her knees, she reached for the bottle on the side table. "Only if we were found out, and we won't be," she said as she clumsily refilled both their glasses. "Now drink up and stop being boring. If I want to honour a hero, I should be allowed to." She took a few gulps of her wine, then wiped the back of her hand across her mouth as she put down the glass and kicked off her shoes, the leather pumps landing with soft thuds on the woven mat beside the bed.

"At least you're going to dance with me this time, Stuart. No excuses." Disappearing into the corner of the room to reposition the needle on the vinyl, she turned with an even wickeder grin as she grabbed his hands.

Stuart resisted, then gave in. He would not let her accuse him of having no sense of fun. He'd dance with her, but that's where it would end.

As he swung her into his arms in time to the beat, he eyed the bed balefully. He could hardly return to the house and ask to be accommodated there. Unfortunately, there was no sofa or armchair since the room was so small, but if they put a bolster of pillows down the middle of the bed, he might ensure honour was maintained.

After dancing—numerous times—to 'Yellow Polka Dot Bikini', the bottle was finished, and he was feeling almost as high-spirited as Philippa. The small space had grown warm from their exertion, the night air outside seeming cool by comparison as it drifted through the slightly open window.

He'd always enjoyed dancing. The rhythm spoke to him,

and Philippa was well matched for she never missed a trick as he spun her round and back into his arms, tossed her over his arm, caught her again and swung her out again, no mean feat considering the tight dimensions of the room. Her laughter filled the space, bright and infectious, making him forget for precious moments about propriety and consequences.

They were both breathless when they finally collapsed, laughing on the bed, too exhausted to stop the record player until Stuart finally stretched out an arm and set it on its cradle. The sudden silence seemed profound after the music, filled only with their heavy breathing and the distant call of nightbirds.

"My word, but you dance well," Philippa gasped in the silence, snuggling against his side on top of the bedspread. "Who would have guessed?"

"You're not so bad yourself." Stuart smiled up at the ceiling, idly stroking her cheek. Her skin was impossibly soft, warm from their dancing.

"You think so?"

She rolled over, her face above his now, her lips inches away. He couldn't keep his eyes off them. Like mulberries. Or blackberries. Moist, inviting and ... kissable.

Reaching up, he cupped her chin, and she closed the distance, her mouth flowering against his, her breasts pressing against his chest as she lowered her body the length of his.

The kick of desire banished every hesitation as the kiss, deep and all-consuming, sucked him into the abyss. He wrapped his arms around her as he kissed her back. Her lips felt like rose petals; her breasts, pressing against his chest, begged to be explored for their own sake, for it was clear that was what she wanted.

He grasped her shoulders gently and flipped her over so he was on top, his breathing as ragged as hers, his seeking hands encountering no resistance. Her body was all contours—soft and hard in all the right places. He was hard in all the right places. Blood roared through his brain as desire coursed through his body.

Then common sense kicked in. With the greatest effort, he pulled himself back.

"Where are you going, Stuart?" Philippa's arms tightened around his neck and her body cleaved to his.

"We can't do this. It's not right," he ground out, unclasping her hands and sliding to the floor, standing a moment as his brain reeled and he tried to snatch back some sense of being in control. But the sight of her, kneeling in the middle of the messed-up bedding, her expression in the dim light showing genuine devastation, had him seriously questioning his efforts at nobility.

"I don't want you to go. Don't you... don't you have... you know?"

He tried to remind himself that she was the DC's daughter, not some fly-by-night he'd never see again. More than that, she was someone who mattered to him in ways he was only beginning to understand. He shook his head, forcing himself to imagine the next time he'd have to look Charles Tremain in the face if he gave in and did what Philippa wanted? And why did she want it? Why had she chosen him? Surely she understood the dangers?

"Philippa..." It was all he could manage as he stood by the bed, looming over her, his breath coming in short bursts, his cheeks hot and the rest of him disordered and restless.

And she looked so damned sensuous in the dim light, her cheeks flushed, one side of her blue skirt rucked up so that he could just see the suggestion of flesh above her stocking top.

"Don't you like me, Stuart?" Her eyes were wide with worry, and her mouth trembled. "Is there something wrong with me?"

"Of course not. You're... exquisite." He swallowed as he took a step back, running one hand through his hair, pushing back the cowlick. He cleared his throat. "Everything that's happened today has been one big accident. I'd be taking advantage if... this went any further." He paced so he wouldn't have to look at her, stopping at the small, curtained window where he could see nothing but darkness beyond. "You must be in shock. Yes, I'm sure that's it. In the morning, you'll thank me." He turned and tried to smile but couldn't. "Besides, your father trusted me to look after you."

"Goodness, Stuart, it's not 1850!" She rolled her eyes and threw herself onto her back across the bed with a short laugh. "Half the girls in my year at varsity aren't virgins." Pointing one stockinged toe at the ceiling, she wiggled her foot slowly, then swivelled her eyes to see his reaction.

Stuart swallowed, his attention riveted, but he couldn't reply. The casual way she spoke of such things reminded him again how much the world was changing, how the old rules his foster parents had drummed into him seemed to be crumbling around the edges.

She giggled. "I didn't expect today to turn out like it has either, but you've got to admit it's been fun." She raised her eyebrows, demanding a response, and he gave a hollow laugh, despite himself.

She looked so kittenish and ridiculously sexy as she added, "I say, let's make the most of this incredible opportunity!" that he nearly joined her on the bed. But he was sticking to his principles.

She made a pretence of pouting before her eyes flashed; her smile wicked. "I've had a crush on you since I can remember, and you've surely done this before." She indicated the bed and then herself with a sweep of her hand. "I want to know what it's like, and I want you to show me. Please, Stuart?"

The silence stretched, her soft, throaty whisper another nail in the coffin of his scruples as she reached out a hand towards him. "Please show me, Stuart."

Slowly, because he still wasn't sure he was going to go through with it, Stuart reached for his jacket hanging over the back of the chair by the bed and felt in the breast pocket for the little metal container Magda had given him the night she'd seduced him over koeksisters. The memory of that first time—awkward, overwhelming, educational— seemed like a lifetime ago.

His fingers closed around a pile of loose change, which he drew into the light.

And there it was. The innocuous-looking silver disc that might be mistaken for a foreign coin. It was certainly discreet enough to take with him wherever he went, but in three years he'd not had cause to use it.

They were both silent as they stared at it in the centre of his palm. When he glanced at her, she was frowning.

"It's not such a good idea, is it?" he asked, waiting for her to nod, for the moment had slipped away from them. He could feel it and sensed her doubt.

"Stuart, I don't know what that is, and I don't know what happens, but... I want to. And I want my first time to be with you. Truly, I do. You're..." She rose onto her haunches and suddenly peeled off her sweater, revealing the delicate shell-pink brassiere beneath. "I've always wanted my first time to be with you." She was growing more eager by the moment, half turning to present him with the back of her brassiere. "If you don't want this because you don't want me, then just say it." Her breasts rose and fell in her excitement, but he couldn't turn away. "If your reluctance is from misguided chivalry, then for goodness' sake, forget all that and... and kiss me."

She'd unclasped her brassiere herself, and as her milky breasts spilled out of the shell-pink, sturdy constriction, he hardened ever more.

"Well?" she asked, smiling coquettishly as she lay on her back and held out her arms to him.

There was no point in further resistance. She wanted this as much as he did. And perhaps in this small lamp-light-filled world, far from the judgments and expectations of their separate lives, they could simply be two people finding solace in each other.

Beneath the sheets they wriggled out of their clothes and as his thigh snaked the length of hers, his arms encircling her, Stuart felt something shift deep within his chest —a recognition that went beyond desire, beyond the physical hunger that had been building all evening. This was more than just passion; this was the culmination of years of unspoken longing. For whom, he had not consciously thought beyond a half-imagined incarnation of the movie poster starlets that had plastered the walls of his teenage prison.

But now he knew.

And she was in his arms now. Beautiful, smouldering, sexy, vulnerable Philippa Tremain, who trusted him to be the man to introduce her to new frontiers.

Her skin was silk beneath his fingertips, warm and

yielding, and when she whispered his name against his throat, it sounded like a prayer. He had imagined some version of this moment countless times over the years, but reality surpassed every fantasy. The way she moved against him, tentative yet eager, her breath catching as he traced the curve of her waist, the gentle swell of her hip—it was as if she were made to fit perfectly in his arms.

"Philippa," he breathed, her name a reverent whisper in the lamplit darkness. When she looked up at him, her eyes were luminous, trusting, and he felt the weight of that trust settle in his chest like an anchor. This beautiful, spirited woman was offering him everything—not just her body, but her heart, her faith, her very essence. The knowledge humbled him, terrified him, and filled him with a tenderness so acute it was almost painful.

He took his time, mapping every curve and hollow of her body with gentle hands and reverent lips, learning the language of her sighs, the rhythm of her breathing as it quickened beneath his touch. When she arched against him, her fingers threading through his hair, he felt as though he were drowning in the sweetest possible way.

The world outside the rondavel ceased to exist. There was only this: the dance of their bodies in the golden lamplight, the gradual building of something so beautiful and overwhelming that Stuart wondered if he would survive it. When she cried out softly against his shoulder, her body trembling in his arms, he felt his own defences crumble completely. He was lost, utterly and irrevocably lost, and for the first time in his carefully controlled life, he didn't care.

Afterwards, they lay entwined in the rumpled sheets, her head pillowed on his chest, his fingers threading through her dark hair. The hurricane lamp flickered lower, casting dancing shadows on the circular walls, but Stuart barely noticed. He was too busy memorising this moment —the weight of her body against his, the soft sound of her breathing as it gradually steadied, the way her fingertips traced lazy patterns across his skin as if she too were reluctant to let the spell break.

"You were incredible, Stuart Price," she whispered into the darkness. Not, 'I love you,' but it would do for now.

When he tilted her face up to his, her eyes held the same truth that was blazing in his own heart—this was real. A love that had come from nowhere, finally given voice in this intimate sanctuary beneath the African stars.

CHAPTER
SIX

PHILIPPA WOKE DISORIENTED, THOUGH HER HEAD CLEARED QUICKLY as the sleeping man beside her stirred. Outside the window, the familiar call of a red-eyed dove reminded her she was not in her usual surroundings.

And she wasn't ashamed in the least.

She stretched luxuriously, her whole body throbbing with pleasure. The morning light filtering through the curtains felt different somehow—brighter, more alive. Everything felt more alive.

Now she knew why Susan and all those other girls took such risks.

Had it been a risk to sleep with Stuart Price? Well, they'd taken precautions.

And it was 1961.

She would not be left behind by Susan and half the other girls at varsity. Yet as she thought this, she realised it wasn't about keeping up with Susan anymore. Last night had been about something far more profound than social competition.

Raising herself on one elbow, she studied the handsome pilot in the sliver of light that fell across the bed from a chink in the curtains. He looked different in repose. More vulnerable, when yesterday he'd seemed all action, his face set and determined. The harsh lines around his eyes had softened, making him seem younger, more approachable than the reserved man who'd saved her life.

She cupped one of her breasts, remembering what it had felt like when it had been his large, calloused hand that had done the same. Closing her eyes, she tried to dampen another heady rush of want.

Stuart might be quiet to the point of reserve on the surface, but he was as passionate as she could ever want when his defences had been breached.

Now, he seemed quite adorably gentle and, for the next little while, he was all hers.

She lowered her face to within inches of his.

She'd known how to change his mind when she wanted something from him.

And she definitely wanted more. Right now.

She shifted position, building up the courage to take him in her arms.

Or maybe just kiss him.

"Philippa?"

He woke at the touch of her lips on his cheek, his expression almost comical, for clearly his immediate reaction was guilt, whereas Philippa was determined she'd never feel guilt for her actions. The worry in his dark eyes made her heart clench unexpectedly.

Live in the moment. Don't let life pass you by.

Her mother had said these words often enough to her when she was growing up, usually while gazing wistfully out at the mountains that surrounded their small world in

Basutoland. Perhaps wondering if she'd made a mistake in choosing to live there.

Philippa snuggled against Stuart and kissed his mouth, stopping him from saying what he'd intended.

Yes, she was following her mother's advice to the letter—even though spending the night with the handsome, rugged pilot she'd had a crush on since she was a schoolgirl wasn't perhaps what her mother had had in mind.

When she'd finished kissing him, she propped herself up on one elbow again and smiled down at him.

He blinked. "You're beautiful."

"Why, thank you. You're not so bad yourself." Smiling, she tapped him on the nose, but something in his expression made her throat tighten. He was looking at her as if she were precious, as if she mattered in ways that went far beyond last night. The intensity both thrilled and terrified her. "I was thinking we should consider last night just a practice run and do it all again."

He sat up suddenly brisk. "Not possible. Though I'm not saying last night wasn't the best night of my life, but... we shouldn't have done what we did."

"Because you're afraid my father will come after you with a shotgun?"

His shocked expression made her laugh, though the sound felt forced even to her own ears. "I'm hardly about to tell him. Or anyone. So, if no one knows, what's the harm in one more time?"

He glanced at the empty metal container that had contained the prophylactic he'd used. "Practicalities, Philippa," he said, and she blushed.

She was disappointed, but perhaps it was for the best. The way he'd looked at her moments before had stirred something in her chest that felt dangerously like longing for things she'd never allowed herself to want. "We could—"

"We certainly could not. Now, would you like to use the bathroom first? We have a plane to get out of a mealie field and, since I couldn't get you to Maseru last night, we're headed to Bloemfontein as you have a train to catch. I think my boss will agree that it's the least Drakensberg Air can do under the circumstances."

But instead of agreeing and entering into the logistics, she sighed. "What about having a bath together, then?"

DEW STILL COATED the long grass, and the sun was rising above the stand of eucalypts by the road as they pushed the plane out of the field. Reluctantly, Stuart had kibosh'd the shared bath idea due to time constraints, he'd said, but mostly because he couldn't trust himself—or her—not to weaken his resolve to do the right thing.

By the time he and Philippa had presented themselves at the main house, Piet and Jacobus had picked up the barrel of Avgas Stuart had ordered and, after the requisite thanking of their hosts, they piled into the *bakkie* and drove out to the plane.

"Can I sit inside? Just for a bit?" asked Jacobus after he'd helped Stuart refuel the plane, which was now lined up on a nice, long straight stretch of dirt road.

It was easy to like the younger van Wyk brother. Stuart was happy to explain what the various knobs and levers in the cockpit did.

Piet seemed disinterested, reluctantly climbing into the cockpit when Jacobus excitedly called him.

Stuart, finishing his pre-flight check walkaround,

signalled to Philippa that they were ready, and stuck his head in to thank the van Wyk brothers.

"I see you fly this in the Drakensberg mountains in Lesotho," Piet said, pointing to the navigation log. "Lots of good diamonds there, man."

Stuart shrugged. "Not for the likes of me," he said. "It's the Wild West up there and the diggings are impossible to get to. A few locals try their luck. Hey, Philippa, are you ready?"

He stepped back to let the brothers descend the steps, and went round to help Philippa.

"Are you ready for the next adventure?" he asked, putting his hand on her waist and smiling down at her.

It was a relief when the engine engaged and the propeller, undamaged, spun into action.

"What an adventure!" Philippa blew out her breath as the plane roared over the gravelled surface of the road—Jacobus having gone ahead to ensure it was free of cars, donkeys and local villagers.

An adventure it had been with so-far, only positive outcomes, for the plane was undamaged, and the beautiful woman beside him had given herself to him, heart and soul.

Well, maybe the heart and soul bit was overdoing it, he thought, as he nosed the plane through sparse white clouds to gain altitude, but last night had been the start of something special. He could feel it.

Her dark tresses, held back by a thin black headband, rippled down the back of her seat, and Stuart reached across to feel its softness.

But although she smiled, her look was suddenly wary,

and the mood, he sensed, had switched from the intimate honeymooner behaviour she'd exhibited right up to her farewell wave to the van Wyks when she'd held Stuart's hand and caressed his cheek briefly before Stuart had helped her into the plane.

"The best adventure *I've* ever had," he said, meaning it and hoping for a signal from Philippa as to what the future held for them. Waking up beside her and being reassured she had no regrets about the night before had altered the landscape of his life. For the first time he could remember, he felt truly hopeful and happy.

"And I'm sure there'll be lots more adventures, Stuart. Who knows what the future holds?"

He glanced at her, trying to interpret her tone, for it hadn't sounded as inclusive as he'd have liked. Nor did she seem to want to make eye contact as she gazed at the landscape.

A few minutes earlier, he'd been feeling on top of the world. Now he asked tentatively, "When will you be back?" *To see your father? To see me?* The sudden shift in her mood disconcerted him.

"Christmas is in a few months," she said. "I'm not sure if Daddy will get much of a holiday, but I'll want to spend Christmas with him, of course."

And Stuart? What about him? His throat felt suddenly dry. "I sometimes have to take the plane to Jo'burg for maintenance or a charter." He cleared his throat. "Maybe next time I could take the train to Cape Town to see you?"

She blinked. "Oh Stuart, I don't know how you could manage that when it's a twenty-four-hour journey one way and... expensive."

But something flickered in her eyes—uncertainty,

perhaps even regret—as she said, "I'll always treasure the last couple of days and... I promise, I'll tell no one."

He didn't know what to say until, filling the awkward silence, she added brightly, "Who would have thought we'd be so lucky as to be taken in by the van Wyks? What a lovely family. And you were so heroic, Stuart, the way you brought the plane down. Susan and Elizabeth will only want to fly with *you* when I tell them what an amazing pilot you are and—!"

He couldn't make her out. She was babbling, and a deep blush had spread up her cheeks as she stopped suddenly.

"And what, Philippa?" he asked quietly. He wished he had the courage to prompt her with an indication of how much he wanted last night to mean more than just a single encounter.

She tucked her hair behind her ear. "And you'll go on to conquer the mountains of the world, and I'll go back to university... And beyond. To live the life I've always dreamed of."

His throat felt dry. The life she'd always dreamed of? But what about the life they might dream of together? Carefully, he asked, "What kind of life is that?"

"Cosmopolitan. It's what I am at heart. I'm not an adventurer like you." She pointed, clearly keen to cut off whatever he was about to answer, but her voice carried a note of something—longing, perhaps, or uncertainty about her own words. "Look, is that Bloemfontein in the distance?"

What would he have answered if she had given him the chance to refute her assumptions about him and to tell her what he wanted out of life? For he certainly had ambitions far beyond navigating the mountainous terrain of the tiny country that had given him so much more than London, the sprawling cosmopolitan city of his birth.

He glanced at her serene profile, watching her expectant gaze as she focused on the town ahead of them—the town where they'd say their farewells and she'd return to her everyday life—and swallowed past the painful lump lodged in his throat.

Philippa had given him a glimpse of an exciting future. A future together, if she'd let him.

They were more alike than she might imagine, both with their dreams of horizons to conquer.

HE WAS on final approach now. She'd be tensing for a thumper of a landing, being used to Lesotho's short, grassy runways. But the stretch of long, smooth tarmac in front of him gave Stuart a rare opportunity to pull off a greaser of a landing.

Not that it would do his cause much good. Philippa was dreaming of the bright lights of cosmopolitan Cape Town. Already he could feel her slipping away, and he had no idea what to do about it.

"When will I see you again?" he shouted over the roar of the engine as the plane neared its final destination.

"I'm sure we'll cross paths next time I come home. There's Christmas. My birthday. Gosh, I can see Mr and Mrs Lehmann waiting for me over there! They must have been so worried! How wonderful to see them!"

Having a welcoming party was anything but wonderful, thought Stuart as he glanced out of his side window to see the DC's elderly neighbours waving from the edge of the apron, the shabby arrivals building behind them, a baggage handler emerging from the hangar.

"Yes, I have no doubt they've been worried sick about you." He heard the edge to his tone, but Philippa was quiet as he backtracked the runway before coming to a stop outside the terminal building, another Cessna temporarily concealing them from sight.

"Perhaps—" He blurted out, not knowing what to say next. "Perhaps you could write and tell me you got to Cape Town all right," he suggested lamely as she reached for her handbag. She was clearly preparing for an immediate and abrupt departure, and the disappointment was crushing.

"No news is good news, Stuart. I'll be fine."

So now she was the Ice Maiden. There was nothing he could do or say to bridge the wall that had gone up between them the moment they'd left the van Wyks.

She turned, gripped her handbag, and then, to his surprise, hesitated. Her carefully composed expression cracked just slightly. "Oh, Stuart," she whispered, then reached across the small space and kissed him full on the mouth.

He'd not been expecting that, and hope stirred him to action. He put his arms about her. There wasn't time to read her expression, and he wasn't about to let her go when she made to pull away. She sagged against him and let him breach the seam of her lips with the tip of his tongue.

Then she drew back quickly, her eyes wide and suspiciously bright. He was conscious of his own ragged breathing as she smiled uncertainly at him. "Thanks for everything, Stuart. For saving my life, for last night—" she was speaking more rapidly now, as if afraid she might say too much— "and for getting me here in time to catch my connection. Keep an eye on Daddy for me. He needs rescuing as much as I do." Her voice caught slightly on the last words.

He didn't say anything before he opened his door and jumped onto the tarmac before coming round to open her door. The warm air of the lowlands rushed into the cockpit, and he put out his hand to help her out of the plane.

"Philippa, can I ask just one question?" His hands encircled her waist, and as he swung her down, he added softly, "Don't worry, no one can see." He could tell she was disconcerted, for her breathing had ratcheted up.

"Yes, of course."

His hands dropped to his sides. "If I do go to Cape Town, will you let me see you again?"

She blushed deeply and gave him a small smile. "Yes, of course, Stuart."

And then she was turning, smoothing her pale yellow and black tartan skirt over her slim hips as she walked away.

CHAPTER

SEVEN

HOURS LATER, RESTING AGAINST THE LEATHER SEATS OF THE Bloemfontein to Cape Town train, Philippa watched the landscape changing from the desert dry of the Karoo to the lush green of the Cape. The rhythmic clacking of wheels on tracks should have been soothing, but her mind refused to settle.

Why did she feel so very different? The porter had just looked in on them and, glancing up, Philippa realised she'd read the same paragraph of her novel three times.

She kept seeing Stuart's face staring at her from the pages; the unruly thatch of dark blonde hair which fell across his forehead and which he was always tossing back.

And which she wanted to run her hands through—if only he were here.

When she doggedly forced her attention back to what was happening in her Georgette Heyer novel, all she could see was the serious look in Stuart's cool blue eyes, and his sensitive mouth curving in admiration as he looked at her. It did strange things to her insides—if she let it.

Other girls from her residence greeted her cheerfully as

she made her way towards her room a few hours later. She wondered if they would notice the change in her. Could they tell that she was now a young woman in control of her own destiny who'd shown strength by taking the initiative?

Or would they only remember the pathetic child weeping in the corridor that terrible night of Angela Myer's twenty-first birthday?

A THOUSAND MILES AWAY, at about the time Philippa was stepping into her bedroom and returning to her familiar old life, Stuart finished filing his official report on the events of the past forty-eight hours. At least, those pertaining to the unscheduled landing of the Cessna.

Nothing could neatly categorise the non-official aspects of all that had occurred.

The cramped office in the terminal building where he filled in the paperwork now seemed suffocating, despite the view from the window promising a majestic kingdom to explore.

With chores to do, and letters to send, he drove into town and parked outside the post office where, stepping out, he encountered, to his discomfort, Lizzie Cameron, the young woman he'd stood up for their Friday night dinner date.

Waiting, frozen on the pavement, for her to reach him, he remembered how close to the edge he'd teetered, weighing up whether or not to ask her to marry him.

Whether or not he could *afford* to ask her to marry him.

Lizzie tucked a strand of dark blonde hair behind her ear as she hurried towards him. Her neat blonde bob bounced on her shoulders, and Stuart couldn't help noticing her voluptuous breasts did the same.

Which made his cheeks burn, for he could only think how different they were from Philippa's. Lizzie's figure was neat and trim, but she was well-endowed, as his mother used to say.

Strange how that didn't seem such an asset when compared with Philippa's smaller, but so much sexier breasts. He tried to rein in his thoughts.

"Stuart, you're back! Oh, my goodness, but I was so worried about you!"

The dimples in her rosy cheeks popped out, and her eyes shone with genuine relief. But his manner must have deterred her from the warmer greeting that would have been warranted if Stuart hadn't met Philippa.

He tamped down his conflicted thoughts and regulated his tone.

"Back on solid ground, safe and sound," he reassured her, his hands at his sides. "I just filed the accident report."

Lizzie bit her lip, and a worried look shadowed the transparent pleasure of a moment before. She was a girl whose emotions were always plain to see. Even Stuart could read her like a book, and he didn't consider himself particularly intuitive. It was one reason he'd taken to Lizzie. He never had to guess what she was feeling, and it was hard not to like a pretty girl who was generally cheerful and who'd clearly fallen for him.

It had seemed like enough, before Philippa had shown him what it felt like when every emotion was heightened, every moment charged with electricity.

"I heard the plane came down in the Orange Free State. Oh, Stuart!"

"These things happen," Stuart told her with a shrug,

turning back to reach into his vehicle for the parcel he was going to post. "You know what the weather can be like."

She nodded, her attention shifting to the red pillar letterbox beside them.

"Stuart, I–"

"Lizzie, I–"

They spoke at the same time, but he let her go first, and she said in a rush, "Pietermaritzburg Hospital really needs an answer." He saw then that she was also holding a letter and knew with a sinking heart how much his response meant to her.

God, this was hard. He hated disappointing her. Lizzie deserved better than being someone's second choice.

Though wasn't he just as disappointed? He felt he'd come through an earthquake these past couple of days. As kindly as he could, he said, "I think a stint at Pietermaritzburg Hospital would be a great opportunity for you, Lizzie."

"You do?" Her head jerked up, the moistness in her eyes almost immediate. Stuart couldn't meet her gaze.

But what else could he do? Philippa might have been prickly when he was saying goodbye, but the physicality between them was electrifying to the end. Just when he'd lost hope, she'd leaned across to kiss him full on the mouth. And he knew she'd felt the connection it had ignited as much as he had. He mightn't be that perceptive, but there could be no faking the look of surprise in her eyes when she'd been forced to acknowledge it.

Perhaps when she had time to think properly about this connection between them, she'd be the first to write and ask him to visit. For she was mistaken if she believed their ambitions were poles apart and that he couldn't give her what she wanted.

Gently, he touched Lizzie's shoulder. "You're a fabulous girl, Lizzie. Maseru is too small for you. You need opportunities to... to grow and reach your potential." Trite, horrible words, but the least brutal he could think of right now.

She blinked rapidly. "So, you think I should accept the nursing position in Pietermaritzburg and... leave Maseru?"

He could barely look at her. She was so sweet. So deserving. He really didn't want to hurt her.

"Meaning... I'd never see you again?" The last came out in just a whisper. He could see the tears wobbling on her lashes.

Stuart shifted the parcel into his other hand and stared at the mountains over her shoulder. "I'd always look you up if I were in town. We'd go out like we do here. You're a good friend, Lizzie."

"A good friend," she repeated softly, turning away from the letter box and tucking the letter she'd been about to post back into her handbag. She cleared her throat and presented him with her back, her voice strangled as she added, half over her shoulder, "I'm sorry, I really must go, Stuart."

He'd been about to take her elbow and say something else bolstering that made him feel less bad about himself, but was glad when she shook him off and started to walk briskly away.

With the way he felt about Philippa, he couldn't compromise what was in his heart and do Lizzie the disservice of pretending something he didn't feel.

As he watched her retreating figure, Stuart wondered if this was how it would always be now—measuring every other woman against the memory of violet eyes and raven hair, against the feeling of coming completely alive in someone else's arms.

Philippa stepped into her room and ran a long look over the familiar pink eiderdown on her bed by the window. Susan's bed, with its blue coverlet, was lined up along the other wall, a shared bedside table between them.

Had it really been less than ten days ago that she'd left this place, her heart eviscerated, her anger towards Susan so intense she thought she could never see her again without causing her harm?

The feelings were still raw but, despite the uncertainty of what lay ahead, Philippa felt a strange calm as she put her handbag on the bed and untied her scarf, dropping it together with her sunglasses and gloves onto the satin eiderdown.

Easing herself into the armchair by the window, she closed her eyes and tipped her head to the ceiling.

She had expelled the awfulness that had preceded her flight to Lesotho. Forever. Her future now was however she moulded it.

"Good trip?"

Susan, wearing a pink flannel dressing gown with a white towel wrapped around her head, opened the bedroom door and paused on the threshold. Her smile was tight and nervous.

As it bloody well should be!

"Yes, thanks." Unable to sit still with Susan in the same room, Philippa rose, her smile cool as she opened the suitcase the porter had put on the bed. She lifted out her blue wool skirt. A mealie husk clung to the hem, and she pulled it off with a mix of emotions. Had she really spent the night with a man? A handsome pilot who'd made a forced landing in a mealie field? The whole crazy, thrilling adventure felt like it had happened to someone else—someone braver, more spontaneous than the Philippa who had left this room in tears.

"You can come in, Susan. It is our room, and I won't bite your head off." It was hard to sound calm when her heart was pounding at the thought of her time with Stuart. "Shall I tell you all about my adventures while I get organised?" She held up the cashmere twinset she'd worn the day before. Would Stuart's aftershave still linger?

She heard the door close and Susan's soft breathing.

"Or perhaps you have more exciting things to tell me?" Philippa turned and looked long and hard at Susan. Oh, how she'd like to scratch her eyes out. Except, strangely, her anger didn't have as much force as she'd expected. "Such as what you and Matthew have been up to and how nice it was to have me out of the way for a while?"

There. The words were out, the challenge issued, sucking the air from Philippa's lungs while she waited.

Through the open window, a gust of wind stirred the curtains, carrying the scent of jasmine from the gardens below. Then Susan put her hands to her face as she sat heavily on her bed.

"Oh, Philippa, I don't know what came over me," she mumbled. "I'm so, so sorry, and I don't expect you'll ever forgive me. We've been friends forever, and I can't bear to think what a terrible time you've had during the past week. When you walked in on Matthew and me and I said what I did, not just at the time but afterwards—" She stopped, waving her hands as if she were the one who'd suffered the most. "Oh, Philippa, I just have to tell you that—"

Philippa sighed. "It's all right, Susan," she said, even though it was not all right. But she was determined to be the bigger person in all this. And perhaps after everything that had happened, it didn't matter quite as much as it had.

"Please, Philippa..." Susan tried again as she removed the towel wrapped around her wet ginger head and ran her fingers through her damp curls. "Matthew and I—"

"Actually, I don't want to hear about Matthew and you, after all," Philippa cut her off, though to her surprise she didn't feel as sick as she thought she would about what Matthew and Susan had been getting up to.

In fact, it was hard to focus on Matthew or Susan because a jumble of images from the past two days were racing through her mind.

And, pinned at the top as the most unforgettable, was the moment Stuart's arms had first gone around her as he'd dragged her from the plane, segueing into the night they'd spent together in the same bed.

Philippa's cheeks burned. Hadn't that been the most thrilling adventure of her life?

Right now, Matthew seemed tame in comparison. Certainly not the man Stuart was.

She took a deep breath and put the best spin she could on matters. If Matthew was out of reach, she would not demean herself by chasing after him. There were other compensations. She could feel her way a little. Her future didn't need to be set in stone as she'd thought it did by the age of twenty-one.

The reflection landed with unexpected clarity.

Why did she want to be like so many of her friends who, one by one, were hooking up and getting married? Hadn't she already proved she was different, more wild, by taking up the opportunity to go to university instead of using a typing job to fill in the short time before marriage and babies?

Raising her chin, she said, "Clearly Matthew isn't worth weeping over and besides, I had far more fun in one night coming back from Mokhotlong than I'd have had in a lifetime with Matthew."

Susan let the towel she'd been vigorously drying her hair with drop to her lap as she sat on her bed. "Not with... Captain Darling?"

"How did you guess?"

"Oh, good Lord!" Susan clapped her hands over her mouth before excitedly begging for more. Suddenly, the air between them seemed clearer. They'd been friends for as long as Philippa could remember. In their childhood, their occasional tiffs had been over dolls and during pretend tea parties.

Now they were adults, and the root of their disagreements might be different, but a lifetime of friendship couldn't be destroyed over something like this—could it? No, not unless Philippa let it.

And despite Susan's treachery, hadn't Philippa now proved that Susan hadn't left her behind? That she was every bit as worldly? And desired?

"Tell me everything, Philippa. And don't you dare leave out a single detail! Do you remember that time you told me you were determined he would be the first man to kiss you? And... he did? Kiss you, I mean. Did he? Did he kiss you?"

Philippa looked up at the ceiling and felt herself blush. "Not only that..." she murmured before turning to look at her friend, adding, "Oh Susan, it was quite the most marvellous night of my life. We crash-landed in a mealie field, and then the family who took us in thought we were married and gave us the guest rondavel and Stuart and I—"

She halted. She hadn't meant to blurt it all out. But

despite everything that had happened, Susan was still her best friend, and she had to confide in someone.

Susan's brows knitted. "You don't mean..." She pressed her lips together. "Oh Philippa, surely you didn't....?"

Philippa hesitated before responding hotly. "Don't take the moral high ground with me, Susan. Who did I catch in bed with Matthew after he'd invited me to the ball—"

"*On* the bed, Philippa. There's a big difference!"

"On the bed, in the bed, what difference does it make when it was so plain to see what you two had been up to? Why, your lips were fused to his!"

"I didn't sleep with him!" Susan glared. "I had too much to drink, and so did Matthew. He went looking for you and staggered drunkenly into the room where I was lying on the bed, and he fell on me." She shrugged. "I don't know quite how it happened. Then we started kissing. And don't blame me for kissing him back because I don't think any girl could resist Matthew. Anyway, you walked in at that point and started weeping and wailing, but we hadn't done anything."

Philippa stared. "But that's not what... you said. You said you had..." Suddenly she felt all hollow inside. "You gloated!"

Susan had the grace to look ashamed. "I shouldn't have, I know. I felt so bad, and my first instinct was to go on the attack." She twisted her hands together in her lap, then began to chip away at her pink nail polish. "It's true I was jealous that Matthew had asked you to the ball, and then when you found us, I let you think the worst." She looked up, adding, "I didn't actually say we'd done it, though."

"But for months you'd been spouting all this female liberation stuff and left all those magazine articles out for me." Philippa's cheeks grew hot. "Of course, I assumed the worst. And I guess those magazines got through to me too… I…"

"Was influenced?"

Susan looked at Philippa as if she were a creature from another planet and not the friend she'd done everything with until she'd betrayed her. Except that Susan was now saying she hadn't betrayed Philippa—not in the way Philippa had thought.

Susan resumed towelling her hair, though she couldn't seem to keep her eyes off Philippa's flaming face. "I can't believe you went to bed with Stuart Price. What was it like? What was *he* like?" She giggled nervously. "Was he as wonderful a lover as we imagined? Remember when we were just silly schoolgirls, we said that if there was any pilot we'd choose to crash land with, it would be Stuart Price… Captain Darling."

Philippa smiled weakly. She'd felt so grown up yesterday as she'd played out the role of the romantic heroine, cast adrift with her handsome rescuer.

Susan's little episode with Matthew had been devastating, and she'd needed to assert her desirability.

But if that's how it had started, it had ended very differently.

She put her hand on her chest and tried to work out how she felt. The answer was complicated—triumphant, yes, but also strangely vulnerable. And missing something, or someone, with an intensity that surprised her.

"If you don't mind," she said, "I'd rather we did not speak of this again."

Susan looked surprised. Then she smiled. "Of course I'll keep your secret, Pippa, if that's what you want. We're best friends." The abject Susan of a few minutes ago was nowhere in evidence as she began to comb her hair. "When are you going to see Stuart again?"

It took a moment for her question to sink in.

Philippa stared out of the window. At majestic Table Mountain, that seemed so small compared to the rugged peaks Stuart had negotiated with such skill such a short time ago.

She'd said she'd see him if he came to Cape Town. And her body had thrilled at the idea, even as she'd been digesting the truth of her extraordinary adventure.

What had happened between them had been an anomaly. Stuart belonged to a world she'd left behind.

A world of danger and adventure. A world her mother had embraced, perhaps because she didn't know any better coming from her safe, privileged world.

It must have been a shock, leaving behind her beautiful clothes, and her busy social schedule with its balls and parties to come to a rugged, unforgiving land, shadowed by strange beliefs. Like culturally sanctioned murder. Her father's *diretlo* investigation was a reminder of how hard it was to quell traditions that had been around since the beginning of time: a chief's belief that the horrific practice of carving body parts from the living flesh of their victims—before hurling the broken bodies into ravines to die—would create potent *muti* for their medicine horns that would frighten their people into submission and abeyance.

As she pondered all this, the light from the window glinted off her grandmother's diamond ring, now back on her right hand. It had precipitated her dangerous, illicit adventure with Stuart after she'd deceived the van Wyks into believing she and Stuart were married, but she had no regrets.

Memories of his handsome face and capable hands kept intruding.

When are you going to see Stuart again?

Susan's question went round and round in her head.

Could there be a future between them? she wondered. She'd been so sure there could never be—

Why? Because the gulf seemed so great between them. He was a loner, an adventurer... A womaniser? She and Susan and Elizabeth had once assumed so, simply because he was so handsome, but she didn't think so now.

She touched the perfect cut stone and tried to imagine the life she'd lead as Mrs Price.

Diamonds? They were just as much a part of the Basutoland she knew, although the diamond on her hand couldn't have come from the diamond diggings at Letseng-la-Terai since prospecting by the local Basotho had only been allowed in the last ten years.

But if she married Stuart, was Basutoland where she'd be destined to live? She didn't know if Stuart had prospects. Or connections.

And at her age, how much time did she have to wait?

Pushing open the window a little wider, she leaned out and breathed in the smell of the ocean.

In the distance, she could just see Cape Town's white-fringed beaches near which were located the city's expensive, established suburbs, like the one where Matthew lived with his father, Cape Town's most prominent lawyer, and his mother, a well-recognised socialite.

Behind her, Susan sighed. "Clearly, you're not listening to a word I'm saying. Here. Matthew gave me this to give to you."

Philippa turned and took the white envelope Susan thrust into her hand.

"He said it would explain to you that things weren't quite like you'd thought." After a minute, Susan put her head on one side and asked, "Well? Aren't you going to read it?"

"I'd like to be alone when I do," Philippa whispered, running her forefinger up and down the smooth, expensive stationery with its embossed watermark. Her head felt strange and heavy, yet light at the same time. Was that hope she felt? Or fear and trepidation? "Please could you go now, Susan?"

When she heard the door close behind her friend, she reached for her nail file on the bedside table and carefully opened the letter.

No doubt Matthew had taken the sheet from his mother's escritoire. Mrs Myburgh would have the most elegant stationery money could buy. Philippa could imagine the woman, exquisitely dressed, writing out invitations to her next society event.

Her breath hitched.

Writing out letters informing her friends of her son's wedding...?

Or wedding invitations if his fiancée didn't have a mother.

She felt the texture of the vellum, closing her eyes as she breathed in its faint perfume. It reminded her of the paper on which her grandmother had written her last letter to her youngest daughter. The letter that had cut ties between Philippa's darling mother and her aristocratic family in England because 'Eleanor had turned her back on kith and kin' by marrying a man the family considered beneath her.

At first it had filled her with rage, for her mother had been exquisite, stoic, delightful and uncomplaining. And her father was a king among men: principled, honourable, loving.

Her parents had been devoted—how dare anyone suggest they weren't made for each other?

But now, having seen how much bigger and more worldly Cape Town was compared with her childhood mountain home, Philippa wondered if her mother had regretted the choice she'd made.

Not about her father—of course—but the life that marrying him entailed. The isolation. The limitations. The small world when she'd been meant for a larger stage.

She heard Susan drop something on the other side of the wall, and quickly Philippa turned her attention to what Matthew had written.

"Dear Philippa, I am so sorry. What you saw completely misrepresented the situation. I thought I was kissing you. Believe me, nothing happened between Susan and me. You're the only girl for me. Can things be like they were before? Please?"

Philippa swallowed, the letter falling into her lap as she looked towards the window.

All she could see was that enormous mountain, staring right at her, which conjured up an image of Stuart, gazing at her with his crooked, enigmatic smile that made her stomach clench with desire.

But when she closed her eyes, she was sure she could hear the roar of the sea.

And suddenly it was Matthew's confident, Adonis-good looks that dominated. And Philippa imagined him writing his letter to her at the urging of his mother, who'd seen the photographs of Philippa crowned Cape Town's Rag Queen, the most beautiful girl in her year.

Philippa, whose mother was one of the famous Richmond sisters, and the granddaughter of an earl.

She took a deep breath as she rose from the bed, the dominating mountain filling her vision.

Was it a sign? Was this mighty mountain staring at her as she held Mathew's apology in her hand a reminder of her true destiny?

To stay here, in a civilised country, and marry a man with all the right connections, who she *knew* could give her the life she wanted?

A man she had feelings for.

Even if it meant turning her back on a pair of gloriously passion-filled blue eyes and calloused hands, and the feeling of being completely, vibrantly alive in someone's arms?

CHAPTER

EIGHT

TWO MONTHS LATER

STUART NOSED THE CESSNA INTO THE WIND AS HE LINED UP HIS approach.

It had been pleasantly warm in Maseru down in the lowlands, but Mokhotlong, at 10,000 ft, would be icy. And at another thousand feet, Letseng-la-Terai would be even more unpleasant when his single passenger disembarked.

It was one reason Stuart was glad he'd be returning to the capital for another uneventful Friday night.

Battling the wind as he came in to land, he glimpsed the DC, Charles Tremain, leaning over the gate at the bottom of his garden and suddenly wondered why the fellow didn't find himself a wife if he was going to stay in this god-forsaken place where summer still could herald snowstorms.

Stuart had reached the point where he thought it would be nice to have a wife just so he had someone to talk to over a shared meal every night, not to mention a warm body next to him in bed.

It had been a blow to receive Philippa's cool, dismissive response to his letter. He'd written to say he'd like to visit her. It had taken him days of negotiation with Dan to arrange time off so he could actually follow through in anticipation of some enthusiasm at the idea from Philippa, for that last, unexpected kiss in the cockpit had given him hope. But Philippa, apparently, had found bigger fish to fry.

The rich, entitled young man who'd apparently—and ever so briefly—broken her heart was back in the picture.

As for the follow-up letter he'd sent her—well, she'd never replied.

Tremain waved as he ambled over to greet them. "Letsi thought you'd forgotten him," he remarked with a laconic grin at the young police trooper at his side. "He's impatient to get to Letseng-la-Terai. Isn't that right, Letsi?"

"Ee, *Rra*," agreed Letsi with little enthusiasm.

"Blasted weather," Stuart muttered in explanation for being late. He hoped Tremain wouldn't start talking about his daughter's latest exploits. Stuart had heard enough in town about Philippa and her diamond-heir boyfriend.

Mrs Lehmann, who'd come in that morning to buy a ticket from Diana at Drakensberg Air, had said she'd eat her hat if the pair weren't engaged before Christmas, launching into an enthusiastic discussion with Diana on Mrs Myburgh's exquisite fashion sense for she was—apparently —frequently featured in the Society column in Fair Lady Magazine. As for her only son, Matthew—Mrs Lehmann had gone on—he'd certainly inherited his mother's good looks, and now that he'd just finished university, he was being groomed to take over the legal division of the Myburgh diamond enterprise.

What chance did Stuart have?

"Let's hope the weather holds for your second flight up

the mountain this afternoon, then," said Tremain. "You've got precious cargo."

"Philippa is back for the summer holidays?" He hoped his blush and stammer didn't give him away.

"And bringing along her fellow, Matthew Myburgh, for us to meet. The young man's just finished his final law exams and wants to see Basutoland's diamond operations firsthand. With the family business so often tied up in negotiations and mining rights, they think a son trained in law will be an asset." Tremain sucked on his pipe. "I'm taking him up to Letseng-la-Terai. Obviously, it's small scale compared to the big consortiums who'd be of most interest to the family business, but we've had our share of impressive finds, and I think the lad should know how we do things here." He sounded proud, and Stuart, from some perverse need to push back, if only to make himself feel better, muttered, "Maybe it's better off as a well-kept secret. You don't want the big guns coming to town and taking away the opportunity for the local Mosotho to strike it lucky."

He knew how much sympathy the DC had for local interests.

"That's getting harder the deeper they've having to dig with their primitive equipment," countered Charles. "Anyway, I'll explain all that to Matthew. Philippa hasn't said much about him, but no doubt he's a smart enough fellow."

"How long's he staying?"

"A week. I'll take him on trek for a couple of days. Best way to see the country, and Philippa assures me he's a good horseman."

Stuart hoped the chap's horse stumbled and pitched him into a ravine, but he said instead, "Philippa doesn't ride?"

"No. Terrified of horses ever since she fell off and broke her collarbone when she was seven. She'll stay at the residence while Matthew gets his education in mountain diamond mining at high altitudes." He grimaced, adding, "And what to look out for when it comes to suspected bogus diamond buyers."

Stuart gave a half laugh and said thoughtlessly, "No, I'd imagine the administration doesn't want another embarrassment."

"Lord, no! Though of course it's only those who breach our defences who get all the publicity. Last week, I apprehended a chap who was trying to channel a diamond illegally obtained from Orapa through one of our miners at the diggings. Anglo American Corporation regulates the diamond markets of the world, and we're in no position to flout the rules of "big brother" South Africa. De Beers takes a dim view of it, and we have to toe the line." He sighed. "I have to have eyes in the back of my head. And it's not just de Beers. The moment the locals see the administration supposedly turning a blind eye to corruption, you're on a dangerous downward trajectory."

The DC switched tack, clapping the young Mosotho on the back. "Off you go, then, Letsie. And keep up the good work."

So Matthew Myburgh was flying up from Maseru this afternoon with Philippa? No way was Stuart going to do that run.

But three hours later and after an unsuccessful attempt at finding another pilot to swap with him, Stuart was duly waiting by the plane for his passengers, and having a hard time remaining impassive as his nemesis greeted with a condescending smile, and a "So, you're the pilot who saved the day when Pippa was sure she was going to die."

Philippa blushed as she murmured a hello, after which she was studiously quiet before she began a forced conversation with her patently unworthy companion while Stuart did his walk-around, checking the plane prior to take-off.

Matthew had *self-entitlement* written all over him. From his perfectly pressed brown woollen trousers to his confident handshake, as if establishing dominance, he exuded the air of a man who'd never had to fight for anything in his life.

Mind you, Stuart had thought the same about Michael Franklin—his so-called foster brother—when Stuart had first arrived in Pretoria to live with the Franklins as a British war evacuee. Back then, he'd used the word *self-entitled* for anyone without holes in their clothes and who spoke the King's English.

But no child of Mrs Franklin—Aunt Edith, as he'd call the good woman who had, figuratively at least, saved his life—could be stuck up. Michael had only been shy.

It was Michael who had taught Stuart to fly, not long after the Franklins visited London and swept him and Gracie away on what they called their Grand Tour of 1952. One moment they were scraping by in a Seven Dials hellhole; the next, they were being ferried through snow-tipped Alps, strolling the boulevards of Paris, and gliding down the Rhine as if they'd stepped out of one of Gracie's fairy stories. For six incredible months, sixteen-year-old Stuart and fifteen-year-old Gracie had lived the high life as if they were Edith and James Franklin's cherished, natural born children and not two slum kids the well-to-do couple had taken pity on.

Adjusting to life when they returned to London had been a battle. Their pa had been surly and resentful while pressing Stuart to do the things Stuart had always hated doing for him—things that were immoral or illegal; and his mother had been as much the harpy as ever. The poisonous combination had been the impetus he needed to put aside every spare penny to save a boat fare to return to South Africa.

Getting away was all he dreamed of.

But of course he had to see his sister Gracie settled first.

"Pippa talks about you to anyone who'll listen," Matthew went on conversationally as he buckled himself into the front right-hand seat. Philippa had quickly chosen the back seat, Stuart noticed.

Glancing over his shoulder to check she was safely secured, Stuart saw her cheeks flame as she caught his look. He didn't return the shaky smile she offered before she countered, "I don't know what you mean, Matthew. You make it sound like I talk behind people's backs."

"You were lauding Captain Price's heroism. That's what I meant," Matthew said with what appeared to be his trademark grin—smarmy and confident. But his abrasive charm and attempt to ingratiate himself were lost on Stuart, who merely grunted when Matthew went on with a puppy-dog edge to his enthusiasm, "Father's very interested in the diamond operations up here. Quite different from the big corporate mines down south, from what Mr Tremain tells me. Must take a lot of skill to fly in this terrain, and to these remote diggings. I'd love some pointers while I'm here if you have the time. I'd pay you, of course."

Stuart ignored the remark. Raising his voice over the noise of the engine, he said, "It'll be cold on the mountain. I hope you've brought something warmer." Matthew was wearing an open-necked shirt. Stuart hoped he froze to death.

No, he hoped he'd soon die in the fiery furnace of hell, Stuart amended when Matthew chuckled and said, "In my carryall. Pippa will keep me warm until it's unloaded." Matthew turned to look over his shoulder, no doubt wondering why his words didn't elicit the expected girlish giggle, and Stuart got some small satisfaction from seeing her squirm instead as she looked out of the window.

How could she favour this trumped-up try-hard? Philippa was far too good for Matthew Myburgh.

But Philippa was too good for Stuart, too. Although she hadn't said it in those words, it's clearly what she'd thought as she'd penned that polite, distant reply to Stuart's letter suggesting that he visit her in Cape Town only days after their encounter.

Encounter. That's all it was to her, he thought bitterly as he adjusted the throttle and nosed the plane up towards the thick clouds, looking for a hole to break through. One night of slumming it with the hired help before returning to her proper world.

Matthew opened his mouth, presumably to say something else inane about his father's business interests, and Stuart reached over to open the air vent. A rush of icy wind blasted through the small triangular window and flooded the cockpit with a thunderous din.

And even though Stuart shivered, it had the desired effect of silencing the most unwelcome of all passengers he'd ever ferried between the lowlands and the mountains.

As they climbed through the clouds, Stuart considered Tremain's oft-repeated opinion about the importance of keeping the diamond wealth in local hands. It was admirable, he supposed, though naïve. Money always found a way to flow towards those who already had it. Men like Matthew's father, who could afford to send their sons on educational trips to remote diamond fields to learn how to exploit new opportunities, would no doubt make good use of the information. The day would come when the bounty from Lesotho's diamonds would no longer be even an optional source of largesse for the local people.

Stuart sent another look at Philippa, who was gazing out at the mountain peaks with an expression he couldn't read. She looked elegant even in the cramped cabin, her dark hair swept back, her profile perfect against the stark landscape beyond the window.

He should accept that she really did belong in Matthew's world of privilege and opportunity, not in Stuart's world of uncertainty and struggle.

How foolish to think that one night—no matter how perfect it had seemed—could bridge the gap between their different spheres. Philippa had made her choice, and it wasn't him.

WHEN THEY LANDED, Philippa jumped to the ground and came round to Stuart's side as he sat recording the fuel reserves, her eyes flashing. "Matthew nearly died of cold up there," she hissed while Matthew, on the other side and out of hearing, unbuckled his seat belt with no-doubt stiff fingers, as Philippa went on, "You had no—"

"I'm the pilot and I always have the side vents open," Stuart replied, not looking at her as he continued to work. To be honest, he was taken aback by her unexpected sharpness, but replied with studied calm, "He should have been better prepared. Or did you not warn your poor chap about what you had in store for him?" He snapped his logbook shut, adding with a cool smile, "I didn't take to him, I'll admit, but I'm starting to feel sorry for Matthew Myburgh."

She drew in a sharp breath, but her look was conflicted as she kept her lips pressed together. For a moment, Stuart thought she might say something; that she might—even obliquely—acknowledge what had happened between them. But then Matthew called her name, and the moment shattered.

Tossing his logbook onto the passenger seat, Stuart got out of the plane, saying to her under his breath, "My lips are sealed, if that's what you're worried about. Charles!" He raised his hand and called across the yellow grass to the DC, who was striding over to meet the arrivals. "You've got your Christmas wish."

"Hello, Daddy." Philippa welcomed him with a hug, smiling as she pretended complicity in Stuart's bonhomie, after she'd introduced Matthew. "Unfortunately, I'm not staying for Christmas." She affected a *moue* of disappointment before adding with more animation, "Daddy, the Myburghs have invited *both of us* down to the Cape to join them for Christmas. Won't that be nice for a change? Do say you can come for a few days? Surely you can manage that with nearly three weeks before to make plans."

"Darling, I'm not sure that–"

"I wasn't referring to that Christmas wish." Stuart cut her off, his voice harder than he'd intended. "Your father wants to keep the illegal diamond buyers at bay through Christmas, and now he has a new right-hand man." He nodded at Matthew. "Someone with fresh eyes and family connections in the diamond trade."

Charles laughed, clapping Matthew on the back. "Well,

I hadn't thought about it in those terms, but if you can add a fresh perspective regarding how illegal diamond buying and trading networks operate, Matthew—and they're growing more devious by the day—then I'd love to join you for Christmas."

"Happy families!" gushed Philippa, presenting Stuart with a shapely shoulder that was immediately commandeered by Matthew's possessive arm as she turned to speak to her—

Boyfriend.

"And where are you spending Christmas, Stuart?" Matthew asked as the four of them crossed the field towards the gate. His tone was friendly enough, but there was something challenging in his look. Did he suspect? Did he see Stuart as a competitor?

He was almost disappointed that the answer was probably 'no' to both, as the young man went on with his perfect manners and just the right degree of feigned sympathy, "I'm sorry to hear you lost your mother recently. Philippa told me. But you have a sister, don't you?"

Stuart, who'd picked up Philippa's bag—for Matthew had left that to the hired help—shifted it to his other hand as he walked at his side. The casual way Matthew wielded personal information—information Philippa had shared with him—felt like another small betrayal. "She's dead."

The words fell like stones into the sudden silence, and Stuart saw Philippa flinch. Good. Let her feel uncomfortable. Let her remember that not everyone lived in her protected world where the worst tragedy was choosing between suitors.

"I'm sorry," Matthew said, though his tone suggested he was already moving past the awkwardness. "One's family is everything, isn't it? Father always says that's why our business works so well—keeping it in the family, people you can trust."

Stuart nodded curtly. How easy that was to say when Matthew was destined to inherit the family's diamond operation that had built a fortune on mining rights and industry contracts.

As they waited for Charles to open the gate, while chatting companionably with Matthew, Stuart stood level with Philippa. She looked awkward at first, raising her chin to meet his gaze with something that might have been regret. But then Matthew's hand tightened on her shoulder, drawing her close, and she turned away.

CHAPTER
NINE

ANOTHER TWO MONTHS LATER

It was hard to believe Christmas had already come and gone. Philippa and her father had enjoyed the Myburghs' hospitality in Cape Town, and now she was back in Maseru, where the late-January heat shimmered off the dusty roads and afternoon thunderstorms gathered and broke with little warning.

How could she not be with her father—and her other best friend, Elizabeth, whom she'd grown up with—for her twenty-first birthday?

Susan had, of course, been invited, but her cousin was getting married the same weekend and, to be honest, Philippa wasn't too disappointed. Though they still shared a room at Fuller Hall, Philippa found she preferred the sophistication of Matthew's friends and family to the sometimes tiring company of Susan.

"Roses would be nice as a centrepiece, don't you think? I've got plenty blooming in the garden, Philippa." Elizabeth Walters stopped by the buffet table Philippa was contemplating in the dining room of the Country Club, her arms full of starched white tablecloths. "We'll bring a bunch when we set up tonight."

"You're very sweet, you know." Philippa had been touched by her Maseru friends' enthusiasm for whipping up what had started as a surprise gathering for her at the Club. They'd heard she was coming home for a small 'do' her father was putting on at the DC's residence in Mokhotlong; an event that would be attended by old-timers, friends of her father, and late mother.

But friends with whom Philippa had grown up in Maseru would also attend this event at the Country Club. Many had gone to South Africa to study or work but had come back for the party, making up a table of eight for her little birthday gathering later that evening.

"You must miss Matthew terribly," Elizabeth sympathised as she caught Philippa gazing through the windows at the mountains. The peaks looked deceptively soft in the late afternoon light, their harsh edges gentled by distance and the golden hour. "He will be back in time for the party, won't he?"

Philippa turned, though her eyes still lingered on the mountain range. Somewhere up there, Matthew was with her father, learning about the country's diamond operations for their trek had been delayed when her father had had to attend court.

And somewhere up there, Stuart was probably flying between the remote airstrips, navigating those treacherous peaks with the same quiet competence that had saved her life.

"Of course." And, yes, she was missing Matthew, though not as much as she'd expected. The realisation unsettled her more than she cared to admit. She cast a final appreciative look around the dining room, forcing herself to focus on the evening ahead. "Let's go back to the cottage and get ready, shall we? Matthew should turn up soon and I need to change. Mind you, he'll be too caught up telling me his adventures with my dad to notice what I look like." She smiled as Elizabeth joined her at the front door and they crossed the verandah, their heels clicking on the polished red concrete, as she tried to inject levity into her tone. "Who knows? Maybe, instead of discovering diamonds, my Matthew has cracked the case to convict the medicine murderer."

Not that Philippa entertained any such idea, really. She'd seen that Matthew wasn't quite as comfortable on a horse as he'd led her to believe. As for convicting Chief Thabo, who'd had charges dismissed three times after witnesses had rescinded their testimony, Philippa suspected that, once again, the dark, cultural underbelly of this country would confound her father's attempts at imposing a justice that not everyone believed in.

Elizabeth was full of excited chatter as they walked towards her parents' home. "Matthew must be as brainy as he is handsome if he plays rugby for CTU *and* is a lawyer. Aren't you clever for catching his eye? How long has it been? You are going to say yes when he asks, aren't you?"

Philippa blushed. "About four months. And yes, of course I will."

"Four months... I wonder why he hasn't asked you before since you're twenty-one and not getting any younger." Elizabeth winked and dug her friend in the ribs. She'd got engaged a few weeks earlier and was eager for everyone else to join the club.

Philippa had wondered the same but said, "Matthew's been very busy since Christmas, working in the family firm, learning the ropes and establishing himself." It sounded important. The truth was, Philippa had seen more of Matthew's mother these last few weeks as Matthew seemed to be at the beck and call of his father, who could be an exacting taskmaster.

"They're awfully rich, aren't they?" Elizabeth's tone was admiring, for Philippa had shown her a photograph of their rambling Kenilworth home she'd taken during one of Mrs Myburgh's tennis afternoons. "And I suppose it's why Mrs Myburgh can dress like she does. I saw her in that wonderful Ciel dress in Fair Lady Magazine when she attended the premiere of King Kong." Elizabeth cast an interested look at her friend. "Your father must approve of them. The Myburghs, I mean, attending a musical with an all-black cast." She gazed about the room adding, "I'm so glad we don't have apartheid in Basutoland."

"Well, King Kong has taken all of South Africa by storm and is now going to London." Philippa tried to deflect Elizabeth's questioning, for Mrs Myburgh had made a few dismissive remarks about her staff. Not exactly derogatory, but Philippa was just glad her father hadn't heard. "And isn't Miriam Makeba's voice to die for?" she carried on, referring to the jazz singer who played the shebeen queen in the musical that portrayed the life and times of South Africa heavyweight boxer Ezekiel Dlamini, whose moniker was "King Kong".

"Absolutely," Philippa agreed as the girls had arrived at Elizabeth's parents' house, a large brick dwelling behind a hedge of bougainvillea whose purple bracts rustled in the evening breeze. Still chatting, they walked up the driveway to the guest cottage in the back garden, where Philippa was staying for the couple of nights she was in Maseru.

"I can't wait to meet Matthew. He sounds divine," said

Elizabeth as they entered the cottage, and she took a seat while Mary, the housemaid, straightened the Sanderson linen covers of the two single beds. The room smelled of lavender and roses. It was where Philippa always stayed when she was in town. "Susan said he was lovely when she was back last hols," Elizabeth went on. "It's a shame she's not here for your birthday. The two of you have been best friends since you were babies."

"Yes, very sad." Philippa was glad she'd not told any of the Maseru gang about her humiliation at Angela Myer's twenty-first birthday party. Although she and Susan had made their peace, the reserve between them hadn't been healed by the amount of time Philippa spent at the Myburgh residence.

Plenty of Philippa's varsity friends had heard about the whole saga, but if tonight went as planned and she returned to Cape Town with an engagement ring on her finger, that would balance the books.

"Oh! I think that's him!" Elizabeth jumped up and got to the door before her, just as Philippa glimpsed a figure crossing the garden before disappearing from view.

The sight of Matthew's tall, broad-shouldered silhouette made her heart skip.

"Hello... darling." She'd been rehearsing the endearment for so long, but it sounded forced as Matthew stepped into the room. Yet not inappropriate, she hoped, considering how Mrs Myburgh had been treating Philippa as an honorary daughter.

And Matthew had certainly been playing his part.

The flowers, chocolates, dinners and meeting his family could be leading to only one thing.

He grinned, and her heart gave another little skip. Yes, he enjoyed hearing her say that—and in company. A bit of the tension drained from her as she stood on tiptoe to kiss him quickly before introducing him to her friend.

"I've told you all about Elizabeth and her lovely family, who always have me to stay when I'm in town." She brushed away a grass seed that had caught in his sweater, the simple domestic gesture feeling both natural and strange. "Are you parked on the street? Yes? And you've met Mrs Walters? Good."

"I have. And she's shown me my room and made sure I know that I'm to be at the Club by six." He transferred his smile back to Philippa, though she was sure something in his expression seemed different—more animated than usual, as if he was bursting with news. "And now I'm all yours."

Philippa couldn't remember when she'd last heard sweeter words.

So why did they leave her feeling slightly hollow?

By 5.45pm, having laddered two stockings in her haste to dress, Philippa was in a less jubilant mood. Her hair didn't seem to work, and her hand was shaking too much to even attempt the cat-eyed look she'd planned. The mirror in the cottage's small dressing room seemed determined to show her every imperfection.

"Philippa, just take a deep breath and sit down for a moment," Elizabeth counselled, rummaging in her friend's suitcase for another pair of stockings. "Anyone would think you were on a first date."

Elizabeth was a practical girl and a good friend. Not as close as Philippa had once considered Susan, but a staunch ally, and certainly proving her worth in her current hour of need.

"Tonight is more important than a first date," Philippa replied, obediently sitting down on the edge of the bed, her hands still trembling.

"Really?" Elizabeth looked interested as she found the spare stockings. "And you're absolutely sure you want to marry him?" She sat down at the Dolly Varden dressing table by the window and dipped the tiny mascara brush into a glass of water before carefully coating it in black powder. Both girls had been doing their makeup in Philippa's room while Matthew had gone somewhere in the car with Elizabeth's dad. Elizabeth giggled, answering her own question. "Well, he's a good catch, that's for sure. And, money aside, he's handsome and charming. What girl with her head screwed on right *wouldn't* want to marry him?"

"He is divine, isn't he?" The words came automatically, but even as she said them, Philippa found herself thinking of a different kind of handsomeness—rugged rather than polished.

"Well, I wouldn't know too much about *that*, would I?" Elizabeth carefully applied eyeliner to Philippa's top lid with steady hands. "Do you think he'll ask you tonight, then?"

Philippa nibbled her lower lip. "Yes, I think he will." In the half hour she'd spent with Matthew after Elizabeth had left, he'd seemed different. Like there was an inner excitement he'd been trying to suppress; and when she'd hinted at it, Matthew's eyes had shone and he'd kissed her even more thoroughly than before and told her not to question him just yet but that he'd satisfy her curiosity later that evening.

Philippa had been sure that when he'd held her tightly

against him, she'd felt the outline of a small box in his jacket pocket.

"And what are you going to answer?"

Philippa laughed. "What do you think? Honestly, Elizabeth, I've never wanted anything more."

"You're sure, sure?" her friend teased.

Philippa shrugged. "Matthew can give me the life I want," she said.

At least that part was true. Even if lately she'd found herself questioning what exactly that life entailed. Even if, in unguarded moments, she found herself remembering what it felt like to want something—someone—with a desperation that had nothing to do with security or status.

PHILIPPA WASN'T one to let nerves discompose her for long, and after a couple of shandies at the bar before dinner, coupled with the general good cheer and the compliments that showered upon her, she was feeling as confident as she ever had. The Country Club had been transformed for the evening, with fairy lights strung between the jacaranda trees outside and candles flickering on every table inside.

"Have I told you that you look absolutely smashing?" Matthew whispered into her ear as he held her close while they danced the cha cha between courses. A lively jazz band from South Africa was playing, and the bar was full of laughter and cigarette smoke and the clink of glasses.

For the first hour, Philippa had nervously scanned the dining room, relieved she'd not seen Stuart. Although he wasn't a club member, he might have heard that a party had been organised for her and got someone to sign him in. The thought both terrified and thrilled her.

During the two months since Philippa had last seen Stuart, she'd done a reasonable job of putting him out of her mind. Time did help, she found, for it had taken a long time before she'd stopped imagining it was Stuart kissing her when Matthew had taken her in his arms.

As she knew it would.

It's why she'd made the difficult decision she had. Marriage was forever, and that's what Matthew—as clearly conveyed by his mother—was offering her.

Or would very soon.

Fortunately, Stuart seemed to have got the message after she'd not replied to his second letter, and following their awkward exchange when she'd introduced Matthew to her father and her home country., and

She'd been glad not to have seen him again during that visit two months ago. Well, that's what she'd told herself.

She tamped down the inconvenient fluttering in her chest at the thought of him while the memory of his first letter—so carefully worded, so hopeful—made her feel guilty in a way she didn't want to examine too closely. Stuart was lovely. Handsome. Heroic. And sexy as anything.

He just wasn't the type of husband she was looking for. That's if he was even in the market for marriage, and she wasn't at all sure that he was.

"You think I look smashing. Why, thank you, Matthew. You have mentioned that a couple of times this evening, yes." Banishing Stuart from her thoughts with more effort than she'd expected, she grinned. Yes, she was happy tonight, Philippa told herself. Matthew had been attentive and complimentary all evening and, when she'd visited the Ladies to powder her nose, Margot and Ruth had sidled up to her and gushed about how gorgeous he was.

If all her friends approved, she must be making the right decision, surely?

Matthew sighed as he raised one hand to briefly smooth back an escaped wisp from her chignon. "And did I ever tell you that you have the most amazing hair?" He was slurring slightly, but if being a little drunk made him want to sing her praises, Philippa didn't mind.

And if he wanted to slip outside for a bit of canoodling, that was even better.

So, when Matthew took her by the hand after the cake had been cut and Happy Birthday had been sung, Philippa exchanged a meaningful look with Elizabeth on her way out.

"We're off to look at the moon," she said in a stage whisper while Matthew offered a theatrical wink. "And... don't feel you all have to wait around here for us to come back," she added over her shoulder, laughing gaily as Matthew pulled her after him.

The anticipation was making her breathing so erratic, she didn't know if she could have walked without his support, even though he was the one who had trouble keeping upright.

The moment was nearly upon her.

Oh, she knew what she was going to say, as an image flashed before her of the view from the Myburgh residence: frothy waves crashing onto the shore. She thought she'd drown in happiness.

"Aha, now I have you all to myself," Matthew chuckled as he pressed her against the club wall, deep in the shadows cast by the overhead lamps and far away from where anyone could see them. The night air was cool against her heated skin. "Surrender!"

"I'm all yours, I promise." Philippa raised her chin to

meet his kiss, her knees going weak as his mouth claimed hers. And if his approach lacked finesse, she could forgive the fact that the reason he'd probably had a bit more than usual to drink was for courage. A chap needed to bolster himself for announcements like the one he was about to make.

After what seemed an interminable amount of time, Philippa had to temper his wandering hands and pull away, just to gasp in a few mouthfuls of air. Matthew seemed to be on a single-minded mission to devour her and the pleasurable tendrils of desire she'd felt initially had given way to, first, stoic fortitude, and then a strong desire that the kissing and breast-mauling would end so that Matthew would cut through all the preliminaries and finally say what he'd brought her out here to say.

His touch felt demanding rather than tender, possessive rather than passionate. Nothing like—she forced herself to stop that train of thought.

"Matthew... darling," she managed as sweetly as she could while she unclasped his fingers from around her neck and wriggled out of his grasp. It seemed ungrateful to tell him he was strangling her, so she pretended to be astonished by the brightness of the moon hanging like a lantern above the mountains.

"Full moon tomorrow. We must go for a drive in the mountains. I'm dying to show you how incredible it looks from up there." She swallowed down her nervousness and managed to add, "Just as you must be dying to tell me your exciting news. You did say you had something to say, didn't you?"

If her invitation for him to speak had as much finesse as his earlier mauling, Matthew would probably be too drunk to notice. The poor darling must be even more nervous than she was.

"Exciting news?" For a second, he looked owlishly at her, his pupils dilated in the dim light. Then his eyes sparkled as he said, quickly, "It came out of the blue, truly it did! I mean, it was the last thing I expected. Grandpa has always been so down on me, but the moment he heard I'd passed my law exams he summoned me to his office in town and, you'll never believe it, but he handed me this!"

While Matthew fumbled in his pocket, Philippa's mind had raced ahead with every possibility. Well, there'd been confusion at first. Matthew hadn't been terribly coherent. But now Philippa knew exactly why Matthew was so excited. His grandfather must have given him a diamond. The box she'd felt would contain an engagement ring that had been in the family, passed down through the generations. And now Matthew was about to flourish the darling thing and slip it on her finger.

Her heart skittered around in her chest so frantically she felt lightheaded.

"It's valid for a full year, so I've decided to go to England first and stay with family."

She stared at him for a second, uncomprehendingly, while, oblivious, he went on, "I mean, I'd always intended to do it but then rugby took over and I wasn't really interested in travel. But now—"

He'd been waving the object he'd whipped out of his pocket with such enthusiasm it took a moment for Philippa to realise what it was.

What she'd quickly realised it was *not* was a diamond ring.

It was a ticket she eventually discovered. A round-the-world ticket because his grandfather thought it was important that his grandson broaden his horizons before returning to his serious career.

"So, I'll spread my wings for a year and then be quite ready to settle down when I get back home."

He stopped, as if to gauge her reaction, his smile slightly uncertain as he added, "Isn't it great news?"

Philippa tried to stop her mouth from trembling while the cold crept up her legs, encasing her in icy shock. "You're going overseas?" she repeated. She'd never felt so deflated in her life. "When?" She stopped. "I mean, when did you find out?" Because the 'when' as in 'when was he going?' was not going to be part of the equation. She was not going to let Matthew do this to her.

"Darling, cheer up. It's not like I'll be gone forever. And you'll wait for me, won't you?"

Her shoulders relaxed, and she let him draw her against him. Slowly, relief filled the void left by devastation. Matthew was going on holiday. She'd misheard him when he'd mentioned the time he'd be away. Soon he'd be back, and they'd be married. It was going to be all right, after all.

She drew in a breath, tilted her head, and smiled up at him. "I will if it's worth my while." Matthew responded well to coquettishness. But perhaps it was only because she was giving him a leash, and a touch of humour was prefer-able to shrewishness. After what he'd termed Philippa's 'overreaction' to the events at Angela Meyer's twenty-first, Philippa was always cautious about how to handle him. Wearing her heart on her sleeve had not gone down well, but she'd thought she'd been playing the situation as cool as a cucumber. Like a grown-up.

"You're a brick, darling! I knew I could count on you to understand. After all, you still have a year to finish your degree and, well, who knows what will happen in that time." He squeezed her shoulders with hands that felt suddenly heavy. "We certainly don't want to get ahead of ourselves. Mummy will still want to see you all the time when I'm gone. And when I come back, then I'd say we're a pretty sure thing... Wouldn't you?"

Was that supposed to be a roundabout way of proposing—*if* she was prepared to wait a year?

Philippa blinked. She found she couldn't stop. First, it was confusion. Then disbelief. And then, finally, it was to keep the tears of mortification firmly at bay so they didn't cascade down her cheeks and further humiliate her.

But finally she found catharsis in anger. "You're telling me you're going away for a year?" she raged.

"Well, maybe not that long. It depends—"

"And you expect me to wait for you?" She heaved in a breath.

"Come on, Philippa, there's no need to get upset. I hardly saw this coming myself." Matthew floundered, his frown belying the soothing stroking of her arm. As if he wasn't sure what to do. "I mean, a round-the-world ticket and a healthy allowance to go with it is what any fellow in my position dreams about. You're surely not asking me to give it up?"

Philippa had heard enough. She stared at him and didn't know what to say. He truly didn't understand. The realisation was like being showered with a bucket of cold water—not just that he was leaving, but that she mattered so little to him that he couldn't even conceive of her as an obstacle to his plans.

When he tried to pull her against him once more, she pushed him away, a fresh wave of mortification swamping her. And, rising above the mortification, was anger as the reality of what he was saying, and of how little she obviously meant to him, began to swamp her. "A week ago, you were telling me something completely different, Matthew Myburgh. You hinted we had a future...on the horizon. Your mother was hinting we had a future! If you can just... do this... just cast me aside, then why didn't you simply let things slide after Angela's birthday? It would have been so much less painful."

The furrow between his eyebrows deepened.

"How could you be so thoughtless... so cruel?" She was gulping in lungfuls of air in between sobs by this stage. In the gloom of the single lamp, a few yards away, Matthew looked stricken, but also frustrated, as if her emotional response was an inconvenience he hadn't anticipated.

"I didn't think—"

"No, you didn't!" Philippa said between sobs. "You thought you could treat me any way you liked. Well, if this is what you really think of me, then you can think again. You can...just get back in your car and drive all the way back to Cape Town and never see me again because I won't be treated like something so... completely expendable!"

She'd run the full gamut from shock to horror to disbelief, but now it was easier to channel all those churning emotions into red hot anger. She wouldn't be the downtrodden wet rag she'd been after Angela's twenty-first. She had her pride.

"Philippa, please—"

She batted away his hand and, with a huge effort, drew herself up and glared at him. "So, you're going overseas, are you? When?"

Matthew couldn't meet her eye. "My flight leaves in a month."

"A month! So, you've been secretly planning this behind my back while letting me believe something completely different?" His perfidy was breathtaking. The casual way he'd let her plan their future while knowing he had other plans entirely made her feel sick.

"No, that wasn't how it was," he protested. "Grandpa told me he was giving me the ticket a week ago, and I was just waiting for the right time to tell you. It was a hard choice, but the only one I could make under the circumstances. Surely you see that?" His voice grew louder as he relayed his version. "I only booked it three days ago."

"Before you'd mentioned any of this to me?" It was worse than she'd expected. Not only had he been keeping secrets, but he'd made the bold and seemingly irreversible move of actually booking his round-the-world flight.

Philippa shook her head and avoided his grasp when he tried to stop her leaving. "I have nothing further to say to you, Matthew Myburgh," she muttered as she turned her back on him and stalked away.

She retained her dignity for a full block. With a straight back and the elegant swing of the hips that all girls strove for in full skirts and high heels, she managed to reach the corner of Lerotholi and Seeiso Streets. And then, as the distance muted the merry din of the club, the pain was suddenly too much to bear. Leaning against the rough trunk of a jacaranda, whose fallen purple flowers carpeted the ground beneath her feet, she covered her face with her hands and howled.

Matthew hadn't even come after her. He'd let her walk away from him, their angry words punctuating the darkness, and he'd not protested his love, his regret or even done the gentlemanly thing, which was to see her back inside to safety.

No, Matthew Myburgh cared only for himself, and

Philippa was better off washing her hands of him, once and for all.

But as she stood there in the darkness, surrounded by the sweet scent of jacaranda and the distant sound of music from the club, unwanted thoughts crept into her mind. Thoughts of someone who would never have let her walk away alone. Someone who had saved her life without thought for himself, who had looked at her as if she was precious rather than convenient.

Someone whose letter was still tucked away in her jewellery box, undeserving of the cold, brief reply she'd sent.

The realisation that she might have thrown away something real in pursuit of something safe hit her with devastating clarity.

But it was too late now.

Stuart Price had got the message that she wasn't interested, and Philippa had thrown away her one true chance at future happiness.

CHAPTER

TEN

AFTER A FEW MINUTES OF TEARS, SHE FINALLY COMPOSED HERSELF and took a deep breath as she tried to decide whether to return to the club or to go back to Elizabeth's parents' cottage which was only a couple of streets away.

She was better off discovering the truth sooner rather than later.

At least, that's what Philippa tried to tell herself as a new bout of tears flowed while she supported herself against the tree.

Matthew's mother might be the most gracious of women who'd clearly welcomed the prospect of having Philippa as a daughter-in-law—or had she got that wrong too?—but Matthew was a cad. Wasn't that the best description of him? An out-and-out cad.

After a few minutes, she realised she couldn't just stay where she was.

If she went back to the club, her pitiful plight and humiliation would become a talking point. If she didn't, she had only the loneliness of her cottage to look forward to, though she had told her friends not to worry if she didn't return.

She chose the club. The pity of a well-meaning Elizabeth or Katherine might be hard to take, but they were her friends, and Philippa needed company more than to be alone in times of crisis. Hopefully, Matthew would have got the message and made himself scarce. He'd hardly distinguished himself through his chivalry.

Sniffing unhappily, she ran her fingertips under her eyes and smoothed her hair before she crossed the road, the night air cool against her heated cheeks.

There was little traffic at this time of night. Just one Land Rover that was slowing as it clearly took into account the fact she was about to cross the road. No one else to observe a young woman dressed to the nines alone in the middle of town, she thought, as she stepped back into the shadows.

The Land Rover went by and Philippa stepped into the street. It was hard to focus, but she managed to put one foot in front of the other, though she wasn't as steady as she'd imagined. Oh, Lord. Surely she hadn't had that much to drink?

"Are you all right, miss?" The vehicle had stopped a little ahead of her, and a man was leaning out of the passenger window. "Do you need help?"

A great rushing noise whistled through Philippa's head as he repeated his concern, and she swayed.

No, it couldn't be. Not Stuart. She closed her eyes, and her breath caught in her throat.

Wracked with indecision whether to bolt, Philippa watched the vehicle reverse, until Stuart had drawn level, frowning at her in the dim light cast by the street lamp.

"Philippa?" He withdrew his head and cut the engine,

getting out of the car while Philippa looked down at her feet.

Why was it that Stuart, of all the people in Maseru, should drive by at this moment? The universe seemed determined to mock her careful plans and throw her into situations where she felt completely out of control.

She couldn't meet his eye as he loomed up before her, but she felt his assessing gaze keenly. Her head was swimming, and she was embarrassed he might think her tiddly —which she was not, she assured herself. All that excess of emotion had to find an outlet somewhere.

Still, shame swept over her as she stumbled a little.

"You don't look all right," he muttered, taking her elbow when she stumbled again. His touch was gentle but firm, steadying her in a way that was so comforting it made her want to lean into his strength. Except of course she couldn't do that. "Get in and I'll drive you home. Where are you staying?" He opened the passenger door. "Or shall I take you back to the Club?"

Philippa allowed him to help her in, while the curtness of his tone caused another wave of self-excoriating disgust. Matthew had spurned her, and now she could feel something guarded in Stuart's manner. What would he say when he learned Matthew had passed her over a second time? Well, she didn't have to tell him that.

"I don't want to go back to the Club. Just drive... anywhere," she managed once he'd got into the car and started the engine. She was having a hard time keeping it all together but when Stuart asked, having released the accelerator so that they lurched into the night over the rough dirt road, "Has that boyfriend of yours been causing trouble again?" the answer she tried for turned into a wail of distress.

And while she sobbed, Stuart said nothing. Just drove on in silence out of town and towards the mountains. Over the flat, stony track and into the shadows of the peaks that the huge, yellow moon threw into such sharp relief. The landscape looked otherworldly in the moonlight, all silver and black shadows, beautiful and wild—like everything she'd been trying to avoid in her carefully ordered life.

"So... you really want to marry him, do you?"

"Yes." Philippa sniffed and made a quick, fruitless search up her sleeve for a tissue. She hadn't brought her bag, and her nose was dripping, and her eyes streaming.

Stuart dug one hand into his pocket and handed her a handkerchief. "I don't know how clean it is. I used it on the engine this morning, but it's better than nothing."

In the ghostly light, he looked rather magnificent with that determined jaw silhouetted against the sky, his eyes steely grey rather than blue right now. There was something about him in profile that reminded her of the carved saints in the cathedral back in Cape Town—beautiful and remote and infinitely patient.

Philippa dabbed her own no-doubt bloodshot eyes with the handkerchief, her nostrils twitching at the strong smell of avgas. "Better not light a match in here," she whispered, "or we'll all go up in flames." She giggled and immediately felt her mood shift. Glancing across at Stuart and seeing him smile, she felt an unexpected jolt of pleasure. Stuart was a good sort. He hadn't pressured her before, and he wasn't doing so now. It would be a relief to bare her soul to someone. And Stuart was a good listener.

"Are you going to give him another chance?"

Philippa blinked at the question. "Well, it looks like he's already made his decision." She took a shuddering breath before adding, "I was sure that was where we were heading." The knowledge that Stuart wasn't too angry to continue to speak to her eased the pain of her humiliation a little. "Matthew hinted he was going to ask me tonight. He's just spent a week with Daddy on trek in the mountains and came down tonight for my party at the club. He was going to go back up the Sani Pass with me tomorrow for the party Daddy's organised with his old friends, and I thought that's when we'd tell my father that—" Her voice broke.

"Except that it doesn't sound like that's going to happen now," said Stuart. He didn't sound the slightest bit sympathetic.

Philippa sent him a narrow look before she went on. "His mother has taken me shopping every week for the past month. I've become part of the family. Mrs Myburgh said I was like a daughter to her. She's a wonderful woman and..." Her voice wavered again, "it's so nice to have that since I don't have my own mother anymore."

Stuart shrugged, his hands tightening on the steering wheel. "She was a great lady, your mum. But you're not marrying this bloke's mother."

"I like spending time with Mrs Myburgh." Philippa sniffed, ignoring his remark. Something about the way he'd said it—with a kind of rough gentleness—made her throat tighten. He understood what it meant to be alone, she realised. "I think she expected Matthew to propose this trip. I mean, judging by some of the things she's said to me. But at my birthday dinner at the club this evening, Matthew told me he was going overseas for a year. His grandfather has bought him a round-the-world ticket, and he's leaving in a month." She wiped her eyes again.

"Can you remind me why you want to marry Matthew Myburgh?"

Philippa's mouth dropped open. "Because... he offers

me everything I want. I tried to tell you in my letter. And everyone at varsity expects me to go back next term with a ring on my finger. Half of our friends are engaged. Matthew has been best man three times this term, and everyone assumes we'll be next. Tonight was... not just a shock, but humiliating as well." Even as she said the words, they sounded childish to her own ears. Since when had other people's expectations become her reason for wanting something?

"It doesn't sound like he's treated you very well."

Philippa didn't want to hear her boyfriend criticised. At least, not by Stuart. The criticism felt too close to her own growing doubts. "The first time was a misunderstanding. I overreacted," she said defensively. "And I behaved out of character. You and I should never have—" She felt herself burning with embarrassment and broke off.

"But we did." There was no embarrassment in his look, and something in his steady gaze made her pulse quicken. "I don't regret it."

In the spotlight of his clear-eyed scrutiny, Philippa floundered. "Well, I do because—"

"Because?" he prompted when it was clear Philippa wasn't going to continue.

"Because I misinterpreted what I'd seen in Cape Town. I... I should have been more trusting of Matthew."

"Who has let you down again," Stuart said baldly.

"He's treated me just fine until now. Well, after we made up last time." She cleared her throat, hating how defensive she sounded even to herself. "Which I also told you about in my letter to you. And if we were married, I'd have none of the complaints I have now because the only complaint I have is that he's leaving."

For the first time, Stuart laughed, and the sound sent an

unexpected warmth through her chest. "Oh, Philippa, you should hear yourself. He's a no-good boyfriend, and you're kidding yourself if you think you can turn him into what you want."

"It's not just him. It's everything. His family, the life we'd live, where we'd live. Everything!" Her words echoed in her head, and she added quickly, "I mean, I love him, of course, but one doesn't just marry one person, you marry their family and get absorbed into the life they live. Matthew offers just...everything I want," she repeated.

But even as she said it, surrounded by the wild beauty of the moonlit mountains and sitting beside a man who'd helped her more than once, she wondered if what she wanted was really what she needed.

"Except that he isn't offering."

Philippa huffed out a breath, but managed a shadow of a grin. "I suppose you think being brutal is going to help?" She caught his gaze and her grin broadened as she batted her eyelashes. "A bit of sympathy wouldn't go astray."

"Oh, I don't intend to give you a jot of sympathy. Why should I? I don't like Matthew, and I think you'd be selling yourself short if you married him." Then, quietly, he added, "You know what I feel about you."

Something in his voice—raw and honest in a way that Matthew never was—made her breath catch. "I think you'd better take me home now," Philippa said, her smile freezing. If this was the way Stuart was going to be, she wished they hadn't travelled so far out of town. The intensity in his eyes was both thrilling and terrifying.

Without a word, Stuart turned the car about and, in stony silence, they travelled through the bleak, beautiful landscape, Philippa resting her cheek against the cold window. The mountains looked different at night—mysterious and untamed, like the feelings Stuart stirred in her that she didn't want to examine too closely.

"And what have you been up to, Stuart?" she asked with false brightness after about five minutes.

"Oh, the usual, Philippa," he replied, matching her tone. "The nights are long and cold, so after a drink at the bar I go back to my empty room at Mrs Henderson's lodging house and sleep until I wake up to go flying. I lose myself in another world high above the mountains because it's the best way to get over life's disappointments. That's been pretty much the way of it for the past four years."

The loneliness in his voice made something clench in her chest. She'd never thought about Stuart's life outside their brief encounters—the isolation, the emptiness he was describing.

"Then why do you stay?"

"Where do you think I should go, Philippa?"

She slanted a look at him, uncertain about his irony. "Don't you miss England? Your family?"

"I don't have any family. Not in England, anyway."

"What about your foster family in South Africa? Pretoria? Have you seen them?"

"No, and I doubt I ever will."

Philippa drew in a quick breath, surprised at the bitterness in his tone. There was pain there, carefully hidden but unmistakable to someone who'd just experienced her own kind of rejection. "I thought you liked them."

"I do. Best people ever. Changed my life; taught me how to value it. If ever there was a woman who deserved to be sainted, it was Mrs Franklin. Aunt Edith I called her. I adored her. Still do. But I messed up and, if you don't mind, I'd rather not talk about it."

With her gaze trained on his face, Philippa slowly put

her hand over his as it gripped the gear stick. She saw the rise and fall of his Adam's apple, but there was no other sign that he registered her touch.

He stared rigidly ahead as he continued to drive on in silence. But he did not move his hand away.

A myriad of thoughts flitted through Philippa's mind. She wanted to quiz him, but he seemed in more pain than she was. Or had been.

As they reached the straggling rondavels on the outskirts of town, Stuart said, "You'll have to direct me. I don't know where you're staying."

"Elizabeth Walter's house. Just near the corner of Kingsway," she replied.

He pulled up outside the hedge and cut the engine. Philippa looked awkwardly at his hand on the gear stick as she removed hers. The street was dark, and the driveway to the cottage behind was long.

"I'll walk you to the door." It sounded like he was performing a reluctant duty, but something in the careful way he said it suggested otherwise.

Side by side, saying nothing, they navigated the brick path until they reached the cottage. The night air was fragrant with jasmine and the distant sound of crickets, the atmosphere intimate. And Philippa was acutely aware of Stuart's presence beside her.

"Nessie must have forgotten to turn on the light," whispered Philippa as she stood on the step, feeling about for the doorknob, then opening it into the dark room. She felt hot and unexpectedly breathless. She put it down to embarrassment, for she wished Stuart gone, of course. "I'll have to find the switch."

Wordlessly, Stuart followed her in, running his hand along the wall until he found it, flicking it on so the room was bathed in a dim, golden light that made everything look soft and intimate.

"Sorry about the mess." Philippa waved a hand at the bed by the window, which was strewn with discarded stockings, makeup, and various articles of underwear. The sight of her intimate things scattered about made her blush.

Stuart smiled unexpectedly, and for a moment his face looked younger, more vulnerable. "It's nice. It reminds me of my sister's room." He scanned the small space with an expression she couldn't quite read. "She was untidy, too."

The past tense didn't escape her notice, and she felt another piece of the puzzle that was Stuart Price try to find its place.

"You've not been very complimentary this evening, Stuart," said Philippa, pretending a touch of indignation when she was in fact relieved that she'd be parting from him on decent terms. She wanted his good opinion more than she knew she ought.

"Well, I was not going to give you the sympathy you were after. You're far better off without Matthew Myburgh, you know." His face softened, and he put a hand on her shoulder, the weight of it warm and steady. "But if it's compliments you're after—" His voice softened and grew husky—" then I think you are the most beautiful, fascinating, intoxicating woman I've ever met."

With each adjective, Philippa moved closer. Well, she must have, for she wasn't sure how else she found herself in his arms, her face tilted upwards, her lips tingling with desire. Actually, everything was tingling with desire as she twined her hands behind his neck and their mouths fused.

She didn't stop to think she must be losing her mind to be kissing Stuart so soon after weeping over Matthew's letdown. It just felt right. Natural in a way that her carefully orchestrated moments with Matthew never had.

And as she pressed herself against him, his hardness set off an even greater surge of desire. Suddenly her mind was spinning with unsated cravings, so that when his hands began to contour her hips, her bottom, her breasts, her own hands began a similar journey of exploration.

His chest was firm. A manly chest. The memory of its contours and the light dusting of hair made her tremble. She smoothed her hands upwards until they were cupping his cheeks, smoother than the first time she'd done this all those months ago, but with the first signs of stubble.

Mindlessly, she matched his growing ardour, pressing harder and harder against him in her frustrated desire to feel more, until he reached the edge of the bed and fell backwards, Philippa on top.

Philippa looked down at him as she scrambled onto her knees beside him. She froze as she took in the situation. His eyes were bright with desire, and his chest rose and fell as if he'd just been running. But there was something else in his expression—a kind of desperate restraint that made her realise he was fighting himself as much as wanting her.

She blinked, about to slide off the bed, but suddenly she felt suspended above a perilous chasm. The wild landscape outside seemed to have followed her into this small room, making her feel reckless and alive in a way that terrified and thrilled her.

She knew she wasn't thinking as clearly as she ought, but an inner voice told her that either choice would be equally terrible.

She could angle herself off the bed and back to safety— back to the predictable world where she waited for Matthew to decide her worth.

Or she could surrender to the feelings pulsing through her body and live with the consequences.

"Your choice," he whispered, as if he could read her thoughts. He didn't move except to run the tip of his tongue over his top lip while his Adam's apple indicated the strain he was under.

He cleared his throat. "But whatever happens, I will always be here for you."

His words snaked their way beneath her defences, clamping her heart in irons. She couldn't deny the physical desire she felt, but it was his pledge of fidelity that her barren soul craved. Here was someone offering constancy when everyone else in her life seemed ready to abandon her the moment something better came along. Matthew had just proven that love could be conditional, but Stuart was offering something different—something unconditional and honest and real.

She shifted quickly, caging him with her body to kiss his eyes, his cheeks, his neck.

He sighed softly. Then groaned when she fumbled with his belt before he flipped her onto her back and set upon her neck, kissing her with a growing ardour as she made a second, concerted but ultimately futile attempt at the buckle.

With a grunt of frustration that tickled the silence and matched his short laugh, he moved his hand from where it had been roaming up her inner thigh to whip off his belt while she arched her back and wriggled out of her panties.

Her body was on fire, and she wanted him now. She reached for him, grasped him to guide him inside her, then sighed with pleasure as she felt the size and weight of him.

Every movement was like exquisite torture, fast, furious and fantastically satisfying, long past the moment of climax with an aftermath just as mind-numbingly wonderful before Stuart rolled over, drew her against his side and stroked her cheek.

"There, I told you she'd have gone back to the cottage."

Elizabeth's voice sounded clearly from outside as she and a companion approached from the direction of the street.

With a gasp, Philippa sat up hurriedly, smoothing her skirts as Stuart leapt to his feet, fumbling to do up his trousers. Frantically, she looked around the room, quickly kicking her panties beneath the bed as Elizabeth knocked lightly on the door, opening it at the same time as she said with relief, "Philippa! You poor darling, are you all right? Matthew was worried and sent us to look after you. He said you'd had a bit of a tiff. Oh... Stuart, I didn't see you there." Elizabeth, and Margot behind her, peered at Stuart with curiosity.

"Stuart drove me back," Philippa mumbled, hoping her hair didn't give her away. "He saw me crying in the street. Very embarrassing." She couldn't meet their eyes, terrified they'd see something in her face that would give away what had just happened.

"I was helping her to find the light switch," said Stuart. He sounded awkward as he inched towards the door, and Philippa caught something almost protective in the way he positioned himself between her and her friends' curious gazes.

"Stuart's flying me to Mokhotlong tomorrow," Philippa said quickly. She didn't want to see him go. The thought of facing tomorrow, facing her father and the questions about Matthew, without Stuart's steady presence, felt impossible.

"Actually, Dan's rostered on the morning flight." Stuart brushed back his wayward cowlick, and she caught a glimpse of something that might have been regret in his expression. "Sorry."

The disappointment was crushing. "Oh," was all she could manage as he said his goodnights and Elizabeth and Margot came to sit on the bed once he'd gone.

Inside, Philippa cringed with embarrassment, and with fear that they might suspect. Strangely, she didn't regret what she'd done in the slightest. It had felt like the most natural thing in the world. Her body and mind still hummed with the joy of it all.

But then, with a start, the enormity of everything that had happened tonight hit her. "Where's Matthew?" she asked, sitting up straighter as she chewed her hand. Oh, what had she done? What had she done? "Is he still here?" He was going to walk through that door and tell her he was sorry and ask her to forgive him. She began to breathe rapidly.

Elizabeth put a comforting hand on her back. "I'm so sorry, Philippa. He's gone back to Cape Town." There was silence except for the sympathetic tuttings of Elizabeth and Margot.

"If it's any consolation," said Margot, "he said he felt a real heel. He told us what happened. About his going away and hoping you'd wait for him."

"While everyone else I know gets married? What does he think I am? A fool?" Philippa rose and went to the dressing table, where a surreptitious check reassured her there were no telltale signs of the terrible sin she'd just committed.

In the harsh light of reality, it seemed *truly* terrible, though she wished she felt guiltier than she did. What kind of woman fell into bed with one man hours—no, minutes —after being rejected by another? The kind of woman her grandmother would have disowned, just as she'd disowned Philippa's mother.

The mirror's reflection was reassuring. She didn't think they'd guessed. Her hair was a little mussed, and her cheeks were flushed. She'd look like someone would if they were discomposed after the kind of let-down Matthew had inflicted.

"Oh, Philippa, don't be too downhearted." Margot sighed. "Maybe it just wasn't meant to be. Maybe there's someone else waiting for you right around the corner. Someone who sets your heart on fire even more than Matthew." She shrugged and stared at the ceiling. "I can't think of anyone just now. But I feel sure you won't have to wait too long to find someone who is... just perfect for you."

If only she knew, Philippa thought, her body still humming with the memory of Stuart's touch.

PHILIPPA HARDLY SLEPT. She wept, and she tossed and turned and wept some more. Wept for all the might-have-beens with Matthew, wept for her sluttish behaviour with Stuart, who obviously didn't respect her any more than Matthew did, or he'd have leapt at the suggestion that he fly her home.

But underneath the self-recrimination was something else—a stubborn warmth that refused to be extinguished. The memory of Stuart's words: "I will always be here for you" was a refrain that would not die. The way he'd looked at her. The gentle way he'd touched her, held her, after their incendiary moments before.

And then he'd sidled out of the room and said he wasn't flying her up the mountain.

She'd all but convinced herself that Stuart must be notching her up as another of his conquests when she arrived at the airstrip.

And there he was, doing his pre-flight walk around the Cessna, and grinning at her when she stopped in her tracks to put down her heavy suitcase, having just farewelled Elizabeth, who'd dropped her off before heading to work.

"I swapped with Dan," he said, laughing at the look on her face and coming towards her as he shoved an oily rag into his back pocket. "And now I'm not sure if you wish you hadn't suggested it last night."

"I'm thinking how glad I am that I did," Philippa said shyly, reaching up to brush an imaginary speck of dust from his shoulder. The simple touch sent a thrill through her, and she saw his eyes darken in response.

"Really?" He looked pleased, and something in his expression—surprised gratitude, as if he hadn't expected her to want to see him again—made her chest tighten. "So, it's just the two of us for the next half an hour."

"And you'll stay?"

"In Mokhotlong? No, I've got some other pickups."

"You could always find yourself weathered in on the return journey," she suggested. "Daddy's having a few old friends over for my birthday celebration. I'd love you to come. I know the guest rondavel is free."

Stuart slid his hands down to grip her forearms and put his face closer to hers. "Do you really mean that?"

She nodded.

"You don't hate me for last night?"

She shook her head. Very decided. "Not in the slightest. I was afraid you... wouldn't respect me."

He laughed, and the sound was full of something that made her pulse quicken. "I don't know what came over me. Well, I do. I just can't seem to resist you, Philippa Tremain, even though I know you are a very, very bad influence." He nuzzled her nose quickly and then picked up her suitcase and turned back to the plane, saying over his shoulder, "But I know to be careful this time."

"Careful? What do you mean?" she asked, following him as he loaded her bag into the pod.

"Careful not to get my fingers burned a second time. Knowing I'm the rebound fellow to help you heal your broken heart."

The words stung because they held a grain of truth, but as she watched him securing her luggage, she realised that what she felt for Stuart wasn't about healing from Matthew's rejection. It was something entirely different— something that had been growing since the night they'd crashed in the mealie field.

"Oh, let's not worry about that, shall we?" Philippa could sound light-hearted when Stuart seemed to be taking everything in such good part. He'd been so grim during their night drive, but passion had sizzled the moment they'd stepped into her guest cottage. And now the banter was easy, while the chemistry fairly hissed between them as he strapped her in.

She liked it.

And she liked the conversation that followed take-off, the easy way they talked over the drone of the engine, the comfortable silences that felt natural rather than forced.

"Please try to stay for tonight," she pleaded when he dropped her off in Mokhotlong and they waited for her father to greet them. "I really want you to."

"Then I'll stay. I'll make a plan." He glanced over his

shoulder and, when the wing obscured them momentarily from public view, kissed Philippa quickly on the lips. "I was only going to if you asked me three times. And you just have."

Philippa felt her mouth stretch into the broadest, happiest smile she'd managed for two days. She reached out to squeeze his hand.

"I'll remember that, Captain Price," she said. "I'll remember that you need a lot of persuading if you're to believe a word I say."

But as she said it, looking into his steady blue eyes, she realised that, unlike Matthew, Stuart clearly understood her worth.

CHAPTER

ELEVEN

The stirrings of excitement were beginning to take hold.

Philippa recognised the sensation—first from their shared adventure all those months ago.

No, even earlier, when she'd been a schoolgirl and he a shy young pilot of few words, yet with a charisma that had enveloped her like the promise of adventures to come.

No, this feeling was nothing new. Not when Stuart was near.

And it certainly compromised her ability to look suitably heartbroken when she explained to her father why Matthew had not accompanied her up the mountain.

"He's decided to go to England for a year," she told him, surprised at how calm she sounded as she signalled to Francina, who was in the kitchen preparing *Devils on Horseback* for her party that night, that she'd want some help to arrange her hair as soon as she was free.

"My darling... I'm so sorry." Her father clearly didn't know what else to say and Philippa was happy to spare him. He'd always known how to appease Philippa's mother, who could be exacting on occasion, but she knew he was uncomfortable speaking of matters of the heart.

"Yes, a very horrible, decisive row during my party at the Country Club. Clearly, he was holding this information pretty close to his chest if he didn't even mention it to you during your trek. So, if you don't mind, I'd rather not talk about it."

Let him believe she was more heartbroken over Matthew than—to her surprise —she felt. Yes, Matthew had led her up the garden path. She was furious with him for that. But she didn't actually miss *him*.

She'd miss the future they'd have had, and she'd miss his mother. But Matthew wasn't the adoring, attentive boyfriend she'd hoped he'd be, and he didn't make her legs buckle and her insides quiver with longing.

Not the way Stuart did.

"By the way, Stuart's coming to my party tonight," she added over her shoulder as she stepped into the passage with Francina following, drying her hands on a tea towel. "He can stay in the rondavel. He has to be up here first thing in the morning anyway to do a pickup at Letseng-la-Terai, so it's convenient."

Convenient. Her whole being hummed in happy expectation. But when her mind wandered any further along the path she and Stuart had embarked upon, she closed it down.

One day at a time.

Enjoy it while it lasts.

See what happens. Something? Nothing?

After all, she was, as he correctly put it, a girl on the rebound.

WHEN SHE AND Francina reached her bedroom, Philippa sat down at her dressing table and rummaged in the drawer for some hairpins while Francina picked up her Mason Pearson boar bristle brush after settling herself on a chair beside her.

"I see Mpho's back from boarding school, but he doesn't look very happy," remarked Philippa as Francina began to work on her hair, just as she had every evening when Philippa had lived at home. Mpho, the second born of Francina's three children, was usually a smiling, sunny-natured fourteen-year-old, and a favourite of Philippa's. "Mary hasn't put a hex on him, has she?"

Francina looked offended, and Philippa laughed. The year before Philippa's mother had died there'd been a huge ruckus in the household when Mary—the wife of John-the-Gardener—a *ngaka* had supposedly put a curse on Francina. The two women hated one another.

Philippa twirled a piece of hair around her finger and reminded herself to tell Stuart the story.

When Francina didn't answer, just looked miserable, Philippa said, "You know that old witch with her bag of bones can't actually do any harm. Mpho should know it too with all his schooling. He's a bright boy. How's he doing?" She hesitated. "Or didn't he do so well on his test?"

It did not surprise Philippa to see Francina stiffen. The DC paid for Francina's two oldest boys to board at a mission school near Roma, and Francina was intensely proud of their academic efforts yet terrified they'd let her down.

Many Basotho boys spent their younger years tending the family's goats so the fact that Francina's two sons, who had no named father, were being educated for government jobs rather than having to fend for themselves in the mountains for months at a time, would have been a feather in their single mother's cap.

Francina shook her head. "Mpho tells me that one of the boys who was given a scholarship to a place called Moscow has come back to the mission school. Mpho says this boy knows all about politics and is very fierce about what is the right path to follow."

Philippa raised her eyebrows, and although she felt a frisson of concern, she tried to sound reassuring. "I'm sure Mpho knows in his heart that the right path is *not* what fiery boys from Moscow would have him believe." She patted Francina's hand and, with a jolt, realised it's just what her mother would have done. "The Canadian priests teach the boys right from wrong, so Mpho will know what to do."

Francina continued to look unhappy. "Mpho tells me this young man wants to talk to him always of independence; of the elections and what is the right way to vote."

"Elections are years away. Mpho needn't worry about that yet." But Philippa was conscious of the growing political fervour and excitement each time she returned to the tiny British Protectorate, landlocked by Apartheid South Africa. Perhaps it wasn't right to brush off Francina's concerns. She traced the kidney-shaped outline of her dressing table with her forefinger. Perhaps she should relay to her father these whispers of discontent at the mission school. "What else does Mpho say this boy tells him to think?"

"That the Russians give the Basutoland Congress Party a lot of money, so their party will win and make Basutoland great. But Mpho knows the *Morena* favours the Basutoland National Party. He knows the party of the chiefs will make

Basutoland great, but he's afraid of making this boy angry if he says it."

Philippa enjoyed politics as little as Francina did. Sometimes she felt guilty that she didn't care more, for it was her father's life. But her student existence in faraway Cape Town was comfortable and shielded, for the most part. She didn't have to worry about politics there. It was only when Francina talked of uncomfortable topics like now that she was reminded the world was not as comfortable for everyone else. She squirmed, not liking the vague unease and guilt in the pit of her stomach. "What did you advise Mpho?" she asked.

Francina kept her eyes averted as she smoothed her apron over her blue cotton work dress.

"I told him it was easy to know what he must think. He must think what the *Morena* wants him to think, for the *Morena* is a wise man. A man who has come so far is a wise man who knows which is the party that will lead Basutoland to greatness."

Philippa nodded as she toyed with a black velvet ribbon. "Yes, you tell Mpho that if he is ever in doubt, or has a problem, he must talk to the *Morena*. That's what I do." She raised her eyes and tried for a confident smile—one like her wise, experienced mother's smile—even though she felt very young right now. "He can fix anything."

Francina nodded. "Yes, I am sure you are right."

But when Philippa saw in the mirror that the deep line remained between Francina's eyes as she brushed her hair, she felt a stab of foreboding and asked, "Was there anything else that Mpho is worried about? I think you must tell me, Francina." She swallowed and for a moment her fears for the future were much deeper and more complex than lamenting the fact that if she married Stuart, she'd not live in a grand house by the sea with a swimming pool and wear Ciel gowns for *Fair Lady* magazine photoshoots.

Resting her hand on Francina's forearm, she said, "If my father is to help, he needs to know what radical talk is being spoken at Mpho's school."

Francina cast down her gaze as she shook her head. Then she whispered, "This boy says it's unfair that there are two sets of laws in Basutoland. One that imprisons men like his uncle on suspicion of *diretlo* when how else is a chief to get the powerful *muti* he needs to be strong for his people?"

Philippa's internal stirrings intensified, and although Francina still didn't look at her, she knew she had to learn the rest.

"And?" she prompted.

"And another that turns a blind eye to the white man who steals the wealth from the country, forcing the Basotho to work in the gold mines of South Africa instead of enabling them to grow rich from Basutoland's diamonds."

CHAPTER

TWELVE

A JAZZ QUARTET ON THE WIRELESS AND THE SMELL OF COOKING
had Philippa in a more carefree frame of mind half an hour
later as she dropped into the kitchen to check on progress.
Francina was grating the cheese for her famous cheese
souffle, which she'd serve as part of the buffet. Meanwhile,
the products of the afternoon's labour—trays of mushroom
vol au vents and *devils on horseback*—were ready to go into
the oven.

"My darling, you look sensational!" Her father, who was
on his way up the passage, put his head round the kitchen
door to voice his praise. He hesitated. "How are you bearing
up?"

At first, Philippa didn't know what he meant. She'd
spent all afternoon in a fever of excitement at the thought
of Stuart's imminent arrival, so his words brought her up
short. After a second's reflection, she decided that anything
that didn't accord with heartbreak must be due to delayed
shock.

She sobered for his benefit. "I'm trying not to dwell on
it. But thank you for asking, Daddy." Then, unable to

155

contain her excitement, she threw her arms wide, just like she used to as an overexuberant child. "Tonight is going to be wonderful! Francina is going to wow everyone with her cooking, and Mrs Oosterhuisen is going to have too much sherry, and everyone will have the most marvellous time. Don't you think?"

Her father looked relieved. "Good girl. That's the spirit. Stiff upper lip and all that. Matthew was a nice young man. I enjoyed his conversation when we were on trek but there'll be someone out there much more exciting and suitable. Now, come along and let's choose some records to put on, shall we? The guests are due any minute."

They chose Frank Sinatra, and soon the crooning of her father's favourite ballad made Philippa want to slowly circle the dance floor in the arms of someone young and handsome.

Someone exciting and...

Well, unsuitable because Stuart was the only man Philippa could conjure up when she thought of being wrapped in anyone's arms and slowly circling a dance floor.

But—

Was he really that unsuitable? she had to ask herself.

Philippa remained by the record player when her father left to see to the drinks; staring out through the window across the colourful flower beds to the rugged mountains beyond.

In the distance, a car door slammed, and the loud, plummy voice of Colonel Buxton heralded the beginning of the party.

Soon Stuart would arrive. Handsome, unsuitable Stuart, who made her body tingle and her heart skitter in her chest.

And even though it would be a small gathering of

mostly Philippa's parents' old friends, Stuart's arrival would make it the most exciting event on the horizon.

Why? Because there was a raw danger Philippa felt whenever she was close to him that made her feel like she was living on the edge. It was exciting and intoxicating.

But it surely couldn't last forever…

Could it? She shook her head to clear it. What did it matter? Live in the moment, she heard the echo of her mother's voice.

"CHARLES! HOW ARE YOU?" Colonel Buxton and his wife burst through the lead light doors. They'd always been ones to make a loud, theatrical entrance for as long as Philippa could remember.

"Never better," her father replied, raising the cut-glass decanter he was holding before preparing four gin and tonics. "Who'd have believed my little girl would have grown up so quickly?"

"Philippa, darling, let me see, let me see!" With her scarlet lips turned up impishly, Mrs Buxton hurried across the room to seize Philippa's left hand, tutting as she dropped it with the look of a disappointed Pekingese. "Poor darling, just be patient. It's only a matter of time."

"Matthew and I called it off last night, I'm afraid." Philippa's announcement was made just as Mrs Oosterhuisen arrived, clicking across the room in a pair of spotted high heels to match her blouse, joining in the gasps and commiserations of the consensus. "What was that boy thinking?"

"That he'd rather go around the world for a year than make a two-minute trip up the aisle with me, I suppose."

Philippa tried to sound blasé. "Now, here's to other things." She raised the glass her father had just handed her before taking a sip, her ears suddenly attuned to the sound of an engine just overhead.

Stuart. Without warning, she needed to sit down. Her legs felt like jelly, and her heart was racing like a steam engine. She knocked back her drink in one and put down the empty glass, saying to the ladies as she stepped back, "Please excuse me. I won't be long."

Hurrying out of the sitting room and onto the veranda, she traversed it to reach the rear of the house, then ran across the back garden, her heels sinking into the soft grass, arriving at the airstrip just as Stuart was nosing the plane up by the garden gate.

Philippa tucked an escaped strand of hair behind her ear as she waited for him to shut down the engine, trying to decide whether to show her eagerness or to play it cool. She could see him through the whir of the propeller and the windscreen, handsome in sunglasses as he took off his headset and put it on the dashboard.

What would he really think after last night? Did he want to be here?

But Stuart was unequivocal about his feelings as he jumped lightly to the ground, slamming the door and striding towards her with a broad smile to follow a wolf whistle. "My word, don't you look a picture?" he said, which was all she needed to throw herself into his arms, kissing him quickly before stepping back, for they'd be on view to anyone who looked too closely from the veranda.

"Audrey Hepburn would have had a run for her money if she were here," he said over his shoulder as he retrieved his bag. "Now, I'm not even going to ask if you've had second thoughts about inviting me because I am ready for a party!"

"With ten elderly people and just you and me?"

Stuart snorted. "I don't think your dad would be too pleased to hear himself described as elderly. He's only fifteen years older than me."

Philippa blinked. "He was very young when Mummy had me. Poor thing. He seems so much older since she died."

"Loneliness does that," said Stuart, flinging his arm about Philippa's shoulders. "It makes people into someone they're not. Sorry—you don't like that?"

Philippa felt herself blushing as she put a little distance between them. "You can squeeze me and do whatever you like when we're alone. It's just that everyone is talking about how bereft I must be over Matthew right now, and it would just seem a little odd if—"

"Of course."

They walked on in silence, Philippa wishing she hadn't knocked out some of his gaiety when Stuart was so charming in this mood. But there'd be all evening to build up to whatever might happen later.

A couple of drinks, starting with the gin and tonic her father thrust at Stuart as he greeted him on the stairs, would oil the wheels. It was a party and the night was young and the world was full of promise, and soon Stuart had stepped into the thick of it, and Philippa was laughing, happy just to be at home and in the company of people she'd known since she'd been a child.

"Here comes Drakensberg Air's handsomest pilot!" Mrs Oosthuizen had clearly had a few in quick succession.

"I don't have much competition." Stuart grinned. They

all knew he was referring to the fact that his fellow pilots were several decades older.

"And not here tonight either." Mrs Buxton's deep, throaty voice sounded in Philippa's ear, and Philippa turned to see her mother's old whisky-drinking, bridge-playing friend indicate the few aged men in the room with a sweep of her arm. "You obviously know poor Philippa is nursing a broken heart. Matthew was a very handsome man, but so are you, Stuart, and you have a duty to pay court to this young lady tonight to help take her mind off her troubles."

"If you insist, Mrs Buxton," said Stuart with a wink that made them both laugh, "though you make it sound such a chore."

"I assure you, the chore will be when you are reminded of your manners and take an old lady for a spin around the dance floor after you've done your duty by young Philippa." Mrs Buxton sent an arch look at her husband's clubfoot. "I always loved to dance, so I don't know what came over me when I said yes to old George over there."

Philippa knew they were a devoted couple, and Mrs Buxton was only teasing. "You don't?" she asked, entering into the banter.

"Well, I do. George was rich. I mean, rich enough." Mrs Buxton tapped the side of her nose as she settled into her Sanderson-covered wingback armchair. "A girl's got to think of the future. Stuart, what about you? Working hard?"

"Always, Mrs Buxton."

"Still chasing South African Airways, or are you planning to return home? Only thirteen hours to London these days. I can't see there's much for you here in the Colonial Service's remotest outpost."

Philippa felt his glance upon her before he answered, "Africa is my home."

"Ah yes, once Africa is in your blood, it's always in your blood. And your mother so recently gone, I hear. I'm sorry. So hard when one is an only child."

"Stuart and his sister were evacuees here during the war," Philippa said, sitting on the arm of the chair, wishing she'd kept her mouth shut when she saw Stuart's face.

"So you have a sister in South Africa? And where does she live?"

Philippa glanced at Stuart.

"Grace died in an accident a few years ago."

Philippa stiffened as she saw his jaw clench.

"I'm so sorry." Mrs Buxton looked dismayed, and Philippa was about to interject when Mrs Oosterhuysen, who'd been eavesdropping, joined the circle, saying brightly, "A blessing, then, to have a foster family in South Africa. Now, I don't quite remember you saying where they lived?"

"I didn't."

"But it was somewhere close. Well, not more than a few hours' drive, if I recall."

"They live in Pretoria." Stuart's stance was almost combative, all his earlier bonhomie evaporated. Philippa just wanted to get him out of there.

"Pretoria? The jacaranda city." Mrs Buxton was too tipsy to pick up on his reluctance to answer their questions. "Your foster family must be so proud of you. What do they think of Basutoland?'

"Ah, Philippa!" Her father came up beside her and patted her shoulder. "Mrs Clements has brought you something. Colonel Buxton is putting it on now." He grinned as

Frank Sinatra's crooning was abruptly replaced by the familiar beat of *Yellow Polka Dot Bikini*.

"Come on, you two. Dance!" Deaf Mrs Clements' baritone boomed at them from across the room. "Show us oldies how it's done! Come on Doris, you were complaining you never get to dance!"

Relieved she'd changed the subject, Philippa tried not to laugh as she stared at Mrs Buxton's green crepe skirts swirling about her as she kicked her feet and wiggled her hips in a parody of the jitterbug.

"Well, doesn't this bring back memories?" Stuart murmured in her ear as he took Philippa's hands and pulled her into the centre of the room to a smattering of applause. "You're blushing." Then louder for the benefit of the oldies, "Come on, Philippa, show everyone how it's done."

Philippa laughed as Stuart spun her around, and her second gin and tonic went to her head. She laughed even more when Stuart did a short imitation of the young Van Wyk lad as he rolled his shoulders and nodded his head. Then grinned as Mrs Oosthuysen tottered into the centre of the room and entreated Stuart to partner her.

There was much hilarity at the spectacle, which both dancers intended to be comedic, for Mrs Oosthuysen was always a crowd-pleaser when she'd had a couple.

Now back on the outer, Philippa clinked glasses with her father when he leaned over to remark, "Not too dull for you, darling?" He pointed at Stuart. "That's a surprise. I didn't know he could dance. Stuart's more of a card than I'd thought. Certainly knows how to seize the moment and please the ladies."

Philippa gave her empty glass to Francina, who was doing the rounds, and cooled her warm cheeks with her hands.

"And what about you, Daddy? No one here for you?" She looked about the room, populated with the couples with whom her parents had regularly socialised.

"I don't need anyone else." Her father sent her a genial look. He seemed relaxed. "Your mother was enough for me. My perfect match. Not everyone is lucky enough to enjoy twenty years of wonderful marriage."

"But you're still young, Daddy." Philippa put her hand on her father's arm. "I can't bear to think of you being lonely."

"Don't worry about me. One day, perhaps. In the meantime, I enjoy my solitude and I enjoy my work."

"And you've done a wonderful job, by all accounts." Philippa ran her hand up and down the smooth wool of his jacket, fine quality but threadbare now. She wondered if he'd bought anything new to wear since her mother had died. "I hear the police have finally brought Chief Thabo in for questioning. Do you think he's guilty?"

"That's not for me to say, darling." Her father turned as the Colonel addressed him from across the room. He nodded to Philippa. "Let justice take its course."

Philippa made a noise of frustration. "Really, Daddy, I can't compete with you when it comes to being a model of discretion and decorum. You might offer me a wink or something just to indicate what you believe. Don't you trust me?"

"It's not about trust, and what I do or don't believe. It's about the law and about justice." He raised an eyebrow. "The rules are the rules, and you know I never bend them."

"How about we go for a drive—if your father lets me borrow his Land Rover?" Stuart stood by Philippa's side on the top step of the veranda, staring at the waxy yellow moon while the party continued indoors.

"It's magnificent, isn't it?" Philippa murmured, staring up at the sky and leaning unconsciously into Stuart before remembering herself and glancing over her shoulder.

"Don't want to be caught out?"

"Too early."

"To know?"

"To know?" She looked quizzically at him.

He patted his heart. "Come." He turned. "I'm going to ask your dad for the keys. You can answer me later."

It felt cosy and companionable being in the Land Rover with Stuart, even in the chill and silence until Stuart took his foot off the brake and the vehicle moved forward, crunching over the gravel, the moon's shadow looming large as they slowly followed the uneven track out of Mokhotlong.

Philippa rested her elbow against the ledge of the open window, her chin in her hand as she gazed at the light-flooded landscape, a strange cocktail of emotions swirling around inside her. Before them stretched endless mountain ranges. Dark and brooding. Not at all like the flat-topped mountain she'd become so familiar with since she'd become a student. Table Mountain was majestic, but it had become ubiquitous. No matter how many times she returned home to Mokhotlong, she was struck by the magnificence of the mountains that surrounded her on all sides. When she'd been young, she'd believed everything she'd been told by her playmates, Francina's children, Mpho, Muketsi and Ann-Bubba; that the mountains were the keepers of dark and dangerous spirits ready to unleash their anger upon anyone who did them wrong.

As they drove slowly around the hairpin bends with ravines plunging to infinity, she felt a surge of homesickness. This was the wilderness for Matthew and her varsity friends, but it was home to her. And one day all this would be just a memory. Her father wouldn't always live in Mokhotlong. Postings were only for a few years. Philippa had spent her earliest years in the capital, Maseru, but her first memories were of these mountains. Her parents had loved the remoteness and requested a second posting when Philippa was a teenager.

Stuart broke the silence as he slowed the vehicle to take a bend that required some tight reversing. The moon had popped into view again behind another mountain peak while to their right the mountain track plunged hundreds of feet to the valley floor, but Philippa wasn't afraid. Stuart had lived here long enough to know the dangers.

"You did well tonight," he said.

She liked the sound of his voice; a sort of hybrid since he'd picked up some of the local accent. "I did?"

"For someone nursing a broken heart."

Philippa gave a short laugh and turned to look at him. "It was easy to forget that when you were dancing with me. I'm on the rebound, remember. Your job is to flatter me and make me feel like I have a future when I've convinced myself I don't. And—"

"Kiss you?"

"Mmm."

He cut the engine as he drew to a halt where the road was wider and Philippa leaned across, snuggling against him, inhaling his aftershave as the gear stick dug into her ribs while she offered him her lips.

"That's nice," she whispered through the kiss. It was soft but full of promise. She supposed that indulging in anything more passionate with a thousand feet plunge by their left wheel might not be wise. She nuzzled his smooth-shaven cheek, feeling lightheaded with the familiar feeling he invoked. It made her dizzy with want.

After a while, he drew away. "So, what do you think?"

Philippa's heart, which was beating erratically enough already, ratcheted up. "About what?" she whispered.

"Don't pretend you don't know what I'm talking about." Stuart's look was serious. He cleared his throat. "You know what I feel about you. How I've felt about you since...since we landed in that mealie field and one thing led to another." He stroked her cheek, adding softly, "Led by you, I might add."

Philippa nodded once slowly as she moved her head to kiss his fingertips. "You make me feel things here—" she touched her heart—"that don't make sense...here." She touched her head.

"There's a remedy for that?"

"Mm-hmm?" She closed her eyes and leaned in, thinking he'd kiss her again; that that was what he meant.

Instead he said, still in that thoughtful tone, "Yes, it's called 'getting to know each other.' "

She blinked open her eyes. His words were both thrilling and terrifying. Did she really want to commit to something more serious with Stuart?

But there was something magnetising in his look. She swallowed, her throat dry, while her body thrummed with so many things: excitement, terror, hope, fear. And a lot more.

"I'm recovering from heartbreak," she whispered nervously, "and I don't know that I can trust—"

"Me?"

"No, me," she said, more worried now as she looked up at him, and continued in a rush, "I like you so much, Stuart, I really do. I want to do all these things with you, but then —" She broke off while she tried to make sense of her jumbled thoughts. "All those things aren't what I'd planned. And...I'm a planner of life. I always have been."

"You didn't plan on ditching in a mealie field with me, but you didn't seem to mind the bit of adventure that followed," he replied, adding, reasonably enough, "Maybe you're more of an adventuress than you think."

She relaxed back in her seat, her smile turning into a gentle laugh. "While I ponder whether that could be true or not, how about we do the bit before?"

"The 'getting to know you more' bit?"

She nodded, leaning across the centre console so she could put her arms around his neck and her lips against his.

"Good idea," he murmured, his words vibrating gently against her mouth, which opened up to his. The kiss deepened, and Philippa felt herself melting into him, her carefully constructed defences dissolving as if they'd been nothing more than a mirage. His hand cupped the back of her neck, his thumb tracing gentle circles against her skin, and she heard herself make a soft sound of surrender that seemed to come from somewhere deeper than thought or reason.

When she finally drew back, she felt breathless and slightly stunned, as if she'd been caught in a whirlwind that had rearranged everything inside her. The world beyond the car windows seemed impossibly distant, while her heart hammered against her ribs with a rhythm that felt entirely new.

"Wow."

She turned to look at Stuart, his soft, stunned murmur echoing what she was feeling.

"Wow," she repeated, nodding, her tone equally serious, her hands now clasped in her lap as she gazed at the surrounding mountains, dark and majestic. She was in familiar landscape. And yet, she felt like she'd fallen into another world.

Finally, he broke the silence. "I want you to think about what I said. But for now, I suppose we should get back." He sounded regretful. "We don't want to worry the oldies."

"Or give them too much to talk about," she added, wishing she'd not said that when she saw his suddenly shuttered look.

But then he grinned. "Home then, madam." The engine shuddered back to life before he began the laborious task of turning the vehicle one hundred and eighty degrees. "I am at your command."

***

When they drew up in front of the house, Philippa thought there must have been an accident, for Mrs Oosthuisen stood on the veranda steps anxiously scanning the road for them.

"Quick, Philippa! Inside!" she cried, descending the steps at an angle with difficulty in her high heels, then opening the Land Rover door before Stuart had a chance.

"What's the matter?" Philippa cried, alarm making her voice crack as she clambered out. "Is Daddy all right?"

"Yes, yes, of course he is! You'll never guess, my dear—"

"Philippa!"

Philippa stopped at the bottom of the steps, staring up at Matthew, tall and smiling. Colonel Buxton and his wife tottered through the double doors behind him to see what the excitement was all about.

"Philippa darling! I've been a fool!" said Matthew as Mrs Oosthuisen hustled Philippa forward.

Her throat felt dry, and her heartbeat was erratic. She didn't know whether to laugh or cry as Matthew patted his chest pocket, then withdrew a small blue velvet box.

Whichever emotion she chose, she'd still not know whether delight or dismay was the motivator.

"I've come back to ask you what I should have last night if I'd not been such an idiot and forgotten to bring this with me."

The remaining guests had now emerged from inside to gather behind Matthew, for it was clear by his tone and manner that his presentation was intended to be public.

And for maximum effect.

There was a collective gasp as Matthew raised the lid of the box, now resting in the palm of his hand, and moonlight glinted on the biggest, most beautiful, diamond Philippa had ever seen. *Obscenely* beautiful, was her first thought as Francina's words flitted through her mind about white men stealing the wealth from the country.

But this was swept away as Matthew's smile broadened and he dropped to one knee and raised his face to hers, his look one of happy expectation.

"Philippa, will you marry me?"

THIRTEEN

AN HOUR LATER, PHILIPPA PRESSED HER KNUCKLES AGAINST HER eyelids as she leaned her elbows on her dressing tabletop. Matthew had just retired to his room, kissing her lingeringly in the passage, telling her how happy he was that she'd agreed to marry him but that he was so exhausted he'd be passed out by the time his head touched the pillow; that it had been a gruelling journey, squeaking across the Caledonspoort border crossing near Buthe-Buthe just before the 10pm closing, risking his neck on the bad roads in the dark after his mother had 'talked sense into him'.

How could Philippa possibly sleep?

The house seemed unnaturally quiet now that everyone had gone home. With a strangely heavy heart, Philippa had watched Colonel Buxton weave his way to the car, his wife telling him she ought to drive—if she only knew how. The others had left at the same time, some to travel only a few minutes away, others a couple of hours. But the moon was large and full.

The white community did not fear going out after dark. *Diretlo* wasn't a threat to them—the ritual murders were confined to the local population, where chiefs selected victims from their own people for the powerful *muti* their body parts would provide.

It was only the administration's problem to prosecute.

Shrugging on her dressing gown and feeling like a caged bird was battering against her ribs, Philippa stepped out onto the veranda. The night air was crisp and thin at this altitude, carrying the distant smell of wood smoke from the village below. Above, the Milky Way arced over her like a giant swathe of smoke.

Or, when she looked more carefully, like scattered diamonds, brilliant in the clear mountain air.

And that's what Stuart had done to her: make her look at life more carefully.

Just because *Matthew* had decided to reframe his return as that of the returning conqueror or hero didn't mean she'd just meekly melt into his arms.

And yet that's what she'd done.

Because what else could she do with everyone watching her as if she were the heroine of some epic romantic drama on the big screen?

"Couldn't sleep?"

She took another few steps forward, putting her hand on the back of her father's chair as she asked softly, "Daddy, what are you doing alone in the dark?"

"Nothing better than a whisky, my pipe, and my own company on nights like this." The red glow of his pipe bowl illuminated his features briefly before fading back to shadow.

"Then I won't intrude."

"Don't be silly. Tell me your plans. Matthew? Do you want to marry him?"

Moving forward to lean against the window opposite

him, Philippa wrapped her arms about herself to stop from shivering; and not just from the cold. Around them, the mountains rose like sleeping giants, their peaks silver-edged in the moonlight. "I said yes, didn't I?"

"There wasn't much else you could say under the circumstances."

She shrugged, glancing towards the guest rondavel, dark and silent at the bottom of the garden. Had Stuart left immediately after Matthew's dramatic proposal? Was he lying awake in there, as sleepless as she was? The thought made her chest tighten with something that felt dangerously like regret.

Or was the chest-tightening something else? Relief that Matthew had changed his mind and returned? She didn't think so.

Slowly, she said, "I've wanted Matthew to ask me to marry him for months." She could see her breath frosting in the night air, a strange miasma in the semi-light from the moon. Fancifully, she could imagine it was her soul doing some kind of contorting dance; trying to be someone she was not. No. Trying to work out *who* she was. "After our disagreement outside the Country Club... after he left... I thought my dreams had gone up in smoke."

She heard her father draw on his pipe. He didn't answer immediately, then said, "That's not always such a bad thing. Heartbreak can sweeten happiness. Don't think I don't understand, my darling." She looked out at the mountains. Somehow, it was easier to talk when they weren't looking at each other, with only the distant call of a nightjar, and the rustle of small creatures in the undergrowth, filling the silence between them. "I thought my heart would break when your mother's parents refused their blessing."

Philippa nodded. The story of her mother's defiance was a familiar one, though she still wondered at the lingering regrets her mother may have harboured after being consigned to such a spartan environment compared with the glamorous world she'd come from.

Philippa had never thought of herself as the adventuress her mother had clearly been. But *did* her mother have regrets? It's what Philippa feared more than anything: discovering that she'd made the wrong choice. But perhaps her mother's regrets weren't about love itself, but about the reduced circumstances—the isolation, the lack of society, even the worry about money—that had marked Philippa's childhood despite her father's best efforts.

She went on, trying to tease out her feelings as truthfully as she could. "I wasn't so much broken-hearted as that I felt a failure. That's not how I should feel, is it?" She turned and touched her heart. "I should have felt it here, but it was more... more hurt pride, I think."

Her father took his time replying, the cicadas loud in the rockery that fringed the veranda. "Is it that young man, Stuart, who's making you question everything?"

Philippa made a noise of frustration. "Yes! I suppose.... No... I don't know." She felt embarrassed and ashamed at what her father would think of her if he knew how much Stuart featured in her life when, as far as he was concerned, she'd only ever pledged herself to Matthew.

She took a deep breath. "When you marry, you're not just marrying a person, you're marrying their life." She'd said it to Stuart. She needed him to understand how much this worried her. "After the first throes of love have faded, what's left? The life you've married into. Their family. The way they've been brought up. Not just the person."

"That's rather sobering coming from one so young. I hope your mother and I didn't make you feel that way."

"No, but it's true. When I first met Matthew, I was mad about him. Just like I'm mad about Stuart now. I'm ashamed I feel that way, but I can say it because you can't see me blushing. Stuart is exciting and adventurous, but Matthew offers me everything I've ever wanted in life. And I love Matthew's family. That's important, too. If I made the mistake of throwing in my lot with Stuart, it wouldn't last. Lord, he won't even talk about his family, so there must be bad blood there."

Even as she said it, she felt a pang of guilt. Perhaps she was being unfair—perhaps Stuart's silence came from pain rather than shame. And really, she'd not probed him more deeply. But she couldn't help the way her mind worked, the way she'd been trained to think. People from good families talked with pride about their families. It was what people like her did. Stuart's reticence felt like a warning that there were dark, threatening shadows in his past. Whereas Matthew was an open book. She knew exactly what she was getting herself into if she married him.

"I worry that the moment the novelty wore off, I'd resent him for the rest of my life because he'd swayed me from following my instincts." She rested her head against the upright beam as the tear that had been gathering in the corner of her eye spilled down her cheek. "I want the life Matthew can offer me. It's why I went to Cape Town to study. So I could marry someone just like him. I'm no different to most of my friends. A good marriage is every-thing." She put her hand against her chest as if she could still her beating heart. "But Stuart makes me feel things that Matthew doesn't."

She heard him draw on his pipe once more before

remarking, "It seems you know Stuart more than any of us might have supposed."

Philippa drew in a short breath. "He's exciting, Daddy. I don't know how else to explain it. He makes me want to throw in all my sensible dreams of choosing the sensible path by marrying Matthew. And yet, what do I know about him other than whispers and rumours that he's not...not really our sort?

"I wasn't your mother's family's 'sort'. "

"I'm sorry, Daddy. I didn't mean to sound so snobbish." She gave a small sob, and in the distance, she thought she heard the soft closing of a door. The rondavel? Gasping, her ears strained while her heart clenched at the thought that Stuart might have heard her words.

"So...you're telling me that you're not sure if you want to marry Matthew, after all?"

She hadn't realised she'd been holding her breath until her shoulders slumped with her defeated sigh. "I don't know what I want."

"Well, I can't tell you that, my darling, and I can't tell you what to do, but you know you can tell me anything." He reached for her hand and gave it a squeeze. "Sleep on it. You'll feel more settled in the morning."

Her father's voice was just as she needed it to be: warm and comforting.

"Don't rush into hasty decisions. Just because you said yes to Matthew tonight doesn't mean everything is set in stone." A note of concern crept into his tone as he added, "But you will have to decide one way or another before Matthew returns to Cape Town. If you're going to break an engagement, it's better that you do it in the immediate aftermath."

She knew he was trying to give her the best counsel, but

she balked at the idea he seemed almost to promote that, after tomorrow, everything *was* set in stone.

"Stuart is a very charming young man, and a good pilot, and I've heard no rumours that reflect poorly on him, if that helps." He dropped his hand to his lap, adding, as she stepped forward to go inside, "But Matthew is the sure option when it comes to providing for you. It's not my place to tell you what to do—and, believe me, I'm not, for you must follow your heart—" he hesitated— "like your mother did." He cleared his throat. "But Matthew does offer material advantages that Stuart clearly doesn't. I just don't want you being impulsive and then regretting it, that's all. But it's your decision, Philippa, and I'll back you, whatever you decide."

CHAPTER

FOURTEEN

Stuart lay on his back on top of the bed, still fully clothed, his head resting on his folded arms as he stared at the seventeen poles that supported the thatch of the rondavel above him.

He'd counted them at least three times. As if it were important to make sure he hadn't miscounted them the first time. That his mind was where it should be. That he could think and function properly and still have perspective.

Earlier that night, he'd recognised shock and confusion in Philippa's stance as Matthew had asked her to marry him. She hadn't thrown herself joyfully at him. In fact, there'd been something more contained and proud than jubilant about the way she'd let Matthew slide that ostentatious engagement ring onto her finger before showing it to the admiring older contingent who'd seen it as 'their' girl's dream come true.

Yes, it had been Matthew who'd held Philippa's hand out on display so everyone could marvel over how much that diamond must have cost.

177

Stuart had melted into the shadows. There was no place for him in the gathering.

As he'd made his way across the lawn in the direction of his rondavel, had Philippa even looked for him?

In the moment of her greatest victory?

Or was that not how she really felt? It wasn't if she'd been truthful during their drive through the mountains just now. And he really thought she had.

But even if she was confused, she'd still asserted how much the idea of marrying Matthew Myburgh appealed to her.

Just as she'd confessed to feeling the same undeniable, sizzling chemistry between them that he felt, even if she made clear it was inconvenient.

Ever since that fateful day when he'd brought the plane down in the mealie field and they'd spent the night in the van Wyk's guest rondavel, there'd been an undeniable connection that she'd admitted she couldn't discount when she weighed up the advantages between her two suitors. For that's what Stuart realised he was.

Philippa knew she had a choice. Stuart couldn't have been clearer that he was making a serious play for her.

But could he really win her? After Matthew's grand gesture tonight, could he really compete?

And did he even deserve her?

With a frustrated grunt, Stuart slid off the bed and put on his shoes. He wasn't much of a smoker, but maybe a cigarette beneath the stars and the moon would help him decide his strategy.

Philippa was quite open about the fact that marrying Matthew gave her access to the life she wanted.

The life she *thought* she wanted.

But Stuart had exerted sufficient charm to sway

Philippa. Money wasn't everything. When it came to attraction—even if it was inconvenient—then Stuart was definitely in with a chance.

Beneath the moon, breathing in the clean mountain air, he was about to strike a match when he heard his name.

He realised he wasn't being addressed personally, but the faint murmur of voices on the other side of the rhododendron bushes indicated he was the topic of conversation.

He moved forward quickly, realising he was eavesdropping on a conversation Philippa was having with her father, for he heard her say, "Stuart is exciting and adventurous, but Matthew offers me everything I've ever wanted in life. And I love Matthew's family. That's important to me, too."

He tensed, knowing he should move away; that it was wrong to listen in on what Philippa and her father were saying about Matthew. And Stuart. But shouldn't he know what Philippa really thought about him?

Philippa thought Matthew offered her everything she wanted, but she hadn't heard Stuart's offer. That's what he intended to do in the morning. Make a compelling counter-offer to Matthew's, which would force Philippa to evaluate just how important the heart was.

Telling her that while he wasn't in a position to offer her marriage just yet, he soon would be.

Stuart's prospects might not be as glittering as Matthew's, but during the past few months he'd built his twin engine time. In a few months more, he'd have a real chance as a First Officer with South African Airlines.

Stuart took a careful step backwards, his excitement growing. He had a case. A compelling case and he was in with a chance.

Now he must go back to bed and try to sleep.

A snapping of twigs made him stop and tense. But

Philippa and her father went on talking. They clearly hadn't heard, for Philippa was now speaking in impassioned tones. "If I made the mistake of throwing in my lot with Stuart, it wouldn't last. Lord, he won't even talk about his family, so there must be bad blood there. I worry that the moment the novelty wore off, I'd resent him for the rest of my life because he'd swayed me from following my head and my instincts."

Family.

If ever there was a word that had the power to make Stuart doubt himself, that was it.

His father's thin, dissatisfied face, with its shifty eyes and curled lip, loomed before him, quickly followed by his mother's: red, blowsy, her eyes small and piggish. Had she ever loved him? She'd railed at him often enough for being born too early and ruining her life.

And finally, there was sweet Grace, looking at him with those luminous blue eyes and that lovely smile of hers: trusting that he'd look after her.

But he hadn't.

Family.

It's what Stuart wanted more than anything, too.

But what Philippa wanted when she spoke of family was something Stuart could never give her.

He was starting to realise that.

She was right about the bad blood—not just because his parents were criminals and alcoholics, but because they represented everything her world would instinctively reject. And worse, because the guilt he carried over Grace's death made him unworthy of someone as pure and bright as Philippa.

He slunk into the shadows, not wanting to hear any more, and certainly not her painful parting shot, not intended for his ears, of course, as she said plaintively, "I want the life Matthew can offer me. It's why I went to Cape Town to study. So I could marry someone just like him. Not someone like Stuart, who's a closed book—!"

The truth of it hit home with devastating clarity. She was right, of course. He was a closed book because opening it would reveal pages no decent woman should have to read. Pages stained with poverty, crime, and worst of all, the death of the one person who'd ever loved him unconditionally.

Fortunately, he wasn't able to hear anymore.

Thrusting his fists into his pockets, Stuart returned to his empty room, already formulating a plan that had nothing to do with winning Philippa's heart and everything to do with protecting what was left of his own.

IT WAS NEARLY dawn when Philippa finally fell asleep. And it seemed only five minutes later that the first pale light was creeping across the mountains. She was woken by the distinct sound of an engine. Not a car engine, her groggy brain deduced, but a plane's engine.

And now it was above the house, she was sure of it.

Snatching her dressing gown from the end of the bed, she didn't stop to find her slippers before running outside, her bare feet slipping on the dew-covered lawn as she sprinted across the garden. The morning air was sharp and thin, cutting through the silk of her nightgown and making her gasp.

The garden gate onto the airstrip was latched shut.

And Stuart's plane was gone.

Devastation at seeing the airfield empty crashed over

her. Where the Cessna had sat just hours before, there was only trampled grass and the lingering scent of aviation fuel on the morning breeze.

"Captain Price remembered something he had to do," Francina told her, when Philippa rushed into the kitchen to find the maid preparing her father's breakfast tray. The familiar smell of bacon and eggs and fresh bread should have been comforting, but instead it made her feel ill. "He said to say goodbye in case he doesn't see you before you go back to Cape Town."

Philippa felt winded. "But... he's picking up some passengers from Mokhotlong later today. He'll be back, won't he?"

"Captain Woods will fly back and do it." Francina didn't say any more as she passed Philippa bearing her tray full of eggs and bacon and tea and toast up the corridor to her father's room. Clearly, Francina had no idea that this piece of information signalled the end of the world to Philippa.

What was she thinking? Philippa drew herself up short as she went out onto the veranda to stare at the empty airstrip once again, the mountains beyond seeming to mock her with their eternal indifference.

Anger and indignation were surging up from the ground, through her legs, filling her chest to bursting.

What kind of man wouldn't stay and persuade her of the advantages of being with him if he cared enough for her?

After everything he said to her yesterday? After all his sweet words trying to persuade her?

Had he woken up realising the dangers of going too far?

Was he terrified that now she really *would* break off her engagement with Matthew and throw in her lot with him after ? And then Stuart would be pressured into marriage when suddenly the idea terrified him?

She clutched an upright beam to keep steady. To keep the axis of her world where it ought to be while tears stung her eyes.

How could Stuart do this to her this morning after doing all those things to her heart last night?

He'd pretended to be her champion. And then he'd failed spectacularly by simply... leaving.

"Darling, what are you doing up so early?"

Philippa swung round, forcing a smile. At least, she was trying to smile and not grimace as Matthew approached, looking perfectly groomed even at this early hour.

He took her in his arms. "All forgiven, baby-cakes?" he asked.

The unfamiliar term grated horribly, but now was not the time to tell him.

Now wasn't the time to tell him a lot of things. Like how she wished he wouldn't squeeze her so hard. Or how she disliked it when he spoke to her like she were a child if she didn't agree with him.

But she'd agreed to marry him last night because that's what she'd told everyone she wanted.

Submitting to his embrace, she stared once more at the empty sky. No sign of a plane. No sound of one returning.

It looked like Stuart had definitely withdrawn from the race.

So she sagged against Matthew, trying to like the feel of his lips on her forehead. His arms felt solid around her and, she liked to think, dependable. That was a good thing. His mother—clearly Philippa's greatest champion—was obviously a strong influence on her only son, so that was something, too.

But what was wrong with her? If this was what she'd pinned her entire future upon for as long as she could remember, why did she feel like she was talking herself into the consolation prize?

Perhaps Matthew felt her reserve, for he drew back a little and tipped up her head so he could look at her.

"Happy?"

Yes, she was happy. Very happy, she told herself grimly. She had what she wanted. She had Matthew and the life he promised. She had a secure future brimming with promise. She had a mother-in-law whom she respected and wished to emulate and who liked her.

A future mother-in-law who was as glamorous as her own mother had been, and who'd been filled with admiration when Philippa had told her about her aristocratic grandmother in England.

A future mother-in-law who'd sent Matthew back to Philippa on bended knee.

She sucked in a lungful of cold air. "I couldn't be happier, darling." There. Her decision had been made. She'd marry Mrs Myburgh's son. She'd make Matthew happy, and she'd have his babies, and those children would have the brightest of futures. She'd have the life she'd always planned...

Though why did everything feel suddenly hollow at the edges?

He set her away from him and looked into her face, and she blinked a little. He'd think she had something in her eye or that at least the moisture gathering there were tears of happiness. He certainly wouldn't imagine they'd stem from anything else. Matthew didn't think that deeply, and he'd be pretty certain he'd bestowed upon her the greatest of gifts. "How could I not be the happiest woman in the world?"

How could she not?

"Then kiss me properly."

Obediently, she pressed herself against him and opened her lips to his. His kiss was practiced, confident, but it lacked the desperate hunger that had characterised every encounter with Stuart.

Then, twining her arms more tightly behind Matthew's neck, she deepened the kiss, and imagined she was kissing Stuart. Imagined it was Stuart's hands on her waist, Stuart's mouth moving against hers with that barely controlled passion that made her feel truly alive.

"You do this beautifully," she murmured, not thinking properly.

Not thinking of anything except...

Of the man she did not have right at this moment. The man who would soon be miles away, carrying with him any chance she might have had at real happiness.

If she allowed her heart to rule her head.

FIFTEEN

Two weeks later, Philippa was back in Cape Town having heard not a peep from Stuart.

So that was how it was? He'd withdrawn from the race. He wasn't prepared to fight for her. He'd abandoned her because he'd got cold feet at the fear she might hold him to what he'd pledged to her on their mountain drive. His love. His desire to be to her what Matthew was.

Well! Now she was vindicated, she thought, as she leaned back in her dining chair and surveyed the table, laden with candelabra and Villeroy & Boch bone china. The crystal stemware caught the light from the chandelier above, casting tiny rainbows across the starched white tablecloth.

But why did she feel like crying?

Twelve people were seated for a lavish dinner. Most had finished the crème brûlée, and a comfortable bonhomie pervaded the room, in part due to the fine Nederburg which had washed down the fillet mignon.

Philippa had participated as best she could in the

conversation, but mostly Matthew had talked for her. He liked finishing her sentences.

But the topics were sophisticated and interesting, and she felt grown up and important, seated amongst the dinner-suited gentlemen and designer-clad women. It was the kind of conversation she'd dreamed of having when she was a lonely teenager in the mountains, listening to her father discuss administrative matters with visiting officials.

The occasion was Mrs Myburgh's birthday, and Philippa wore a tight-waisted long pink satin gown, her hair in a chignon, like her future mother-in-law's, she now realised. Gosh, perhaps she was emulating her unconsciously.

Yes, a girl could get used to this, she thought grimly, trying to whip up her anger towards Stuart for letting her down so badly.

"Oh, Philippa, did you get your father's letter?" Mrs Myburg asked her suddenly from across the table. "Marielle was supposed to give it to you."

Her father? Her father rarely wrote, for they exchanged most of their news during their weekly phone calls.

"It had a Basutoland stamp on it at any rate," Mrs Myburgh said absently before turning her attention to the gentleman on her left.

Suddenly Philippa's heart was beating like a drum. *Stuart?* Could Stuart have written to her? She wanted to leap up and run to the sitting room, where all correspondence was kept in Mrs Myburgh's roll top desk.

"There's no better place in the world to live than Cape Town, eh?"

Philippa had half risen to go and find this letter when the elderly barrister on her left detained her with his question.

"Er, it's a wonderful place," she said, sitting down though more desperate than ever to discover who had written.

"I have a place on the Wild Coast I like to get away to when the hustle and bustle gets too much. One needs that," her companion went on, taking a contemplative sip of his wine, before adding that it offered him something for which his heart yearned: a certain roughness, lack of sophistication and... dare he say it, danger and adventure.

Philippa thought longingly of Stuart, and her expression must have betrayed her, for Mrs Myburgh's voice cut briskly through the conversation. "You really are the most marvellous clothes horse, Philippa." Her future mother-in-law had just risen, a signal for the rest of the ladies to join her and retire to the sitting room while the men began on their cigars and brandy. "And you will make the most striking bride. Won't she, Connie?" she added to her companion as the two women waited at the door for Philippa, who felt an odd mix of pride, distaste, and queru-lousness.

At the moment, Philippa was staying at the Myburgh's after Mrs Myburgh had insisted Philippa stay in a guest room at their home. It was the summer holidays after all, and Mrs Myburgh was an enthusiastic hostess. She seemed to want Philippa by her side as she organised tennis parties, drinks parties, card parties.

As if she were putting Philippa through an apprentice-ship in becoming the perfect society wife, while Matthew would have his own apprenticeship in learning the ways of the world when he departed for England for the trip that was suddenly looking uncertain due to his grandfather's health.

Certainly, he would *not* be going for a year; his mother had made that quite clear.

And tonight, there had been this lavish dinner with some of Cape Town's most well-known socialites and industry figures.

It was everything Philippa had ever dreamed of.

Well, she'd thought it was. All her aspirations were being met.

In between the bouts of boredom.

"Come, Philippa!" Mrs Myburgh's tone was commanding before a cloying tone crept in as she added, "You can talk to Matthew later."

Really, she hadn't wanted to talk to Matthew at all, but she sent him a suitably lovelorn smile before obediently following the ladies out of the dining room. Sometimes she felt as if she were on a fast train from which she couldn't disembark.

"Miss Tremain, there's a telephone call for you from a Mr Price." Marielle, the Myburgh's maid, put her head out of the study as they passed.

Philippa hoped her companions didn't notice her reaction as she tried to look mildly surprised, hiding how desperately she wanted to take the call.

"Rather a late hour to disturb anyone," said Mrs Myburgh, clearly disapproving. "Who is this Mr Price and what does he have to say that can't wait until tomorrow?"

"Just...a family friend," Philippa managed, her heart thundering as she added, faintly, to Marielle, "Tell him I'll call him back some other time."

"And quite rude at this time of night unless it's an emergency, which it clearly is not or he'd have said," Mrs Myburgh went on, linking arms with Philippa's as they entered the sitting room, oblivious to Philippa's distress. "Now, remember that you have a dress-fitting appointment for your going-away ensemble the day after tomorrow. Does that suit? I'm waiting for confirmation regarding your wedding gown appointment in Johannesburg in a few weeks. Matthew thought it would be nice if we all had lunch together after your Thursday fitting."

Philippa tried for as considering a look as would be required by Mrs Myburgh's questioning tone. In reality, her brain was whirling with the ramifications of Stuart's call.

He'd called her here? He'd tracked her down to ask her... what?

"Philippa?"

She snapped back to the present at Mrs Myburgh's tone while Connie laughed, saying with slight condescension, "Wedding Fever. Your mention of her wedding dress fitting has Philippa dreaming about it too much to actually answer you."

And although the atmosphere seemed light-hearted, Philippa's heart was far from light-hearted as she tried to hide her feelings beneath a veneer of superficiality as she took a seat on the sofa, agreeing with most of what Connie, and her future mother-in-law, and the other women, were saying.

But it was torture to have to sit, quiet and demure, nodding at conversations about the staff, and social engagements, when all she could think about was what it would have been like to have heard Stuart's voice on the telephone.

If she'd had the courage.

And of the letter in the study.

Matthew's arrival was a relief. He'd come to walk her to her room, he said.

And maybe they'd step out onto the verandah and talk

about something that would reaffirm that he really was the one for her.

"Goodnight, Mrs Myburgh, and thank you for a lovely dinner," Philippa said, casting a longing look about the beautiful room. She did so want to live in a house like this one and have such an elegant woman as Mrs Myburgh to call mother-in-law because even though Mrs Myburgh was direct and superior, she clearly did like and admire Philippa and that was such a good feeling.

The kind of maternal approval she'd been craving since her mother died.

Now, with Matthew's arm about her as they wandered up the passage, she felt slightly better.

Well, good enough to think everything would be all right, she told herself, as he steered her past her room towards his.

"I don't think I'm supposed to go this far," she told him playfully, as he opened the door to his bedroom and, with his hand on her bottom, gave her a gentle push.

"I don't know where else I'm going to get away with kissing my future wife in this house," said Matthew, immediately pushing her against the wall and putting his mouth to hers.

Philippa closed her eyes and tried to let herself drown in the sensations.

This was her future husband. What could Stuart's letter —presuming it was from him—or his phone call say to prove otherwise?

And as Matthew kissed her, she felt her arousal growing. It was nothing like the adrenaline rush she felt with Stuart—nothing like that desperate, all-consuming hunger —but maybe that was a good thing. Marriage was for the long haul. Better to burn long and slow than combust and die in a passionate conflagration.

Matthew aroused her just enough for her to consider that she'd made the right choice. Matthew was the husband for her.

They'd sunk to the floor now, and Matthew was on top, straddling her as her head was pushed against the wall, her neck at an awkward angle. She could feel his erection straining against his trousers, pressing into her stomach, and she feared he might rip her dress. That would take some explaining to the maid. Except she wouldn't do that, of course.

"Just feel you, Philly. God, you're sweet," he murmured into her ear as his hands roamed over her breasts and up her thighs.

Philippa's insides seemed in revolt as his ardour grew, but she told herself this was normal pre-wedding nervousness. Should she let him? Shouldn't she?

He made the decision, tearing himself from her and standing unsteadily as he adjusted himself with a sheepish grin, pushing back his hair. "Mother would kill me if I deflowered you before the big day." He reached for her hand and hauled her to her feet. "Did you like that?"

Philippa nodded. Of course, she had to, but she also wasn't sure how much she'd liked it. With Stuart, she'd never had to question whether she liked it. Her body had responded without hesitation.

"Good. I did. You really are beautiful," he said, putting his hands on her shoulders. "I'm a lucky man. I hope you know that I know it. And if I could take you to England with me, I would."

"Would you?"

"Yes, but I can't," he said quickly, stepping back and

thrusting his hands into his pockets. "Not with grandfather funding my trip, and it's really just one final chance to sow my wild oats before I settle down."

"And what does that mean, exactly?" Philippa asked. "It doesn't sound like the sort of thing a man about to be married should be doing."

"Ah, Philippa, you're a funny girl. I can promise you that what happens in England stays in England." He laughed as he went to sit on the arm of a chair. "And nothing that you need to worry your pretty little head about will happen. Anyway, I think it'll just make me more than ready to come back to pick up my responsibilities—*if* I go," he said with a gloomy sigh before adding, "I know I've had it easy." He indicated his surroundings, adding, "I don't want to be regarded as the rich kid who had it all handed to him on a platter. You're the perfect wife for me because you look like you're one of us. Rich and spoiled, I mean. Except you're not. You remind me that I'm one hell of a lucky *oke*." He grinned at the slang for a bloke, and Philippa tried to, also.

The words should have been complimentary, but something about being called the "perfect wife" because she looked the part while not actually being spoiled did not sit well with her.

"I should go." She raised her face for his kiss, anxious to be gone.

Anxious to read her letter from Basutoland.

CHAPTER

SIXTEEN

FEELING SICK WITH DISAPPOINTMENT, STUART CRUMPLED THE paper on which he'd written the phone number of the Myburgh residence where Susan had told him he'd find Philippa.

He carefully replaced the receiver on the handset then leaned against the wall of the tickey box.

What now?

He'd opted for a station-to-station call rather than person-to-person—at least he could ask for Philippa directly rather than through an operator. Not that it mattered. The maid had simply relayed Miss Tremain's message that she was occupied.

Stuart straightened, about to step onto the pavement when a thought occurred to him.

He was in Pietermaritzburg.

So was Lizzie.

Yesterday, when he'd medevacked a missionary family's

ill child to Grey's hospital, he'd actively resisted contacting Lizzie. He'd wanted to talk to Philippa first.

But the sickening disappointment of Philippa's refusal to take his call or answer the letter he'd written two weeks ago had created a void he needed to fill.

He looked up the number. "Nurse Cameron is off duty, sir," the hospital operator said. "I can try the nurses' home."

Lizzie was there, and unlike Philippa, couldn't have been more excited to come to the phone. After a brief chat, they arranged to meet the following morning.

And now, here he was, saying to the pretty young woman opposite him in a small teashop in town, "It's good to see you again, Lizzie. You look lovely."

And she did. Rosy cheeks, shining hair the same shade as Gracie's. The same blue eyes too, though Lizzie's serene gaze lacked the wicked sparkle that had got his sister into trouble.

Lizzie wasn't the kind of girl who courted danger like Gracie. Or Philippa.

"Oh, Stuart, what a lovely thing to say." Lizzie beamed. "I can't tell you what a thrill it was when the ward sister said you were on the phone. I can't think of anyone I'd want to catch up with more," she added boldly, unable to meet his eyes. "You're such a...gentleman. I don't think there's anyone who makes me feel...as happy."

It was nice to hear something nice for a change. Something that made him feel like... a man. And valued. "Quite so... *what?*" he prompted, wanting to hear it again.

She blushed. "I shouldn't have been so... familiar," she mumbled.

There was something to be said for being with someone who clearly desired his company and who looked at him as if he could do no wrong. Lizzie made him feel protective and needed—emotions that had nothing to do with lust and longing and everything to do with marriages that actually worked.

He looked at her hands resting on the tabletop and wondered if he should rest one of his over hers.

No, too soon, he thought while he wondered if perhaps Philippa was right to choose practical considerations over passion.

"When are you likely to return to Maritzburg?" Lizzie asked hopefully.

He prevaricated, afraid suddenly of being tied down to anything. "It all depends on my roster, and quite often there are unexpected emergencies or charters. I usually don't know until the last minute. Sorry."

She nodded. "Actually, an old nursing friend has invited me to her baby's christening this Sunday in Maseru. I have three days off, but I'm still deciding whether to go." She looked at him as if her decision rested on his response.

Stuart felt cornered. "If she's an old friend, why don't you?"

"Well, it's all day by train with four connections to get there, but a friend might be driving—" She hesitated. "I just need to make a plan to get home."

Suddenly Stuart decided he really did want to see her. "Why don't you just come? I'm afraid I'm away on Saturday, but I'll be in town on the Sunday evening, so we could make it a date." He hesitated. "That's if you think it's worth an all-day trip back to Maritzburg the following day."

"Of course it would be!" She was animated now. "If you'd like to go out on Sunday evening, then I'd be glad to get a lift from my friend on the Saturday and take the train back on the Monday."

Her excitement at spending time with him really was beginning to ease the ache in his chest.

He thought it again as he flew home the next morning.

In fact, as he soared above the clouds on his return to Maseru, he thought a lot about loneliness, and companionship, and the benefits of marriage. Lizzie was born to be a wife and mother. She was a natural. Kind, nurturing, patient. The type who'd welcome children and create the warm home he'd never had. Maybe that was worth more than the dangerous attraction he felt for Philippa—the kind that had destroyed his parents' marriage when his mother fell pregnant and found herself trapped with a man she'd never really loved.

But the moment he opened the door to Mrs Henderson's Lodging House, all thoughts of happy families deserted him as he saw on the hall dresser a letter addressed to him in the familiar spidery handwriting that made his skin crawl.

He was shaking so much he had to sit on his bed before he was able to slit the thick envelope and extract the short letter together with a small velvet box.

In all his years away—when he was an evacuee living in Pretoria, and even in the four years since leaving England to return to fly in this beautiful, desolate wilderness—his father had not written once.

So he wasn't surprised that the tone was begging and querulous. That his father had only written because he wanted something.

His father was dying. Coughing and spewing his guts out—was the way he'd put it—which was not surprising since he'd been a two-pack a day Woodbine man for most of his life.

Then the date caught Stuart's eye. He did a double-take

when he realised how long the letter had taken to reach him as his eye skimmed the words *Airline Ticket*.

"Bloody hell!" he cried as he extracted two first-class tickets: one to get him to London and one to bring him home a week later.

The old bastard always was determined to have the last laugh.

Just as he was determined to see his son for the last time, though Stuart was quite certain there'd be no fond farewells.

As with all their communications, the last one had been bitter before Stuart left England.

The Franklins, his father had maintained, had been cruel rather than kind, giving a slum kid a taste of privilege that would give him ideas above his station.

Stuart had pondered the truth of this these last few months as he'd tortured himself over thoughts of Philippa. But his foster parents hadn't just given him a taste of privilege, they'd modelled the fact that two people could exist in a state of marital harmony for, literally, a lifetime.

Pushing away the pang that always intruded when he thought of the happy home Edith and Ernest Franklin had given him for those precious few years, he reflected on their respective natures: kind, considerate, and practical.

Like Lizzie.

Slowly, he placed the airline tickets on his bedside table, though his heart was racing.

Philippa... Lizzie...

With a sigh, he leaned forward to put his head in his hands.

Maybe it really was better to aim for a steady drip feed of contentment than try for the dizzying heights of possibly unsustainable passion?

Maybe he really would be happier over the long term… with Lizzie.

Nevertheless, he wasn't ready to give up without one final fight.

Three days ago, Philippa had declined to take his call but admittedly, the hour had been unfashionably late—though only because it had taken the operator three hours trying to get a phone line through.

If he could get hold of her earlier in the day, his chances of speaking to her personally might be greater. That—he'd decided—would be his line in the sand. He needed to speak to her.

Letters went astray, phone calls could be logistically difficult to answer if one was staying at someone else's house.

But if Stuart could speak to Philippa personally, and hear from her own lips her true feelings, then he knew in which direction he could move on with his life.

So, with his father's letter tucked into his pocket, Stuart walked to Stephen's Hotel, where it took less than an hour before the telephonist was able to connect him to Cape Town.

While waiting, he passed the time reading the Himeville Times which, today, was doing a retrospective on the Colonial Administration's failure to apprehend the 'criminal mastermind de Vries' who'd stolen several valuable diamonds from under the noses of the investigators who'd thought they were onto the heist.

He stared at a photo of the two missing diamonds and thought about the size of the diamond Matthew had slipped onto Philippa's finger. A stone like that would buy a house, a car, a future. It would buy the kind of security that meant never again having to count every penny, never again wondering if he could afford to take a girl to dinner or buy a decent shirt. The kind of security that Philippa took for granted and that he would never have on a bush pilot's salary.

The irony wasn't lost on him. While investigators fumbled around trying to catch diamond thieves, men like Matthew's father grew rich from the legal diamond trade, offering their sons lives of endless privilege while men like Stuart scrambled for the crumbs.

But all that was irrelevant because until Stuart ascertained from Philippa whether she'd received his letter, and what her true feelings were as of this moment, he had no real interest in anything.

He just had to make sure there was...

Literally no hope for him.

He chewed the end of his pen as he tried to concentrate on the crossword instead of casting his mind back to the intimacy they'd shared the night of her twenty-first.

She'd been honest. But she'd also been conflicted.

And she'd been conflicted when she'd accepted Matthew's public proposal. And when Stuart had overheard her speaking about it to her father in the immediate aftermath—

Stuart hadn't waited around to try to persuade her— and he wished he had.

He'd slunk away like a coward, but he'd written two days later. He'd bared his soul.

She hadn't responded.

The operator finally connected them. "Stuart?"

She sounded too calm and collected, and his heart plummeted.

"Philippa." He swallowed. "How are you?"

"Well. And you?"

How clinical and sanitised. Her greeting rolled off her tongue as if she were already the society hostess she aspired to be.

And that's what he had to remind her. That he, too, had prospects. That she could still play that role in a different context once he became what he aspired to be.

She just needed to be patient.

"Philippa—"

"I got your letter. Thank you for that. It was good of you to write."

"Can't you talk? Could we maybe meet up?" He was feeling more desperate than ever. He imagined her in an elegant day dress with her hair done up and her sweeping eyelashes framing her violet eyes, revelling in her luxurious surroundings. Probably sitting in some beautifully appointed room where the furniture cost more than he made in a year.

But those trappings of wealth couldn't make up for what he could give her: a reason to live. Love. Passion. Something real.

Or could they?

"Philippa. You haven't walked down the aisle yet. I'll get myself to Cape Town somehow, and we can thrash this out together if you just say the word. I didn't know how else to contact you, but if you don't have any privacy to say what you really feel—"

"Yes, I can speak. I appreciated your letter and its senti-ments." She swallowed, and he heard the first wavering in her voice but then thought he must have mistaken it when she resumed quite smoothly, "But with my wedding to Matthew in eight weeks, I have a lot to organise."

"Philippa, please. I'll fly all the way down to Cape Town if you'll only grant me an hour just to...talk about this. Do you remember what you said when we were driving through the mountains? Just before we came back and Matthew proposed? You said—"

"I remember it well. But I think it would be pointless you coming all this way just for a chat when we can say all we need to say right now."

It was an elbow in the gut. She was shutting him down like she had before.

But he had to try one more time.

Just in case she might suddenly give in to her real feelings like she had done so unexpectedly in Maseru, and then again in Mokhotlong, only three weeks ago.

"Philippa, I love you." Despite his inner turmoil, he lowered his voice, pausing as a hotel guest passed within earshot. "If it's security and pretty dresses, I can give you what you want. I just need...a bit more time. I know I can't offer you what Matthew does, but I do have prospects. Please, Philippa. Can we just talk? God, I want you, Philippa. Only you! In two years we could be living the high life if that's what you want. Don't throw me over because of Matthew's money—" He'd never let himself go so completely, but if it was the only way—?

"My decision has nothing to do with...that!" she bit back. "Now, please! I have to go." There was a pause before she added in a more measured tone, "It was so lovely of you to call. Please send my love to everyone back home."

And there was the rub, he thought, as the line went dead.

There was no 'back home'. And there was no 'everyone'. Not even one person.

Well, there was Lizzie, he supposed. Sweet, uncomplicated Lizzie, who thought he was a gentleman, who made him feel valuable and needed. Who would probably be thrilled to marry a pilot and start a family, who wouldn't care that he didn't have money or connections. Who would love their children unconditionally, the way his mother never had.

He dug his hands into his pockets and fingered the surprising little accompaniment to the airline tickets that his father had sent him—something that might change everything, or might damn him completely.

Maybe it was time to stop reaching for stars that were beyond his grasp.

Weighed down by a sense of the destiny his father had thrust upon his shoulders, he walked out of the hotel where, in a few days, he would have dinner with Lizzie after she attended the christening of her friend's baby.

The evening air was sharp and cold against his cheeks, and only when he felt the sting did he realise it was the night wind drying his tears. He wiped them away with savage swipes of his hand—as mortified by this display of weakness as he had been when his father's belt had taught him that tears were shameful.

He didn't think he'd let emotion get the better of him since then.

No, that was a damned lie. What about Gracie?

Drawing in another deep lungful of air, he forced himself to keep walking, forced himself to push away any feeling except grim stoicism.

His future was in Lizzie's hands now. Not because he loved her the way he loved Philippa, but because love wasn't everything. Security, companionship, children, a peaceful home—maybe those things mattered more than the kind of desperate passion that had destroyed his parents and now threatened to destroy him.

Maybe Lizzie was exactly what he needed to finally put the past behind him and build the kind of life that was actually within his reach.

MEANWHILE, Philippa carefully replaced the handset with trembling hands and tried to steady her breathing.

"Who was that, my dear?' asked Mrs Myburgh from the nearby sofa where she was reading a magazine.

"Just an old friend," Philippa managed faintly.

"Is everything all right?" Mrs Myburgh raised her head and fixed Philippa with an enquiring look.

"Oh, yes," said Philippa. She knew she couldn't risk rising and walking across the room to resume her previous seat. She needed distance to compose herself. The things Stuart had said— her brain could barely comprehend them —though he'd laid out some of it in his letter.

"If your friend wants to visit you, there's no reason to say no on our account, Philippa."

How much had Mrs Myburgh overheard? she wondered.

"Of course, Mrs Myburgh. I can see...my friend any time," Philippa said, trying so hard to smile but afraid that the result was a parody, for a faint line of worry appeared between Mrs Myburgh's elegantly shaped eyebrows.

"Come and sit by me, Philippa." Mrs Myburgh patted the sofa, her demeanour almost maternal.

Obediently, Philippa crossed the room and sat down.

"It's really nothing, Mrs Myburgh," she began, while her mind screamed that it really *was*. How could Stuart's letter have taken two weeks to arrive? The post was usually so reliable. But it was what Stuart had written that had caused her such anguish. All those feelings that she thought he'd dismissed the moment she was out of his orbit.

Yes, she wanted him to come down so they *could* 'thrash' this out together. She *needed* to see him. But she could hardly have told him that with Matthew's mother just a few feet away.

"Philippa." Mrs Myburgh had taken her hand between both of hers, her smile sympathetic.

No, warm. In fact, Philippa couldn't remember when there'd been *such* warmth in the older woman's smile. It did strange things to her heart. It made her remember her own mother with the most terrible longing.

"Are you happy here?"

Philippa gasped. "Of course!"

"Do you feel you have the freedom to do what you want to do? I realise I have been somewhat exacting with the number of social engagements I've imposed upon you. It's just that I thought you enjoyed them."

"Oh, I do, Mrs Myburgh!"

"And Matthew hasn't done anything to upset you?"

Philippa shook her head. He really hadn't.

"My son loves you very much, you know." Mrs Myburgh squeezed her hand. "And so do we. I know his father isn't around very much, but Richard couldn't be more delighted with his future daughter-in-law. He was saying so only last week. And he's very keen on getting to know your father better and...advancing their mutual interests."

Philippa nodded again. "I'm sure Daddy would like that very much," she said lamely.

"Good." Mrs Myburgh dropped Philippa's hand. She stood up and went to the door. "I just wanted to make sure there was nothing else we could do to make you happy." She put her hand on the doorknob and then added over her shoulder, "You know, you really are like the daughter I never had."

CHAPTER

SEVENTEEN

MASERU

"Stuart!" Lizzie looked up, his name almost a squeal of excitement as he arrived in the dining room the promised Sunday four days later.

"I should have picked you up at your place. Not very gentlemanly. Sorry."

"That's all right. Like I said, I think you're the perfect gentleman." Her dimples popped out as she looked up into his face. "And I have a surprise to tell you."

Stuart raised his eyebrows enquiringly as he sat down opposite her.

"At the christening this morning, I spoke to the Mokhotlong District Commissioner, Mr Tremain, who told me he was looking for a nurse at his vaccination clinic in Mapolaneng and did I know anyone who was a competent horsewoman."

"That's a rather odd job requirement for a nurse."

"Apparently it's an hour by Basuto pony over a rough bridle trail from Roma Cathedral and mission school." Her eyes gleamed with excitement. "I love horses, and I love babies. And I definitely don't love Sister Patterson, who makes my job a nightmare on the ward at Grey's Hospital."

"Surely you haven't got the job already?" Stuart asked as their drinks order was taken.

"I might have. I hope so." She sighed. "Stuart, I've tried to adapt to Maritzburg, but the truth is, I just love Lesotho. I was so excited when Mr Tremain and I discussed the position."

"But won't you be afraid in such a remote location?" He toyed with the small item in his trouser pocket and felt both excited and sick with terror at the same time. Lizzie's job offer might not come to anything, but there was an inevitability to what he was about to say, as soon as she'd stopped talking.

Yes, he was terrified, but there was fatalism too. He'd not regret the answer—though he was fairly confident of a positive—but he *would* regret losing another opportunity to move forward with his life.

"Afraid? No, I just want to come back here to live, and I want to work with babies. What's there to be afraid of?" She smiled, putting her head on one side as she explained further, and he had to admire her courage and commitment.

That's what he needed right now, he told himself, his hand sweating as it enclosed the object he was about to whip out and put on the table. Courage and commitment.

He didn't need to question himself, though. This would be catharsis to the throbbing pain and emptiness that hit him at alternate times—and had done for the last four months since he'd fallen so hard and fast for Philippa Tremain.

Really, the question he was about to ask Lizzie was a

common-sense response to the fact that he wanted someone to share his life with. He'd hoped it would be Philippa. But she was like a firefly, always darting about as she teased him with evidence that she more than liked him…only to then reassert her core values: Matthew's money—and whatever else Matthew offered—would always trump whatever she felt about Stuart. Or whatever Stuart offered her: his heart, his determination to give her what she did want—if she could only be patient for a short while.

"Lizzie," he finally said, when he was able to change the subject. "I've been meaning to ask you—"

"Yes, Stuart?" She cupped her cheek in her hand and smiled. She looked so sweet and innocent when she did that. And he should want sweet and innocent. Most men would feel pretty good having a woman look at them the way Lizzie was looking at him. As if he really were her hero.

"What is it?" she prompted, and in a rush of adrenaline-fuelled bravado, Stuart pulled out the engagement ring his mother had once worn and which his father had sent to him, and reached for her hand.

"Will you marry me?"

Her eyes widened, and her gasp and joyous smile said more than words, before she breathed, "Oh y—"

And then her eyes widened even more, if that were possible, and he suddenly thought she was about to cry.

"Lizzie? What is it?" he asked as the most awful disappointment sliced through him. "You…you don't want to?"

She gripped his hand in both of hers and leaned forward, her voice barely above a whisper. As if she were in pain. "I do want to, but…but Stuart, I…I just—"

He thought she was going to cry and wondered if she had some terrible secret she was about to divulge. Like she was already married. And then she forced out the words, "Stuart, please tell me if the reason you wanted me to accept that nursing position in Pietermaritzburg a few months ago was because there was someone else?"

He didn't know what to say. It was as if the air had been knocked out of his lungs.

Clearly, his expression said what he could not voice, for Lizzie nodded slowly. She took a deep breath, exhaled slowly, then said softly, as she looked down at their hands, now limp on the tabletop, "I thought that was the reason. I cried over it a lot and then I accepted that I couldn't make you love me if you loved someone else—"

Stuart was not going to lose another woman if he could help it. Her reluctance had fired him up even more to deny to the ends of the earth that there was anyone else more important to him than the woman sitting opposite him. "Lizzie, it was a flash in the pan. Something so brief and... unimportant compared with...with you." It didn't matter how true or not the words were, he wanted Lizzie in that moment like he'd never wanted anyone more. He just had to make her believe him. Gathering up her hands, he squeezed them as if the gesture could emphasise what he was about to say. "I love *you*, Lizzie. Only you, and thank God I realised that in time."

For a long moment she looked at him, as if searching his face might reveal a hidden truth. Then her shoulders sagged and, putting her forehead against his, she whispered, "Then, yes, Stuart, I will marry you," before leaning back a little to let Stuart slip the ring onto her left hand.

"It's a sign of the future, Stuart, for it fits perfectly," she whispered. "Oh, but you've just made me the happiest girl in the whole wide world because I'm going to marry the most incredible, manliest, bravest pilot in the whole world!"

"Who's the manliest, bravest pilot in the whole world?" Without asking if he could join them, Stuart's laconic friend, Lawrence, a sheep farmer from the lowlands, who'd appeared seemingly from nowhere, grabbed a free chair from the adjoining table and sat himself down. "I don't think we've met," he said, nodding at Lizzie. "Don't know why, because a fellow usually knows every pretty female for a hundred miles around. I'm competing with too many bachelors in these parts. I'm Lawrence. What's your name?"

"Lizzie," she replied, blushing. "And Stuart's just asked me to marry him."

Lawrence's jaw dropped. "Dark horse," he said, looking at Stuart. "I didn't know you liked blondes. I certainly do."

"Well, Lizzie is taken," said Stuart, "and if you don't mind, we're about to plan the rest of our lives."

But Lawrence didn't reply, for his attention had been diverted. His brow darkened as he stabbed a finger in the direction of a thin, dark-haired newcomer who stood framed in the doorway, surveying the dining room.

"Not a local, to be sure. See over there?" he said, pointing to the new arrival. "IDB. Sniffing out diamonds for a bargain. Place is crawling with them since that de Vries character made the Colonial Administration look like amateurs. Word's getting around that Basutoland's an easy target."

"More likely a grazier from across the border who's come to Maseru to pick up some sheep for a good price." Stuart exhaled in exasperation, though he found himself studying the stranger more carefully. "Trust you to come up with a conspiracy theory for anyone you haven't seen drinking here before. Now go away. I've only just asked this beautiful woman to be my wife, and you are adding nothing to the romance of the moment."

But Lawrence, who had the social graces of a warthog, ignored him as he continued to stare at the doorway. "Fellow's on his own and you have to be shady if you can't find a friend in this place. I tell you, the guy's got illegal diamond buyer branded on his forehead. And with all this political unrest brewing—did you hear about that Moscow-trained agitator stirring up trouble at the mission schools? What's his name? That's right! Moses Shakane!— the government's got their hands full. Perfect time for the diamond thieves to move in."

Maseru was a repository of odd characters. Political activists—those opposed to the Apartheid regime who, in the eyes of the South African government, therefore plotted against it—often crossed the border into Basutoland.

Illegal diamond buyers were just another category of undesirables. And, although the diamond trade was heavily regulated, unlicensed diamond buyers often took a sniff around, believing the gullible Mosotho miner easy pickings when it came to getting a diamond on the cheap or funnelling through Letseng-la-Terai an unregistered diamond from elsewhere.

Not that any of this really concerned Stuart just now. He wanted Lawrence gone so he could start planning for the rest of his life with Lizzie.

Her acceptance of his marriage proposal hadn't made him feel nearly as panicked as he'd thought it would.

Lawrence began to rise.

And then he sat down again when they were addressed by the very fellow against whom Stuart believed false accusations had been levelled.

A fellow whom Stuart now realised was not a political

activist, potential terrorist, or illegal diamond buyer, but a lanky Boer farmer—or motor mechanic—with whom he was acquainted.

"What a surprise to see you here, Captain Price. You don't remember me, do you? Piet van Wyk." The fellow grinned at Lawrence and Lizzie. "Life is full of *blerry* coincidences." He stabbed his thumb in Stuart's direction and said, "I met this *oke* when he ditched just up the road from my place. Mind if I sit down?"

Dry-mouthed, Stuart nodded, for he could hardly refuse. He managed a smile for Lizzie's benefit as a kernel of not quite realised fear began to form in the pit of his stomach. "Piet helped me pull the plane from the mealie field," he explained, just as Lizzie gasped, "Of course! That was the night I thought Stuart had died because he failed to show up for dinner with me!" She sent Piet a disarming smile. "So, you're the fellow who helped rescue Stuart and Philippa?"

Piet frowned, as if he couldn't quite assimilate what she was saying. "Philippa? Ah yes, that was her name if you mean the girl in the passenger seat. Lovely dark-haired young lady, as I recall." He flashed Stuart a knowing look as Lizzie went on in a tone that was both excited and grateful, "Yes, Philippa's the District Commissioner's daughter. She's marrying into the Myburgh family in Cape Town. You've probably heard of the Myburghs. Everyone has. And I—" She drew herself up and thrust out her left hand, upon which flashed a small diamond, as she beamed with pride — "I am marrying Stuart."

Stuart felt as though he were drowning as Lizzie's voice washed over him, chattering away to Lawrence and Piet like they were dear friends, while the full weight of this unexpected meeting settled over him and he tried to formulate some coherent damage control response.

Lizzie's bright hair and sudden animation blurred into an incarnation of Grace, so desperate to be rid of the taint of their ma and pa and the rot of Seven Dials, and knowing how attractive she was to the fellows, used to bare her soul like this when she had an audience.

He tried to interject, but Lizzie continued to chatter, unfiltered, while the potential ramifications of this meeting with Piet started crystallising with horrifying clarity.

"Oh yes, there's room going to Mokhotlong," Stuart heard Lizzie telling Piet, and Stuart jerked forward, saying, "No, there's not!"

Lizzie looked surprised. "I thought you said you were flying an almost empty plane when you head for Mokhotlong tomorrow."

"It's too late for Piet to buy a ticket."

They all looked strangely at him. But what else could he say?

Taking a breath, Stuart said as calmly as he could, "Diana at Drakensberg Air can organise a ticket for...for Tuesday." He'd not be the pilot rostered that day.

"But, Stuart, Piet wants to go tomorrow," said Lizzie. "He has to be back at his farm by Tuesday."

Piet nodded. He looked supremely comfortable as he leaned back in the plush green chair, his hands folded across his lean stomach while Lizzie unknowingly did his work for him.

Then he slowly got up and stretched. "Ack, man, it's OK. I think it's time we left the lovebirds to it." He winked at Lawrence, nodded at Lizzie and Stuart, then stalked out of the room.

Lawrence whistled. "Well, what do you make of that, eh?" he asked.

Lizzie leaned across the table and put her hand over Stuart's. "I think he must be wonderful to have helped Stuart, who might have been stranded all night in the freezing cold."

"And I think you should leave us to finish our dinner so Lizzie and I can plan our wedding," said Stuart, looking at Lawrence, and then meaningfully at the door.

Lawrence rose with a shrug. "Congratulations," he said. "I know I shouldn't say it, but just make sure you're not making the biggest mistake of your life." He winked broadly, then walked away, chuckling.

CHAPTER

EIGHTEEN

MISTAKE OR NOT, THERE WAS NO TURNING BACK. STUART WAS going to make the best of things, and he was going to be happy.

He was going to make Lizzie happy.

But he was not going to make Piet van Wyk happy. He was not going to fly him to Mokhotlong. Because he had a horrible suspicion that that was not where it would end.

He tried to push the thought away.

Who was Piet anyway? If he'd come to Maseru just for 'a squiz', as he'd told Lizzie, then no harm done. He might even be secretly applauding Stuart for his success with the ladies.

Or not, for Stuart didn't feel terribly successful right now. He felt like a fraud and a liar, sitting across from this sweet, trusting woman who deserved so much better than a man determined to forget past mistakes and start afresh.

He smiled and squeezed Lizzie's hand, agreeing that a honeymoon spent driving the Garden Route and exploring beauty spots along the way could be idyllic.

In fact, a driving holiday was far from his idea of an

idyllic honeymoon, but Stuart could see its merits. It would keep him busy. No lolling about on beaches, itching for something to keep his mind from straying to violet eyes and raven hair.

He'd be hunched over the steering wheel, searching out stunning landmarks to keep Lizzie entertained and his mind where it should be.

"The garden route is a wonderful idea," he enthused as he considered the cost benefits and the fact he really didn't have enough in the bank to get married. The irony wasn't lost on him—here he was, proposing to one woman while calculating how little he could afford to spend on her, when his first choice was planning a wedding that probably cost more than he made in two years.

He'd have to explain to Lizzie that things would be tight and give her the chance to change her mind.

"Of course I know that!" she exclaimed in response, her eyes shining with such genuine affection that Stuart felt another stab of guilt. "You didn't think I was marrying you for your money, did you?" She laughed, and the sound was so different from Philippa's—so innocent and hopeful. "We'll be poor and happy. And besides, it won't always be like this. You won't always be a pilot in Lesotho unless you want to. I've pegged you for great things, Captain Price."

Her faith in him was both touching and devastating. She believed in him completely and had no idea that he was settling for comfortable love over passion just as surely as Philippa had settled for Matthew's money and status.

She bit her lip and looked suddenly coy. "Perhaps we're getting ahead of ourselves to be talking about the honeymoon when..."

She trailed off, clearly too embarrassed to articulate what he should have thought of.

"When we haven't set a wedding date. Of course! But Lizzie, there's something else I have to tell you."

She blanched at his serious tone, and he saw fear flicker across her features—as if she was bracing for him to take it all back, to reveal this was some cruel joke. The vulnerability in her expression made him hate himself a little more.

He patted her hand and said, "Don't worry, I don't have any awful secrets, but I do have to see my dad in England."

"England!"

No doubt she imagined he'd be away for months, not weeks, so he said quickly, "He's not well and time's running out, so he's sent me an airline ticket." He cleared his throat and went on, "He's dying. I can't refuse."

"Oh Stuart, that's awful!" she whispered, squeezing his hand. "I'm so sorry. Of course you can't refuse when—"

Stuart stopped her. "He's not a nice man, and I wouldn't be going if I could help it. In fact, I would be quite happy never to see him again. Except that—"

She frowned, clearly not sure how to respond. Her eagerness to comfort him, to say the right thing, was almost painful to watch.

"He's sent me a first-class ticket to London. It leaves Johannesburg on Tuesday. He was taking a chance, and it only just got to me, otherwise it would be a small fortune down the drain, but he obviously doesn't care since he's dying." He tried not to sound as bitter as he felt and went on quickly, "And the return is for a week later. So, we'll just work around that, but as far as getting married, I don't know what you want, but I'd like to do it as quickly as possible."

And he did. There was no point in wasting time and agonising over possibilities that didn't exist. The sooner he married Lizzie, the sooner he could stop himself from thinking about what might have been with Philippa.

"But maybe you want something—" he swallowed— "bigger, or in a church and with your mum."

"I don't think so! She's not travelling from Australia to see her least favourite daughter get married." The casual way Lizzie dismissed her own worth made Stuart's chest tighten. Another woman who'd been taught she wasn't enough, just like he had been. "Oh Stuart, I'd marry you tomorrow, I'm so in love with you."

The words should have filled him with joy. Instead, they suddenly felt like a weight around his neck. She was so completely, utterly in love with him. Was he using that love as a bandage for his wounded pride?

But he grinned, trying to match her enthusiasm, and then found that, despite his reservations, he really was growing excited. Yes, this might not be such a bad idea. Lizzie might just be the perfect wife for him. After all, passion and drama and fireworks were all very well for the short term—look where they'd got him with Philippa. But he really did want a partnership, for the long haul, that was more successful than that of his parents.

And sweet, kind Lizzie couldn't be more different from his own ma.

"Then we'll get married as soon as possible," he said, "though to be honest, I have no idea what we have to do."

"My friend Clodah works at the local magistrate's office in Pietermaritzburg. She registers weddings all the time. I'll write to her tonight and ask what forms and documents we need. And then when you come back from England, maybe I'll have finished my first stint in the mountains and had a real taste of my own adventure. Mr Tremain said to see him tomorrow." She hesitated, and he could see her trying to read his mood, to be whatever he needed her to be. "But Stuart, I think we shouldn't tell anyone until...until maybe it's done, otherwise I might not be allowed to work if they know I'm engaged."

Stuart brought her hand up to kiss her knuckles, the gesture feeling both tender and hollow.

"All right, we'll keep mum for now and look at getting married as soon as I return. Dan has given me three weeks' leave."

Rising, he added, "I'll be back in a minute. I just need to organise something."

Lizzie deserved some kind of extra surprise and acknowledgement. A word in the waiter's ear and he might be able to get the chef to rustle up something special. It was the least he could do when he was giving her so little of what she actually deserved.

"Captain Price, I hoped I'd see you again." A figure emerged from behind the wooden partition, and Piet smiled his oily smile. "I wanted to bring up again my simple little request to hop aboard your plane and take a trip high up in the mountains."

Stuart stiffened and glanced to the side. There was no one in the vicinity, and he didn't want to draw attention to himself, just as he didn't want to engage in conversation with Piet. The man's presence felt like a snake sliding into his carefully constructed new life.

"I'm sorry, that won't be possible. There are no tickets available," said Stuart stonily, taking a step past him.

Piet put his hand on his shoulder. "I was thinking maybe a ticket would be unnecessary. I'd rather not share the trip up with anyone, even your fiancée, sweet though she is." His eyes bore into Stuart's with the calculation of a predator who'd found wounded prey. "I was thinking that a nice, private little flight, with no one the wiser, would make us even, Captain Price. And if anyone asks, then you can vouch for me. There's always a need for a good mechanic where there's a dirt-sieving machine or similar that needs tending." He held up his oil-stained fingers. "That's the thing about the diamond diggings, remote though they are —lots of equipment breaks down." His smile grew oilier. "You just need to fly me there and back, unscheduled, and I'd be happy to keep my mouth shut about you and your lovely dark-haired little lady on the side."

Stuart swallowed. "I don't know what you're talking about."

"Don't you?" Piet raised his eyebrows in mock surprise. "See, the thing is, me, and my ma and pa, remember that night very clearly. How you and that pretty girl introduced yourselves as husband and wife after your plane unexpectedly landed in our mealie field. How she flashed that nice diamond ring on her finger so that my kind-hearted ma treated you *honeymooners* to your own, cosy...*married*... accommodation." His voice dropped to a whisper. "You lied to my family. Made us accessories to whatever game you were playing with the District Commissioner's daughter —" He straightened, then added ominously— "who's about to marry Cape Town royalty if what your sweet little *real* fiancé says is true."

Stuart felt the walls closing in. "We didn't do anything wrong."

"Charles Tremain might see it differently, don't you think? A lowly pilot taking advantage of his daughter? Compromising her reputation? Using false pretences?" Piet's eyes glittered. "And then there's your employer. Drakensberg Air probably wouldn't like knowing their pilots are playing marriage games with passengers. Bad for business, that." He grinned. "And that's before we even get to what the Myburgh family would think."

The implications hit Stuart like physical blows. His job, his reputation, any future with Lizzie—all of it could be destroyed by a few well-placed words from Piet.

"What do you want?" Stuart asked, though he already knew.

"Just a little trip to Letseng-la-Terai. No questions asked, no passenger manifest, no witnesses. Think of it as... payment for my family's hospitality that night." Piet glanced toward where Lizzie sat waiting, probably wondering what was taking Stuart so long. "Your sweet fiancé seems like the trusting type. Shame if she found out her hero wasn't quite the gentleman she thinks he is."

Stuart felt trapped, just like he had as a child when his father would corner him with impossible choices—steal or be beaten, lie or face consequences he couldn't handle.

"I need time to think about it."

"Of course you do." Piet straightened, his manner becoming almost jovial again. "Take all the time you need. But not too much time. These mountain routes can be so dangerous—the weather changes quickly, equipment fails. Would hate for something unfortunate to happen to anyone's reputation... or career... or happiness."

He patted Stuart's shoulder one more time. "You know where to find me when you've made up your mind, Captain Price. I'll be around Maseru, finding things to do." He paused. "And people to talk to," he added with an ominous look.

CHAPTER

NINETEEN

MOKHOTLONG

Stuart had caved and now he was in Mokhotlong—with company he'd sworn he'd avoid.

Unloading supplies from the pod, he uncomfortably aware of Charles Tremain's arrival before Piet's lanky figure had disappeared down the road towards the town. The DC's enquiring glance made Stuart's collar feel tight around his neck.

He'd told the fellow how strictly scrutinised every visitor was to Letseng-la-Terai and that every miner who found a stone was required to declare it to the District Commissioner before selling to a licensed buyer. Charles Tremain took his oversight duties too seriously for a man like Piet to operate with impunity.

"And who is that visitor to our remote empire?" Charles asked, frowning in Piet's direction.

"A mechanic here on business," Stuart replied, trying to sound casual. "I didn't get the details." He hesitated, watching Piet's retreating figure and willing it to be swallowed up in the distance. Though he wished it would be swallowed up more than just figuratively.

"What have you got on these next couple of days?" Stuart tried to turn the topic and was surprised by Tremain's sudden smile.

"I'm seeing the Resident Commissioner in Maseru this afternoon after you fly me down, and then a certain Miss Cameron will meet me at my office to discuss the details of a possible job at the medical clinic at Mapolaneng." His tone carried unexpected warmth. "Delightful young woman. A nurse. Perhaps you know her?" He raised his eyebrows. "That's right! She said you were acquainted. Also, she said she was an excellent horsewoman, which I hope is not a lie as I've decided to offer her the job since she said she'd be happy to start as soon as possible. We'll start out in the Land Rover to Roma, where the road ends, so the rest is trekking overland."

"So, you'll accompany her?" Stuart knew how much Lizzie wanted this job. Yet he felt an unexpected jolt at the thought that in just over three weeks she would be his wife, and here he was facilitating her journey into the mountains with Charles, who had no idea of this.

"I'm sure Miss Cameron wouldn't lie about her ability to ride," he said. "She's not that type."

"Oh, so you do know her?" Charles was watching Stuart carefully. "She says her two great loves are horses and babies. We certainly are desperate for a nurse at the vaccination clinic as soon as possible."

When Stuart mentioned he was leaving for Johannesburg the following day to catch a BOAC flight to London—his father was dying—he noticed Charles's shoulders ease almost imperceptibly.

Was that relief? The thought lodged uncomfortably in

his chest. How much did Charles suspect regarding his feelings for his daughter? Stuart had probably worn his heart on his sleeve the night of her twenty-first.

Well, the man needn't worry, he thought grimly. Stuart was marrying Lizzie and couldn't be happier about it.

Stuart had planned to bid Lizzie farewell before her mountain journey, but Diana hurried out from the Drakensberg Air office as soon as he touched down in Maseru.

"A sick miner has chartered the plane," she said breathlessly. "Sorry, but you're needed to pick him up in Letseng-la-Terai and bring him down to the hospital."

Stuart's heart sank. Another trip to the diggings meant another opportunity for Piet to approach him. He'd hoped the Afrikaner would give up and find his own way back to the lowlands.

When Stuart landed the Cessna back at Mokhotlong to collect the miner's son who would accompany the sick man, his worst fears were confirmed. Piet was waiting by the airstrip, leaning against the fence with that calculating smile.

"It's fate, isn't it?" Piet said, approaching with a laugh. The miner's son stood nearby, clearly having accepted some payment to allow the extra passenger.

Stuart didn't reply. The threat to Philippa's reputation hung over him like a sword. Charles Tremain would have him horsewhipped if word got out. "Twenty minutes at the diggings," he said finally. "That's all."

Piet's grin widened. "That's all I need, Captain. Like I said, I just want a quick squiz."

THE FLIGHT to Letseng-la-Terai passed in tense silence.

When they landed amidst the usual crosswinds, Stuart taxied toward the large tin shed where some miners had gathered. The place looked as barren and unforgiving as always—a moonscape of rocky ground and desperate men scratching for their fortunes.

"*Blerry* strange place," Piet commented as he stepped onto the dirt, his lip curling. "I didn't think it'd be like this. I'll just take a bit of a walk."

"See you back at the plane in twenty minutes," Stuart called after him, busying himself with organising the interior for the prone passenger. He'd have insisted on accompanying Piet if he hadn't had to prepare for the injured miner, but perhaps it was better this way. Twenty minutes of looking around, and then Piet would realise there was nothing here for him.

Stuart glanced up at the sky. While it had been clear over Maseru, storms could move in quickly at this altitude. He didn't want a repeat of his mishap-laden journey with Philippa.

Well, the truth was, he did—if it meant reliving the best twenty-four hours of his life. But Philippa was marrying into Cape Town aristocracy, and Stuart was marrying Lizzie. When all was said and done, Lizzie was far more suited to a fellow like him. Stuart had been a fool for making a play for someone like Philippa—someone so far out of his league.

Twenty minutes felt like hours. When Piet finally appeared, striding through the dirt from behind the shed, his casual demeanour did nothing to ease Stuart's suspicions.

"I nearly went without you," Stuart shouted over the engine.

"You'd have been sorry if you had," Piet shouted back. "That place is like a frozen desert."

During the journey back, there was little noise other than the groans of the injured miner and the reassurances of his son. Stuart wished he'd put out the word for Piet to be searched—the DC often did this when visitors returned from the diggings.

But Piet just raised his hand in thanks when they landed, hopping to the ground and walking towards town without a backward glance. Not even offering to help get the injured miner out of the plane and into the station wagon that the Queen Elizabeth II Hospital had sent.

It was too late in the day to bid Lizzie farewell before her journey to Mapolaneng. She and Charles would already be well on the way to their destination by now, and Stuart was surprised to feel a pang of disappointment.

Good. He didn't want to believe that comfort, companionship, and a clean start were his main motivations in proposing.

CHAPTER

TWENTY

"Philippa! Did you even listen to a word I said?"

Philippa jerked her attention back from the fountain in the park and plastered an interested look on her face as she turned to Matthew sitting beside her on the park bench.

The truth was that she hadn't listened to a word Matthew had said because he had been incredibly boring, talking about his disappointment at having to give up rugby which he loved so much that he'd even contemplated failing his finals last year so he could continue playing for UTS.

Not that she'd minded him droning on because it meant she could continue to ponder over Stuart's phone call and letter as she decided what to do about the things he'd said.

Five days ago he'd told her he loved her. She'd not taken those words lightly. Then Mrs Myburgh had told her she loved her like a daughter. Again, not words to easily dismiss.

So, when Matthew carried on like a spoiled child, it was

just one more reason to consider Stuart's offer more seriously. She was engaged to be married with glittering prospects on the horizon. But there was so much more at stake than simply choosing between two men.

"Yes, Matthew, I'm sorry you had to give up your rugby, but look what you got instead." She opened her hands in a gesture to reveal her beautiful self, expecting him to laugh.

Instead, he glowered, staring into the middle distance, before snapping rudely at a vendor who tried to sell him a beaded key ring shaped like Africa.

"There's no need to take your bad mood out on others," Philippa reminded him, watching the vendor's face fall as he moved on to another bench.

Now Philippa wondered how much compassion and humanity Matthew could show in any situation that didn't prioritise himself.

"Don't tell me what to do."

Philippa's mouth dropped open at his tone; quiet and dangerous and not the petulant rejoinder she'd expected.

He must have registered her look, for he sighed, his shoulders slumped, and he muttered, "God, I'm sorry. I'm just sunk right now because grandfather has to go into hospital and so he's postponed my trip again."

Philippa felt an extraordinary maelstrom of emotions. "Postponed it? You mean until after we were married?" A slow fizzing of excitement pushed away her earlier disenchantment. "But that's good, isn't it? We could both go together. I have family in England. My grandmother—"

"Yes, yes, you've told me about your grandmother and I suppose we could go together but Pippa—" he sent her a long, forlorn look — "this was supposed to be my chance to have a bit of fun before I tie myself down. Oh, don't look at me like that. You know what I mean. What do you girls say? Kick up your heels? Well, a bloke needs to do that, too."

Philippa didn't know what to say. And whatever she did say was not going to be taken the right way by Matthew in the mood he was in. She most certainly did not like the casual way he spoke of their marriage as 'tying himself down'.

So when Mrs Myburgh remarked on Philippa's lacklustre looks that afternoon, finally getting her to recount her conversation with Matthew on the park bench, she merely laughed.

"Oh, Philippa! Get used to it! Grown men are just little boys inside." With an elegant hand on Philippa's shoulder, she pushed her down onto the cream silk sofa and took a seat beside her, her Chanel perfume enveloping them both.

"Consider yourself lucky that Matthew is so easy to manage. He likes the trappings of success, like his father. Like me and like you. He loves you, and he's secretly pleased that you reflect well on him."

Philippa pressed her lips together and listened. She didn't know what to say.

Mrs Myburgh's brittle smile softened a little. "Don't let him break your heart, Philippa. Matthew will make a wonderful husband. You will want for nothing—"

"But I'm surely allowed to tell him when I don't like something?"

"Of course! But learning how to do that the right way is vital for a marriage like yours to work."

Correctly interpreting Philippa's frown at the term 'like yours', Mrs Myburgh smiled again. "While I'm sure there are some men — softer emotionally, or more principled, or less invested in wanting the outside of their marriages to reflect well on their business interests—men who would allow more ..." She struggled to find the word, then settled upon, 'honesty', adding, "Matthew, and his father, are simpler souls in the domestic sphere."

She squeezed Philippa's knee, and now her smile was sympathetic; and Philippa, who'd felt a great sense of revolt at what she was being told earlier, warmed a little.

Until Mrs Myburgh said, "It doesn't take too much to learn the rules, but as long as you reflect well on your husband, you will be given the world."

Smoothing her cashmere skirts as she rose, Mrs Myburgh made to leave, pausing in the doorway to add, "Now, cheer up, Philippa, and go and find Matthew, who has been moping about the house like a bear with a sore head. He'll get over his disappointment, but it's up to you to discover the right way to tackle him in a mood like this. You do understand what I'm saying, don't you?"

Philippa rose slowly. "But Matthew... he does love me, doesn't he?"

"Of course he loves you!" Mrs Myburgh said it on a laugh, but there was a note of exasperation, too. "I'm just giving you some invaluable advice on how to keep Matthew —and this applies to all husbands—where you need them to be, in order to enjoy all this." And with her elegant, bejewelled hands, she indicated the luxurious trappings of the exquisite beachside home that Philippa would once have given her eyeteeth to inhabit.

Philippa felt a strange sense of abandonment as the French doors closed behind her future mother-in-law. Beyond, she could see the pristine garden, and beyond that, the sparkling sea that had once represented everything she'd dreamed of. Now it looked as cold and distant as the life being mapped out for her.

Why should she be the one who always had to drag Matthew out of his stupid, selfish doldrums?

With a furtive glance about her, she made her way to the telephone, then stopped. It could take hours to put a call through to Basutoland.

"Marielle, I'm going for a walk," she told the maid, snatching a scarf and sunglasses. "I might visit a friend on the way, so I probably won't be back for afternoon tea."

A few minutes later, she was at the tickey box asking the operator to put a call through to Stuart, her hands shaking and her heart quailing as she contemplated where this talk might take them.

When she learned the surprising news from Diana at Drakensberg Air that Stuart had flown to England the previous day, the disappointment was a sudden, sickening plunge, as if the ground had fallen away beneath her.

CHAPTER

TWENTY-ONE

LONDON

Stuart barely recognised his father in the frail, shrunken body beneath the heap of dirty bedcovers. The basement room reeked of unwashed flesh, stale tobacco, and something medicinal that couldn't quite mask the underlying smell of decay. When it had become clear the old man had been unable to look after himself, Stuart's Aunt Thelma had been prevailed upon to come down from Newcastle, where she'd escaped some decades before. However, having fallen on hard times herself following the death of her husband, Bert, brother to Stuart's father, the promise of a small retainer had lured her back to London where, surely by the look of Reggie Price, she'd only have to stay a few months.

"You came then. Wasn't sure you would," the old man wheezed as Stuart stood in the doorway to his bedroom. "You couldn't be bothered to see your old ma before it was too late. That's why I sent you the ticket."

"You took a risk. I only got it barely the day before I was due to fly."

Reggie twisted his head. "I'm a gambler. 'Sides, I can't take me pot 'o gold wiv me. That ticket came out of what'll be left to you. Didn't leave much." He sucked on his gums. "'Spose that's the reason you came, eh? You wanna know what you'll be getting."

Stuart lowered himself onto the seat of a broken chair after removing the mouldy remains of a sandwich.

"I don't want anything to do with your ill-gotten gains. The only reason I'm here is because—" Quite frankly, he didn't know what to say, for he felt no affection, nor any reason to soften what would be their final farewells. "Well, you asked me, and the least I could do was tell you that despite all your dire predictions, I'm managing just fine without the proceeds of crime."

The old man narrowed his eyes. "How old are you now? Twenty-six? Twenty-seven? Not got yersel' a parcel o' kids? A handsome chap like you? No grandkids to tell me about?"

Stuart shrugged. "I'm getting married when I get back to South Africa."

"Getting hitched, eh?" His father took a laboured breath. "Got some girl in the family way, eh? I picked you as a bounder, so it weren't that surprising you left town wivout so much as a goodbye. Lot of scummy water under the bridge since you abandoned me and your mum."

Stuart closed his eyes. He'd waited too long when his mother had written to tell him she was dying. Stuart had not wanted to see her again, and it was only when Dan had heard she was on his deathbed that Stuart had finally booked his passage.

Getting belted by his dad was expected, but his mum had been mean and shifty about it. He'd learned the dictionary meaning of the word sadist when he was twelve. He'd been a lot younger when he'd learned that was what his mother was.

"You were too late to say your farewells to your mum, for all her beggin'. Broke her heart, you did." Reggie shifted and, when Stuart didn't bite, wheezed, "So, tell me about yer girl."

Stuart wondered whether telling his father about Lizzie was such a good idea. He decided not to. It would only taint her goodness. After his long flight, he was finding it hard to remember what she looked like, but her sweet nature still shone bright in his memory.

And surely that counted for more than the smouldering image of Philippa imprinted on his brain?

"Not giving away much, are you? Perhaps you *do* have a parcel of kids I don't know about." His father tried again. His watery blue eyes tried to focus on Stuart. "*Do* I have any grandkids?"

There was a plaintive note to the question. Stuart felt himself relenting until his father's bitter, whiplike addendum. "Poor Gracie didn't get a chance. You saw to that." His lips trembled. "She'd have made a fine mum...once she calmed down a bit. But my princess is dead." A tear escaped and rolled down his cheek. "Get me a light, will you?"

"Dad, I don't think—"

"I don't care what you think!" his father managed through his coughing fit, and Stuart dug into the mountain of pills and filth and sundry items cluttering his bedside table to find a half pack of Lucky Strike.

After helping his father to light his fag, he rose to draw the curtains, but the windows were so grimy that very little extra light penetrated the basement bedroom. He leaned against the cold wall and watched his father draw in lungfuls of tobacco smoke, then exhale in a series of phlegmy wheezes and coughs.

"Don't have anything to say for yourself?" his father finally barked.

"The room stinks. Does no one clean for you? I don't wonder Aunt Thelma stays out of here."

"Does no one clean for you?" his father mimicked. "What a la-di-da you've turned into. I don't recognise me own son. But then, you always liked to lord it over the rest of us after you came back from those do-gooders who thought they could turn you into something."

"At least they tried."

"Easy to buy loyalty, boy, when you're loaded. I gave you what I could. What I had. Street smarts."

Stuart stared at the rotten stumps of teeth as his father smiled. "I was never more proud of you than when you acted as decoy for that job Bert and I did in '39. The coppers was after us but you well and truly got 'em. Remember? Tripped 'em up with a basket of fish from Middy O'Brien's barrow. Only a little 'un at the time, you was. 'Course I had to fix up Middy, but Bert and me got that little consignment buried under the coal, sweet as pie." He took a long, laboured breath, but the obvious pleasure from these reminiscences pushed him on. "Thought me lad was cut from the same cloth as his Da, back then, I did. Thought you'd be someone like me, I did. Someone I could be proud of."

Stuart stooped to remove the smouldering cigarette his father had dropped.

"Then the bloody war come and off you went to that family in South Africa what ruined Gracie and you. I heard old man Franklin carked it last year." Speculation crept into his tone. "Leave 'is fortune to you, eh? That why you didn't need to see your old man?"

Prickling heat, despite the frosty room, made Stuart run a finger around the inside of his collar. He didn't want to go there. "I haven't seen the Franklins since I returned."

"What? You didn't go to old man Franklin's funeral?" His father looked genuinely surprised. "After he took such a shine to you and Gracie? Good lookin' missus," he added with a grin that managed to appear lascivious, despite his sunken mouth. "Though she looked like she'd eaten a prune when she stepped over our front doorstep."

"You wouldn't remember that, Dad. You were in gaol."

"Yer mum told me. Anyway, didn't they just love our Gracie, though nice they took you on that grand old Froggie, snail-eating tour when you was teens. Missed yer too much, they said. Thought they were gonna adopt you, I did. Well, you must have disappointed the old man big time. And I don't jes mean what you did to Gracie. Oh no. Disappointed everyone, you did."

The old man's hacking cough resumed. Without enthusiasm, Stuart leaned forward to wipe the drool from his mouth.

"I'm getting married as soon as I get back," Stuart said. The old man would be dead soon anyway. He might as well know what Stuart intended doing with his life.

"What's she look like? Don't tell me. Black-haired siren, like all them posters you had on your wall. Yer mum was like that. A black-haired siren. Well, she was for about five minutes until she got preggers wiv you and her dad came after me with a shotgun pointed at me head until I marched her up the aisle."

Stuart was wondering if he was expected to apologise when his father barked out the question again: "Go on, tell me I'm right." His mouth twisted into a grin. "The girl you love is a black-haired siren."

Stuart rolled his eyes, and when he met his dad's look he couldn't help grinning. There had been some good times growing up when his dad had teased him and taken an interest. "Yes, the girl I love is a black-haired siren, if you want to know." The pleasure drained out of him as he added, "But I'm marrying a blonde."

"Interestin'." His father worried at a scab on his lip with his tongue. "So the girl you love wouldn't have you, then? Too good for you, eh? You not flyin' that jet yet, I take it?"

"Not yet, Dad." He rolled his shoulders. "It'll happen, though."

"Jest not quick enough for your black-haired siren. Ah well, it wouldn't have lasted. Good thing you disappointed her early in the piece." His voice became peevish again as he struggled to roll over. "Better that than after a parcel o' kids what desert you in old age."

His aunt met him in the passage, a dusting rag in her hand. Stuart didn't think the place had been dusted since his mother had died. Longer, probably. His mother was not known for keeping a clean house, either.

"Not staying?" Aunt Thelma asked as he picked up the suitcase he'd left by the front door.

Stuart shook his head. "I'll visit every day, but I'm staying with friends." That wasn't true, but he'd rather find cheap lodgings than stay under the same roof as his father amidst the squalor and memories. "My plane leaves on Friday."

"Haven't we come up in the world, Stuart Price?" His aunt propped herself up against the dingy wall. "You come all this way and barely darken the doorstep. Don't fancy them long, cosy chats your dad was so lookin' forward to?" Her tone was snide.

"If he wants to see me, he only has to ask. You can get a message to me at Jimmy's, in case he worsens. He hasn't got long, has he?"

Aunt Thelma shrugged. "That's what I thought for three years before his brother died. They're a tough lot, these Prices. A tough, cruel lot." Her smile was bitter. "You're about the best o' the bunch, I reckon. Liked you as a little 'un. Your sister, too. Couldn't imagine how Reggie and Mavis got kids like you. Decent kids." She paused. "You goin' to see your sister's grave?"

Stuart nodded.

"Hope your dad didn't make it too hard for you." His aunt blinked, as if she had something in her eye. She worked at her gums before lowering her gaze. "It weren't your fault."

Stuart supported himself on the doorframe and studied her expression for signs of lying. "You're the only one who thinks that."

"I saw the coroner's report. She'd already bled out before the car rolled. I know you was tryin' to get her to the hospital before it was too late. Stupid Gracie! Why didn't she tell *me* when she got herself up the duff? I'd a known who to send her to." His aunt pulled a cigarette out of her cardigan pocket and lit it with trembling hands, drawing in deeply. "Your dad didn't know nuffink about Gracie. She called you from that back-alley butcher, didn't she? Asked you to fetch 'er, didn't she?"

Stuart let Aunt Thelma talk. It'd probably be the last time he saw her. She was wheezing just like his Da.

"Your dad likes to blame you cos' he can. Cos you were driving. The fall guy. You know your dad." She grimaced as she touched her broken nose. "He and his brother always had to have someone to blame for whatever didn't go right in their lives."

Her words brought some solace. But in his heart, Stuart knew he was to blame. Not because he was driving but because he'd refused Gracie help when she'd asked for it.

"I don't know why you didn't leave Uncle Bert years ago," he said instead. The Price brothers had lived a stone's throw from each other until Bert's death from lung cancer. The same cancer that was killing his father. As a child, it had been common to see Aunt Thelma with a black eye or a cut lip. Stuart's mother used to be scornful of the fact Thelma stayed.

"And where would I 'ave gone?" Thelma arched a brow. "Oo would 'ave 'ad me? I ain't got no family." Her face softened. "Like you, Stuart, I'm all alone in the world. I'm like a discarded old shoe. No kids, no parents, and—thank the good Lord—no husband. But it's a lonely place to be when you ain't got your looks, neither, and time is ticking. That's what makes you the lucky Price out o' the two of us."

Stuart put a hand on her shoulder, but she pulled away. There was moisture in the corner of her eye. "You go and put some flowers on yer sister's grave for me. She didn't deserve to die like she did, though everyone'll say it were no-one's fault but her own." Aunt Thelma rolled a scrawny shoulder, her mouth like a downturned sliver of moon between her jowels. "Yes, got herself into trouble, didn't she, though no one'll mention Jimmy Mcgee's part in it. Jest that young Gracie reckoned she were too good for 'im *an'* the rest of us when them la-di-da Franklins invited her to live with 'em and nothing was going to stop her, specially not the bub she reckoned Jimmy forced on 'er."

Stuart paused, his hand on the doorknob. "The Franklins invited her to *live* with them?"

"They was going to pay for her education. Well, somethin' that were goin' to get Gracie out of this stinking rat hole of a place." Aunt Thelma sent him a narrow look. "What? Ya didn't know that? All hurt they forgot to invite you?"

Stuart shook his head. "They did more than enough for me. The old man paid for my flying lessons—"

"Then I don't know why you 'aven't traded more on the association. Yer dad might sneer at 'em for being toffs but 'e reckons you're a fool for not takin' advantage. Reckons the old man woulda left a fortune to you if you'd played your cards right."

"The Franklins have a son and daughter of their own." Stuart forced out the words. He was still digesting what his aunt had said about Gracie.

He switched his suitcase to the other hand and opened the door. "But they loved Gracie like their own," he conceded. "I always knew that." His throat felt thick as he paused, then added, "I couldn't go back and see them after Gracie died. How could I explain?"

"That it weren't your fault when it looked like it was?" Aunt Thelma shrugged. "You and your high and mighty morals, Stuart Price. If there's one thing me and yer dad are agreed on, it's that your high and mighty morals were always goin' to be the downfall of you!"

CHAPTER

TWENTY-TWO

It was dawn when Stuart blinked open his eyes, instantly wide awake.

In a few hours, he'd be married to Lizzie—a good woman who deserved the best.

He really hoped he was up to the task. He'd returned from England even more determined to make a success of his upcoming marriage than he had been before he left.

Lizzie was his future because he'd accepted that Philippa was in the past, and because Lizzie loved him. He'd sunk his pride, and he'd sworn to himself to be a good, honest husband.

He stared at the ceiling of his hotel room, listening to the sounds of Pietermaritzburg waking up beyond his window. A thousand miles away, in South Africa's glittering coastal city of Cape Town, Philippa was planning her future with Matthew Myburgh. The thought made his chest tighten with a familiar ache, but he clenched his fists and told himself he'd made the right choice.

What other choice could he make when Philippa had so categorically made hers?

In the bathroom, he studied his reflection and tried not to see a fraud staring back. Clean-shaven, respectable-looking, about to make promises he would't have dreamed of making only weeks before. Lizzie deserved a devoted husband, and that was what Stuart was determined to give her.

Not a man whose thoughts would always drift to violet eyes and raven hair.

At least with Lizzie, he could be honest about his limitations. She knew he wasn't wealthy, knew he was still chasing his dream of flying jets. She'd agreed to marry him, anyway.

And maybe that was a good enough start. Maybe love grew from kindness and shared goals rather than the desperate hunger he felt for Philippa. Maybe Lizzie's faith in him would be enough to build something real.

AT THREE FIFTEEN PRECISELY, Stuart knocked on Lizzie's hotel room door, carrying a bouquet of pale pink roses he'd bought that morning. When she opened the door, radiant in cream silk, he felt a stab of guilt that immediately turned to tentative hope and, finally, delight at the joy shining in her face.

"You look lovely, Lizzie. You haven't changed your mind?" He handed her the flowers, noting how her hands trembled slightly as she took them.

"They're beautiful!" She kissed his cheek, and he caught the scent of her perfume—light, innocent, nothing like the sophisticated Chanel that haunted his dreams. "No, I haven't changed my mind. I'm so happy!"

The word 'happy' hit him like a club, reminding him that she deserved someone who could match her joy, not someone going through the motions.

"I'll make you happy, Lizzie," he promised, meaning it. "We'll be a good team. Basutoland is remote, but soon I'll be in Johannesburg, and I'll be flying a jet, and we'll have all the babies you want, and we'll be happy. I promise."

Lizzie's face lit up at the mention of babies, and he forced himself to smile back. Children would make a difference. Perhaps becoming a father would finally silence the voice in his head that whispered Philippa's name.

THE CEREMONY PASSED IN A BLUR. Lizzie's friend, Clodah, had organised the registry office and was one of the two witnesses.

Stuart heard himself repeating vows, felt Lizzie's small hand in his, watched her face glow with happiness as they were pronounced man and wife. It should have been the happiest moment of his life. He told himself it was.

So why did he feel like he was watching someone else's wedding, detached and hollow?

"Time for the champagne!" he declared with forced enthusiasm, taking Lizzie's hand as they ran down the stone steps. If he could just keep moving, keep performing, maybe the feeling would catch up with the actions.

They returned to the hotel for their wedding dinner, where Stuart drank more than usual. The champagne helped blur the edges of his feelings, making it easier to smile and play the devoted bridegroom. Lizzie chattered happily about starting their driving honeymoon the following day, and of the sights she couldn't wait to see, and about her new job in the highlands at the vaccination clinic.

Stuart knew he should be impressed by her adventurous spirit and grateful at her desire to maximise her financial contribution—all without even implying that he ought to be more financially stable than he was.

"You're not afraid?" he asked.

"Of what? Being in such a remote location?" She shook her head. "There's a thriving community and school at Roma, which is only an hour away."

"By Basuto pony," Stuart said with a grin. "I take it you showed the DC just how well you handle a horse and tricky terrain?"

Lizzie really was remarkable. He was sure his admiration would turn to full-blown love before very long.

Especially after Philippa's wedding put the final nail in the coffin and consigned her to a distant memory.

"What are you thinking, Stuart?" She put her head on one side and touched his sleeve.

He thought quickly, and came up with, "Oh, just something I read in the newspaper about a troublemaker. A political agitator Charles Tremain mentioned a while ago," Stuart replied. "Moses Shakane. He was once a student at Roma."

"Well, that must have been a while ago and nothing to concern yourself over," Lizzie reassured him. "Mr Tremain said that his maid's son, Mpho, goes to the convent school and that we're to take the boy a box of school books and food that his mother will prepare for the two of them on my next stint at the clinic after our honeymoon."

"And you haven't told him about...us?

Lizzie reddened. "I wasn't sure how he'd take it. You know, he could be the old-fashioned type who'd think I had to stay at home the moment some man put a ring on my finger. I don't know how strict the administration is about the Marriage Bar and allowing married women to work."

"Oh? So, you take off your engagement ring when you're at work?"

"Would Sir like another?" The waiter hovered with a fresh bottle, and Stuart glanced at Lizzie.

"What do you think, Lizzie? Perhaps it's time to go back to the room."

The words came out more roughly than he'd intended, weighted with implications they both understood. Lizzie's cheeks flushed pink, but she nodded, suddenly shy.

Stuart opened his wallet to pay the bill and his heart nearly stopped. Out with the money came a photograph of Philippa he'd taken during her twenty-first.

"I've never seen a picture of Gracie," Lizzie said, leaning forward with innocent curiosity. "May I see?"

Panic shot through him and he pushed the photograph out of sight, saying as he rose, "Time for bed, Lizzie!" But his smile was unsteady, and Lizzie's face had already changed, confusion replacing curiosity.

"Why not have that extra bottle of champagne after all?" he said desperately, trying to recapture the earlier mood. "I'll order one for the room. We've got a big night ahead of us."

The forced joviality rang false even to his own ears, but Lizzie managed a smile and took his hand.

———

LATER, as Lizzie slept peacefully beside him, Stuart stared at the ceiling and wondered what kind of man he really was. He'd been gentle with her, kind, but even in their most intimate moments, his mind had wandered to another woman. To memories of passionate encounters that bore no resemblance to the careful, considerate coupling he'd just shared with his wife.

The photograph felt like it was burning a hole through his wallet, lying on the dresser across the room. Tomorrow, he'd destroy it. Tomorrow, he'd start his new life properly.

Tonight, though, he allowed himself one last moment to remember the feeling of silky raven tresses and the taste of forbidden kisses, before closing that door forever.

CHAPTER
TWENTY-THREE

MOSES SHAKANE WAS A SIXTH SON WITH GOOD LOOKS, THE ABILITY to sway others, and a status far outstripped by his soaring ambition.

The family was well off—each night his father locked thirty sheep into the kraal next to the family's four rondavels. The rondavels were made of mud brick and thatched with wheat straw: one for his mother and father, another for the six boys, a third for the two girls, and the fourth for cooking. There was also a large fireplace outside where the cooking was done when the weather was fine, the smoke carrying the scent of roasting maize and samp across the mountainside.

Moses was now in his mid-twenties with a decent education behind him. He'd attended the Mission School at Mapolaneng, reaching Standard 8 before going down to Natal where he'd found work in a trading store. There he'd learned to speak reasonable English—and more importantly, he'd learned to recognise the hunger in white customers' eyes when they looked at what they couldn't have.

Since he worked in the Richmond area populated mainly by Xhosas, he'd learned to speak that language, too. Languages were power, and Moses collected them like his father collected sheep.

Moses had saved hard and after a couple of years had acquired enough money to buy a Land Rover—secondhand, but it ran, and ownership of any motor vehicle in the mountains marked a man as someone to watch.

It was time, he decided, to return to Mokhotlong.

There he'd got work in another trading store and, on a couple of occasions, had attended Congress meetings in the Mokhotlong District. The taste of political discourse had been intoxicating—men with serious faces discussing the future of their people, speaking of independence as if it were not just a dream but an inevitability.

Working in South Africa, he'd been enraged by the injustice of apartheid. It offended him enormously that he couldn't go into a hotel bar or step foot on the beaches, use the toilets and other venues in South Africa reserved for Whites Only. The humiliation burned in his chest like swallowed fire, fuelling ambitions that grew larger with each slight.

The apartheid system did not operate in Lesotho, but that didn't mean the politics of the country were sound. The British still pulled the strings, still decided who would prosper and who would not.

So, while selling Basuto blankets and sacks of mealie meal at Frasers Trading Store, he'd jumped at an unexpected opportunity that would change his life and give him a voice in the running of his country: a one-year scholarship to study political science in Moscow.

The Russians had been generous teachers. They'd shown him how power worked—not just the power of words, but the power of fear, of organisation, of knowing exactly which pressure to apply to make a man bend.

Now Moses was back home, and on a mission to achieve justice for his people. Not only his people collectively, but a minor chief currently under investigation for medicine murder.

His chief. His uncle.

The multiple hangings some years ago of a number of chiefs and their supposed accomplices for medicine murder was a frightening reminder of what possibly awaited his uncle, Chief Thabo. The colonial government had made examples of those men, their bodies swaying from British ropes as a warning to any who might challenge the new order.

Moses wished the old man had accepted his brother Tumelo's offer to go halves in a mechanically operated sieve and try his luck at Letseng-la-Terai. At least diamonds were a clean way to power—cleaner than the old methods that had served their ancestors for generations.

Moses wished Tumelo would one day enjoy the luck of his friend at the diggings who had found a big diamond which he'd sold to a diamond buyer who'd arrived unexpectedly in Letseng-la-Terai, recently, saving him the trouble of going down the mountain to sell it. He'd received a big deposit with the remainder to come in a few days. Smart man, his second uncle. He understood that the future belonged to those who could adapt. Good fortune was sure to come to him in time.

But instead of finding diamonds like his brother, Chief Thabo was more concerned with shoring up his power base through the old ways.

Moses knew his uncle did not understand their

changing society. He knew the old man was frightened by the young and educated Basotho who had different ideas on how to run things and who should rule: the educated ones who'd seen the world beyond these mountains and returned with dangerous ideas about democracy and human rights.

Moses and his generation scorned the old ways and were becoming skeptical about the power of human flesh as strong *muti*. Not because they didn't believe in its potency—Moses had seen enough in his travels to know that power took many forms—but because such methods were a liability now, drawing the wrong kind of attention from colonial authorities.

While it was no doubt true that his uncle had ordered the murder of the imbecile Ntsu Kwele for such purposes, Moses didn't believe justice would be served by holding him to the Colonial Administration's values. White man's justice was not Basotho justice, and never would be.

Today, as he stood in front of a crowd in the mission school he'd once attended at Mapolaneng, Moses scanned the faces of the boys and girls he'd just addressed at an evening forum. The excitement in the small fibro and tin classroom was palpable, thick as the smoke from paraffin lamps that cast dancing shadows on eager young faces. Moses felt his own veins bubbling with it as he contemplated the possibilities that could start from here.

"Independence and justice for the Basotho is within our grasp, but we have important decisions to make." He paused so his words could sink in, watching as several students leaned forward. The atmosphere was close with so many bodies pressed into the small space, and flies buzzed above the eager heads of the students ready to give Moses their full attention. The air was heavy with the scent of young sweat and anticipation, the particular energy of youth ready to be harnessed. He'd never felt so powerful. "And it is up to us to decide who will lead us."

He knew there were disparate allegiances among the thirty or so students—some still loyal to the chiefs, others drawn to the moderate voices calling for gradual change. His job was to ensure they realised there was only one party who could do the job when the first free and fair elections were held in Lesotho within the next few years. Only one party had the strength to take what was rightfully theirs.

He started with persuasion, drawing in the more resistant with his compelling rhetoric, weaving stories of what he'd seen in the outside world—the wealth that existed, the power that could be theirs. Then he accelerated the pace and passion, his voice rising and falling like a preacher's, like the orators he'd studied in Moscow. He'd become a good speaker, and more importantly, he'd learned the art of intimidation—when to use honey, and when to show the sting.

During his fiery speech, Moses had become conscious of an earnest-looking boy in the front row. Small for his age, perhaps fourteen or fifteen, with intelligent eyes that seemed to see too much. While the other students had cheered when he'd exhorted that strong measures might be needed to establish the dominance of the 'true leaders,' this boy had remained unmoved, his expression thoughtful rather than swept up in the fervour.

Now his gaze narrowed as he focused on the boy, enjoying watching him squirm under the scrutiny before he demanded, "What is your name and which is the party that we must all vote for?"

The boy hesitated, and Moses sensed his fear and reluctance—but also something else. A stubbornness that reminded him uncomfortably of his own younger self, before he'd learned when to bend and when to stand firm.

In a quiet but steady voice, the boy answered, "My name is Mpho Ramotla."

Moses took a step forward, pushing his head close to Mpho, whose eyes flickered to the right, unable to meet those of his interrogator. The boy's breathing was shallow, but he hadn't looked away entirely. So! He had an intransigent before him. Moses glared as he drew himself up, his scrutiny of the boy more intense now, letting the silence stretch until he could hear several students shifting uncomfortably in their seats. "What is the party we must all vote for?" This time he barked it harshly, his voice echoing off the tin walls.

He saw Mpho swallow, saw the whites of his eyes as he held his panic at bay, but also saw the slight lift of the boy's chin—defiance, however small. "The BCP," the boy said, too faintly and after too long a pause, but there had been no tremor in his voice.

Moses shook his head, reining in his anger, suspecting that anger would not work with this particular boy. Some responded to the stick, others to the carrot—but this one might require more subtle handling. "Wrong answer, Mpho," he said very softly, smiling in that effective way that didn't reach his eyes. "We will talk together afterwards."

The boy's face was rigid with fear, but he nodded once, meeting Moses's gaze directly for the first time.

There was much work to be done, Moses thought, but perhaps this Mpho Ramotla would prove more interesting than he'd first assumed. The boy had spine. Properly directed, that could be useful. And if not properly directed... well, Moses had learned in Moscow that examples were sometimes necessary to teach the larger lesson.

The future of Lesotho would not be decided by the weak.

CHAPTER
TWENTY-FOUR

MOKHOTLONG

Francina eyed her son with the usual disquiet she felt when he came home these days. The boy who used to bound through the kitchen door with stories of his lessons now entered quietly, his school satchel seeming to weigh him down.

Mpho was the most pliant of her children. Ann Bubba, who still bore the moniker though she was now a round and bouncing nine-year-old, was her helpful little treasure for half the time while making mischief the other half. Yesterday she'd been found feeding the Morena's prize roses to the neighbour's goat, claiming she was "helping it grow bigger."

Moeketsi, meaning 'another boy' in Sesotho, was the typical second son, always finding ways to gain her attention. He was not studious like Mpho, preferring to chase chickens and practice his slingshot rather than bend over his books by candlelight. She didn't expect him to go as far as Mpho. Few boys had her eldest's gift for learning.

255

So when Mpho showed signs of disquiet, when her gentle scholar came home with worry lines creasing his young forehead, Francina took notice.

"What troubles you this time, my son?" she asked, casting a concerned look at the beginnings of the dessert she was making in advance for the special dinner the Morena would enjoy for his birthday. There was no one else who would mark the day for him, but Francina knew this date.

Miss Philippa was supposed to have celebrated with him, but she was too busy with the plans she needed to make so that everyone would be able to talk about her wedding as the greatest celebration Cape Town had seen.

Francina didn't know why Miss Pippa was getting married in Cape Town when all her family and friends were here in the mountains.

She'd told the Morena so, too, and also how disappointed she was that Miss Pippa had changed her plans for bringing her young man to the top of the mountain.

But then the Morena had told her that he was quite glad Miss Philippa's young man was no longer driving them both to Underberg in an open-topped sports car before borrowing a Land Rover in which they were to travel to the top of the Sani Pass.

And Francina understood and agreed with him. The drive to the top of the Sani Pass, navigating the steep and treacherous mountainous approach from Natal, had claimed too many vehicles tumbling into ravines, when young men's confidence proved no match for mountain weather and treacherous paths carved from solid rock.

Francina didn't trust a young man with no experience of the harsh terrain to take her young Madam to the top of anywhere, and especially not to the top of the Sani Pass.

Miss Philippa was as precious to her as her own children. She'd raised that girl from a baby, had sung her to sleep, strapped to her back by a Basuto blanket, with the same lullabies she'd sung to Mpho.

Handing over to Dolly the job of caramelising the apples, Francina took a seat at the kitchen table and gave her sensitive son the sympathetic ear he needed at this important time.

Mpho looked down at the table, his fingers tracing the grain of the wood. "It is the young men who have seen great sights and learned many things in Moscow that trouble me. Now they are back and want to persuade us that their vision of Lesotho, free of the white man, is the right one." His shoulders slumped as he played with his pencil, defacing the clean, lined pages of his exercise book. Mpho, who took such care with everything, always.

"And what is their vision for our future?" Francina was defensive as she deferred to the vision of her Morena. The DC had explained it to her many times, his voice patient and kind as he spoke of the gradual change that would come, the way independence would unfold like a flower opening to the sun. "We will make our own laws and be our own rulers, but we will do it in peace and in consultation with our fellow Basotho. Surely it is the only way?"

Mpho's mouth turned down, and in that expression she saw the ghost of the little boy who used to cry when other children were unkind. "These soldiers of our future preach a doctrine called Communism. They say it is the only way for all Basotho... all mankind... to be equal."

Her boy was so clearly troubled that Francina's heart went out to him, even though she didn't understand this thing he spoke of called Communism. It sounded foreign and harsh on her tongue, like words that didn't belong in her clean, ordered kitchen where everything had its place and purpose.

Idly he began to sketch a line drawing as he continued, his pencil moving without conscious thought across the page. "They say the white man is our enemy."

Ignoring his mother's sharp gasp of outrage, he went on, his voice dropping to barely above a whisper, "They say the white man exploits the black man for their own gain. That they use every opportunity to advance themselves while grinding us, the Basotho, the Black man, into the earth so that we will forever be their servants."

The words hung in the air like smoke from a badly tended fire. Francina felt something cold settle in her stomach. Not just at the words themselves, but at the way Mpho spoke them, as if he were testing their weight on his tongue.

"This does not sound like the future our Morena speaks of, where we will vote for the party and its prime minister and make our own laws." Her voice was firm, but inside she felt the first tremor of real fear. Not fear of the DC—never that—but fear that the world she understood, the world where loyalty and hard work were rewarded, where kindness flowed both ways between master and servant, might be changing into something she couldn't recognise.

Mpho slumped even more in his chair, and he looked so despondent that not even the hiss of a bubbling pot on the stove could rouse Francina to put her cooking duties at the forefront of her maternal responsibilities. Even though she sensed Dolly had forgotten her important task, this was more important than burned sauce or curdled custard.

"These men speak of revenge against the white man who will cheat us of our riches. Our diamonds."

The word 'revenge' was frighteningly disconcerting.

Francina rose to wield the wooden spoon once more, stirring not just the caramel but trying to stir some sense into this conversation that was moving in directions she didn't like. "The Morena says there are laws to prevent that happening. He prosecutes these bad men when they break those laws." She thought of the DC's tired face when he returned from difficult cases, as if he carried the weight of justice on his shoulders. "But you are right to confide in me, my son. I shall speak to the Morena so he knows what dangerous forces threaten our peace." She reached across to pat the tight curls on his head, feeling how much he'd grown, how his childhood was slipping away like water through her fingers. "In the meantime, my son, you will keep out of such discussions because you will build your future in this country through hard work. The Morena can see it. He will reward it. Let us talk of reward, not revenge."

They were fine words, and she was proud to use them as a fitting termination to an uncomfortable conversation. Words that belonged in her ordered world, where good service was acknowledged and children grew up to be better than their parents.

But Mpho had more to say.

"Revenge is talked about if the white men do not keep their promise to pay men like Moses Shakane's uncle, Tumelo and his friend, what their diamonds are worth."

At the mention of Moses Shakane's name, Francina felt her blood cool. She'd heard whispers about that young man, seen the way other women's faces grew guarded when his name was mentioned. Francina made a tutting noise, the sound sharp in the warm kitchen. "Violence is not the way of the Basotho." By making it a definitive statement she hoped it would be true, but she was not ignorant of the rumblings of disquiet after the diamond thief de

Vries had used a fishing rod to reel away his ill-gotten diamond gains from under the noses of the police.

That had been the start of something that felt like the unravelling of everything she'd believed about how justice worked in their world.

Now her heart felt dangerously pained to hear criticism of the Morena for not doing more after the unknown White man had flown into Letseng-la-Terai to cheat the miners of their hard-won gains only recently. How could they blame the Morena? He was one man, trying to hold together a system that seemed to be cracking under pressures she couldn't fully understand.

Mpho sounded dubious, his young voice carrying such uncertainty she wanted to gather him close like she had when he was small and frightened by thunderstorms. "Perhaps it is not wrong to punish men who have done harm to our people."

Francina rounded on him, her wooden spoon pointed like a weapon. "It is for the law to punish. The chief, the police and the Morena can talk about delivering justice. Justice is not for the likes of you or me—or your friends—to dish out." The words came out fiercer than she'd intended, born of a fear that was growing like a weed in her chest.

She saw Mpho look relieved at her certainty, and was glad. The boy needed boundaries, needed to know that some things were fixed and unchanging in a world that seemed determined to shift beneath their feet.

Mpho had clearly wanted reassurance when the hotheaded youths he studied with tried to fill his head with their dangerous nonsense. These boys, who thought they knew better than their elders, who'd learned just enough to be dangerous but not enough to be wise.

As he picked up his pencil and began to carefully write

in his exercise book, forming each letter with the precision she and the mission school had taught him, Francina felt a weight rise from her shoulders. Mpho was a good boy. He understood reason, and he would use it against the fiery boys who wanted to stir up trouble.

But as she turned back to her caramel, she couldn't shake the feeling that the conversation was far from over.

Or that the unknown white man who'd flown into Letseng-la-Terai and cheated Chief Thabo's brother, Tumelo's friend, of his valuable diamond, had unleashed something unknown, but fiery and terrible.

Outside, the wind was picking up, rattling the windows with a sound like distant thunder. She gripped the wooden spoon so hard her fingers ached.

CHAPTER
TWENTY-FIVE

THE WEDDING DRESS WAS WASP-WAISTED AND FULL-SKIRTED WITH a modest neckline edged with heavily worked Guipure lace and long sleeves with a vee at the wrists. Just like in the illustrations of Sleeping Beauty Philippa's mother had read to her as a child.

"Oh, Pippa, I think that's the one," breathed her friend Catherine, as they flipped back through the pages of Madame Fontaine's sketchbook to return to the lovely wedding dress. "You've got just the sort of figure that will carry it off."

"I like it and, fortunately, Matthew's mother approves, as she's the one who has organised the dressmaker in Johannesburg. Yes—" Philippa gave a wry smile and shrugged. "I'll be going there for a fitting in a few days, now that I'm no longer at varsity."

Catherine sighed as she hugged herself. "Lucky you. What a dream wedding it's going to be. Matthew will swoon when he sees you walking down the aisle."

Philippa tried to keep her smile in place. The perfect wedding dress to make up for a less-than-perfect wedding. To a less-than-perfect groom. For a bride who was feeling her life was less perfect by the day.

Glancing at her watch, she said in a rush, "He'll be furious with me for keeping him waiting! Goodness, is that the time? I promised I'd meet him for lunch at Finnigan's ten minutes ago."

Catherine smiled beatifically as she watched her friend gather up her handbag and smooth her white gloves. "Matthew would forgive you anything, Philippa, and you know it."

That did seem to be true these days, Philippa thought as she went towards the door. Matthew was a changed man, she reflected, hurrying up Adderley Street through the light drizzle that seemed to mirror her mood perfectly.

More attentive, more considerate—someone had clearly been coaching him in the art of being a proper fiancé. The transformation was so complete it sometimes felt like she was marrying a stranger, which perhaps made the whole charade easier to bear.

Charade? No, she'd *chosen* this. Stuart was in England. He'd moved on with his life, and if that was Philippa's fault, maybe she'd done him a favour.

Matthew rose from the table he'd reserved for them by the window, and Philippa sat down, still catching her breath, apologising for being late and noting, absently, that his brief kiss had done nothing to ratchet up the speed of her heart—and that she was quite pleased about this.

Now that she'd experienced the heady throes of passion and all its inconvenient trappings with Stuart, she felt it was far more desirable to face the future with Matthew that had been allotted to her in a calm and steady fashion.

Passion, she'd learned, was dangerous. It made you do foolish things, made you forget who you were supposed to be.

She was going to be one of Cape Town's leading society matrons, usurping—when the time was right—Matthew's exquisitely manicured and coiffured mother. It was a role she'd been trained for since birth, one that would suit her perfectly. Safe. Predictable. Respectable.

She was not an adventurer like her mother had been.

As soon as he returned from his truncated trip to England, Matthew would join the family business, and he and Philippa would move into the lovely home his parents were gifting them for their wedding. Everything planned, everything proper, everything exactly as it should be.

It wasn't large, but it was their first home, and it was not too far from his parents', who had decided that proximity to their future grandchildren was an important consideration. The thought of children—Matthew's children—sent an odd little flutter through her stomach that she chose to ignore.

"What will you have, darling?" Matthew leaned across the table to point at her menu, his voice taking on that carefully solicitous tone she'd noticed lately. Was that his mother's doing? "The steak is always excellent."

"I think I'll have something light." Philippa took a sip of water as her vision wavered slightly, though she maintained her smile. This had become her new mantra: that nothing could make her stop smiling these days. If she could pretend enough, it might become real. If she could just keep performing the role of the happy bride-to-be, eventually the happiness might follow. "I'm feeling a little off colour today."

"All this galloping about in pursuit of the ultimate

wedding gown and perfect reception." Matthew smiled. "You'll be utterly ravishing, whatever you wear, darling."

She accepted the compliment with a nod as she studied the menu, the words swimming slightly before her eyes. When had the print become so difficult to focus on? She glanced up to see Matthew's look of sympathy, noting how he seemed to have matured a great deal over the past few weeks—or else he'd been taking advice from someone who understood women better than he did.

"I'm so sorry you won't have your mother with you to share the preparations for your big day." His voice was gentler than she'd ever heard it. "Darling, are you all right? I didn't mean to upset you by bringing it up."

The mention of her mother felt like the reopening an old wound.

The thought of the decisions she'd made to be here was like rubbing salt in it.

What would her mother have thought of Philippa choosing to follow her head not her heart? Of Philippa choosing to reclaim the life her mother had given up—so that she could be safely insulated from the dangers that falling inconveniently in love?

But now Philippa didn't feel safe at all—even though Matthew was everything a young woman on the cusp of marriage could want from her fiancé. He promised security, and a wonderful lifestyle. And now he was covering her hand with his large, warm one, his expression as concerned as she could want it to be.

Philippa pulled her hand away as she rose hastily to her feet, waving aside his concern as she hurried toward the ladies' room. Suddenly her stomach had chosen to behave in a most uncharacteristic and unsettling way, rebelling against her careful composure with a violence that brooked no argument.

Good Lord, was she really going to be sick? In public? In Finnigan's, where half of Cape Town society might witness her humiliation?

She made it into a cubicle just in time before hurling up her breakfast, clinging to the seat on her knees while she gasped and choked, conscious enough of appearances to be heartily relieved no one else was occupying the powder room and could hear her. Her white gloves were ruined, her carefully arranged hair coming loose, her dignity in tatters.

Finally she rose and, rather shakily, crossed the white-tiled floor to wash her face and hands, watching the water swirl down the drain and wishing she could disappear with it. She pulled out her compact to powder her face and reapply her lipstick, going through the familiar motions that had always restored her equilibrium before.

She peered at her reflection, hoping Matthew wouldn't comment on her pallor, then used a touch of lipstick to colour her pale cheeks. The face that looked back at her seemed like a stranger's—older somehow.

She stood a minute longer, gripping the marble edge of the vanity as she continued to stare at her reflection. The woman in the mirror looked perfectly composed again, but something fundamental had shifted.

Somehow she looked different. More fragile, perhaps. More haunted.

She certainly felt different. This was not the first time she'd felt queasy—there had been mornings this week when the smell of coffee had sent her running, afternoons when exhaustion had hit her like a physical weight.

She drew in a shaking breath as she ran an experi-mental finger down her pale cheek, then lower, contouring her collarbone. Across her breasts, which felt very tender today, fuller somehow, sensitive to even the lightest touch of her fingers.

Her fuchsia-pink lips parted in a silent gasp, and her hand dropped to grip the edge of the vanity as the first tendrils of dread and dismay began to curl around her entrails like poisonous vines.

Slowly she breathed in, exhaling as she mentally calculated the timing of her spontaneous, thoughtless fling with Stuart—that magical, wonderful night that had felt like stepping into another world—and the physical changes in her body she'd been experiencing lately. Changes she'd hitherto given no thought to, dismissing them as wedding nerves or the stress of keeping up appearances.

The mathematics were simple and devastating.

She stared at the horror reflected in her eyes, watching as understanding dawned. Terrible and final. The little kernel of fear, which had lodged like a walnut in the pit of her gut, flowered into full-blown panic, and she began to hyperventilate, her carefully controlled breathing dissolving into short, sharp gasps.

Oh, my God, was all she could think as she closed her eyes and held on for dear life, feeling her carefully constructed world tilt and crack around her. Her thoughts fragmented into a million ghastly scenarios: Matthew's face when he discovered the truth, her father's disappointment, society's whispered condemnation. The scandal that would destroy not just her but everyone she loved.

What do I do now? The question echoed in her mind like a prayer with no answer, like a scream with no sound.

How could she marry Matthew carrying another man's child? How could she not?

The bathroom door opened with a soft whoosh, and

Philippa heard the click of heels on tile. She forced herself to straighten, to arrange her face into the mask of composure she'd perfected, to become once again the woman everyone expected her to be.

But inside, everything had changed. Inside, she was falling through space with no idea where she might land.

"You're looking a little pale, Philippa, my dear." Her mother-in-law, who had just joined them at the table, waved a languid hand to summon a waiter so she could order her lunchtime gin and tonic. Her frosted blonde hair was perfectly coiffed in the latest bouffant style, teased high at the crown and smoothed into elegant waves that just grazed her pearl earrings. She wore a dove-grey Chanel suit with the signature braid trim, its pencil skirt precisely was tailored to mid-knee, paired with patent leather pumps and a matching handbag. A silk scarf in muted pastels was knotted artfully at her throat, and her makeup was flawless —pale pink lipstick, subtly winged eyeliner, and just a hint of rouge on her high cheekbones.

She looked exactly as Philippa would want to look at her age.

But right now, Philippa's mind was on anything but superficial elegance.

"Matthew, you haven't said anything to frighten your new wife to be?" Levity was obviously Mrs Myburgh's intention, but the look Matthew gave her suggested his mother really had been giving him a talking to.

"Wedding nerves, I suppose," Philippa said by way of excuse. If Mrs Myburgh noticed the blankness in her eyes and recognised it as real fear, she might get away with it.

Only subconsciously, she realised something else was required, but her voice sounded wooden to her own ears as she went on, "I'm glad you like the wedding gown I picked out, Mrs Myburgh. My friend Catherine thought—"

"Yes, but I'm not sure I like the pointed sleeves. A little outdated. Madame Latoufe can make those refinements when we go to Johannesburg next week." Smiling as she reached into her handbag, Mrs Myburgh added, "I went ahead and organised train tickets for next Thursday. I do hope that's convenient, but as you're no longer a student, what more important things do you have on your agenda than planning your wedding? And the date is changeable if you prefer to move it back or forward a couple of days."

Philippa didn't know what to say as she accepted the ticket, but it seemed Mrs Myburg was not finished. Reaching across to rest her hand on Matthew's jacket sleeve, she went on, smiling at Philippa, "We can all travel to Johannesburg together. Matthew has business there on behalf of his father, so you and I can spend the next couple of days seeing Madame Latoufe and planning the wedding, Philippa, darling. How does that sound?"

CHAPTER

TWENTY-SIX

Stuart woke in the grey pre-dawn darkness of their hotel room at Plettenberg Bay, the sound of waves rolling against the beach below filtering through the open window.

Beside him, Lizzie slept peacefully, her blonde hair spread across the pillow, one hand curled beneath her cheek. She wore an expression of such trusting innocence that his chest tightened with guilt. The Indian Ocean stretched endlessly beyond the white sand, its surface dark as pewter in the early light, while the Tsitsikamma mountains rose like sleeping giants along the coastline.

This was supposed to be paradise—the Garden Route's most romantic destination—and Stuart was determined that this morning, at least, he would show her he was the husband Lizzie deserved. He slipped quietly from the bed, careful not to disturb her, to organise what he hoped would be the perfect romantic gesture: sunrise, a thermos of tea, and a picnic breakfast.

And he would try to have the kind of intimate conversation that real lovers shared on their honeymoon.

Yes, he wouldn't close down when she brought up

important topics. Such as why he hated his father so much. He'd made that clear enough at dinner but then diverted the conversation when she'd started asking questions.

But maybe his final visit to his father really had exorcised the hate that had been a canker in his breast for so long.

Because he was as unlike his father as could be. He was not a thief or a liar like his dad.

So, if Lizzie had questions, he was determined to answer them, however hard it might be.

Quietly, he packed the picnic blanket he'd picked up from reception.

Then his wallet to check if he'd have enough to get through the next couple of days.

When his thumb snagged on the stiff corner of that photograph, he pulled it out one last time and he held it towards the pale light by the window so he could remember, one last time, the happiest night of his life.

Then, slowly and deliberately, he began to tear it into tiny pieces.

"Stuart, you're up early. Is something the matter?"

Guiltily, he thrust the pieces into his wallet and moved over to the bed.

"It's a surprise," he said, bending down to stroke her cheek. He was glad he was already dressed so she wouldn't get any ideas. "I know how you love walks on the beach and sunrises, so I thought we would combine the two and have a picnic." He tried to inject enthusiasm into his tone. "The hotel kitchen has put something together that we can pick up at reception. What do you think about that idea?"

It was a relief that Lizzie all but dissolved, gushing at how "utterly, adorably romantic" the gesture was, as she put it, and immediately leapt out of bed to get ready.

Twenty minutes later, they were happily settled on a picnic blanket watching the sun rise over the ocean.

"Oh, Stuart, you are the most thoughtful man I've ever met," Lizzie said, resting her head on his shoulder. "You certainly know how to make a girl feel special."

"Well, it's our last opportunity to enjoy nature's bounty before we hit the big smoke. Two nights in Johannesburg and then it's home to the mountains. Dan wants me to fly the Cessna back that's in for maintenance at Rand Airport." He rubbed his stubbled jaw. "I feel bad that we're not moving right into our married digs—"

"There wasn't time to find anything suitable with us... eloping." She snuggled against him with excitement. "And it doesn't matter with me going straight to the clinic near Roma to work after we get back."

"You have an amazing capacity for understanding, Lizzie Cameron. And hard work. He smiled down at her sweet, trusting face, trying to lose himself in her corn-flower-blue eyes.

"Penny for your thoughts, Captain Price? she asked playfully and he jerked back guiltily.

Then, struck by inspiration, Stuart put her away from him, a grin erasing his frown. "Last one to dip their feet in the ocean can choose what they want to do the rest of the day!" he shouted over his shoulder, sprinting down the sand to get there with a few seconds to spare.

A few seconds to thrust his hands into his pocket, pull out the tiny pieces of Philippa's photograph and toss it into the wind.

Lizzie arrived, panting at his side. "What was that?" she asked, shading her eyes against the weak, rising sun, clearly not sure what she was witnessing.

"Consigning the ashes of my past to the sea for a more

hopeful future," he said, placing his arm about her shoulders and tucking her head onto his shoulder.

"Your...dad?" she asked uncertainly.

"My dad is part of all that...all the bad things he made me do...all the bad things *I* did without help from anyone but myself." Then, with real enthusiasm, he kissed the top of her head before declaring, "All vanished with the wind because *you* are my future, sweet Lizzie."

He pulled her into his embrace and, inspired by the first real flowering of hope since he'd met his new wife, kissed her lustily on the lips.

"Oh, Stuart!" Lizzie sagged against his side and kissed him back with all the fervour of a new bride hopelessly in love.

CHAPTER
TWENTY-SEVEN

There was no way Philippa was going to seek out a doctor in Cape Town when she was so certain she knew the verdict. Word travelled, and the shame and potential damage would be more than she, the Myburgh family, or her father would be able to cope with.

Hoping that sunglasses and a scarf covering her hair would make it harder to identify her, she huddled in a tickey box she'd found in a part of town no Myburgh would be likely to visit and waited for the operator to connect her.

Finally she heard Diana's voice from Drakensberg Air.

"I wondered if you could tell me when Stuart Price will return from London or how I might get hold of him," she said, doing her best to disguise the tone of her voice—and its trembling. She swallowed and went on quickly, "I'm a...a cousin of his."

"Oh, Stuart is already in Johannesburg. He'll be flying one of our planes back to Maseru in three days."

The sense of relief was so heady—both at how forthcoming Diana was and that Stuart was, in fact, back in the country—that Philippa's knees nearly gave way.

"Oh, that's wonderful news," she said, as calmly as she could. "Do you know where he's staying?"

Diana thought for a moment, then said in a tone of regret, "Sorry, I have no idea. I imagine he'd be at a hotel in Germiston since he's got an early start out of Rand Airport."

The moment she put the receiver back, Philippa leapt into action, hurrying back to the Myburghs where she encountered both Matthew and his mother in the sitting room discussing the wine that would be served at the wedding.

"Philippa, is everything all right? You look flustered," Mrs Myburgh remarked, and almost immediately Matthew followed with, "Quite pale, in fact, my darling. I hope you're not coming down with something."

Philippa felt like a deer caught in the headlights. She hadn't prepared for this, but immediately the most convenient lie came to her lips. "I just learned that my great-uncle is very ill in hospital in Johannesburg and not expected to last the week." She fidgeted with her handbag, rushing on to say, "I really want to see him, and I thought...I thought I could go ahead to Johannesburg a couple of days early."

Her desperation not to be thwarted was so intense that Mrs Myburgh's calm acceptance came as such a surprise that, once more, relief nearly made her knees give way while a burst of hope flowered inside her like a ray of sunshine.

There was no objection? From either of them?

She felt something shift inside her. Was she the only one standing between herself and what she, as an independent young woman, wanted to do?

Of course, she should have agreed with Stuart that they could 'thrash it out'—his words—long before this. The truth was, she'd been too afraid to see him again. Whenever she was in his orbit, he made her forget herself.

And why was that so terrible? She straightened her shoulders. It wasn't. In her heart, she knew unequivocally what seeing him would do to her—and suddenly she was glad to give herself up to it.

"Thank you for being so understanding," Philippa said faintly, her mind already racing ahead to their imminent meeting and how she would say all she had to—and all that was in her heart.

Of course, he might not be so jubilant when she told him about the baby.

But then, that would be the test, wouldn't it?

Stuart had said he loved her. His words over the phone had been conflicting but powerful, and she'd held them close to her heart, knowing that as the days passed and her wedding grew nearer, she always had an out if she got cold feet and discovered she couldn't—

That she couldn't love Matthew like she loved Stuart, and that was the most important lesson she needed to learn, wasn't it?

Yes, suddenly she realised that in her heart of hearts, she was never going to marry Matthew.

It was always Stuart.

And although telling Stuart she was pregnant wasn't obviously the best way to announce her change of heart, was it such a bad thing to have it act as a catalyst?

"Leave as soon as you need to, Philippa," said Mrs Myburgh. "I'm very sorry to hear about your great-uncle, but the ticket I gave you is changeable, so Matthew and I will just meet you up there in a few days."

Philippa thanked her, blinking away tears that were real.

In a few days, she'd learn just how much Stuart really loved her. Which meant she doubted Matthew and his mother would be meeting her in Johannesburg after all.

She hurried to her room to pack, while liberation coursed through her.

It was terrifying being pregnant, but she wasn't alone. She had Stuart. And Stuart's love.

And a whole lifetime ahead of her being Stuart's wife.

A LITTLE MORE THAN 48 hours later, Philippa was in the bustling metropolis, sitting in an unexceptional café, having just received the diabolical confirmation of her worst fears.

She'd trawled through the phone book to find a doctor in Germiston because, if the worst came to the worst and she couldn't locate Stuart, at least she'd be able to intercept him when he turned up to fly Drakensberg Air's plane back in two days.

Nervously, she gnawed at her thumbnail while staring blankly at the menu in front of her. Her desperation for a glass of milk—yes, her milk cravings were ridiculous!— meant she'd slipped into the first café she could find. The faded red and white checked curtains blocked out the street and, as she rested her face in her hands, she went over the multiple ways she could convey to Stuart her regrets, her hopes, and her fears.

She'd demolished the eggs and bacon that had been put in front of her, but she was still hungry. The nausea that plagued her mornings had given way to an almost voracious appetite by afternoon.

"Philippa?"

The familiar voice sent her heart into such violent palpitations she nearly knocked over her water glass. When she looked up, Stuart stood beside her table like an answer to her most fervent prayers.

Just seeing him was like a curtain being lifted from in front of her eyes. How handsome he looked with his beautiful blue eyes staring at her as if she was an apparition, his chiselled square jaw and that well-built, athletic body. Just feasting her gaze upon him gave her heart palpitations.

"Stuart!" She clasped her hands to her chest. "I can't believe it! I...I was looking for you, and here you are!"

"You were looking for me?" he repeated, and she noticed that delight had not yet replaced shock.

Nervously, she twisted her hands in her lap. She needed to say this right so that he didn't think she was only prepared to marry him because she was carrying his baby; that it was so much more than that. It was discovering she was pregnant that had opened her eyes to how she'd felt about him all this time.

"Yes, Diana from the office said you were flying one of the planes back from Rand Airport in a few days—"

"And you came all the way from Cape Town looking for me?" The furrow between his brows deepened, but he didn't sit down. Nor did he follow up his question with another, which would have made it easier for her to say the words she wanted to—so badly.

"Aren't you going to ask me why?" she prompted, but to her dismay he shook his head and said, "No, because it's too late—"

"Too late to hear me say I love you?" she burst out, gasping at the shock of his words. But the way he was looking at her didn't match his harsh sentiments, and she drew comfort from what she could see in his eyes: the longing, the acknowledgement of the connection that burnt so fiercely between them that surely neither could deny it.

"Please, Stuart—won't you sit down and talk to me?" She gestured to the chair across from her, trying to keep the pleading from her voice. Was he punishing her? Surely that was not Stuart's way?

He glanced toward the window, then back at her, clearly torn. "I'm meeting someone. They should be here any moment."

But then he lowered himself onto the seat, shaking his head and saying in a low voice, "I must say, your timing leaves something to be desired."

"Stuart, I'm sorry—" She choked on a sob. "I know I was cruel. But I was so confused. Matthew's mother—"

"You never answered my letters. And you refused my phone calls until the last one, when you made your feelings quite clear."

Heat flooded her cheeks. Unconsciously, she pressed her hands against her still-flat stomach. "I've had time to think, and I—"

"Stuart? Stuart Price?"

They both turned as a handsome, well-dressed woman in her mid-thirties, with a dark brown bob and a Roman nose, approached their table, a small boy's hand firmly grasped in hers. Philippa bit back a curse at the interruption, surprised to see how the woman's rather stern features had lit up with genuine delight.

"It *is* you! Mummy will be so delighted!" Turning to Philippa, she introduced herself. "I'm Margaret Franklin, Stuart's adoptive sister for want of a better term. I'm sure Stuart would have mentioned us." She smiled at Stuart as if she truly was a fond and loving sister, and Philippa felt both surprise and something like trepidation as she witnessed the way Stuart's lips pressed together while Margaret went on, for Philippa knew there were things about his past Stuart didn't want to talk about. "Stuart and his sister, Gracie, lived with us during the war—and after, too—though I was at boarding school most of that time."

"I'm...Philippa," Philippa mumbled, omitting her surname, wondering why Stuart looked less delighted to see Margaret than she'd have expected. But then, she supposed he was still digesting Philippa's bombshell opening of her heart. No doubt he wanted Margaret to be gone as much as Philippa did so they could resume their conversation.

"You're looking well, Margaret. And how is...your mother?"

"She's your mother, too," Margaret said, adding for Philippa's benefit, "At least, that's what she's always called herself. Stuart and Gracie's mother." She turned back to Stuart. "Lonely, though, since Daddy died. She'll be so happy to hear you're back in the country. When are you going to see her?"

Stuart looked uncomfortable, ignoring the question to say, "I was sorry not to make it to...your father's funeral."

"Yes, but I understand you were out of the country. He asked for you, even on the day that he died, but we didn't know how to contact you. All our letters to your old address were returned. But what are you doing here? You must come to dinner. I live in Jo'burg now."

Stuart cleared his throat. "Unfortunately, I have to return to Maseru in a couple of days."

"Maseru? What takes you to the back of beyond, then?"

Philippa hesitated. "Stuart flies for Drakensberg Air."

Margaret looked surprised. "Oh!" She looked down at her son. "This is James. He's eight. He wants to be a pilot, too." She smiled, but pressed her lips together as if she were suddenly on shaky ground. "Daddy would have been so proud if he'd known you'd..."

When it seemed she couldn't find the words, Stuart supplied, "Made something of myself?"

But she shook her head, frowning. "Oh, we all knew you would."

Finally, Margaret left with promises to tell her mother where Stuart could be found, and Philippa was trying to gather her courage to press her point, when Stuart leaned forward, his eyes oddly bright. "I'm sorry, Philippa, but you made it quite clear that I was nothing more than a pleasant interlude before you returned to your real life."

Philippa put her hand to her breast, as if to protect her heart from the pain of Stuart's unexpected—

Rejection? No, she had to talk him round. His words didn't accord with the pain written across his face. He did still love her. He did.

"Stuart—"

But before she could answer, another voice interrupted. "Oh! What a lovely surprise! Another who hails from the mountains!"

This time it was Lizzie Cameron. Philippa vaguely remembered the nurse from Maseru. What she hadn't remembered was how pretty she was. She'd always thought her plain in a dumpy, pasty way. But today, she seemed positively radiant.

"Sorry I'm a bit late, Stuart," Lizzie continued after properly greeting Philippa. "I got chatting with my friend Clodagh."

Something in Lizzie's manner—a possessive quality in the way she moved closer to Stuart—set off alarm bells in Philippa's mind. Then she saw it: the small diamond ring catching the light as Lizzie's left hand came to rest on Stuart's shoulder.

The café seemed to tilt around her. "You're engaged?" The words came out as barely a whisper.

Lizzie's smile was incandescent. "Married, actually! Just last week. We're still in that wonderful daze, aren't we, darling?"

The roaring in Philippa's ears nearly drowned out the rest of Lizzie's words. Married. Stuart was married. To this vapid, undeserving creature now flaunting her wedding ring as if she wanted to drive home the fact that she had been victorious when—

Oh, stop it! Philippa screamed to the voice inside her head. She'd brought this on herself, and she had no one else to blame. Stuart was with this no doubt deserving and uncomplicated young woman because Lizzie had had no compunction in accepting an offer made from the heart.

No! Stuart's heart belonged to Philippa. Philippa had claimed it. How could he have married Lizzie so suddenly and without a word to her?

"How wonderful," Philippa managed, the words scraping her throat raw. "Congratulations to you both."

She had to get out of here before she humiliated herself completely. Rising on unsteady legs, she gathered her handbag. "I'm afraid I've just remembered an appointment. So lovely to see you both."

"Philippa, wait—" Stuart half-rose from his chair, but Lizzie's hand on his arm stopped him. "Let me walk you out," he said quietly.

"That's not necessary." She couldn't bear his pity on top of everything else. "I hope you'll both be very happy."

Outside, the Johannesburg afternoon sun felt harsh and unforgiving. Philippa walked blindly up the street, her carefully laid plans crumbling around her. She'd been too late. By mere days, it seemed. Stuart had moved on, found someone who could give him the love he deserved.

And now she was truly alone, with a secret that would have to remain buried and a future that stretched before her like a prison sentence.

She pressed a hand to her stomach, where Stuart's child grew in secret, and tried to imagine a world where she could raise this baby. The scandal would be hugely damaging to her father's career, exile her from everything she'd ever known.

That's if she could even keep the baby. She knew what happened to unmarried mothers. They were shipped off to institutions, their infants removed from them the moment they were born.

Lowering her head against the wind, she continued to walk, heedless of where she was going.

What could she do? What could she do? Stuart was married. Stuart was out of reach. How could she tell him now?

But keeping such a secret felt like a betrayal of the tiny life inside her—and of the man who would never know he was going to be a father.

TWENTY-EIGHT

The nurse behind the reception desk looked up as Philippa entered. With her starched white uniform, greying hair swept into a neat chignon, and the fine lines that crinkled at the corners of her eyes when she smiled, she exuded just the kind of reassuring comfort the doctor had not.

"Back so soon, miss?" she asked. "Did you forget something?"

"I need to see Dr Van Der Merwe again," Philippa said, her voice trembling so much she could barely push out the words.

"I'm afraid the doctor has no more available appointments today," the nurse said, consulting the appointment book in front of her. But then her brow cleared, and she looked up as a patient passed through the waiting room. "Actually, I've just remembered that Dr Van Der Merwe's four o'clock has cancelled. Would you like to go in now, Miss Brown?"

If Philippa had been hoping for compassion from the doctor who'd confirmed her pregnancy only hours earlier, she was bitterly disappointed. Dr Van Der Merwe was a thin, austere man with silver hair slicked back with pomade and pale eyes that seemed to look right through her.

She had barely begun to stammer her desperate question when he raised his hand to cut her off.

"Young lady, I am a physician, bound by the Hippocratic Oath to do no harm. What you're asking is not only illegal under the laws of this country, it is morally reprehensible." His Afrikaans accent lent weight to each condemning word. "I will not compromise my professional standing or my soul for the convenience of wayward girls who find themselves in predicaments of their own making." He leaned back in his leather chair, his expression carved from granite. "You made your choice when you conducted yourself without regard for propriety or consequence. Now you must live with the result."

His dismissal was a cruel, visceral shock. She had expected refusal, perhaps even judgment, but not such condemnation. Stumbling from his consulting room, she had to grip the reception desk on her way out to steady herself as the room seemed to tilt around her.

"Miss, are you quite well? Would you like to sit down?"

Initially, Philippa tried to wave away the nurse's concern, but the woman's gentle touch on her elbow and the genuine worry in her voice nearly undid her completely.

"Is someone collecting you, dear?" the nurse asked, guiding Philippa to a chair in the corner. "Your mother, perhaps?"

"She's dead." The words came out flat, drained of emotion.

The nurse's expression softened further. She excused herself briefly to settle the next patient in Dr Van Der Merwe's office, then returned. "Perhaps a cup of tea while you gather yourself," she suggested. "Come along."

Sister Margaret—the name embroidered on her uniform badge—led Philippa down a narrow corridor to a small staff room. The space was cramped but spotless, with a tiny electric kettle on a corner table and two mismatched chairs that had seen better days. Filling the kettle, Sister Margaret fetched proper china cups and saucers from a cabinet, then measured the tea leaves with the sort of maternal care that made Philippa's chest ache with longing.

When the nurse finally sat down across from her, cradling her own cup, her gaze was direct but not unkind.

"I know what you asked the doctor," she said quietly. "And I can see from your face how he responded."

Philippa's composure crumbled. "I don't know what to do. I truly don't know where to turn."

"The father—is he not able to help?"

"He's married. To someone else." The admission felt like swallowing glass.

Sister Margaret nodded slowly, unsurprised. "I see. And your family?"

"My father—" Philippa's voice caught. "It would destroy everything he's worked for. He's a respected man, and I'm his only daughter. The scandal would ruin him professionally, socially. I'm engaged to be married, but if this comes out..." She pressed her hands to her face. "I've considered adoption, but that means months in a home for unmarried mothers. The shame would follow me forever."

The sobs came then, great shuddering waves that seemed to tear from somewhere deep inside her chest. When she finally looked up, Sister Margaret was holding out a folded piece of paper.

"There's a woman named Mrs Simmons," she said carefully. "Discreet. Professional. She'll listen to you. You can't rush into something like this unless you've exhausted all options. But she will be able to help you—whatever you decide."

Philippa took the paper with trembling fingers. "I don't have much money. What would something like this cost? I have to do this. I have no choice."

When Sister Margaret named the figure, Philippa felt the blood drain from her face. It was an impossible sum.

"I could never raise that amount. And I have to return to Cape Town in a few days." Panic clawed at her throat. "There's nothing I can do. Nothing."

Sister Margaret glanced toward the door, then leaned forward and pressed a second piece of paper into Philippa's hand.

"Mrs Thompson," she said in a voice barely above a whisper. "She charges less than half of Mrs Simmons' fee, but..." She paused, choosing her words carefully. "The conditions are more... modest. The risks are correspondingly higher. But she's helped other young women in circumstances similar to yours."

She squeezed Philippa's hand briefly. "I trust you'll keep this conversation between us. If it became known that I'd provided such information, I would face immediate dismissal and possible criminal charges. But I've watched too many lives destroyed by situations beyond a woman's control to stand by and do nothing."

Philippa clutched the papers as if they were lifelines thrown to a drowning woman, which, she supposed, they were.

CHAPTER

TWENTY-NINE

STUART HAD PLEADED A HEADACHE AFTER HE AND LIZZIE HAD LEFT the cafe.

While she'd clucked sympathetically, and said she wasn't surprised since he'd done such a tremendous job with all that driving around the country, he'd remained distant and uncommunicative.

And the next day was no better; so he completely understood Lizzie's worried glances and hated the fact he was the cause of them.

Why now? The question chased itself around his head. Why had Philippa suddenly and unexpectedly sought him out with no warning? It didn't make sense.

But then again, Philippa was like a wil o' the wisp, darting wherever her fancy took her. She'd probably had a tiff with Matthew, jumped on a train, and thought that a weekend with Stuart would salve her hurt feelings before she returned to Matthew in Cape Town in time for the wedding.

No, the fact that Stuart was married made no difference to how he ought to be feeling about her bombshell declaration of love. He was simply lucky that he had a defence against Philippa's seductive, dangerous allure so that he wasn't drawn back into the same destructive, painful attraction he felt for her that never—and, now, *could* never—go anywhere.

Lizzie—the lovely, kind-hearted, generous creature who was his wife—ought to make him feel the luckiest man in the world.

So, now it was time to atone. Standing by the door to their hotel room, he dragged in a breath, offered her a smile, and said, "Would you like to meet me for lunch at that cafe just round the corner after I've run a few errands for Dan?"

She thawed immediately. As he knew she would. "Oh yes, please!"

Her smile was radiant, sending guilt shooting through him. In his pocket was his father's silver fob watch. It ought to fetch a bit. Enough for a nice late wedding present, he hoped.

Lizzie deserved far more than he could give her, but whatever money he could make from the sale of the watch would be a start.

⁂

THE BELL above the door gave a sickly chime as Stuart stepped into Goldstein's Pawnbrokers, squinting as his eyes adjusted from the harsh Johannesburg sunlight to the shop's dim interior.

He sniffed. The place reeked of desperation. Dusty musical instruments hung from the ceiling, and jewellery glittered forlornly behind smudged glass cases.

As far as Stuart's inheritance went, the old fob watch in

his pocket was really his father's only possession of any value. Distrusting lawyers and accountants, the old man had died intestate. Stuart doubted there'd be much from his meagre estate anyway, and even if there was, it would be tied up in probate for months.

Lizzie had mentioned a leather handbag in Stuttaford's window—crocodile skin with an elegant handle. She deserved so much more but he could manage that much, at least. He might suggest a shopping trip later so she could choose it.

Approaching the counter, he heard a customer already in negotiations with the pawnbroker—the trade seemingly not going the young lady's way.

"I'll give you fifteen pounds for it, no more," came the pawnbroker's nasal voice from behind the counter. "Take it or leave it, miss. I've got bills to pay same as everyone else."

"But it's worth at least two hundred!"

Stuart froze. He'd recognise that voice anywhere—cultured and light, but now edged with desperation, trying so hard to sound composed. He'd heard it only yesterday—telling him what was in her heart.

When it was already too late, he thought bitterly.

He took a few steps forward to peer past a stuffed bear holding a ukulele.

"It's been in my family for generations," Philippa was saying, her back to him as she leaned over the counter, her shoulders rigid with tension. The diamonds alone—"

"Diamonds?" The pawnbroker—a thin man with suspicious eyes and stained fingers—picked up a jeweller's loupe. "These are paste, love. Pretty paste, I'll grant you, but paste nonetheless."

Stuart watched as Philippa reached for the ring the man held dismissively between thumb and forefinger, and something twisted in his gut. What was she doing here?

"That can't be right," she whispered, her voice breaking slightly. "My grandmother always said—"

"Your grandmother was having you on, or someone had her on first." The pawnbroker shrugged. "Fifteen pounds. Final offer."

Stuart pushed past the stuffed bear and went up to the counter. "There's nothing paste about that stone," he said, fixing the pawnbroker with a combative glare.

"Stuart!" His name escaped her lips in a gasp that held both relief and mortification. This wasn't the kind of establishment where someone like Philippa should find herself, and they both knew it.

"I know a good diamond when I see one." It was easy bluster—he'd have said anything to rescue her from this sordid transaction. He nearly placed a protective hand on her shoulder before catching himself. Even now, married to another woman, touching Philippa felt like lighting a fuse. "Come, I know somewhere they'll give you a fair price."

She looked paler than he remembered, violet shadows smudging her eyes like bruises, but she followed him with the docility of someone who'd exhausted all other options while he wondered why she was so desperate for money when she was about to marry the son of one of the richest men in Cape Town.

"You won't get a better offer than fifteen!" the pawnbroker shouted after them, his voice echoing off the grimy windows. "That's my final offer!"

But Botha's Exchange, three doors down, proved just as heartless. Their proprietor examined the ring before delivering his verdict with something close to satisfaction.

"See here," he said, breathing on the stone before

holding it under his loupe. "Real diamond would clear immediately. This stays fogged." He scratched it with a steel file, creating tiny glass particles that glittered mockingly in the afternoon light. "Weight's wrong too. Pretty piece of work, mind you. Whoever made this knew their business. But it's paste, sure as I'm standing here."

"I thought you said you recognised a good diamond?" Philippa whispered to Stuart, her voice hollow.

Stuart felt heat rise in his cheeks. "I have no idea, actually. I just didn't want to see you robbed."

"Except it seems my grandmother was the one who was deceived." She stared at the ring as if it had personally betrayed her. "All these years, thinking it was valuable..."

"Not interested, then?" Mr Botha called after them as Philippa led the way to the door. "All right, I'll give you fifteen!"

Stuart expected her to walk away—surely fifteen pounds wasn't worth salvaging her pride?—but Philippa hesitated at the door.

"You're not seriously considering giving it away for that price?" he asked. "It has sentimental value, doesn't it?"

"Sentiment won't help me as much as fifteen pounds," she said, and the flatness in her voice alarmed him more than tears would have. She looked as if she were about to step away from him, out of the shop and into the street, but his hand on her shoulder stopped her.

He felt her flinch. And then almost immediately lean into him before she took a quick step backwards.

"Philippa, what's happened?" He hesitated as he studied her face, seeing past the careful composure to the desperation beneath. The shadows under her eyes weren't just from sleeplessness. "What's so urgent that you'd sell your grandmother's ring to these... vultures?" He hesitated, trying to hide the bitterness in his tone as he added, "If you're that desperate, why not pawn the engagement ring Matthew gave you?"

She wrapped her arms around herself and stared at the wall. Anywhere, it seemed, than at him. "It's being resized in Cape Town."

"Why don't you just ask Matthew for money?" Stuart persisted.

"I can't... Stuart, please. Just go away and forget you saw me here."

"You know I can't do that!" The vehemence in his voice startled them both. He was married now, to a sweet woman who trusted him completely. Philippa's problems should no longer be his concern. But he understood Philippa far more deeply than he understood Lizzie, and every instinct screamed that this was more than just a tiff with Matthew.

"Has Matthew hurt you?" he pressed.

Her laugh held no humour. "No."

"Then what—"

"Leave it alone, Stuart." She turned back towards the counter, her expression bleak. The pawnbroker was out of hearing, polishing a ship's bell. "You're married now. To a woman who deserves better than a husband who entangles himself in other women's troubles."

The words hit him like a slap, not because they weren't true, but because they were devastatingly accurate. What was he doing? Lizzie was waiting at their hotel, probably getting ready to meet him at the cafe. He'd promised himself to be the husband she deserved.

But as he really looked at Philippa, he saw the haunted quality in her eyes. This wasn't ordinary desperation. This was the look of someone cornered, with no way out.

Despite everything—his marriage, her previous rejection, all the rational reasons to walk away—Stuart heard himself say, "Tell me what you need, Philippa. Whatever it is, I will do what I can to help you."

She stared at him for a long moment, her violet eyes swimming with unshed tears. When she finally spoke, her composure cracked as she sagged against the wall, dropping the ring that clattered to the floor.

"I'm...pregnant."

The simple statement was like a fault line cracking through the foundation of his world. The pawnshop seemed to tilt around him, dust motes dancing in the afternoon light like tiny witnesses to the moment his world shifted on its axis. "What?"

"I'm pregnant," she repeated, her voice barely audible above the street noise. "And before you ask—yes, it's yours."

"Mine." His voice sounded foreign to his own ears. He didn't have to spend a second trying to recall the occasion. The joy of being wrapped in each other's arms was constantly with him. As was the pain of parting. "Your birthday."

She nodded, pulling her arms tighter around herself as if she could hold the pieces of her life together through will alone. "I thought... I hoped it might resolve itself naturally. Sometimes it does in the early weeks. But it hasn't, and now..." Her voice broke. "I'm running out of time."

"Time for what?" But even as he asked, understanding crashed over him like a cold wave. The desperation, the pawnshop, the terrible finality in her voice. "Philippa, no."

"I don't have a choice!" The words burst out of her. "Do you think I want this? Do you think I planned it?" She was shaking now, her mask of composure finally shattering. "I'm twenty-one, unmarried, and my father has an important, public position. The scandal wouldn't just devastate him—it would do great harm to his career. And me…" Her voice dropped to a whisper. "It would break his heart. After losing my mother, to lose me too, to shame…"

Stuart bent to retrieve the ring, his mind reeling. A baby. His baby. The family and loving connection he'd dreamed of during those lonely nights in Lesotho. And she was talking about…

"There has to be another way," he said roughly, gripping the ring so tightly it bit into his palm. "Adoption. There are places—"

"Where?" Her laugh was bitter. "Do you think I haven't considered every possibility? Even if I could hide a pregnancy—which I can't, not for much longer—where would I go? Who would take me in without questions? The gossip would reach my father within days, and Matthew…" She closed her eyes.

The brutal logic of her situation settled around Stuart like a shroud. In their insular colonial world, secrets were impossible. Such a scandal would indeed impact Charles Tremain's career and exile Philippa from everything she'd ever known.

Stuart's mind raced through alternatives, each more impossible than the last. Marriage—but he'd destroyed that option in a moment of desperate loneliness. He could…

"What about going through with your marriage to Matthew?" The words tasted like poison, but desperation made him voice the unthinkable. "If you… if you convinced him…"

Philippa's eyes snapped open, filled with such anguish it nearly broke him. "He's made a point of 'preserving my purity for marriage,' " she said, her voice hollow. "He'd know immediately that the child wasn't his."

Of course. Stuart closed his eyes, remembering their nights together—the only times Philippa had ever... The weight of responsibility crushed down on him.

"The money from the ring—" He wasn't sure how to phrase the question.

She looked away, unable to meet his eyes. "There's a woman. Mrs Thompson. The nurse at the doctor's rooms gave it to me. She said she'd help me."

"Philippa—"

"Don't." She held up a trembling hand. "Don't make this harder than it already is. I've considered every angle, every possibility. There's no other way."

"There's always another way." But the words sounded hollow even to him. In 1962, for a woman in her position, the choices were brutal and few.

"Is there?" She finally looked at him again, and the raw desperation in her eyes nearly brought him to his knees. "Because I've been searching very hard, and this is all I can find. Unless you have a miracle hidden somewhere?"

He didn't. They both knew he didn't. The social conventions that governed their world were as rigid as iron bars, and having a child out of wedlock was a transgression that destroyed everything it touched.

"When?" The word scraped his throat raw.

"Tomorrow afternoon. That's if I can find the money in time." Her voice had regained some steadiness, as if speaking the words aloud had given them terrible finality.

Stuart stared at the ring in his palm—a beautiful deception, just like the careful life Philippa had built around herself. "And if you can't get it?"

Time was slipping away. Lizzie would be wondering where he was, and lying to her felt like another betrayal in an already impossible situation. But looking at Philippa—

seeing the woman he loved facing the destruction of everything that mattered to her—he knew he'd move heaven and earth to help her.

Even if it damned him.

"I'll take the fifteen pounds and find someone cheaper." Her breath hitched.

Stuart's mind flew to Gracie—sweet, lost Gracie, who'd faced the same impossible choice and paid the ultimate price. He'd failed his sister when she needed him most, driven by judgment instead of love.

He wouldn't fail Philippa too.

"Come with me," he said, pressing the ring back into her hands. "I think I can help you."

The hope that flickered in her eyes was worth whatever price he'd have to pay.

THIRTY

MIND RACING, STUART LED PHILIPPA ALONG THE BUSTLING Johannesburg street.

"Where are we going?"

"Looking for a tickey box." Stuart turned, Philippa's lost yet hopeful look making it difficult to sound dispassionate. "I'm supposed to be meeting Lizzie for lunch in half an hour. I'll phone reception so she gets the message before she leaves."

"Oh." She followed him, silent until he completed his mission, before asking, "Now what?" as he emerged onto the street.

"A taxi to Rand Airport," Stuart replied, just as one pulled over to the kerb the moment he raised his arm. "Tomorrow I'm supposed to fly one of Drakensberg Air's Cessna back to Maseru. It's been down for maintenance, and…" He helped her into the cab, his mind working furiously. He had half a plan but as to how the rest might unfold, he had no idea. "Mrs Oosthuizen—yes, one of your parents' old family friends and the district's more… eccentric residents—put in an order for fresh flowers for a garden party she's having on Saturday."

"You want me to help you choose flowers?" Philippa's puzzled frown and her tone of voice suggested neither mockery nor dismay. She seemed too dazed to be able to respond with much clarity to anything.

"She's chartered the plane to bring up all the flowers it can fit and has forwarded her order to her favourite florist in Johannesburg. There should be an envelope of money tucked in the plane's console for the purchase."

Philippa turned to stare at him. "You're going to steal it?" she gasped.

"Borrow," Stuart corrected, though the distinction felt thin. "I'll give you the money and then ask the florist to put it on tick."

"How—?"

"I have no idea and... one thing at a time. You'll leave Rand with the money you need, and I'll be as persuasive as I can when it comes to the florist."

"But how will you replace the money? Oh, Stuart!" Philippa put her face in her hands."

"I can sell my watch, my camera. I have a few other things, too." He leaned forward to brief the driver, who looked like he was suddenly heading away from the airport in Germiston, then settled back, trying to project a confidence he didn't feel. "Mrs Oosthuizen would want only the best for you and your family—though of course she'll never know the truth."

He shuddered at the irony. Barely two weeks into marriage, he was already planning to steal for another woman. How his father would laugh. No. He'd mock and say those terrible words that had haunted him since he'd been a child: *The apple doesn't fall far from the tree.*

But as he drank in Philippa's beautiful profile as she stared out of the taxi window, he knew he'd rob the Bank of England if it would help her. And dear God—he was the one who had put her in this position.

They were silent as the taxi wound through the industrial outskirts of Johannesburg.

Finally, she said, "Stuart, I can't let you do this. If you're caught—"

"I won't be caught," he said with more conviction than he felt. "And even if I were, it's just money. Mrs Oosthuizen has plenty of it."

"That's not what you really think, though, is it? You're making light of it...for me. This could jeopardise your job. Your reputation." She turned to face him fully. "Your marriage." Then she shrugged, looked at her clasped hands in her lap and whispered, "Though I don't care about that. I wanted you to marry me."

It was hard to respond due to the roar in his ears. "Not now, Philippa," he managed, and with a half sob, she threw herself against the side of the taxi to rest her cheek against the window.

"Sorry. That was unfair," she gulped. "I should never have told you. This isn't your responsibility."

"Isn't it?" Stuart heard the roughness in his voice. "It's my child too, Philippa. Do you think I could live with myself knowing I let you face this alone?"

The taxi pulled up to the airport gates, and Stuart paid the driver, then helped Philippa out. "There she is," he said, pointing to the small plane in the distance as they began to walk across the tarmac.

Before he reached the Cessna, he was waylaid by a couple of mechanics who were concerned that he was here to pick up the plane when they'd not yet started the maintenance work. Stuart assured them he only needed some-thing from inside and would be back tomorrow.

So they left him alone, and he climbed into the cockpit, locating the envelope, tucked into the console exactly where Dan had said it would be.

Feeling sick with relief and disgust in equal measure, he jumped down onto the tarmac. "I told Lizzie on the phone there was a change of plan and I'd pick up the money now as the maintenance guys wanted to talk to me about some problem," he said, as he counted the crisp notes before handing them to her. "Looks like Mrs Oosthuizen's obsession with exotic blooms is going to save us both."

"Stuart? Stuart Price, as I live and breathe!"

The jovial voice from the other side of the plane made Stuart's blood freeze. He knew that accent—Afrikaans, tinged with the particular smugness that came from getting away with something. Flicking Philippa a worried look, he waited for Piet van Wyk to appear.

Piet had transformed himself from the farm mechanic Stuart remembered. Gone were the oil-stained work clothes and scuffed boots. Now he wore a sharply tailored charcoal suit, crisp white shirt set off by a burgundy silk tie, and black Oxford brogues.

His once lank, oily hair had been slicked back with pomade in the Continental style favoured by successful Afrikaner businessmen. But it was the accessories that really sold the performance: a leather briefcase that looked both expensive and well-used, the kind a man might carry to important meetings with mining executives, gold cuff-links, and a cigarette case that protruded from his breast pocket.

The only thing that hadn't changed was the look in his pale grey eyes, which were predatory, watchful, his smile too calculated, the confidence just a shade too aggressive. To someone who knew what to look for, Piet van Wyk still looked exactly like what he had proved himself to be last time: a very dangerous man. This time, he was a very dangerous man wearing a very expensive costume.

"What brings you to Johannesburg, Captain?" Piet's gaze flicked to Philippa, who stood frozen a little behind Stuart. "Business or pleasure?"

Stuart forced his voice to remain steady. "Picking up the plane. Maintenance check."

"*Ja*, I can see that." Piet's smile was wolfish. "But that doesn't explain the lovely company." He offered Philippa an exaggerated bow, taking her hand briefly, and saying as he rose, "I believe congratulations are in order, Miss Tremain. Great things have happened since I last saw you. Word is that you're marrying into Cape Town royalty."

Philippa pulled away. The threat was subtle but unmistakable. She clearly understood that Piet's appearance had just complicated everything exponentially.

"What are you doing here, van Wyk?"

Piet laughed. "Straight to business. I like that!" He glanced around the hangar, as if to check the mechanics were out of earshot. "Actually, I was hoping to run into you. Funny how fate works, hey?" With a smile at Philippa, he asked with exaggerated courtesy, "I wonder if the young lady would allow us men a moment to discuss a little business matter?"

Stuart's jaw tightened. "I'm not interested in whatever scheme you're running."

"Scheme?" Piet looked wounded. "Captain Price, you cut me to the quick. I'm a legitimate businessman these days. Diamond buying, all above board." He leaned closer, his voice dropping to a conspiratorial whisper. "Well, mostly aboveboard. And that's where you come in."

From the corner of his eye, Stuart saw Philippa take a step deeper into the shadows of the hangar. She looked frightened.

"I need transport back to Lesotho," Piet continued conversationally. "And not just to Maseru—all the way up to Letseng-la-Terai. There's a miner there I met last time you were so obliging as to fly me. Tumelo and I had a good old yarn, and he was very grateful when I told him I could take a stone that one of his cronies had found, down the mountain and save him the trouble...for a good price of course. Turns out, old Tumelo, himself, has now found something special. Something that requires... immediate attention."

"Find another pilot."

Piet's smile widened. "But you see, I need a pilot with discretion. Someone who understands the value of keeping certain things quiet." His gaze flicked meaningfully toward Philippa. "Someone who might have secrets of his own to protect."

Stuart already knew the pieces had fallen into place the moment Piet had seen him with Philippa. Piet had also, quite likely, seen him handing her the banknotes.

He could almost hear his dad's maniacal laugh in whatever unearthly place he occupied now. Stuart couldn't have made a worse job of trying to do the right thing by doing the wrong thing, even if he tried.

And Piet couldn't have stumbled upon a better time to waylay a pilot who already was compromised.

But who was now married, alone with a beautiful woman who was not his wife. A woman on the cusp of her own society wedding—yet who clearly needed money urgently. It all painted a picture that could destroy Philippa's future as well as Stuart's marriage and career with a few well-placed words.

If he could have just turned on his heel, and ushered Philippa away, with an unequivocal rebuff of Piet's request, he would have.

Instead, he said, his voice too low for Philippa to hear, "What *exactly* are you proposing?" Though he already knew he wouldn't like the answer.

"Simple business transaction. You give me a ride to the diamond fields, I help you with whatever financial difficulty has brought you here." Piet's eyes glittered with malicious satisfaction. "Everyone wins."

Stuart felt the walls closing in. Refuse, knowing Piet had the capacity to see Stuart and Philippa lose everything. Accept, and compromise everything he believed in.

But as he looked at Philippa, and saw the fear and desperation she was trying so hard to hide, Stuart realised he didn't have a choice.

"I don't want your money. But I'm leaving in the morning. First thing," he heard himself say.

Piet's grin was triumphant. "Tomorrow is it, Captain. I'll be waiting. *Baie dankie!*"

"Oh, Stuart!" Philippa was at his side the moment the Afrikaner had left. "What did he say?" She gripped his arm. "I recognised him. It was one of the van Wyk brothers, wasn't it?" She watched as the Afrikaner sauntered away. "The not-so-nice one." There was a quaver in her voice.

"Yes, the not-so-nice one," Stuart confirmed.

THIRTY-ONE

"I'M SO SORRY I'M LATE, DARLING," STUART SAID. "I WAS HELD UP by the traffic, but I thought that if you went ahead to the florist with the list for Mrs Oosthuizen, I could catch up with you and then we'd have a something to eat. You must be starving."

The lie did not sit well with Stuart, but he was out of options. And fortunately, Lizzie was pliant and unquestioning. He hated that this worked in his favour.

"The cafe around the corner?" she asked, taking the envelope Stuart handed her. It was only a fraction of the amount needed to pay the florist for Mrs Oosthuizen's order, but he had the workings of a plan.

"No, let's make it a proper lunch." He smiled, opening his suitcase to find his camera. If he could make her feel special, it would be one small victory. But guilt curdled in his belly. "Let's walk there now, and you can look at the menu while I nip around the corner to pick up a few of the things Dan asked for."

Really, he had to nip around the corner to Botha's Exchange where he'd take whatever he could get for his camera and his father's watch in order to try to make up the shortfall to give the florist. Mrs Oosthuizen's order had been eye-watering, which had had its benefits in the short term—

"And then we buy Mrs Oosthuizen's flowers, or do we do that tomorrow morning before we fly?"

"No time in the morning. We'll buy them this afternoon and take them to the airport, where we'll get them put in buckets of water ready for the flight back. For a while, you can feast your olfactory senses on the best blooms Johannesburg has to offer." He squeezed her hand as they set off to the restaurant, where he settled her before heading off to do his errand.

Returning ten minutes later, he sat down opposite Lizzie and smiled. There was slight relief in feeling he hadn't been completely cheated on the price of his Leica camera. Then, after a reasonably substantial meal of beef stroganoff and apple strudel, they set off to visit Blooms & Botanicals, presenting the proprietor with Mrs Oosthuizen's lengthy list of demands.

It took a while for the blooms to be cut and prepared in water ready for the trip into the mountains the following day, by which time it was nearly closing hour.

"Thank you so much for your help," Stuart said, handing the proprietress the envelope, depleted by what he'd given Philippa but now augmented by the proceeds of his camera sale, and adding, "Please count it. Mrs Oosthuizen gave me this just as I was leaving, so I hope everything is in order."

The profusion of proteas, bird of paradise, and white orchids was now in the hands of Mrs Van Der Merwe's helpers, two young Zulu girls who were about to follow Stuart and Lizzie out onto the street to catch a taxi.

Stuart's smile was bland, but he managed to inject it with a touch of surprise when Mrs Van Der Merwe said, with a tone of slight embarrassment, "I think there's been a bit of a misunderstanding. The amount here doesn't cover the blooms I've given you."

He saw Lizzie blush before he said, "Oh dear, I shall have to give you back whatever flowers are necessary."

"No, no, of course not! I normally don't extend credit, but Mrs Oosthuizen is a loyal client. I will let her know how much the shortfall is."

"That's fine, just write it down for me," Stuart said quickly. "I'll be back in a few days and can bring you the cash."

"That was an embarrassing situation for Mrs Oosthuizen to put you in," Lizzie remarked as they headed to Rand Airport in the back of a taxi. "But, oh my goodness, how lucky there are only the two of us since the flowers will fill up the back seat."

Stuart nodded. "Mrs Oosthuizen is obviously a good customer. She'll make up the shortfall straight away, so no harm done," Stuart said, his first thought being that the flowers offered an opportunity to deny Piet passage to Lesotho. Then he realised Piet might be safer where Stuart could monitor him rather than operating independently. And the flowers might well provide an opportunity to screen their passenger when they arrived in Mokhotlong—if Charles Tremain was at the bottom of the garden when they landed.

Anxiety tightened in Stuart's chest as he watched the suburbs flash past the taxi window.

When they reached the airport, Lizzie turned to him with one of her radiant smiles. "Thank you for lunch, Stuart. And getting the flowers... It was such fun!"

Fun? He'd never felt more conflicted and on the back foot in his life. Nevertheless, he managed, "You're welcome," as he helped her from the taxi and then the airport workers relieved them of the fragrant cargo after instructions regarding its care.

Tomorrow, he thought, as they returned to the taxi to take them back into town, this would all be over.

CHAPTER
THIRTY-TWO

It had taken a long time before Philippa finally slept, the envelope of money tucked beneath her pillow. She'd counted the notes three times, enough to pay Mrs Thompson and still have something left over—though for what, she couldn't imagine. A future seemed an impossible luxury now.

The light tapping at her door pulled her from lost dreams of mountain peaks and the sound of aircraft engines. She wrapped her silk dressing gown around herself, noting absently that her hands no longer trembled. Perhaps there was peace to be found in having made an irreversible decision.

"Who is it?" she called, though her heart already knew.

"It's Stuart."

The sound of his name in his own voice made her pulse leap so violently she had to grip the door frame for support. She threw it open, drinking in the sight of him—rumpled white shirt, jacket slung over one shoulder, dirty blonde hair falling across his forehead in the way that made her fingers itch to smooth it back.

For one wild moment, she almost threw herself into his arms until she saw his expression. Careful. Guarded. The look of a man who'd already said goodbye.

"Lizzie's still sleeping," he said, his voice carefully neutral. "I walked here. I wanted to—" He stopped, seeming to search for words. "I needed to see you. Before..."

Before he left with his wife. Before she kept her appointment with Mrs Thompson. Before their lives diverged forever onto paths that would never cross again.

"Come in," she whispered, stepping back to let him enter her small hotel room. The space felt even smaller with him in it, charged with the electricity that always sparked between them.

He stood in the centre of the carpet, hands thrust deep in his pockets, looking everywhere but at her. "I wanted to make sure you had everything you needed. That you'd be... safe. That this woman is trustworthy."

The concern in his voice nearly undid her. How was she supposed to let him go when he looked at her like that? When every instinct screamed that they belonged together?

"I have all the money I need," she said, touching the envelope in her pocket. "Thank you. I know what it cost you to get it."

"Not just the money." His eyes finally met hers, dark with an emotion she couldn't name. "Are you certain this is what you want?"

The question hung between them like a bridge she was afraid to cross. What she wanted was to rewind time, to make different choices, to find a world where loving him didn't require destroying everything else. But that world didn't exist.

"What I want is impossible," she whispered. "This is what's necessary."

Stuart's jaw tightened. "Philippa—"

"Matthew called last night," she interrupted, unable to bear hearing him try to talk her out of a decision that was already breaking her heart. "I think I told you he'd planned a trip to England to see his grandfather. Apparently, the old man is dying. He's leaving his entire estate to Matthew."

Stuart went still. "And?"

"Matthew wants us to live in England now. London. He says we could have the life my mother gave up when she married my father." The words tasted like ashes. "Isn't that ironic? I could finally have everything I thought I wanted."

"Could have?" Stuart's voice was carefully controlled. "You mean you will have. Once you... once this is behind you."

"Yes." But even as she said it, she knew it was a lie. How could she marry Matthew now, knowing what actual love felt like? How could she pretend to be happy when her heart would always belong to the man standing three feet away from her, close enough to touch but impossibly out of reach?

"How neat," Stuart said, his tone bitter. "You can have the life your mother abandoned. The grand house, the society connections, the money. Yes... Everything you've always wanted."

The accusation in his voice made her flinch. "Yes, that's what I thought I wanted." She paused, her throat tight with unshed tears. "Before I met you."

He shook his head, taking a step back as if she'd struck him. "Before you realised you couldn't have me. I think you're missing the difference, Philippa. It's safe to say these things when I'm a married man and marrying me isn't possible."

Philippa flinched. "That's not fair."

"Isn't it?" His control was slipping. "You made your choice, Philippa. You chose Matthew and his money and his family's position. I was just… what? A fun little fling before you settled down to serious business?"

Hot tears stung her eyes as something fierce and desperate rose in her chest. "That's not true," she said, closing the distance between them before he could retreat further. "I'd marry you tomorrow if it were possible. I'd give up England and the money and all those things I thought I wanted if I could only be with you."

His hands came up to grip her shoulders, whether to push her away or pull her closer, she couldn't tell. "But it's not possible, Philippa. I'm married. To a good woman who doesn't deserve—"

"I know," she whispered, reaching up to cup his face in her hands. "I know all of that. But I also know that I love you. I love you more than I've ever loved anything or anyone, and I can't let you go without telling you that. Even if it doesn't change anything. Even if it only makes this harder."

For a moment they stood frozen, her confession hanging between them. Then Stuart's careful control finally shattered.

"God, Philippa," he breathed, and then his mouth was on hers, desperate and hungry and full of everything they'd never been able to say. She melted into him, her hands fisting in his shirt, trying to memorise the taste of him, the feel of his arms around her, the way her heart seemed to restart whenever he touched her.

When they finally broke apart, both breathing hard, Stuart rested his forehead against hers. "This doesn't change anything," he said, but his voice lacked conviction.

"I know." Her fingers traced the sharp line of his jaw,

cataloging every detail for the lonely years ahead. "But I needed you to know. I needed you to understand that if I could choose differently—if there were any other way—"

"I've made my vows to Lizzie. There *is* no other way." His words were barely a whisper, but they fell between them with the finality of a closing door.

"No," she agreed, though it felt like agreeing to her own execution. "There is no other way."

He pulled back, his hands dropping to his sides, and she saw him rebuilding his walls in real time. The careful pilot, the dutiful husband, the honourable man who would do the right thing even if it destroyed him.

"I should go," he said. "I left Lizzie asleep. I need to get back before she notices I'm gone."

Philippa nodded, not trusting her voice. She watched him walk to the door, her heart breaking with each step that took him further away.

At the threshold, he turned back. "If you need anything —anything at all—"

"I know," she said. "But I won't. After today, I know we can't..."

"No," he agreed. "We can't."

The door closed behind him with a soft click that sounded like the end of everything. Philippa sank onto the bed, the envelope of money staring accusingly at her, and finally let herself cry for all the futures they would never have.

THIRTY-THREE

MASERU

Stuart and Lizzie were back in Maseru before lunchtime the following day, the flight from Johannesburg passing in strained silence, Piet sitting in the back. Gloating. Deadly.

At breakfast, Lizzie had been strangely withdrawn and it had taken all Stuart's courage to ask her if anything was wrong.

Had she known he'd left her for an hour in the middle of the night? Had she—God forbid—smelt Chanel No. 5 on his shirt collar?

But she'd maintained she simply had a headache. And each time Stuart had tried to make conversation since, her responses had been clipped. Not that he'd been much better, he was so distracted and filled with self-disgust at what Philippa was going to do—because of him.

Finally, both had given up, staring out at the passing landscape with hurt confusion.

Their parting in the car had been strained, Lizzie's kiss no more than a peck on the cheek before Stuart watched her walk towards the administration building to report for work, bumping into Charles's secretary, Marjorie, at the gate.

Stuart had overheard the exchange, Lizzie claiming to have enjoyed her holiday, omitting mention of her marriage which they'd decided they'd still keep secret because of the Foreign Service marriage bar which made dismissal possible if word got out that she and Stuart had tied the knot.

Of course, it would have to come out eventually when it was discovered that Lizzie had moved into Mrs Henderson's Lodging House with Stuart. But a couple more stints at the vaccination clinic would give her a taste of the adventure she craved.

And to be perfectly honest, they needed the money.

Now, standing at the bar in Lancers, berating himself for the relief he felt that Lizzie would be away for the week in Mapolaneng, fear of what Piet would require of him to keep his silence weighed Stuart's shoulders down.

He'd charmed Mrs Oosthuizen's florist into extending credit—apparently his father's gift for deception ran in the blood after all. But that minor victory felt hollow.

That gave him a few days to come up with the shortfall. But, by God, whatever Piet wanted, the trade would not involve Stuart taking his money.

It had been a relief to overhear Marjorie say that Charles Tremain himself would take Lizzie to Roma as he was driving the government Land Rover there that afternoon.

Charming though Charles was, the DC was a wily,

sharp-eyed administrator, and Stuart did not want to possibly be subject to his scrutiny.

But Piet would only be in town for a day or so and once he was gone, Stuart could get back to what he'd promised.

Being the husband Lizzie deserved to have married.

Unlike his father, Stuart took his vows and his responsibilities seriously.

An hour later, Piet was waiting patiently at the air strip when Stuart returned to pick up the two paying passengers departing Maseru for Semonkong.

He said nothing as Piet climbed into the back, the Afrikaner remaining silent as the two Oxfam workers chatted during the flight, before disembarking.

The following leg of the journey to Letseng-la-Terai took them over terrain that had once filled Stuart with excitement—the soaring peaks and hidden valleys of a country he'd come to love. Now the mountains looked like tombstones marking the death of his integrity.

Piet sat beside him, radiating satisfaction. Now that it was just the two of them, he'd been talking since takeoff from Semonkong, spinning justifications for his actions.

"These people, they don't understand money the way we do," Piet was saying, gesturing toward the windscreen as the mining settlement came into view. "Give them too much and they'll only waste it on drink. We're doing them a favour, really."

Stuart's jaw clenched. "They're not children, van Wyk."

"Aren't they?" Piet's laugh was ugly. "Look at them down there—scratching in the dirt like animals. They need someone with proper business sense to help them get fair value for their finds."

The irony was breathtaking. Stuart said nothing, focusing on his approach to the treacherous mountain airstrip. Below, figures emerged from tents and makeshift shelters, shading their eyes against the sun as the Cessna circled overhead.

These were good people. Hardworking people who'd carved an existence from one of the harshest environments on earth. And Stuart was about to help rob them.

The landing on the short runway was as rough as usual given the wind gusts at nearly eleven thousand feet, and Stuart's concentration was fractured by the war raging in his conscience. As they taxied to a stop, Piet was already unbuckling his harness, eager as a hunting dog scenting prey.

"Right then, Captain. Time to make some money."

Stuart wanted to tell him to go to hell. Instead, he cut the engine and—because he needed to minimise as much potential fraud on the Afrikaner's part as possible—followed Piet across the windswept plateau, feeling like Judas walking to his thirty pieces of silver.

Piet navigated the maze of claims. He'd done his homework. Clearly, he knew where to go as he made his way to a sandy hollow where an elderly Mosotho worked alone except for his wife, who sat atop a mound of earth beneath a faded blue umbrella, patiently sifting gravel through a makeshift sieve.

"Howzit, Tumelo?" Piet called out in joking familiarity, as if greeting an old friend rather than a mark he was about to fleece.

The old miner straightened, wiping sweat from his

weathered face. His gap-toothed smile was genuine, trusting. It made Stuart sick.

"I'm hoping those sheep I sent are doing well?" Piet continued, clapping the man on his shoulder with false bonhomie. "Spotter's fee, we call it, for you did well telling me about your friend's diamond during my last visit. And now you're the one who has found a big stone. Your family must think you're quite the successful businessman now."

Tumelo's wife looked up from her sifting, her dignified face creasing into a smile at mention of the livestock. "They are very fine sheep, *Morena*," Tumelo replied. "My family is very happy."

"Excellent! Now then, my friend—" Piet's voice dropped to a conspiratorial whisper, though he pitched it loud enough for Stuart to hear every damning word. "I've been speaking with Mr De Beers himself about this magnificent stone you've found. He's very excited. Very excited indeed."

Stuart saw the old man's eyes widen. Even in this remote outpost, the De Beers name carried mythical weight.

"You know Mr De Beers?" Tumelo breathed.

"Know him? We're business partners now!" Piet's grin was predatory. "He's asked me personally to come and see this diamond of yours. Word has reached Johannesburg, you know. They're saying it might be bigger than anything ever found here."

The lie rolled off Piet's tongue like honey. Stuart watched, horrified, unsure whether to step in and stop any transaction, or whether to just file it away to be used against Piet.

That is, after Philippa's situation had—he swallowed,

the thought making him feel ill and desperate—resolved itself.

Hating himself, he kept silent as he watched the miner and his wife exchange excited glances. After years of back-breaking labor, scraping a living from the unforgiving mountain, they dared to hope their fortunes had finally turned.

"Would you show me this stone?" Piet asked, his voice reverent now, as if he were a priest requesting to see a holy relic.

Tumelo hurried to his tent while his wife climbed down from her perch, both behaving as if this miraculous opportunity might evaporate like mountain mist.

When Tumelo returned with a battered box, Stuart's breath caught. Even from several feet away, he could see the size of the stone nestled inside. It was enormous. And even if it was encrusted in oxidised kimberlite and clay—Stuart could tell that Piet spoke no lie. This might well be the next Pride of Lesotho.

And Piet was about to steal it for a fraction of its worth. Again, he opened his mouth to say something. And then closed it.

By God, he couldn't let Piet get away with this—and he'd bear the consequences—but there was not a thing he could do right now.

"Magnificent," Piet breathed, holding the diamond up to catch the mountain light. "Absolutely magnificent. Mr de Beers will be overjoyed."

He reached into his jacket, withdrawing a substantial roll of notes. Stuart, who'd flown enough wealthy clients to recognise real money, could see it was far less than the stone deserved. A down payment on a king's ransom.

"Now, as Mr de Beers' representative, I'm authorised to

make you an immediate offer," Piet continued smoothly. "Cash today, no waiting, no complications."

The old couple watched with wide eyes as Piet began counting out notes. More money than they'd likely seen in their entire lives—but still a pittance compared to the diamond's true value.

Finally Stuart could stand it no longer. "Wait," he said, stepping forward. "Tumelo, you should get a proper valuation before—"

"Captain Price is quite right to be cautious," Piet interrupted smoothly, shooting Stuart a warning look. "Which is why I'm prepared to be even more generous than originally planned."

He added more notes, and Stuart watched Tumelo's face transform with wonder and disbelief. The old man probably thought he was witnessing a miracle.

"You're still cheating him," Stuart said quietly, but his words were lost as Tumelo reached out with trembling hands to accept Piet's blood money.

The transaction was over in minutes. Piet pocketed the diamond with the casual air of a man completing routine business, while Tumelo and his wife stared at their sudden wealth with stunned gratitude.

"Pleasure doing business," Piet said, shaking the old man's hand one final time. "Give my regards to those sheep."

Walking back to the plane, Stuart felt like he was drowning in his own complicity. "That stone was worth a thousand times what you paid."

"Two thousand times, actually," Piet replied cheerfully, pulling out the box to admire his prize. "Maybe more. Depends on the clarity, but from what I can see..." He whistled appreciatively. "This little beauty is going to set me up for life."

"You're a thief."

"I'm a businessman. There's a difference." Piet's eyes glittered with malicious satisfaction. "Besides, what's your alternative? Turn me in? Explain to the authorities how you came to be here with me? I'm sure your wife would love to hear about your romantic troubles, and I'm equally sure the DC would be fascinated to learn what his precious daughter has been up to—not to mention what the Myburgh family might think."

Stuart clenched his hands, but they both knew he was trapped. Piet had played the game perfectly, using Stuart's own desperation against him.

"Here," Piet said, separating a few notes to press into Stuart's hand. "Your cut. Call it consultant fees."

Stuart stared at them, bile rising in his throat. Blood money. Payment for his soul. Payment for the shortfall Mrs Oosthuizen supposedly owed her florist.

"No thank you," Stuart muttered, forcing Piet to take the money back. "You know, you won't get away with this forever."

Piet shrugged. "If I go down, I'm taking you with me, Captain. After all, we're partners now."

Stuart sent a pointed look at the money he'd refused to take and which Piet was now tucking into his wallet. "We'll never be partners," he said.

THIRTY-FOUR

LEAVING THE CAPITAL NOT LONG AFTER MISS CAMERON HAD reported for duty, Charles navigated the winding track southeast from Maseru in the government Land Rover towards Roma.

Beside him, Lizzie—she'd asked him to call her that—gazed out at the changing landscape with the wonder of someone still relatively new to this remarkable country.

"It's quite something, isn't it?" Charles remarked, pleased by her fascination as they crested a rise. Below them, the road descended into a broad valley where traditional rondavels dotted the hillsides like scattered coins, their thatched roofs catching the sunlight.

"I never tire of it," Lizzie replied. "The way the light changes everything. One moment the mountains look purple, the next they're gold."

Charles smiled, remembering his own first impressions of Basutoland twenty-five years ago. The landscape ahead began to shift as they approached Roma, the fertile valley broadening between sandstone cliffs topped with basalt mountains. Then, as they rounded a final bend, Roma rose majestically before them—the mission buildings spread across the valley floor like something from a medieval illumination, amidst the green of cultivated fields.

"There she is," Charles said. "Rather impressive for the middle of nowhere, wouldn't you say?"

The Catholic University buildings dominated the settlement, their Gothic Revival architecture transplanted incongruously but beautifully into the African highlands. Bell towers pierced the morning sky, and Charles could see figures in brown habits moving between the buildings like industrious ants.

"I can see why they chose this spot," Lizzie murmured. "It's like a hidden kingdom."

Charles brought the Land Rover to a halt in the main courtyard, where Brother Augustine was waiting for them, his weathered face creased in a welcoming smile.

Beside him was the Mosotho doctor, whom the elderly Oblate introduced as Dr Lehlohonolo Molapo, a lean, earnest-faced young man with wire spectacles, wearing a perfectly pressed dark suit, to whom Lizzie would be reporting. He'd been employed since Lizzie's last stint.

"Dr Molapo is a recent graduate of the University of the Witwatersrand Medical School in Johannesburg. Doctor, would you like to explain to Nurse Cameron the vaccination schedule for the week?" Brother Augustine said as he led them into the cool interior of the main building.

The young doctor smiled, and Charles was relieved to see Lizzie's unquestioning acceptance of the hierarchy as Dr Molapo spoke. "Word has spread about the new clinic, which is a new outstation of Morija. Families are walking for days to bring their children. We must make sure we have enough syringes so we don't have to send a runner back to Roma for more supplies. Now, perhaps Dr Molapo can take you to the stables to choose mounts. I'll meet you there in about ten minutes as I have some other matters to go over with Brother Augustine."

As soon as they were alone, Charles got straight to the main reason for his visit.

"Moses Shakane," he began. "He was formerly a student at one of the French mission schools, I believe?"

The brother's expression darkened as they sat down and the sisters served them tea and biscuits. "Ah, yes. Moses. I got your message, but I hardly needed to research. I know the man well. A brilliant mind, but..." He shook his head. "He was expelled from the Protestant mission school at Morija some years ago. Troublesome even then, but his recent activities are far more concerning."

"What more can you tell me?"

Brother Augustine stirred his tea thoughtfully. "He's twenty-five now, I believe. Went to Moscow for his university education. Came back full of dangerous ideas about revolution and the overthrow of traditional authority. He's been touring the districts with a megaphone, stirring up resentment."

"Yes, of course. The rally in Quthing—"

"Yes. But it's not just the political agitation that worries us." The brother's frown deepened. "I daresay you know that Moses' uncle is Chief Thabo, who I believe is currently under investigation for medicine murder."

Charles nodded. "The albino villager found at the bottom of a ravine." He cleared his throat. "My police troopers are doing an excellent job of investigating..." He hesitated. "But Chief Thabo is powerful. He's been acquitted of murder once already. His people are afraid, and so far, none of his villagers are prepared to testify."

Brother Augustine nodded. "And there's another uncle,

as you probably know. Tumelo, Chief Thabo's younger brother." Brother Augustine adjusted the rope cord around the middle of his brown habit. "I heard word just this morning that Tumelo provided information to an Afrikaner diamond buyer who recently did a recce at the diggings—"

"What?"

"Yes, I wondered if you knew."

Charles was going to ask how he got there but checked himself. He should have been across these details. "Go on," he said slowly.

"Just last night, it was communicated to me that there were rumblings that the man Tumelo introduced to this buyer several weeks ago was cheated."

Charles ran a hand across his forehead. "Then he wasn't a licensed buyer. I knew nothing of this."

Brother Augustine nodded. "Yes, I suspected as much."

"The miners should know they must trust no one unless—" Charles stopped. Any non-local who visited the diggings was carefully scrutinised. Often searched. Only those with legitimate business were permitted. Yet, somehow, someone had navigated bridle paths and ravines to get to the remote diggings.

Unless he'd been flown.

He didn't put it into words. The thought was too chilling. For now he let Brother Augustine go on.

"It didn't take long for Moses to use this as evidence of colonial exploitation and to show that a white man—"

"What evidence does he have?"

Brother Augustine chose his words carefully. "The evidence is flimsy, I'll admit—if you could call it evidence, even. Apparently one of the miners wanted to document the 'great moment' when Tumelo's friend sold his diamond for great riches."

"He took a photograph?"

"Yes, but of course it's taken some time to be developed and it's only just now surfaced in view of the rumblings that the amount paid is a pittance compared with its value."

"Can I see the photograph?"

Brother Augustine shook his head. "I believe it's in the hands of Moses Shakane."

"Is the Afrikaner who purported to be a licensed dealer identifiable?"

Again, Brother Augustine shook his head. "Unfortunately not. The photo focuses on Lehlohonolo holding his diamond. In the background, we can see the plane and a European, presumably, the pilot who flew the Afrikaner to Letsing-la-Terai. But the photograph is grainy, making it difficult to identify him with any reliability."

Charles felt hollow. He was on good terms with all four pilots who flew for Drakensberg Air. Surely it was none of them.

"The plane could have originated from anywhere across the border, could it not?" he said. "It does not mean the pilot in the photograph is one of ours."

"I wish I could say that was the case," said Brother Augustine. "But, using a magnifying glass, the three letters that can be discerned on the Cessna's registration are the same as one flown by Drakensberg Air."

"And the pilot?"

"He appears to be a man in his twenties, though the photograph is, as I say, grainy and not well developed." He cleared his throat. "I believe only one of the company's pilots is ...er... under forty or so."

"You have done your homework," Charles remarked drily. Indeed, his throat was very dry.

Stuart Price? He was the only pilot under forty, and he couldn't believe the man would do such a thing.

"I was obliged to discover what I could before handing over to your capable hands," said Brother Augustine, "given the unrest the circulation of this photograph has caused. Shakane has been brandishing it about, claiming the incident proves the Administration doesn't care about justice for the Basotho people."

Charles nodded, already anxious to be gone. "I'll investigate the matter as soon as I return to Maseru. What else can you tell me?"

Brother Augustine pushed forward a folder. "There are no names we can ascertain with any certainty, but word is that an Afrikaner first went up to the diggings a few weeks ago as a mechanic to fix a sieving machine. Sister Mary Palesa reports she was told this man has transformed himself into a so-called buyer for de Beers. All the information we have is in this dossier."

Charles ran the back of his hand across his forehead. "Damn!" he said softly. "I thought dealing with Moses Shakane was bad enough."

Brother Augustine sighed heavily. "When you combine legitimate grievances about economic exploitation with Moses's revolutionary rhetoric..." He spread his hands helplessly. "It's a dangerous mixture. The young man was always rebellious, even as a child. Intelligent, passionate, but completely unwilling to accept any form of authority—traditional or colonial."

Charles stared out through the window at the peaceful surrounds and thought of his own maid, Francina's good, obedient son, Mpho. "I wonder where Shakane's radicalisation began. It takes only one hothead firebrand to stir up a hornet's nest."

"I suspect it began with his expulsion from school. And he saw the lengths to which his uncle Chief Thabo would go to gain power over his people—not that anything is proved, I know. But his uncle undoubtedly wields power through fear," said Brother Augustine. "I've seen it before, though not as extreme. The boy felt betrayed by the mission education system, saw it as just another form of colonial control and when the opportunity came to study in Moscow..." The brother shrugged. "Soviet ideology provided him with a framework for his anger. Now he sees everything through the lens of class struggle and anti-imperialism. And he knows how to wield fear."

"Yes, his family connections make him even more dangerous."

Brother Augustine nodded. "He'll use Chief Thabo's legal difficulties and Tumelo's diamond grievances as proof that the colonial system is fundamentally corrupt. Whether his uncles are guilty or innocent becomes irrelevant, Moses has turned their troubles into political capital."

Charles rubbed his temples. "I hope the press doesn't get wind of this before we've got the investigation under way with something in our favour to report," he said, recalling the article in the Bloemfontein Friend that had poked fun at the administration thanks to de Vries and his fishing rod that had, quite literally, hooked a small bag of diamonds from safe keeping and reeled them in.

Of course, that would be the least of his troubles.

Thank you, Brother Augustine," he added, rising, holding out his hand. "You have been most helpful."

Stuart Price. Could he really be involved?

When the young man had arrived in the country four years ago, he'd been an unknown. His boss, Drakensberg Air's pilot Dan Greene, spoke of him as reliable and competent. Charming, too, for he'd exerted considerable charm over his daughter.

Philippa had been desperately smitten, though Matthew Myburgh had won the day.

Nevertheless, Charles had always liked Stuart Price. And as he'd got to know him better, his impression had become even more favourable. He treated the Basotho with genuine respect rather than the patronising courtesy many whites affected.

Word was that the fellow came from a rough background. His accent was difficult to place with the occasional Cockney slang giveaway but for the most part it was a pleasant English, slightly South African accent—probably due to his connection to the prominent Franklin family in Pretoria who'd looked after him as a war evacuee, though Price himself never spoke of his past.

If Stuart were involved in illegal diamond trading, it would be a profound disappointment.

But then, weren't the most devastating betrayals always committed by those one would least suspect?

"Any sign of trouble in this vicinity?" he asked, rising with a sigh. "Nurse Cameron is in no danger?"

Brother Augustine gave a reassuring smile as he rose. "Judging by her accent, Nurse Cameron is from Australia and far removed from the administration or the perpetrators who have stirred up the ire of Chief Thabo and Moses Shakane and the hotheads they influence."

CHAPTER

THIRTY-FIVE

On impulse, Charles decided that instead of returning to Maseru, he'd personally accompany Lizzie from Roma to the vaccination clinic. Dr Molapo, he suggested, should go ahead.

In the next few days, after he'd dealt with several matters relating to the investigation into Chief Thabo in Mokhotlong, he'd return to Maseru and invite Stuart to his office for a "friendly chat" in the hopes he might be able to "clear up some confusion" regarding flights—and supposed diamond dealers—to Letseng-la-Terai.

Yes, that's how he'd frame it.

In the meantime, he convinced himself it would be a dereliction of duty not to ensure Lizzie was safely settled at her new place of work and that her basic living quarters were adequate. That Lizzie was utterly charming meant the task was hardly a chore.

But he must remind himself not to be tedious. Philippa teased him gently, often enough, about his tendency to hold forth on the country's history when not everyone shared his enthusiasm.

After half an hour of trekking across the country, he finally found the courage to be more forthcoming. And following a brief history lesson about the area through which they were passing, he shared with Lizzie Philippa's gentle reproach about his verbose tendencies.

She laughed. "I like your anecdotes. Basutoland is so remote and rugged. So different from where I grew up in South Australia, and I love hearing your stories of the pioneers. Those who were as stupid as they were intrepid ended up at the bottom of the ravine, though of course that part is sad. But the other stories—"

Lizzie's laughter rang out across the mountain air, emboldening Charles even further.

When had he felt as carefree since Eleanor's death?

He caught himself up and reminded himself that Lizzie was thirteen years younger than he was and in his employ. Yet he couldn't help himself as they dismounted for a rest and a cup of tea. "Now be sure to admire the glossy coat of Father O'Brien's Alsatian," he said with a wink. "He'll tell you the secret is half a rat a day."

He laughed when her mouth dropped open. "Well, Lizzie, I have it on good authority that Father O'Brien takes his pellet gun to the rats on the church rafters several times a week for Rusty's benefit."

Lizzie shuddered. "How perfectly revolting. But now, the cathedral. Oh, my goodness, I've never seen anything so beautiful."

"Penance labour is a wonderful thing," Charles said drily. "A week's hard work rather than a few Hail Marys for your sins and in a few years a building like this one has risen from the dust."

Lizzie smiled. "I'm so happy I got this job. Living in Maseru is all well and good but to come here every few weeks to do a stint at the clinic is my idea of heaven. I couldn't imagine living anywhere that answers so much to my soul."

Surprised, Charles didn't know what to say as he boiled water over a small fire of sahalahala bushes when they stopped for a cup of tea. He wanted to extend the moment, but suddenly shyness had kicked in. Even so, the silence wasn't awkward. Miss Cameron seemed to have a character that perfectly complemented his, and Charles was conscious of a feeling of wellbeing and happiness he hadn't felt in a long while.

"I think someone's spying on us." Lizzie smiled, pointing at a little herd boy in a ragged Basuto blanket. He was crouched behind a rock, and when Lizzie beckoned him over to give him a biscuit, she admired his shoes made out of an old tyre.

"This boy will probably start school at Mapolaneng Mission when he's fourteen or so or when his younger brother can take over herding his goats," Charles explained.

"I get the impression the children are good students when they get the opportunity to learn."

"There's no shortage of eager students, my own maid's son, Mpho among them. Mapoloneng is run by dedicated teachers. Nuns and priests and, yes, education is highly prized." He hesitated, unsure if he should elaborate. Although he'd established that Miss Cameron was in no danger, he did have a duty to explain some of the political background.

"What is it?" she prompted.

"Lately there've been rumblings. A few hotheads have returned from scholarships in Moscow."

She sent him an enquiring look and he noticed how blue her eyes looked beneath the clear sky as she asked,

"You mean with Independence looming, they want to impose their revolutionary ideas?" She was thoughtful. "The Basotho are hardly what I'd call a warlike people. Not like the Zulus or the Shona."

"Or the Ndebele and so on, no. Chief Moshoeshoe was a wise ruler. When he feared the Boers would dispossess them of their land, he sought Queen Victoria's protection and in 1868 she made Basutoland a British Protectorate."

"And now you're giving it all back to them," Lizzie murmured, warming her hands over the flames.

"We never had the right to own the land," Charles replied. "I love this country, and I like to think that after Independence the Basotho people will regain full rights to a country with improvements. We've built roads, schools, hospitals and clinics in the most remote areas. Life expectancy is rising. Literacy is very high." He paused, choosing his words carefully. "Call me a good colonial servant when it's becoming a dirty word, but I think our approach has been rather more responsible than some."

"The Belgian Congo?"

Charles shuddered in agreement. "Precisely. But there are some radicals here who want to poison the people's minds against us, regardless."

She smiled. "Should I be afraid?"

"You've nothing to worry about here, Lizzie," he said, and without thinking, put his hand over hers in a brief and impulsive effort to reassure.

The flare of surprise in her eyes echoed his own shock, and he quickly drew back, saying, "The chieftainship has exercised authority over the Basotho for hundreds of years. From the most senior chiefs right down to the village headmen. Now their authority is being challenged by politicians who believe they can bring in a new regime, but the troublemakers are in the minority."

He stopped, afraid of boring her, and ashamed that he'd crossed professional boundaries, but her eyes were bright. "Go on."

"The political situation is being driven by outside funding. Russian and Chinese. Both are in an expansionist mood throughout Africa." Charles added more fuel to the fire, sending sparks spiralling upward. "Meanwhile, South Africa is terrified of Lesotho providing a haven for what they call terrorists. Our mountainous terrain makes it ideal for that sort of thing, and of course we're completely landlocked by apartheid South Africa."

"I've never seen anyone in this country who looks Chinese or Russian," said Lizzie.

Charles smiled at her innocence. "They entice promising young Basotho to their countries with scholarships—ostensibly for education, but really for indoctrination. These radicalised elements return home with deep pockets and revolutionary ideas. So we have not just the traditional contest between chieftainship and modernity, but rivalry between Russian-funded and Chinese-funded factions."

He drained the last of his tea and started to rise.

"No, don't stop. I want to know more...I want to know everything about this country, and I could listen to you talk all day."

Her words sent warmth through him that had nothing to do with the fire. He settled back down, making himself more comfortable. He hadn't talked so much since Eleanor had died. "A further complication is that tensions aren't confined to this country. Look at South Africa. Look at Sharpeville just a few months ago."

Lizzie frowned. "That was terrible! I know that Black people protesting were killed, but I don't know exactly why."

"Sixty-nine were massacred protesting the pass laws—Verwoerd's way of controlling movement under apartheid. Segregation based purely on skin colour." He shook his head. "It's all such a bloody mess and one day there'll be more bloodshed, though hopefully not in the new democratic republic of Lesotho."

"How recent is apartheid?"

"Just over ten years since this government got in. At Cape Town University I attended lectures, played rugby and socialised with black students." Charles began to put away the tea things. "That doesn't happen anymore, I'm afraid. Come." He reached out his hand to help her up, his reaction as her fingers clasped his dismaying him.

She was so much younger than he. He had no right to think she would be remotely interested in him.

And yet, the blush that sprang to her cheeks when he looked at her suggested she might be.

CHAPTER

THIRTY-SIX

Philippa didn't know if she'd survive the pain. A few hours earlier, she'd got as far as stepping across Mrs Simmons' threshold but had not been able to go through the procedure. In fact, blind terror had taken over the moment she'd registered the kitchen table, surgical instruments laid out on the white sheet.

Yes, she'd run, with no thought as to what she'd do next.

However, it was during the journey home that she'd felt the first sharp, menstrual-like cramps that intensified progressively, followed by lower back pain that radiated down both legs. Curled up in the back of the bus, she'd barely managed to disembark before the pain nearly brought her to her knees.

Was this what she thought it was?

In a public toilet, she received confirmation and, with the help of the single sanitary pad she'd found at the bottom of her handbag, she'd made it to the chemist for reinforcements before she'd finally been able to collapse onto the bathroom floor in her dingy hotel room, closing her eyes against the nausea and dizziness while the pain came in waves, building to peaks before subsiding.

For the rest of the day, she'd hugged her belly, wrapped in her dressing gown and two bath towels, both now covered in blood.

Throughout the night, the bleeding continued, but she dared not seek help. An unmarried young woman in a shabby hotel room having a miscarriage was more likely to receive censure than compassion—not a tradeoff she was prepared to make in return for medical help.

With a shudder, she recalled Sister Margaret's words about prosecution. The phone numbers of two abortionists in her possession would be enough to convict her by authorities who might believe she'd brought this on herself.

The fact that she hadn't would be of little account.

But as she drifted in and out of consciousness, she didn't really care if she lived or died. What was the point of living when everything that mattered had been torn away from her?

Reaching up a flailing hand, she gripped the bathroom vanity and managed to haul herself to her feet. The cold porcelain felt solid beneath her palm, an anchor in a world that seemed to tilt and sway around her.

But then she collapsed over it as her vision swam, and she was afraid she might black out and crack her head on the tiles.

Blinking open her light-sensitive eyes, she stared at the mess around her. The harsh fluorescent light made everything look stark and clinical, like a scene from a medical textbook she'd rather not have opened.

So, that was her baby. Or, all that was left of it. The baby she and Stuart had conceived with such love—their love made flesh, however briefly. The baby that might have been their salvation, their reason to fight for each other against all odds—if Stuart hadn't been married.

She could almost see the child they might have had: dark hair like hers, Stuart's blue eyes, perhaps?

Now there was nothing. No baby to consider, no desperate reason for Stuart to choose her over duty and honour. She was simply a woman who loved a married man —the oldest, most sordid story in the world.

Shuddering with pain and loneliness and despair, Philippa burst into tears just as she heard a knock on the door. The sound echoed through the small room like a gunshot.

"Madam, room service," said the voice on the other side.

"Not right now," she managed, her voice hoarse from crying. "Can you tell reception I'm unwell and don't want to receive visitors?" She sank to her knees, the thin carpet rough against her skin, for the effort of standing was too great. "And...please could I have another couple of bath towels?" she managed, fortunately while the maid was still within hearing.

The worst of the bleeding seemed to have subsided. The bathroom looked like a scene of carnage, but after a few more hours, she felt it was safe to now drag herself to the bed, curling up amidst the sheets that smelled of her own desperation and covering her face with a pillow that was damp with tears.

She'd never felt so drained in all her life. The exhaustion went bone-deep, as if her very soul had been hollowed out.

All she wanted to do was sleep for eternity. And maybe it would be better if she never woke up.

"Madam."

Would people only stop interrupting her descent into blessed oblivion?

"Madam, I have a telegram for you."

Blearily, Philippa forced herself to sit up. The movement sent fresh waves of pain through her abdomen. She felt a little alarmed because no one sent telegrams unless it was urgent.

Could Stuart have found a way to extricate himself from Lizzie?

"Push it under the door," she said, her heart hammering as she crawled towards the paper that emerged a second later, yellow and official-looking against the worn carpet.

Her hands were shaking as she read the words, hope and dread warring in her chest.

Stuart loved her. She knew he did.

But when she saw it was from Matthew, bile rose up in her throat as she tossed the telegram away from her. How had he tracked down the fact that she was here? In this dingy hotel?

Oh, if only he'd leave for London soon, though that was suddenly all up in the air—

Then she remembered that she didn't have Stuart. She'd given up her studies. She didn't have the baby. She began to sob once more.

What *did* she have left? She drew in a shuddering breath and thought of the only support that was unwavering in her desperately untethered world.

Mrs Myburgh.

But was that enough to justify Philippa marrying her son when she knew she didn't love Matthew?

Ha! Matthew. Who represented everything she'd thought she wanted before she'd learned what real love felt like. Before Stuart had shown her what it meant to be truly alive, truly connected to another soul.

The telegram fluttered onto the floor, and Philippa, lying on her stomach over the bed, only had to open her eyes to see the words:

Philippa. Arriving Jo'burg tomorrow. Can't wait to see you.

Right, she thought. Sleep first. Maseru next. Before Matthew arrived.

Matthew would just have to follow her to Maseru instead of taking her down to Cape Town because she had a duty to fulfil.

Determination had filled the vacuum left by despair and misery. If there was one task that was more important than any other, it was to return Stuart's money—the blood money that had cost them both so much.

Reaching across to the bedside table, she pulled open the drawer, her fingers closing over the fat envelope Stuart had given her two days ago. The bills represented a fortune to most people, but all she could think of was the price Stuart had paid to obtain it.

It was a lot of money, and he needed it back. She would not be accused of ruining his life more than she had already.

If she couldn't get it to him tomorrow by leaving before Matthew arrived, she didn't know when she could.

But despite her noble intentions, Philippa was thwarted at every turn.

Having finally drifted off to sleep after a warm bath,

and a reasonable attempt at cleaning—or, at least, minimising the mess she'd made—an insistent rapping on the door at eleven o'clock the following morning jerked her awake, and she opened her eyes to a full ray of sunshine penetrating the curtains.

At first she assumed it was room service—though she'd ordered nothing—but then someone was calling out her name in tones that brooked no argument. She could make no sense of it in her groggy state, and without thinking, staggered to the door, opening it a crack.

To her utter horror, there were Matthew and...

His mother!

"Oh my goodness, Philippa, you are a lie-a-bed this morning. What have you been up to?" Arch disapproval tempered Mrs Myburgh's supposedly playful tone.

Behind her, Matthew had the expectant but somewhat disappointed look of someone who had been expecting a welcome far beyond the underwhelming "what a surprise this is" that Philippa offered when she opened the door after having done a panicked check that the bloodstained linen was firmly behind the bathroom door, and she, herself, was clean enough to pass inspection.

Mrs Myburgh swept past her, her sharp eyes taking in every detail of the shabby room—the rumpled bedding, deep in shadow thanks to the drawn curtains, the general air of despair that clung to everything.

Philippa saw exactly what she was thinking while she prayed no one would want to use the bathroom.

Or maybe it was better to have everything blow up in her face right now so as to end it sooner rather than later.

Gripping the edge of a table, Philippa closed her eyes briefly. What would be, would be.

"Clearly you were not expecting us, so Matthew and I

will return in twenty minutes. Philippa, get yourself ready. I'm taking you out to lunch. I couldn't believe it when Marielle reported back that after half a dozen phone calls she'd located you at The Transit Hotel. My dear, if money was a problem, why didn't you tell me and I'd have happily extended credit for The Carlton, which is where we'll be going shortly. A Myburgh wouldn't be seen dead in a place like this."

"Mrs Myburgh, I don't think I—"

"No time, Philippa! Your final wedding gown fitting is tomorrow, and I want to go through a few things before then. Come, Matthew, we'll leave Philippa in peace. Twenty minutes, my girl. No more. I'll meet you at reception."

Philippa wasn't sure how she summoned the energy to shower, dress herself, and apply makeup to hide the ravages of her ordeal. Her hands shook as she applied lipstick, and her reflection looked like a ghost of her former self—pale, hollow-eyed, diminished. The hot water helped somewhat, but by the time she dragged her weary body downstairs, she still felt as fragile as spun glass.

She was not surprised when Mrs Myburgh voiced shock at her appearance.

"Good heavens, Philippa, you look positively ghastly! Have you been ill?"

"Yes, I've been ill," Philippa said weakly, grasping at this lifeline. "Goodness, I hope I am not still contagious. Perhaps I should go back to bed." Why had she not thought of this excuse before? Because she had been numb, her mind responding as usual to Mrs Myburgh's authority.

"Nonsense," Mrs Myburgh declared. "Fresh air and proper food will set you right. We have far too much to discuss to waste time with vapours. Far too many details still to be settled."

Matthew, who had been studying the reception area with obvious distaste, finally spoke. "Mother's right, darling. You do look rather peaked. But nothing that can't be fixed with a good meal and some colour in your cheeks."

Hustled into a taxi, Philippa felt herself being swept along by forces beyond her control. But she was beyond resistance. She'd lost her baby. She'd lost her true love. Did it really matter what happened to her now?

"First lunch, then we'll visit Mrs Latoufe—"

"No, please, not today!" Philippa cut her off, thinking of white dresses and blood flow over which she had no control. "Please can we do that tomorrow?"

Mrs Myburgh frowned, as if Philippa's wishes were an inconvenience to be overcome before she finally conceded. "Very well. But I've taken the liberty of making some adjustments to your original design, nothing drastic, mind you, but something more suitable for photographs. Then we'll discuss the reception arrangements. I've had to make several changes to accommodate the additional guests Matthew's grandfather has insisted we invite. You heard how ill he is. Poor Matthew is so disappointed he's had to postpone his visit."

The restaurant Mrs Myburgh had chosen for lunch was the sort of establishment where appearances mattered more than appetite—all white tablecloths and hushed voices. Philippa, seated between her captors, felt increasingly like a prisoner being marched to execution, and afraid that her body might betray her, though she'd chosen a thick black skirt to wear and had already made one trip to the bathroom.

"Maybe you could go to London right after the wedding," Philippa said, without thinking.

"Good Lord, what are you suggesting?" Mrs Myburgh

said, as Matthew told the waiter their wine order. "Mind you, this is just the time to bring up the subject of the expectations people will have of you as Matthew's wife."

Matthew nodded. "Philippa, of course I wouldn't leave you right after we're married," he said, frowning. "Maybe later—"

"Enough, Matthew! Neither of you will be going anywhere until you have established yourselves," Mrs Myburgh continued, warming to her theme. "Matthew will start work with the family firm as soon as you are back from your honeymoon. And that's when your work begins, Philippa. A wife's primary duty is to reflect well upon her husband. The way you conduct yourself, your friends, even your interests—all of these must be carefully considered. We can't have any hint of scandal or impropriety as a result of unwise connections."

Philippa stared down at her lap, praying she'd taken sufficient precautions to avoid an embarrassing break-through bleed. The word 'scandal' seemed to hang in the air like a sword.

"I also want to discuss your future plans," Mrs Myburgh pressed on, apparently oblivious to Philippa's distress. "Matthew's grandfather has been most generous in his will. As it stands, his entire estate will come to Matthew, including the London properties. However, I've advised against any plans to live abroad."

"Have you?" Philippa managed, though her voice sounded foreign to her own ears.

"Yes, Matthew's future is here in Cape Town, taking over his father's practice. And frankly, my dear, I intend to be very involved in my grandchildren's upbringing until it's time for them to go to boarding school."

The mention of children threatened to bring Philippa's

world crashing down around her ears once more. Her hand instinctively moved to her still-tender abdomen, and she had to bite her lip to keep from crying out.

"Are you all right, my dear?" Mrs Myburgh sounded more irritated than concerned. "You've gone quite pale again."

"I'm fine," Philippa whispered, though she was anything but. The restaurant suddenly felt stifling, the air thick with the scent of expensive perfume and barely concealed ambition.

"Mother's right, of course," Matthew said. "I was jumping ahead of myself, suggesting we decamp to London."

But even as he said it, Philippa could see the resignation in his eyes. His mother had spoken, and Matthew would obey. They would stay in Cape Town, in the house Mrs Myburgh had chosen for them, living the life she had mapped out.

Mrs Myburgh smiled. "Exactly. And Philippa, I trust you understand the importance of presenting a united front in all things. A marriage requires mutual support, and above all, a clear understanding of one's role."

Philippa saw with crystalline clarity the life that stretched before her: endless dinner parties where she would smile and nod at appropriate intervals, charity committees where she would organise events for causes she'd never chosen, and always, always, the watchful presence of Mrs Myburgh, ready to correct any deviation from the approved path.

She thought of Stuart, probably at this very moment flying through the mountain peaks of Lesotho, free and alone in the vast African sky. She thought of the passion that had blazed between them, the way he'd looked at her as if she contained all the mysteries of the universe. She thought of the baby they'd created in love, lost before it ever had a chance to breathe.

And she thought of the years ahead, playing the role of the perfect wife to a man who saw her as an ornament, supervised by a woman who viewed her as raw material to be shaped according to her own specifications.

"I'm sure Philippa will be a credit to our family," Mrs Myburgh was saying, though her tone suggested this was more command than confidence. "Won't you, my dear?"

Philippa looked up from her untouched bread roll, meeting those calculating eyes with a spark of something that might have been defiance—or perhaps just the dying embers of her former self.

"Of course," she heard herself say, though the words tasted like ashes. "I wouldn't dream of being anything else."

But in her heart, she was already saying goodbye to the woman she might have been.

CHAPTER
THIRTY-SEVEN

MASERU

Stuart hesitated before the polished brass nameplate that bore Charles Tremain's name on the door of his Maseru office.

Usually, he met Charles unofficially or casually at the airstrip at the bottom of the DC's Mokhotlong residence. He'd come to like and respect the man during the years he'd lived here. He hoped Charles respected him too.

But this meeting was unnerving.

Lizzie had been gone for four days, so Stuart had had breakfast at a cafe in town. He'd literally bumped into the DC as he'd stepped outside, a collision resulting in a mumbled apology that had ended with Charles's easy smile and invitation for "a friendly chat over tea."

Nothing to indicate Charles harboured any suspicions of Stuart's involvement with Piet van Wyk.

So, Stuart had no reason to worry. It was unlikely van Wyk's crime had yet come to light.

But *friendly?* The word had seemed genuine enough, accompanied by that charm that made Charles Tremain so effective in his role.

Now, standing before the wooden door, Stuart wondered what Charles *really* wanted.

He straightened his shoulders. It reminded him of the days of putting up a front to carry him through the worst of London's East End. At least he could take comfort in one crucial fact: he'd received no financial reward from Piet's diamond theft. The moment Philippa was safely married to Matthew—less than ten days now—he intended to alert the authorities about van Wyk's criminal activities.

Ten days. The thought should have brought relief, but instead it opened a chasm in his chest. Ten days until Philippa became Mrs Matthew Myburgh forever. Ten days until he lost her completely to a world of garden parties and society columns, of everything he could never give her.

He pushed the thought away. What was done was done. He'd made his choices: marrying Lizzie, helping Philippa with money that had come from Piet's schemes, allowing himself to be compromised step by careful step until he stood here, outside the DC's office, wondering if his carefully constructed life was about to collapse around him.

Stuart knocked twice and entered.

"Stuart, good to see you!" Charles rose from behind his desk, extending a hand in greeting. The office was quintessentially colonial. Dark wood furniture, hunting prints on cream walls, and the lingering scent of pipe tobacco mixed with the leather bindings of legal volumes. Through the tall windows, the Maluti Mountains stretched endlessly, their peaks sharp against the afternoon sky.

"Marjorie will be through with tea and scones shortly."

The warmth in Charles's voice should have been reassuring, but Stuart found himself analysing every nuance, every pause. *Very hospitable,* he thought, settling into the offered chair. *But is that good or bad?* If Charles suspected half of what Stuart was guilty of, this civilised veneer would evaporate faster than morning mist on the mountains.

"I suppose you're wondering why I've asked you here?" Charles settled back into his chair.

Stuart forced his voice to remain steady. "I wasn't sure, no." He hesitated, then took a punt, wondering if Lizzie had let slip that the pair of them had just got hitched. He didn't think she'd be able to keep such a secret. So he said, "But perhaps you wanted to reassure me that all was going well with Lizzie. Communications are difficult at the best of times, and it's a challenging posting, but then she's an intrepid young woman."

"Yes, indeed, she is." A subtle warmth crept into Charles's voice at the mention of Lizzie's name. "Miss Cameron has exceeded all expectations. The vaccination program needed someone just like her, and she's shown tremendous initiative by preparing some rudimentary health education sessions for the mothers. She told me how much she looks forward to her work at the clinic."

The soft knock on the door interrupted them. "Come in," Charles called, and Marjorie entered bearing a silver tray laden with bone china and what appeared to be fresh scones still warm from the oven.

"Thank you, Marjorie," Charles said. "That'll be all for now."

As the secretary arranged the tea service, Stuart used the respite to study Charles's face. The DC's expression had shifted almost imperceptibly. The warmth was still there, but tempered now with something else. Curiosity? Suspicion? It was impossible to tell.

Marjorie withdrew with a soft click of the door, leaving the two men alone.

"Sugar? Milk?" Charles's voice was perfectly normal, but Stuart caught the way his eyes lingered a moment too long, as if cataloguing every reaction.

"Just milk, thank you." Stuart accepted the cup, his hand trembling almost imperceptibly.

Charles settled back with his own cup. Through the windows, Stuart could hear the distant sounds of Mokhotlong going about its business.

"I've had some interesting reports lately," Charles began, his tone conversational. "About activities up at Letseng-la-Terai."

Stuart's blood turned to ice water, but he kept his expression neutral. "Oh?"

"Yes. It seems there's been some... unauthorised trading." Charles took a deliberate sip of his tea, his eyes never leaving Stuart's face. "Diamonds changing hands at prices that don't reflect their true value."

The scone turned to ash in Stuart's mouth. He forced himself to swallow, then reached for his teacup so he could avert his eyes. "That's concerning. The miners work so hard for their finds."

"Indeed, they do." Charles's voice carried a subtle edge now. "Particularly troubling when the perpetrators appear to have used official transport to facilitate their schemes."

Official transport. The euphemism hung between them like an accusation. Stuart felt sweat gathering at his collar despite the cool air drifting through the window. Every instinct screamed at him to confess, to throw himself on Charles's mercy and hope that twenty-five years of colonial service had bred some compassion along with the authority.

Instead, he heard himself say, "I hope you catch whoever's responsible."

Charles smiled, but it didn't reach his eyes. "Oh, I intend to. You see, Stuart, I've spent twenty-five years learning to read people. It's an essential skill in this job—knowing when someone is telling you the truth, when they're holding something back, when they're calculating their next move."

Stuart set down his teacup with excessive care, afraid his shaking hands might betray him completely. "I'm sure that must be invaluable."

"It is." Charles leaned forward slightly, his gaze intensifying. "For instance, I can usually tell when someone is carrying a burden that's eating them alive from the inside. When they're involved in something that goes against every principle they hold dear."

Stuart's throat felt like sandpaper. "Charles—"

"I'm not making accusations, you understand." Charles's voice remained perfectly pleasant, but there was steel underneath now. "Merely observations. Sometimes good men find themselves in impossible situations. Sometimes they make choices they never thought they'd make, for reasons that seem compelling at the time."

The silence that followed was deafening. Stuart stared into his teacup as if it might offer some escape, some explanation that would make everything right again. But there was nothing. Just the reflection of a man who'd compromised everything he'd once believed about himself.

"Is there anything you'd like to tell me, Stuart?" Charles's voice was gentle now, almost fatherly. "Anything that might be weighing on your conscience?"

For a moment, Stuart teetered on the edge of confession. He could tell Charles everything. About Piet's threats, about Philippa's desperate need for money, about the impossible choice between helping the woman he loved and maintaining his integrity.

But then he thought of Philippa, probably at this very moment choosing flowers for her wedding or discussing reception details with Mrs Myburgh. In ten days, she'd be safely married, beyond the reach of scandal. If he confessed now, everything would unravel. Her reputation would be destroyed along with his own.

And the love and respect of her father—the man speaking to Stuart right now—would be irretrievably damaged.

"No," he said finally, the word scraping his throat raw. "Nothing comes to mind."

Charles studied him for a long moment, his expression unreadable. Then he sat back with what might have been disappointment or relief—Stuart couldn't tell which.

"I see." Charles reached for the teapot, refilling both their cups with movements that seemed designed to fill the uncomfortable silence. "Well, if anything does occur to you —anything at all—I hope you'll feel comfortable coming to me. I've always believed that honest conversation can resolve most difficulties."

"Of course." Stuart's voice sounded foreign to his own ears as he forced himself to drink.

"Excellent." Charles glanced at his watch. "I'm afraid I have another appointment shortly, but I'm glad we had this chance to chat."

Stuart finished his tea, then rose on unsteady legs. "Thank you, sir."

"My pleasure." Charles stood as well, extending his

hand in farewell. His grip was firm, his smile warm, but his eyes remained watchful. "Take care of yourself, Stuart. These are dangerous times for those who find themselves on the wrong side of justice."

Stuart nodded, not trusting his voice, and stepped into the corridor.

THIRTY-EIGHT

Two days later, the interview with Stuart was still playing in Charles' mind as he worked late. He was in Maseru this week but had been in communication with his right-hand man in Mokhotlong, Sergeant George, who was optimistic that a potential key witness to Chief Thabo's alleged crime was on the point of offering a sworn statement.

In front of him were several other testimonies—as yet, unsigned—from villagers who'd allegedly heard Chief Thabo delivering orders that would ultimately see the unfortunate albino victim at the bottom of the ravine.

But it was hard to concentrate, for he kept replaying the conversation with Stuart over and over in his mind.

Marjorie put her head around the door to tell him she was leaving for the evening, and Charles glanced up. Through the windows, he could see the afternoon light beginning to slant golden across the mountains, painting the peaks in shades of amber and rose.

He gathered up the files scattered across his desk: reports from the diamond fields, witness statements, fragments of a puzzle that was slowly taking shape.

These investigations weren't about illegal diamond buying and *diretlo*, in isolation. They touched every facet of Basotho culture. The cultural practise of medicine murder the British Administration was trying to stamp out using the harshest means possible would never be extirpated if the Basotho people saw double standards in the dispensing of justice for another crime: one law for the white man, and a different one for the Basotho.

Stuart? Could he really be involved in something so abhorrent?

Never in a million years would Charles have thought it, yet his mind kept drifting to the way Stuart's hands had trembled when he'd reached for his teacup, to the way he'd looked at him. Guilt had radiated from him like heat from a forge.

And then there was the photograph. Until Charles saw it, he would give Stuart the benefit of the doubt. However, Brother Augustine had seemed certain.

Good men in impossible situations. The phrase echoed in his mind as he locked the files in his desk drawer. Twenty-five years in the Colonial Service had taught him that few men were entirely good or entirely evil—most existed in the grey spaces between, making compromises they could live with...

Or that slowly eroded their souls until they no longer recognised themselves.

If Stuart was involved in illegal diamond buying, something catastrophic must have driven him to it.

The question was what—and whether Charles could afford to care.

He took his jacket from the coat stand and checked his watch. Nearly six o'clock, but his work did not end there. He had paperwork to review at home, reports to complete so he could file them with the Resident Commissioner in the morning.

Locking his office, he made his way down the corridor. The building felt different in the evening hours: quieter, more contemplative.

He was crossing the main courtyard when he saw her.

Lizzie Cameron walked briskly down the dusty road, away from the administration offices, her blonde hair catching the last rays of sunlight. She'd changed from the practical clinic attire she'd been wearing earlier into a simple blue dress that emphasised her trim figure.

Charles felt his breath catch in his throat and, without conscious thought, he altered his course to follow her. He told himself it was mere politeness. He wanted to inquire about her work at the clinic to ensure she really was happy to do another stint the following week, for it was remote and isolated. He needed to know she felt comfortable, otherwise he'd have to find a replacement.

But these were justifications for waylaying her. He knew the truth was simpler and more dangerous.

He was falling for her.

The realisation should have stopped him in his tracks. Lizzie Cameron was thirteen years his junior, a professional colleague, someone who deserved far better than a lonely widower with more past than future. But his feet continued moving of their own accord as he maintained a discreet distance behind her.

She turned down a side street lined with jacaranda trees, their purple blossoms carpeting the ground like scattered confetti. The evening air was sweet with their fragrance, reminding him of walks with Eleanor in past years. But those memories felt distant now, overlaid with something immediate and vital.

Lizzie's destination became clear as she approached Mrs Henderson's Boarding House. A utilitarian red brick house with a wide verandah, it housed the overflow of government workers and temporary residents. Charles had been there once or twice on official business.

He quickened his pace, thinking to call out to her, to surprise her with a friendly greeting and perhaps suggest dinner at the Country Club. The words were forming on his lips when he rounded the corner and stopped dead in his tracks.

Stuart Price had just emerged from the boarding house's side entrance, and Lizzie was hastening her pace towards him while Stuart waited.

Charles tensed. The scene felt wrong. Catastrophic. Like a slow-motion walk towards disaster.

He tried to get a reading of Stuart's face but could not in this light. Stuart was merely waiting, and as Lizzie took the steps, his arms went about her and he lowered his face to kiss her.

Before drawing her inside. Out of sight.

Into his rooms and into his clutches.

Charles pressed himself back against the jacaranda tree, his heart hammering against his ribs. The purple blossoms seemed to mock him now. Everything that had seemed so beautiful was now spoiled. How could he have been so blind? So foolishly romantic?

So Stuart had set his sights on Lizzie Cameron? Young, beautiful, innocent—everything a man could want. And Charles had played the perfect fool, developing feelings for a woman who was clearly enamoured of the youth and virility of the dashing pilot.

A man who Charles suspected was a criminal.

The pieces fell into place with sickening clarity. Stuart's

nervous behaviour during their meeting, his obvious guilt over something he couldn't confess. If he were involved in illegal diamond buying, he'd need money—perhaps to impress women like Lizzie...

And his daughter.

He thought he'd be physically ill. Thank God Philippa had escaped his clutches. But how many others were there? How long had Stuart been playing this game?

And Lizzie—sweet, trusting Lizzie—had no idea what kind of man she was involved with. She saw only the handsome pilot with his effortless charm and exciting profession, not the corruption that lay beneath the surface. She was being used, manipulated by someone who would destroy her reputation without a second thought if it served his purposes.

Charles turned away, his hands clenched into fists at his sides as he strode back toward his own quarters, his mind racing with implications and strategies. Any vestige of leniency he might have felt for Stuart Price had evaporated.

The investigation would proceed with ruthless efficiency. Stuart would be prosecuted to the fullest extent of the law, not just for illegal diamond buying but for every crime Charles could pin on him. And when the truth came out—when Stuart's corruption was exposed in open court—Charles prayed to God that Lizzie would be saved in time to see him for what he really was.

CHAPTER
THIRTY-NINE

CAPE TOWN

THE MORNING LIGHT FILTERING THROUGH THE LACE CURTAINS OF the Myburgh guest room felt like rays through the bars of a prison. Philippa sat on the edge of the single bed, still in her silk nightgown, staring at the fat envelope of money that lay accusingly on the Persian carpet where she'd dropped it the night before.

Yes, she'd scribbled a cryptic note telling Stuart that 'matters had been resolved so that no one had blood on their hands'. It had been a struggle to write even that, and it had salved her conscience with regard to informing Stuart, while slicing her heart in two to actually put it into words.

But that's all she'd managed.

Mrs Myburgh, seeing that Philippa was clearly under par, had instructed her to take to her bed as soon as they'd returned to Cape Town a few days before, so Philippa had given her scrappy letter to the maid to post.

But how would she return that wad of tainted money?

Her hands trembled as she reached down to pick it up,

feeling the weight of Stuart's sacrifice. He had risked every-thing—his principles, his marriage, his future—to help her when she'd been desperate.

Which begged the question: how had she got here in the first place?

By choosing the safe path, the expected path, the path that led away from him and toward this gilded cage.

She caught sight of herself in the bevelled mirror across the room and froze. For a moment, she saw her mother's face looking back at her—Eleanor Richmond, who had given up wealth and position and family for love.

Her mother hadn't given up *anything*.

She'd just been brave enough to choose her heart over security, even when it meant exile from everything she'd known.

Live in the moment. Don't let life pass you by. Her mother's words. Spoken so often during those quiet evenings in the mountains when Eleanor would gaze towards the horizon.

Philippa had always thought her mother regretted the choices she'd made. Now she suspected that Eleanor's gentle wistfulness had just been quiet contentment at living a simple life with a man she loved—not regret at all.

For days, Philippa had been trying to escape this suffo-cating house, to return Stuart's blood money before it was too late. But every attempt had been thwarted by Mrs Myburgh in some way or another.

"You are the daughter I never had," her future mother-in-law had said with cloying sweetness just yesterday. Words Philippa had once longed to hear, but now they felt like shackles.

She wasn't Mrs Myburgh's daughter. She was Eleanor Richmond's daughter. And Eleanor's daughter would never have settled for a marriage built on aspiration and position rather than love.

"Oh, my dear, you can't possibly go to town today—the cake decorator is coming to discuss the crystallised flowers," Mrs Myburgh had said another time.

Or, "Philippa, darling, I've arranged lunch with the Pemberton-Smythes. They are such important people for you to know."

Mrs Myburgh had choreographed every minute of Philippa's time with military precision, ensuring she was never alone, never free to slip away.

The irony wasn't lost on Philippa. She was surrounded by luxury—French perfume on the dressing table, a wardrobe full of trousseau garments worth more than most people earned in a year that Mrs Myburgh had bought for her, fresh flowers replaced daily by silent servants—yet she felt more trapped than she ever had in her life. Even in that shabby Johannesburg hotel, facing the most desperate choice of her life, she'd had more freedom than this.

But it's not too late, a small voice whispered in her mind—her mother's voice, perhaps, or simply her own conscience finally finding its strength. *It's never too late until the moment you say "I do."*

A sharp knock at the door interrupted her thoughts. "Philippa? Are you awake, dear?" Mrs Myburgh's voice carried that particular tone of sweetness that meant business.

"Yes, I'm awake." Philippa quickly shoved the envelope under her pillow and reached for her silk dressing gown, her heart already racing with newfound determination.

Mrs Myburgh swept into the room without waiting for permission, immaculate as always in a pale blue Chanel suit. Her silvery blonde hair was perfectly coiffed, her makeup flawless despite the early hour. She carried a leather appointment book and that businesslike smile that had become so familiar.

"I trust you slept well? You look a little pale, darling. Perhaps we should have Dr Morrison look at you before the wedding. Can't have the bride collapsing at the altar!" Her laugh tinkled like breaking glass.

"I'm fine," Philippa said. "Just tired."

"Of course you are, with all the excitement. Now then —" Mrs Myburgh settled into the chintz armchair by the window and opened her appointment book. "I've had to make some last-minute adjustments to today's schedule. The florist wants to see you about the bouquet—apparently the white orchids aren't quite the shade we ordered. And I've moved your appointment with Antoine."

"Antoine?" Philippa asked, though she was barely listening. She was thinking of Stuart's hands in her hair, the reverent way he'd cupped her face, as if she were the most precious creature in the world. And—her heart clutched so she had to stifle a sob—the baby they had made together and which she had lost.

"The hairdresser, darling. Really, you must pay more attention. I've booked you for two o'clock instead of four. He wants to trim at least four inches off—your hair is lovely, of course, but far too long for a modern bride. We want something chic and sophisticated, not all those romantic tresses tumbling about your shoulders."

Shocked, Philippa suddenly paid attention. Her hair—her mother's hair, the one feature that truly connected her to the woman who'd raised her with such love and wisdom. The silky black waves that Stuart had tangled his fingers through on those precious nights when the world had seemed full of possibility.

Something fierce and protective rose in her chest. They wanted to cut away the last piece of her mother she carried, the last visible connection to the woman who she now realised had made the right choice—the only choice—when she'd chosen love over every other consideration.

"No," she said quietly, but with a strength that surprised them both.

Mrs Myburgh looked up from her appointment book, her perfectly pencilled eyebrows raised in polite inquiry. "I'm sorry, dear?"

"I said no." Philippa's voice was stronger now, fuelled by something that felt like her mother's spirit flowing through her. "I'm not cutting my hair."

"Oh, nonsense. It's just a trim, really. Antoine knows exactly what will suit your face shape. Trust me, darling, I know what'll look best for your wedding portraits."

Philippa felt a spark of anger kindle in her chest—the first real emotion she'd felt in days that wasn't despair or resignation.

And suddenly she understood what her mother had felt, all those years ago, when her own family had tried to cut her off from everything that made her who she was.

"I said no, Mrs Myburgh. I'm not cutting my hair."

The temperature in the room seemed to drop ten degrees. Mrs Myburgh closed her appointment book with a soft snap and regarded Philippa with the look she might give a servant who'd broken her favourite china.

"I see." Her voice was silk over steel. "Philippa, dear, I think we need to have a little talk about who really knows best in these kinds of situations."

Mrs Myburgh rose from her chair and moved to the window, her back ramrod straight as she gazed out at the perfectly manicured gardens. When she spoke again, her tone was that of a headmistress addressing a particularly dim pupil.

"You're about to become a Myburgh, which means there are standards to be maintained. Personal preferences —romantic notions about hair and such nonsense— become secondary to the family image. Surely you under-stand this?"

"What I understand," Philippa said carefully, feeling her mother's courage flowing through her veins, "is that you're trying to turn me into someone I'm not."

Mrs Myburgh turned from the window, her smile frozen. "I'm trying to help you become the woman you need to be. The woman Matthew needs you to be. The woman this family requires."

The word 'requires' fell between them like a gauntlet. Philippa thought of her mother, who had been 'required' to marry within her social circle, to maintain family stan-dards, to sacrifice love for duty. Eleanor had been brave enough to refuse. Could Philippa be equally brave?

"And what if I don't want to become that woman?"

"Then you're being incredibly selfish." Mrs Myburgh's mask was slipping now, revealing something cold and calculating beneath the gracious hostess facade. "Matthew is giving you everything—his name, his family's position, a future most girls would kill for. The least you can do is make a few small adjustments to fit in properly."

"Small adjustments?" Philippa's voice rose despite her efforts to remain calm, her mother's spirit burning brighter within her. "You're planning every detail of my life from the moment I walk down that aisle. What I'll wear, how I'll style my hair, which friends I'm allowed to keep, where we'll live, how I'll raise children I haven't even had yet. When exactly am I supposed to be myself in all of this?"

Mrs Myburgh's laugh was brittle. "Yourself? My dear girl, you're twenty-one years old. You barely know who you are, let alone what's best for your future. I'm simply providing guidance based on thirty years of experience in society."

"Experience in controlling people, you mean." The words came out with Eleanor's fearless honesty and hung in the air like a slap. Mrs Myburgh's face went white, then flushed red with indignation. "How dare you speak to me like that? After everything I've done for you, after welcoming you into this family—"

"You haven't welcomed me anywhere!" Philippa was on her feet now, suppressed frustration finally finding its voice. Her mother's voice. Her own voice. "You've been grooming me like a...a prize poodle, trimming away everything that makes me who I am until I fit your perfect little mould. Well, I won't do it anymore. I won't cut my hair, I won't pretend to love your ghastly friends, and I won't spend the rest of my life being your son's ornamental wife!"

"You're hysterical," Mrs Myburgh said coldly. "Classic pre-wedding nerves. Perhaps we should call Dr Morrison after all—he could prescribe something to calm you down."

The casual dismissal of her feelings as hysteria—the same way her grandmother had probably dismissed her mother's objections to an arranged marriage—was the final straw. Philippa felt something inside her snap, like a rope stretched beyond its breaking point.

She thought of the letter she'd found, hidden for so many years; the cruel words her grandmother had written to her daughter, disowning her because she'd chosen love over social standing. She thought of Stuart, flying dangerous mountain routes while she played with the idea of gracing Fair Lady Magazine's social pages. She thought of the baby they'd lost, the future they'd never explored because she'd been too afraid to be brave.

"I'm not hysterical," she said with deadly calm. "I'm clear-headed for the first time in months. And what I see clearly is that I can't marry Matthew."

Mrs Myburgh went very still. "What did you say?"

"I can't marry your son." Each word felt like stepping off a cliff, terrifying and liberating at the same time. Just as it must have felt for her mother, all those years ago. "I won't marry him. The engagement is off."

For a moment, the only sounds were the distant chirping of birds in the garden and the soft tick of the mantle clock. Mrs Myburgh stared at Philippa as if she'd suddenly sprouted horns, her mouth opening and closing like a fish gasping for air.

"You can't be serious," she said finally. "The wedding is in eight days. Eight days, Philippa! The invitations have been sent, the church is booked, the reception planned. My friends, Matthew's grandfather, half of Cape Town society—"

"Will have to find something else to do that day." Philippa moved to the wardrobe and began pulling out her own clothes—the simple dresses and skirts that predated her engagement, garments that belonged to the woman she'd been before she'd tried to transform herself into someone else's ideal. Her fingers shook slightly as she folded them, but not from fear. From relief. "I'm leaving today."

"You most certainly are not!" Mrs Myburgh's composure finally cracked completely. "Matthew! Matthew, come here this instant!"

After her second, more hysterical exhortation, heavy footsteps sounded in the passage, and Matthew burst through the door looking dishevelled and concerned. He'd obviously dressed in haste—his hair was uncombed, his shirt partially unbuttoned, his feet bare beneath hastily pulled-on trousers.

"Mother, what's wrong? I could hear you shouting from the other side of the house—" He stopped short when he saw Philippa folding clothes into her suitcase. "Pippa? What are you doing?"

"I'm leaving," Philippa said without looking up from her packing. Each folded garment felt like another step towards escape. "The engagement is off."

Matthew's face cycled through confusion, disbelief, and something that might have been panic. "You can't be serious. This is about the hair thing, isn't it? Mother, I told you—"

"This isn't about hair!" Mrs Myburgh's voice was shrill now, all pretence of gentility abandoned. "Your fiancée has taken leave of her senses. She's having some sort of breakdown, probably brought on by all the wedding stress. We need to call Dr Morrison immediately."

"I'm not having a breakdown," Philippa said firmly, closing the suitcase with a decisive snap. "I'm making the sanest decision I've made in months. Matthew, you're a decent man, but you're not the man for me. And I'm clearly not the woman for you—or at least, not the woman your mother wants you to marry."

Matthew looked between his mother and his fiancée like a man watching a tennis match, his face pale with confusion. "But Pippa, we love each other. We're perfect together. Everyone says so."

"Everyone except us, apparently." Philippa picked up her handbag and retrieved the envelope from under her pillow. "When did you last make a decision without consulting your mother, Matthew? When did you last stand up for something you believed in, even if she disagreed?"

Matthew's mouth opened and closed soundlessly. The answer was written in his silence.

"That's what I thought." Philippa moved toward the door, but Mrs Myburgh blocked her path.

"You're making the biggest mistake of your life," the older woman hissed. "Do you think you'll find better than Matthew? A man with his prospects, his family, his position? You're the daughter of a colonial administrator, for heaven's sake—this is the best marriage you could possibly make."

"Maybe," Philippa agreed, thinking of her mother, who'd given up an earl's daughter's inheritance for love. "But it would also be the unhappiest. I'd rather be poor and free than rich and miserable."

She stepped around Mrs Myburgh and walked toward the door, her heart hammering but her resolve solid as granite. Behind her, she could hear Mrs Myburgh's voice rising to near-hysteria.

"Matthew! Don't just stand there like a statue! Go after her! She's clearly suffering from pre-wedding nerves, the silly girl. A firm hand is what she needs, not indulgence!"

Philippa paused in the doorway and looked back at the man she'd planned to marry. Matthew stood in the centre of the elegant room, still looking confused and helpless, still waiting for someone else to tell him what to do. Even now, faced with losing his fiancée, he couldn't summon the strength to act independently.

Just like her mother's first suitor, probably. Lacking something, just like all the men her grandmother had probably tried to force on Eleanor.

"Goodbye, Matthew," she said softly. "I hope you find

someone who can be happy in the life your mother has planned for you."

And then she was walking down the corridor, down the grand staircase with its crystal chandelier and Persian runner, past the disapproving portraits of long-dead Myburghs who seemed to judge her from their gilded frames. The servants she passed looked scandalised—word would have spread through the house within minutes. Soon, all of Cape Town society would know.

Let them talk. Let them whisper about the Tremain girl who'd thrown away the catch of the season. Let them shake their heads over her foolishness and her ingratitude. Her mother had endured the same whispers, the same condemnation. And Eleanor had never once regretted her choice. She knew that now.

Philippa pushed through the front door and into the crisp Cape Town morning, breathing deeply of air that didn't smell of expensive perfume and expensive lies. Table Mountain rose in the distance, reminding her of how much more majestic her beloved Maluti Mountains were, of her father, of the world she'd left behind in pursuit of this hollow dream.

In her handbag, Stuart's money felt like a sacred trust—not just the return of a debt, but the first step toward honouring her mother's legacy of courage. She had no idea what would come next. No plan, no safety net, no guarantees. But for the first time in months, she felt like herself again—Eleanor's daughter, messy and complicated and imperfect, but real.

And that was enough to start with.

CHAPTER

FORTY

MASERU

"Darling, how was your day at the clinic?"

Stuart tried to keep up the cheerful front as he drew Lizzie inside and hoped she wouldn't grill him in return. The less asked about *his* day, the better.

Not that he'd quite processed the implications, he realised as he shoved the letter from Philippa he'd only just received into his pocket. To be honest, he felt numb.

"Tiring." She kicked off her shoes as she collapsed onto the bed. They didn't yet have the luxury of a separate living area while they were waiting for married accommodation, and the room that had been Stuart's sanctuary ten minutes ago seemed suddenly far too small for both of them.

"More tiring than working at the clinic?" he heard himself asking, for he didn't quite feel he was operating in the present.

Nevertheless, remembering Charles's remarks about Lizzie's enthusiasm for returning to Mapolaneng had made him uncomfortable.

Though not as uncomfortable as the rest of the conversation.

He didn't want to think about that—

"Stuart—?"

He stopped as he'd been about to turn away and raised his eyebrows enquiringly. Her tone seemed to portend something ominous. Or did he just suffer such a guilty conscience that everything made him feel guilty these days?

"I bumped into Mrs Oosthuizen today..." She trailed off, her eyes following him as he moved restlessly about the small room.

"Oh, yes?" What else could he say?

"She said she had no knowledge of any shortfall in the flower funds." She hesitated as if waiting for him to reply. When he didn't, she said, frowning, "I thought it odd."

"Well, I wouldn't worry. Mrs Oosthuizen is getting on a bit. I'm sure she gets a bit forgetful." He knew that if he looked at her, she'd know he was lying. She'd quiz him about why he was so distracted. And God knew, he was that.

His hand closed around the one-page letter in his trouser pocket once more while he pretended to straighten some paperwork on the small desk.

After a long silence, she sighed. "You're probably right."

"Yes, and you're probably hungry. Shall we get something to eat at Lancers?" The sooner they were out of this intimate setting with awkward questions being asked, the better.

He heard her draw in her breath slowly, and then venture suggestively, "We could always get a late dinner."

When he looked up, he was shocked to see she'd unbuttoned the top of her dress. Her skirts were drawn up around her knees, and she was looking at him suggestively.

The jolt to his equilibrium made him say far more harshly than he meant, "Not now, Lizzie. I'm starving."

To ameliorate her hurt, he went on, as he extended his hand to help her up from the bed, "Sorry, but I'm absolutely ravenous. I won't be good for anything until I've had a good steak."

Of course, she was quiet as they walked around the corner to get some dinner. And Stuart didn't know what to say.

Oh God, being a husband was exhausting.

As for being a good husband… Well, that horse had bolted. *Give it time.* He had to think that.

The sound of cheerful voices hit them as they opened the door, and Stuart relaxed. He wanted to be surrounded by people who were enjoying themselves; to remind him that one day he wouldn't feel as if the world was on his shoulders.

They sat at a table in the corner. Stuart just wanted to eat, talk about simple things that didn't trigger bad memories or feelings of guilt, and then go home and sleep.

"I'm glad you liked your work at the clinic," Stuart said for something to say.

Lizzie's face lit up. "I love it and I love working with all those little babies." A soft faraway look replaced her enthusiasm before she said quickly, "But I completely understand you wanting to wait a bit before we try for children." Fidgeting with the saltshaker, she went on as she stared at the tablecloth, "Sometimes I think that being married is hard. I suppose… we don't really know very much about each other, and now we have to live in each other's pockets."

"It'll be easier when it's not just one room, Lizzie. Things will be better then." By the time they reached the top of the list for married accommodation and could move into something more spacious, Stuart hoped this nightmare would be over. Philippa's wedding would have taken place—

Oh God! It was only now beginning to sink in. In a matter of days Philippa would be married, and she and Myburgh would be on their honeymoon. Stuart could go to Charles and make a full accounting of everything that had taken place. He was prepared to accept responsibility for his part as well as the consequences. He had acted unethically, but hopefully he hadn't—technically—acted outside the law.

"Tell me more," he went on, because if Lizzie was telling him about her world then she wouldn't be asking him about his, and he could think through the ramifications of all that he had learned this afternoon.

"I love the mountains and the freedom," she said. "I love the adventure." A cloud crossed her expression. "I wish I could keep going back there, but I don't think the administration will allow it once they know... " She made a gesture to encompass both of them. "And it won't take long before everyone knows we're married. But at least if I can go back a couple more times, I will be happy. And then I will have you."

"Hello, hello, fancy seeing you in a place like this."

"Oh, Piet, how nice to see you again!" Lizzie's face lit up, and she nodded enthusiastically as the Afrikaner asked if he could join them.

"Piet." Stuart's tone was wooden. "I didn't expect I would see you again. I thought your business here was done." He hesitated, then added, "I wondered if in fact you would find yourself in a little hot water if you came back over the border."

He didn't care that this would inevitably cause Lizzie to gasp and his nemesis to narrow his eyes. He simply could not believe the Afrikaner had the nerve to show his face in Maseru again.

"*Ach*, no man, nothing like that," Piet said with a dismissive wave, though his smile didn't quite reach his eyes. "Just some paperwork mix-up with the customs fellows. You know how it is—bureaucrats making mountains out of molehills." He settled into his chair and made himself comfortable. Oh, he was a man accustomed to talking his way out of trouble. "Besides, I had some unfinished business to attend to."

Lizzie looked between the two men with a slight frown. "What sort of business are you in, Mr van Wyk?"

"Import-export, mostly. Agricultural machinery, mining equipment. Whatever's needed up in the mountains." Piet's gaze flicked meaningfully to Stuart. "Speaking of which, I was hoping I might prevail upon Captain Price here for another flight up to Letseng-la-Terai. Tomorrow, if possible."

Stuart's fork paused halfway to his mouth. "That's not possible. I'm booked solid for the next week."

"Surely you could make an exception? I'd pay handsomely for the convenience." Piet's casual tone carried a steely edge. "I have something I think you'd be very interested in seeing."

"I can't imagine what that would be." Stuart's voice was carefully neutral as he avoided eye contact.

"Oh, I think you'd be surprised." Piet reached into his jacket and withdrew a leather wallet, making a show of checking its contents. "Let me just see if I have enough cash to make it worth your while—"

A small photograph fluttered from the wallet onto the

white tablecloth. Piet made no immediate move to retrieve it, and Stuart's pulse suddenly roared in his ears as he recognised the image: himself and Philippa, laughing together in the lamplight of the van Wyk rondavel, her hand resting on his chest in unmistakable intimacy.

Lizzie's eyes widened as she caught sight of the photograph. "Oh, is that from your family's party? What a lovely—"

"Clumsy of me," Piet said smoothly, snatching the photograph back before Lizzie could get a proper look. But the damage was done—Stuart had seen the recognition in her eyes, the hurt confusion that followed. "Just some old family snap my brother Jacobus developed. You know how it is with young lads and their cameras. They get quite carried away and don't know when to stop." He sent a meaningful look at Stuart.

"Excuse me," Lizzie said quietly, rising from her chair. "I need to powder my nose."

The moment she was out of earshot, Piet's genial mask slipped away entirely. "Now then, Captain. About that flight to Letseng-la-Terai."

"You bastard," Stuart hissed. "What do you want?"

"One more trip to the diggings. There's a miner there. He's found something special. My contacts in Johannesburg are very interested, and they're not the patient type. Besides, time's running out before the authorities get wind of things. Still, if we leave tomorrow—"

"Find another pilot. I'm done with your schemes."

"I don't think you understand." Piet leaned forward, his voice dropping to a dangerous whisper. "My associates know about our previous arrangement. They know about the money you needed to help your lady friend with her... little problem. They know her identity and that of the chap she's going to marry in a few days." He leaned back and smiled, tapping his breast pocket where he'd replaced his wallet. "And they know about this photograph, and that I have others. If I don't deliver what I promised, they'll make sure the authorities know exactly what kind of man Stuart Price really is."

"The authorities—" Suddenly Stuart stopped as the ramifications finally sank in of Philippa's hastily written note he'd opened literally minutes before Lizzie's return.

The 'little problem' that Piet planned to use as leverage over Stuart no longer existed. The 'little problem' that had haunted his dreams and threatened to upend Philippa's hopes and dreams had resolved itself naturally.

Piet intended to blackmail Stuart once again into bending to his will, but...

The realisation washed over him with startling clarity.

Good God! There was nothing over which to blackmail him.

No amount of digging could now reveal a sordid back alley visit to shame and humiliate the district commissioner's daughter and jeopardise...the future she had chosen.

"I'm not doing it, Piet." He smiled, and for the first time in a long while he felt at peace. No, he was not doing it. He'd never do it again, and in a few days he would reveal everything. With Philippa having safely said her vows and secured her heart's desire, Stuart could relax. His conscience—regarding doing his best by her, that is— would be clear.

Something ugly flared in the other man's eyes. "I don't think you quite realise what you're letting yourself in for if you refuse, Captain. Your career, your marriage, your precious reputation—all of it rests on one simple flight."

He turned as Lizzie returned to the table, immediately

shifting back into his charming persona. "Ah, Mrs Price! I was just telling your husband how lucky he is to have found such a lovely wife. You must be so proud of him—flying those dangerous mountain routes, helping people in remote places." His smile carried no warmth. "I do hope you appreciate what a hero you've married."

Lizzie's smile was strained. "Of course I do."

"Well, I must be off. Early start tomorrow, you know." Piet nodded to Stuart as he rose. "Think about what we discussed, Captain. I'll be in touch."

As he walked away, Stuart felt a great weight lift from his shoulders.

Until he took in Lizzie's hunched shoulders as she sat in silence, her face pale, her hands trembling slightly as she reached for her water glass.

"Lizzie—"

"Don't." Her voice was barely audible. "Please, Stuart. Not here. Not now." She drew a shuddering breath. "I know who that girl is now."

Stuart reached across the table, but she pulled her hands away, folding them in her lap. The cheerful din of the restaurant continued around them, but their little corner had become an island of misery in a sea of oblivious happiness.

CHAPTER

FORTY-ONE

Miss Cameron's decision to return to Mapolaneng barely a day after she'd got back to Maseru had taken Charles by surprise, though it would be just like her to have wanted to follow up with a sick child.

As he urged his horse up the rocky path toward the vaccination clinic, he tried to convince himself that professional duty motivated him.

Regardless of his reasons for seeking Lizzie out, there were aspects to the conversation he was about to have with her that made him quite uncomfortable. In fact, he had questioned whether it was right to interfere. But it would be a gross abrogation of moral responsibility if he did not warn Lizzie about the type of man with whom she appeared to have been tricked into some clandestine affair.

It didn't lessen his respect for Lizzie. She was too sweet, too trusting and had obviously been thoroughly groomed and hoodwinked by the man Charles had once liked and, yes, respected.

Just as his daughter had been.

Clearly, Stuart Price was a con artist. A womaniser. A criminal.

His breath misted in the cold mountain air. Under normal circumstances, he would have savoured this journey—the solitude, the magnificent scenery, the sense of being truly alive in one of Africa's most remote regions.

But today, duty weighed on him like lead.

When Marjorie had first placed the newspaper on his desk that morning, he'd been dismayed to discover the story had leaked to the press. Ropable, in fact. The **Bloemfontein Friend** had somehow got hold of that damning photograph from the diamond diggings—the grainy image that showed a pilot in the background of what appeared to be an illegal transaction. While the newspaper had been careful to avoid direct accusations, using phrases like "reportedly involved" and "under investigation," the implication was clear enough.

PILOT SOUGHT IN DIAMOND THEFT INVESTIGATION screamed the headline, and though Stuart wasn't named directly, anyone familiar with local aviation would recognise him from the photograph. Charles had already fielded three calls from concerned officials wanting to know what he intended to do about "his pilot problem."

The newspaper folded in his saddlebag felt like a lead weight. The photograph—poor quality though it was—would be seen by thousands across the Free State and beyond.

Lizzie was innocent. Sweet, trusting Lizzie saw good in everyone. She needed to know that the man she'd obviously fallen for was about to face serious criminal charges. The evidence had been accumulating: two illegal flights to the diamond diggings, collaboration with the Afrikaner now identified as Piet van Wyk, suspicious financial trans-actions.

The moment van Wyk tried to cross the border officially, he'd be apprehended. Unfortunately, Charles knew how easy it would be for him to slip across illegally through the mountain passes.

At least the newspaper hadn't released van Wyk's name—he would have no idea the authorities were onto him. And once Charles brought Stuart in for formal questioning, he'd have a better chance of learning van Wyk's whereabouts and plans.

The clinic came into view as he crested the final ridge, a simple structure of corrugated iron and timber that was both practical and welcoming against the harsh mountain landscape. Smoke rose from the chimney, and he could see several Basotho women with babies wrapped in colourful blankets waiting patiently on the wooden benches outside.

Charles dismounted and tethered his horse to the hitching post, straightening his jacket and trying to summon the right words. How did one tell a woman that the man she...cared for? Loved?...was being investigated for a crime and might end up behind bars? How did one balance duty with the desire to protect her feelings?

But then, he told himself with grim justification, he was protecting her. Protecting Lizzie Price, the young woman for whom *he* had feelings—irrelevant though that was in this instance—from being preyed upon.

The door opened before he could knock, and Lizzie appeared, her face lighting up at the sight of him.

"Charles! What a wonderful surprise!" She stepped aside to let him enter, her blonde hair bouncing on her shoulders. "I wasn't expecting to see you. Of course, you know I came up early. I bumped into Sister Pelesa in Maseru yesterday, who said she was heading to Roma virtually straight away, so I jumped at the chance to hitch a lift. And there's so much to do here. I love it!"

The warmth in her voice made his chest tighten with guilt. And affection. She was so open and giving. She didn't deserve a man like Stuart Price. A man who was smooth and charming on the outside but devious and manipulative on the inside. He'd obviously been paid well by van Wyk to do his bidding.

Nevertheless, he naturally had misgivings about what he was about to do.

"I wanted to check on how you were settling in," he lied, removing his hat and setting it on the small table by the door. "This clinic and the vaccination program are special projects of mine, and I wanted to see how everything was going, now that you've been here awhile."

"It's going wonderfully well. Dr Molapo is so dedicated and hardworking. And the mothers are so grateful. We've seen nearly thirty children since yesterday, and word is spreading to villages even further away." Lizzie's enthusiasm was infectious, her cheeks flushed with the satisfaction of such meaningful work. "Would you like some tea? I was just about to take a break between patients."

Charles nodded, though his stomach was churning with apprehension. Lizzie had found her calling here in these remote mountains. That was wonderful. Perhaps it might mitigate the hurt at discovering she'd been played by the man who'd won her affection but who obviously was taking advantage of her.

"And where is Dr Molapo now?" he asked. He needed to have this discussion in private.

"He's gone to Roma this afternoon. I'm surprised you didn't pass him along the way. But your timing is good because I was going to take half an hour for lunch," she said. "I'd just closed the door to the waiting room because, honestly, I've been going non-stop for five hours and I'm exhausted."

But her smile did not suggest she found the work onerous.

Charles chose his words carefully as he took a seat. "Yes, I imagine it could be never-ending if one didn't know when to stop. Certainly, when I am investigating a case, I completely lose myself in time." He cleared his throat, trying desperately to find a way to elaborate on the real reason he was here.

And then, miraculously, she did the job herself as she took a seat opposite him. With a sympathetic sigh, she said, "You must find this illegal diamond buying business I've been hearing about very challenging. I heard that two miners so far have been cheated by a bogus dealer."

Charles tensed. "Who told you this?"

"A couple of the ladies mentioned it. And Dr Molapo says it's caused great consternation in his village, which is where one of the miners is from."

Charles drummed his fingers on the table as he tried to think of his next line, relaxing only momentarily when Frangini, Lizzie's nursing assistant, brought them both tea before being dismissed to have her own break.

"Have they mentioned any names?"

Lizzie shook her head, guilelessly. "No, you know what rumours are like when they're swirling around. You never know what the truth is until the evidence is presented."

Charles cleared his throat again. Awkwardly, he reached down for his satchel, to pull out the newspaper.

"This was in the Bloemfontein Friend this morning," he said, pushing it across the table towards her. He cleared his throat again, then said, pointing at the European in the front-page photograph, "This is the man who is alleged to have flown that bogus diamond buyer...that criminal dealer... to Letseng-la-Terai." He waited so she had a chance to study the evidence; for it to sink in, then asked, softly, "Perhaps you recognise him?"

The face she raised to his was blanched white, her eyes luminous with horror.

"Stuart?" she whispered. Her hands tightened around her teacup until her knuckles went white. For a moment she was quite speechless. Patiently, Charles waited, and then finally she said in a whisper, "I suspected he'd done something wrong, but I couldn't believe it was truly...*that*."

Charles swallowed. He couldn't admit that he'd spied on Lizzie and seen her in Stuart Price's embrace. Not that it had been spying, exactly. Dully, he said, "I wondered if this man meant something to you."

"You did?" She jerked up her head, then whispered, "I wasn't sure how many people knew...about me and Stuart."

Charles was at a loss how to respond. Clearly, Lizzie was in love with the fellow. He realised it was unprofessional of him to be as affected by the knowledge as he was.

But that was why he'd made the journey. To save her from bad decisions before it was too late.

"Lizzie." Charles reached across the small space between them and covered her hands with his. "You have to understand how serious this is. When the news becomes public—and it will very soon—anyone associated with Stuart will be caught in the scandal. Your reputation, your career, your future—all of it could be gravely impacted."

Tears gathered in her eyes, but she didn't pull her hands away from his.

"But…this isn't proof, is it? It's all just speculation at this point."

So, she was trying to pretend he was innocent? To have hope that he was, at any rate.

He sighed. "I'm afraid there is credible evidence that Stuart Price has made two unlawful flights to the diggings, transporting a felon."

Lizzie gasped and put her hand to her mouth. "But… if he made a terrible mistake—for reasons we don't understand—perhaps there's justification?" She gulped. "Because Stuart *is* a good man. He has to be."

Frustrated, Charles shook his head and tried again. "Lizzie…I know how loyal you are. And if you care for him, this will be difficult. But believe me, you cannot be associated with him. He'll just drag you down with him."

Lizzie was crying now, silent tears that tracked down her cheeks like snail trails in the morning light.

With another shudder, she raised her tear-stained face to him. "It's too late, Charles. You don't understand."

"You must put yourself first, Lizzie." He squeezed her hand. "Stuart Price is no good for you. My strongest advice is that you cut ties between the two of you before he's dragged any further into this. You don't want to be associated with a felon and, at the moment, your…affair" —he didn't want to say the word but he had to be as blunt as possible—"is not common knowledge. The sooner you end it, the better it will be for you."

"Oh, Charles!" The words came out like an animal in pain, and Charles could hardly bear to hear it. Lizzie Price was more emotionally involved with Stuart Price than he'd thought. What a fool he'd been to imagine that her blushes could ever have been for him. Charles.

"There's something I have to tell you. Something I should have told you weeks ago." She took a shuddering breath. "Stuart and I... we're married!"

The words struck Charles like a hammer. He jerked his hands back as if her touch had burned him.

"Married?" he repeated stupidly.

She nodded. "A month ago. The day Stuart came back from England, in fact, we eloped and were married in a registry office in Pietermaritzburg."

"A month ago?" Charles was on his feet now, standing behind his chair, not knowing what to do with himself. "Before or after the diamond theft?"

"I don't know when the theft occurred," Lizzie said miserably. "I didn't know about any of this—" she pointed to the newspaper—"until I started hearing people mentioning it only in the last few days. And of course I had no idea that Stuart might be connected."

"You really did not?" He had to ask it. Had to look her right in the eye to try to gauge if she had somehow had an inkling of her...husband's exploits. But again, her expression was guileless.

"I didn't. But, Charles, please listen to me. *If* Stuart is involved, I believe in my heart that he must have been driven to it by circumstances beyond his control. He's not a criminal by nature."

Charles' composure finally cracked. "You're defending a man who quite possibly will make you complicit in his crimes! Don't you understand? When this comes out—and it will come out—you'll be seen as either his accomplice or his victim. It's going to be very hard for you, Lizzie." He cleared his throat again.

"But I am his wife." Lizzie's voice was quiet but resolute. "He's my husband, Charles. For better or worse, in sickness and in health. Those vows mean something to me—" Giving a little sob, she put her head in her hands—"even if they don't mean anything to him."

Charles stopped pacing. "What do you mean?"

Lizzie's laugh was bitter. "I mean that, even though Stuart married me, I have come to the horrible understanding that, in fact, he was never in love with me."

Charles stared, unable to formulate a response. Her words made no sense.

Outside, the sounds of cheeky Basotho children intruded, while she went on quietly, "I think that, even as we spoke our vows, I knew that was the case. But I was too blindly in love. I couldn't believe that a man as handsome and dashing as Stuart could want to marry someone like me." She shrugged. "Of course I said yes. I'd been looking for love my whole life. Now, finally, it had landed in my lap in the most whirlwind and unexpected way. And I truly thought it would solve all my unhappiness."

"You were unhappy?" he repeated stupidly, barely able to take in her words, because of his own pain.

"I was so lonely." She wiped her eyes with the back of her hand. "I'd been out with a few different men, but nothing came of it. Stuart was the first man who seemed truly interested. Though I should have seen the signs," she added bitterly.

He had to ask, even though it shouldn't matter. But he was more affected by her answers than he cared to admit. "What do you mean?"

"Clearly, Stuart was suffering from a broken heart." She sniffed. "I realise now—only the night before last, in fact, though I had my suspicions before—that he only married me on the rebound."

Charles felt something cold settle in his stomach. He didn't want to ask it. He suddenly didn't want to know the answer. "So...there's someone else?"

Slowly she nodded, her eyes boring into his, her hands gripping her now cold tea. "Yes." She swallowed. "Your daughter."

Charles recoiled. To have Philippa's name brought up like this, amidst all this sordidness, seemed a desecration. He shook his head emphatically. "That was over long ago."

He began to pace, and when he turned to face her again, her expression was wistful. "I don't think it'll ever truly be over," she whispered. "And that's what makes our marriage so tragic. He's tried so hard to be the husband I would want. But always...always he's thinking of her." She stood up suddenly, saying softly as she gathered up the tea mugs, "I can tell."

"Lizzie—"

"Please don't." She held up her hand to stop him. "Whatever you're about to say, please don't. I don't think I can deal with any advice, or sympathy or anything else right now."

Charles nodded.

Outside, he could hear the murmur of voices as more mothers arrived with their children, the normal rhythms of life continuing despite the personal dramas unfolding within the clinic walls.

"What are you going to do?" he asked finally.

"My job." Lizzie turned back from putting the cups in the sink, her professional demeanour sliding back into place. "These children need their shots, and I'm not abandoning my post because my personal life is a disaster."

"I would quite understand, given the circumstances, if you preferred to leave."

"And go back to Maseru? To Stuart? After learning this?" She raised her eyebrows. "Besides, I'm here because I have a job to do. I'll stay until the program is complete or until I'm physically removed from the premises."

THE TREK back to Roma passed in a blur of conflicted emotions. Charles's horse picked its way carefully down the narrow donkey track while his mind churned.

Lizzie was married to Stuart Price. The knowledge sat in his chest like a stone, heavy and indigestible. Even worse, she was married to a man who was about to be exposed as a criminal, a man who would drag her down with him when he fell. His blurred photograph and the allegations relating to his complicity had been published in the press, so there was every chance he'd already done a runner.

But what about Lizzie? Would he try to contact her? Send for her when he was across the border and safely in South Africa or further afield?

The mission buildings of Roma came into view, limned with gold in the afternoon sun.

Brother Augustine was at the stables when Charles returned his mount.

"How did your visit to the clinic go?" he asked as he walked with him towards the government Land Rover. Charles needed to be back in time for his flight to Mokhotlong, where advances on the case against Chief Thabo were suddenly gaining pace.

In the meantime, Brother Augustine's conversations with some teachers at the mission school had yielded some helpful information related to Moses Shakane, though there was still no evidence to suggest Shakane had leaked the photograph to the press.

"Miss Cameron is doing an admirable job. I feel confident the programme is in competent hands," he said as he opened the door of the vehicle and climbed in. "As for Shakane...any sign of where he is?"

Brother Augustine shook his head, then said, frowning, "Sister Mary Palesa did receive several phone calls this afternoon, but there was a lot of static before the line dropped out.

"For me?"

"She thought, at first, the caller wished to speak to Nurse Cameron but then said she said she believed the speaker must have asked for you since the tone of voice sounded—according to Sister Mary Palesa—quite urgent."

"Stuart Price, perhaps?" asked Charles, feeling again that churn of disgust but not yet able to tell Brother Augustine what he'd just learned about the relationship between Lizzie and the suspected criminal pilot.

Brother Augustine shrugged. "If I hear any more information, I think you'll want to know, I'll take notes before I direct the caller to phone you in Maseru."

Charles tapped his fingers on the roof of his vehicle. "I'm heading back to Mokhotlong as soon as I return to Maseru. I need to be back in the district to deal with some other matters in my jurisdiction, and my troopers have finally recorded some very interesting testimony from one more of Chief Thabo's villagers. One who until now has refused to speak. However, on this IDB matter, of course, I'll have Price questioned. That's a priority."

"Then if you're in Mokhotlong, I will radio through whatever I learn."

"That'd be much appreciated," said Charles, closing the door and then rolling down the window. The police radio was a more reliable method of communication than the switchboard, where phone lines frequently dropped out. "Don't worry, we'll get to the bottom of this counterfeit de Beers and these illegal diamond traders."

"You don't think the cuckoo will have flown the nest already, as you might say?" Brother Augustine scratched his scalp.

Charles was careful not to say too much. "If Captain Price is the man in the photograph—and at this stage everything is conjecture with not even the photograph veri-fied as having been taken on the day in question—then he has emotional ties that will keep him, for the meantime, in Basutoland."

It was disconcerting to realise that innocent Lizzie was their best hope of apprehending Stuart Price. *If* he was, in fact, the man they were after.

As an afterthought, he added, "Keep an eye out for any unusual visitors or air traffic in the area. Word has it that Stuart Price has rather a soft spot for Miss Cameron."

The brother blinked, hesitated, then said, "He'd have to land here first and complete the journey overland. We would definitely catch up with him."

"There's no other place he can land that's closer to the clinic?"

Brother Augustine shook his head. "Not unless he'd risk his neck on the stretch of rubble near the summit that one of your predecessors tried to turn into a cricket pitch before realising the folly of the endeavour." He paused. "Do you really think he's some desperate criminal who's a risk to the community?"

Charles turned on the ignition as he pondered the question. "No, I don't. At the moment, he's only wanted for questioning, and he won't get very far. I'll alert the border authorities. And, as I said, he has a rather substantial stake in Basutoland—" He thought of Lizzie which made him feel ill and even more determined to put aside personal animosity—"which means I can avoid the drama of running him to ground in some desperate manhunt. I don't think that would serve anyone's interests."

CHAPTER
FORTY-TWO

MOSES SHAKANE LOOKED WITH SATISFACTION AT THE MORNING'S newspaper that lay on the wooden table, its black and white photograph staring up at him with damning clarity.

He had got this far in his pursuit of justice. For, yes, the photograph was the one he had supplied. Even in the grainy newsprint, there was no mistaking the face. It was the same pilot who had ferried the Afrikaner thief to Letseng-la-Terai, who had helped steal first Lehlohonolo's diamond; then his uncle Tumelo's diamond. The man who represented everything corrupt about the colonial system that ground the Basotho people beneath its boot.

Moses smoothed the paper with trembling fingers, his eyes scanning the headline again: **PILOT SOUGHT IN DIAMOND THEFT INVESTIGATION.** The article was brief but devastating. There were allegations of illegal diamond buying, questions about misuse of administration aircraft, suggestions of a wider conspiracy involving European criminals and their local accomplices.

The irony was bitter. For weeks, Moses had railed

against the Colonial Administration's pursuit of justice against his Uncle Thabo.

But to no avail.

And then...

The diamond. Well, diamonds represented value. A stolen diamond from Lesotho's diggings was bad for de Beers, bad for the reputation of the administration. Much more important, he thought with rising rancour, than the death of a few imbeciles. Nobody cared about them yet the administration cared deeply about administering justice to Chief Thabo.

Their justice.

Yes, the irony would have been exquisite had it not highlighted everything that was wrong with this country.

Still, the greedy Afrikaner had played right into his hands.

He'd given Moses the ammunition to organise meetings, deliver passionate speeches about white exploitation. He had proof, now, that his anger had been justified all along.

But Moses was no fool. The pilot himself was untouchable—protected by his employers, shielded by the very system Moses sought to challenge. Going after Captain Price directly would accomplish nothing but landing Moses in prison.

No, he needed leverage. Something the pilot valued more than his own skin.

Thanks to young Mpho's nervous chatter about the happenings in the DC's household, Moses knew more about the Colonial Administrators' home lives than they might have suspected.

Moses pushed back from the table in the cramped mission school classroom where he'd soon address a crowd of students in a secret meeting. Through the single window, he watched the clouds shrouding the mountain peaks. Stark, dangerous, beautiful structures that had defied the centuries, ever present in his beautiful country. *His* country, bleeding wealth into the pockets of foreign thieves while its own people scratched for survival in the dust.

The door opened with a soft creak, and Jacob Mbongeni entered, his eyes bright with the particular fervour that Moses had learned to recognize and cultivate. Behind him came a handful of other students—young men mostly, their faces eager and angry in equal measure.

"Moses, we heard—" Jacob began, but Moses cut him off with a raised hand.

"You heard correctly," Moses said, his voice carefully modulated. He'd learned in Moscow that the most effective revolutionaries controlled their emotions, channeled their rage into precise action rather than blind fury. "The pilot who helped rob our people walks free while the colonial police chase shadows."

"But the newspaper says he's wanted," protested one of the younger boys, barely sixteen and still naive enough to believe in justice from official sources.

Moses smiled, but there was no warmth in it. "Wanted for questioning, nothing more. White men investigating white men—how much justice do you think will come from that?" He gestured to the newspaper. "They'll ask him polite questions over tea and biscuits, accept his explanations, and send him on his way. Meanwhile, my uncle Tumelo grows poorer by the day, cheated of wealth that could have fed his family for years."

The boys shifted restlessly, their anger palpable in the confined space. Moses could feel their energy like electricity before a storm, dangerous and unpredictable if not properly directed. This was the moment he'd been waiting for—not just their rage, but their readiness to act upon it.

"There must be something we can do," Jacob said, his hands clenching into fists. "Some way to force them to pursue real justice."

"Perhaps there is." Moses moved to the window, gazing out at the mountains that had sheltered the Basotho people for generations. Soon those peaks would witness the birth of a new Lesotho, one free from colonial oppression and foreign exploitation. But first, certain lessons needed to be taught.

"Tell me," he said without turning around, "what do you know about the vaccination clinic at Mapolaneng?"

The question seemed to catch them off guard. "The clinic?" Jacob frowned. "What does that have to do with anything?"

"Everything." Moses faced them again, his expression intense. "Who runs those vaccination programs? Who decides what medicines to inject into our children's veins? Who benefits when our people become dependent on Western medical intervention instead of traditional healing?"

Understanding began to dawn in their eyes, along with something darker. Moses had planted these seeds weeks ago, but they were finally beginning to sprout.

"The white doctors," whispered one of the younger boys. "The colonial medical service."

"Precisely. And who is currently administering these... treatments... to the children of Mapolaneng?" Moses let the question hang in the air, watching as the pieces fell into place in their minds.

"The pilot's wife," Jacob breathed. "The woman from Australia."

Moses's smile was sharp as a blade. *Perfect.* They'd made the connection without him having to spell it out completely. "The wife of a man who steals diamonds from the Basotho people while she injects foreign substances into Basotho children." His voice was soft now, almost conversational, but it carried the weight of absolute conviction. "Do you see the pattern? The systematic exploitation, the coordinated assault on our sovereignty?"

But more than that, Moses thought with satisfaction, he'd identified the pilot's weakness. A man might face consequences for his own actions, but he would move heaven and earth to protect his wife. Especially a wife hidden away in the mountains, vulnerable and alone.

The room had gone very quiet. Through the thin walls, Moses could hear the distant sound of evening prayers from the mission chapel, the familiar cadences of Latin that represented yet another form of foreign domination. How long had the Basotho people accepted such intrusions, such gradual erosions of their independence?

"What are you suggesting?" Jacob's voice was barely above a whisper.

Moses smiled again, and this time there was genuine warmth in it—the satisfaction of a teacher whose students had finally grasped a crucial lesson. "I'm suggesting that sometimes, when official channels fail, the people must pursue justice through their own means."

"You mean…" The youngest boy swallowed hard. "You mean we should go to the clinic?"

"I mean," Moses said carefully, "that the wife of a diamond thief has no business injecting anything into Basotho children. I mean that symbols of colonial oppression should not be allowed to operate with impunity simply because their husbands are white and well-connected."

And I mean, he thought but did not say, *that Captain Price will finally understand that his crimes have consequences—consequences that touch the people he loves.*

The silence stretched taut as a drumhead. Moses could see the conflict in their faces—excitement warring with fear, righteous anger struggling against ingrained respect for authority. This was the crucial moment, the point where rhetoric either transformed into action or died in comfortable inactivity.

"The woman at the clinic," Moses continued, his voice gaining strength, "represents everything wrong with the colonial system. While her husband grows rich from stolen Basotho wealth, she poses as a saviour, poisoning our children with foreign medicines designed to make them weak and dependent."

"Poisoning?" Jacob's eyes widened. "You really think—"

"I think," Moses interrupted, "that coincidences are rare in politics. A diamond thief's wife just happens to be administering injections to Basotho children? Western medicines that our people survived without for thousands of years? Ask yourselves—who benefits when the next generation of Basotho grows up believing they need white doctors to stay healthy?"

The logic was seductive, Moses knew, because it contained just enough truth to seem plausible. Colonial medicine was indeed another form of control, another way of making the Basotho dependent on foreign expertise. The fact that the vaccines might actually protect children from disease was irrelevant. In the larger struggle for independence, every form of Western intervention was suspect.

"What do you want us to do?" The question came from

one of the older boys, a serious young man whose father had been killed in the South African gold mines.

Moses walked to the small blackboard at the front of the classroom and picked up a piece of chalk. In bold letters, he wrote: **JUSTICE FOR THE BASOTHO.**

"Tomorrow," he said, turning back to face them, "the children of Mapolaneng are scheduled to receive their second round of injections. I think it's time we showed the colonial authorities that the Basotho people will no longer accept their poison—literal or metaphorical."

"You want us to stop the vaccinations?" Jacob was beginning to understand, his face flushing with excitement.

"I want us to send a message," Moses corrected. "I want the diamond thief's wife to understand that her husband's crimes have consequences. I want the Colonial Administration to see that the Basotho people will not be passive victims of exploitation."

And I want Captain Price to know, Moses thought with cold satisfaction, *that he cannot hide behind his uniform and his employers. Justice will find him—through the people he thinks he can protect.*

He moved among them now, his voice dropping to a conspiratorial whisper that made each boy feel specially chosen, uniquely important to the cause.

"Think of your brothers and sisters, your cousins, your own children someday. Do you want them growing up in a world where white criminals steal their heritage while white doctors weaken their bodies? Or do you want them to inherit a Lesotho that belongs truly to the Basotho?"

The answer was written in their faces—in their clenched fists and blazing eyes, in the way they straightened their shoulders and lifted their chins. Moses felt the familiar surge of power that came from moulding young minds, from channeling their natural rebelliousness into organised resistance.

"What exactly are we going to do?" The question was asked with breathless anticipation.

Moses smiled and began to outline his plan. Nothing too extreme—he wasn't a fool. But dramatic enough to make the newspapers, to show the colonial authorities that their days of unchallenged dominance were numbered.

And the leverage, Moses thought with grim satisfaction. *Captain Price will learn that his actions have consequences that reach far beyond himself.*

As he spoke, Moses felt the intoxicating rush of revolution beginning to stir. Tomorrow, the children of Mapolaneng would learn that they didn't need white medicine to be strong. Tomorrow, the colonial authorities would discover that their crimes had consequences.

And tomorrow, Moses Shakane would take another step toward the independent Lesotho that his Russian mentors had taught him to envision—a nation free from foreign exploitation, strong in its own traditions, answerable to no one but its own people.

The mountains outside the window stood eternal and unchanging, but tomorrow they would witness the birth of something new. Moses could hardly wait.

CHAPTER
FORTY-THREE

EDITH FRANKLIN WAS NOT A WOMAN WHO ACTED ON IMPULSE. Her daughter, Margaret, had said it a hundred times before.

And Margaret had just said it again as she helped arrange flowers for her mother's monthly mahjong afternoon.

"I don't know why you didn't try to contact him when I told you he was back in the country. You've been looking for him for years. And now, there he is! Stuart! Working for Drakensberg Air! I'd stake my life on it!" Margaret said, stabbing the grainy picture on the front page of the morning newspaper that lay on the table beside three cut proteas.

Edith was silent as her daughter, with a grunt of irritation, returned her attention to the slightly furry, dusty grey and maroon blooms that lasted forever and were South Africa's floral emblem.

Edith wasn't particularly fond of proteas. She much preferred delicate posies in soft colours like pinks and mauves and pale blues—posies that wilted after a few days. This was despite the fact that Edith was a practical and, for the most part, forceful woman, though she believed in letting things be—or rather, letting people be—if that's what they wanted.

It was why she had left Stuart in peace while she warred with her own desire to see him again.

Margaret snapped another stem and said, "Now it turns out that not only has he been working in the country for years—flying! Can you believe it?—but he's been dabbling in some diamond profiteering on the side."

"That's if the newspapers are to be believed," Edith protested finally, feeling ill as she'd dabbed at some spilled water. "They didn't mention his name."

"No, but—" Margaret pushed aside the vase and drew the newspaper in front of them again, pointing as she said, "That photograph, grainy though it is, is Stuart!"

Edith felt uncharacteristically querulous. "Surely it can't be? He'd have contacted me or your brother if he were back in the country, much less working as a pilot. Michael taught him to fly, for goodness' sake!"

Margaret huffed out a breath. "That would be just like Michael—crediting himself with Stuart's success. But now it appears the law is after Stuart, Mum. And who does he have on his side now?" She shrugged, answering her own question. "I have no idea, but you loved him more than you loved us."

"I loved him in a different way—"

Margaret smiled, not offended. "Because he needed you more than we did. That's what you once told me. But after all this time, why haven't you seen him?"

When Margaret had finally finished her dutiful task with the flowers and left, having deposited her son James, who was staying for a couple of days, Edith remained staring at the stern, stiff proteas, feeling a great churning inside that she tried not to identify as guilt.

Or fear. Fear was not an emotion with which Edith was familiar. She had always been in control of her destiny. She'd married well: a lawyer of whom she'd been immensely fond. Together, they'd brought up two successful children. Margaret had eventually found a husband, a placid, earnest accountant of whom she, too, seemed unusually fond, though perhaps that was because he kowtowed to her every command.

Michael had inherited his father's flourishing law practice and was married to a glamorous young woman who had given him two delightful children, a boy and a girl.

But while Edith's natural born children had had every advantage and grown into solid, deserving citizens, it was the children who'd landed on Edith's doorstep in 1940 who had, quite extraordinarily, engaged her love and interest, because, as Margaret had rightly pointed out, they'd needed her the most.

Little Gracie, the adorable, sweet-natured, doll-like child, had—even before she'd been cured of her slum accent and taught to behave—tugged at her heartstrings. The pang Edith felt at her unnecessary death was as fierce and strong now as it had been when she'd learned the grim details.

Stuart, the sensitive, ignorant little street urchin, had engaged a different kind of netterest. Over the seven years they'd parented the pair, Edith and Ernest had taken pride in their belief that Stuart would develop into a fine young man who would undoubtedly achieve worthy goals through grit, determination and honest toil.

When he had stood, fearful and reluctant, on the gangplank at the docks in Cape Town, looking younger than his years as they'd farewelled him back to England, he'd wept bitterly. Edith had tried to tell him that his real mother and father were waiting anxiously for him, but he'd only cried harder and said that Edith and Ernest were his real mother and father.

And indeed, the parental tug had not dissipated. Several years later, Edith and Ernest had come back into their lives, taking the now teenage Gracie and Stuart on a six-month trip through Europe while their own children were just forging independent lives.

So *why* had Stuart never contacted Edith and Ernest if he'd been living in the country for the past four or five years as Margaret claimed?

Edith continued to train her critical gaze upon Margaret's floral display, though her thoughts were far away. She could almost hear the horn of the steamer at the docks, feel the brush of streamers, with little Gracie whimpering that Edith was her real mother. She remembered how, a few months after Gracie had arrived, when Edith had asked her to recount a memory of her mother—to help the child keep the memory of her real mother alive—Gracie had said she mostly remembered her mother chasing her with a broken bottle while slurring her words.

This was what she'd sent them back to? Was this why Gracie had met the fate she had? Because she truly had no one?

Well, Edith was not going to fail Stuart this time.

Her decision was as impulsive as any she'd ever made.

"Mary!" she called to her Xhosa maid, who appeared promptly in the doorway.

"Madam?"

"I can't host Mahjong tomorrow. Please telephone Mrs

Watkins and apologise for the late notice. Tell her that her *melktert* is the only reason anyone comes to tea and if she doesn't believe me, she'll discover it's the truth if she serves it at her house instead of mine tomorrow, as I have to dash out of town."

Mary's eyes grew large. "You are leaving Pretoria so suddenly, Madam? Tomorrow? I will go now to iron what you shall be wanting."

"On second thoughts, Mary, I think I shall leave today. Yes! I have this moment decided to visit a very dear friend in Maseru who needs me. And maybe my help. Perhaps once you've telephoned Mrs Watkins, you could telephone Margaret and let her know that I'm going on a short trip. Oh, and that young James will obviously be coming with me."

It was easy enough to get in the car and head for Maseru, breaking the five-hour journey with her brother and his family on their farm just outside Bloemfontein.

Now she was in Maseru, parked at the airstrip near the hangar with young James asleep on the back seat of the Mercedes.

The receptionist at the Maseru Hotel, which she'd just checked into, had made enquiries on her behalf, informing her that Captain Price was due in about 2.30pm.

Now, with fifteen minutes to spare, Edith was parked and waiting patiently in the shadow of the corrugated iron open hangar which, save for herself, was completely deserted.

The drive from Pretoria to Maseru was the longest she'd ever taken on her own, and it had given her time for reflection as she'd cycled through multiple possible reasons for Stuart's lack of contact. Each one circled back to Gracie's death. Though really, who was she to think she might know? She hadn't seen Stuart for years.

She sighed, closing her eyes briefly as she settled back in the Mercedes.

Through the windows, the airfield stretched toward the mountains. A Cessna, painted blue and white like the one Michael had learned to fly in before he'd been able to afford the fancy Beechcraft he loved to buzz around in, visiting clients, was parked on the apron next to a couple of fuel drums.

Ernest had been an aviation enthusiast, too, and in his latter years, he and Edith often socialised at the local Flying Club. It was there, over long lunches, that the pair would often wistfully recall their two evacuees, wondering if Stuart had followed his dream of becoming a pilot.

But with Margaret having confirmed that, and yesterday's ghastly newspaper article detailing how badly that beloved, hard-worked-for flying career might be about to slip out of his grasp, Edith knew that she'd wait at the airstrip for as long as it took to find him.

And when she did, she'd make sure he knew that she would provide him with every financial and legal resource possible to clear his name using the contacts Ernest, and by extension, herself, had in the legal and aviation worlds.

That's how these things worked. Stuart was just too proud to capitalise on that. And of course, it went without saying that Stuart was not guilty of something as grubby as illegal diamond buying. If anyone knew Stuart, it was Edith. A leopard does not change its spots.

Glancing at her watch and seeing that it was nearly time for the plane to arrive, Edith got out of the car to stretch her legs, checking that James was still asleep on the back seat.

It was disconcerting to feel her heartbeat quicken as she wandered into the hangar.

A few minutes later, she observed someone else approaching. A taxi was disappearing in a plume of dust, and, to her surprise, Edith saw that the dark-haired young woman who'd got out was now running towards the hangar.

What struck her as odd was that the girl, who was well dressed in a blue wool skirt and cashmere sweater, appeared to be in something of a panic, her dark hair tumbling about her shoulders, her heels digging into the soil.

Edith looked about her for a possible reason. There was no sign yet of any plane, and the hangar was deserted.

And then she saw that another car had parked—a smart green MG. A young man had jumped out, and he was now running after her.

When he was close enough, Edith could see that he was tall and handsome with sandy hair, and that his well-cut clothes were obviously expensive. But he looked dishevelled, with his tie loose, his shirt half tucked into his charcoal trousers.

Glancing at the sports car, Edith noticed it was covered in dirt, its windscreen a mess of squashed bugs. As if he'd driven all night.

"Philippa!" the young man cried out to the young woman. "Come back! I've been chasing the train from Bloemfontein for hours, and I'm not giving up until I talk to you. Is this what I have to do to show you how much I love you?"

The young woman—Philippa—slowed her pace but

didn't turn around. She was now standing, staring into the hangar but clearly too light-dazzled to notice Edith just a few feet away.

Tactfully, Edith stepped behind a 44-gallon drum, wondering if she should make herself known.

"How did you find me, Matthew?" The young woman sounded defeated as she turned to face him with obvious reluctance.

"Susan told me you'd stayed the night with her before taking the train to Bloemfontein." The young man raked his hands through his hair. "So then I knew you'd be on your way here to see your father. And that you'd probably be looking for a flight to Mokhotlong. I told you, I've been driving all night." Matthew approached her carefully, as if she were a skittish horse that might bolt. "Pippa, please. Let's talk about this sensibly."

"There's nothing to talk about." Philippa's voice was steady, but Edith could see the tension in her face. "I told you—the engagement is off."

His voice was gentle and coaxing. "You don't mean that. You're upset, and I understand why. Mother can be... overwhelming. But we can work this out."

Transfixed by the drama unfolding before her, Edith watched the young man—Matthew—continue his slow advance. She could see every feature of his handsome face, but he clearly had not noticed Edith.

"Your mother isn't the problem, Matthew," Philippa said, her voice cold. "Well, she's part of it, but not all of it."

There was a long, tense silence. Embarrassed, Edith wasn't sure what to do. It was too late to declare herself. She wasn't eavesdropping, but they clearly hadn't registered she was there, observing their intimate drama.

The young man took another step forward. "It's the

pilot, isn't it?" he asked, his tone hardening. "That's why you've come here. You're not running into your father's arms, are you? You're running to find Stuart Price? Aren't you?" His voice grew harsher while Edith felt her heart miss a beat.

Stuart Price. Had she heard correctly?

Slowly, Philippa nodded.

Matthew sucked in an audible breath. "But he's married, Philippa. You can't have him. And why would you want him when he's nothing but a nobody from the wrong side of the tracks?"

The sympathy in the first part of this revelation—for Edith—very quickly gave way to scorn.

"How dare you say that, Matthew Myburgh?" Philippa reacted fiercely. "He's more of a man than you will ever be! He stands up for his principles. You can't even stand up to your own mother!"

Edith wasn't sure who gasped louder. Matthew or herself. Well, the girl certainly had spirit.

But her Stuart was married? Margaret hadn't mentioned *that*.

And now this poor, beautiful girl was obviously wanting to throw herself at a married man when this clearly very eligible gentleman was giving her an alternative?

Edith wasn't sure what she felt at that moment. Of course she could understand any beautiful young woman being in love with Stuart...

But no one with a ring on their finger should play around.

Nevertheless, the young man's derision had raised her protective hackles.

"I shall pretend you didn't say that," Matthew said, his

voice barely controlled as he pushed out his chest. "I didn't just drive for fifteen hours because my mother told me to. I drove fifteen hours because I love you. We're perfect for each other—everyone says so. The Pemberton-Smythes, the Weatherbys, even Grandfather thinks—"

"I don't care what your grandfather thinks," Philippa interrupted, her voice rising. "I don't care what anyone thinks except us. And when I look at you, Matthew, I don't see the man I want to wake up next to for the rest of my life. I see someone who will *always* let his mother decide for him. Even if he says she doesn't."

Matthew's face flushed red. "That's not fair. I'm trying to build a future for us—"

"No, you're trying to build the future your mother has planned. But that's beside the point, and this is not about your mother. It's about you and me. It's about me realising that I made the wrong decision when I chose you over Stuart, and yes, it's too late, I realise that. I am not about to go and make the oldest mistake in the world and throw myself at a married man—"

Well, that was some relief, thought Edith as she silently cheered the young woman on. For really, there was something about that entitled curl to young Matthew's lip that set Edith's teeth on edge.

"No, I am going to right a wrong!" The feisty young woman went on. "You know what, Matthew? When I got on that train in Cape Town, I knew I had done something terrible. That was bad enough. But then I got to Bloemfontein, and I saw a newspaper, and do you know what else—?" She'd begun to physically shake now. Edith could see it even from here.

The young man took a step forward, but Philippa retreated, her hands in front of her chest as if to defend herself. "That's when I realised that my crime was so much worse! Yes, you'll read it in the paper soon enough. You'll hear it all over town. Captain Price is wanted for questioning over illegal diamond trading. Yes, you'll tell me that's another reason I'm a fool to be rushing up here to see him. Yes, to see him! That's the reason for all this!" Reaching into her blouse, Philippa withdrew an envelope. A fat envelope. "Do you know what is in here? Money, Matthew. A *lot* of money. I made a terrible mistake, and Stuart came to my rescue. He's not a diamond thief; he's a hero. And if any scandal attaches to his name, then the whole reason for that is ... me!"

Matthew was staring at her as if he didn't know what to say.

Edith was just glad she had the 44-gallon drum to hold her up at this stupendous revelation. Really? This young woman was claiming she was at the root of Stuart's troubles?

Holding her breath, she waited to see Matthew's response.

He looked about him. At the desolate field, the dark, brooding mountains looming behind them. At Philippa, breathless and shaking before him. Somehow he still didn't seem to register Edith behind the fuel drum.

And he tried one more time.

"Pippa, please... I don't care what you've done." Matthew's voice took on a wheedling tone that made Edith's skin crawl. "Let's go back to Cape Town. We can work this out. Mother can be overbearing. I'm the first to admit it. But we don't have to live so close to the family. We could get our own place far away."

For a moment, Philippa wavered, but then Edith saw it was from pure exhaustion. No, she was resolute.

"It's not about hair or houses, Matthew." There was a new softness to her expression. As if she were trying to explain something to a very small child who may not have the wherewithal yet to grasp its meaning. "It's about love. Real love. The kind where you'd risk everything for someone. Where you'd choose them over luxury...or even comfort. Where you'd put them before everything. Even oneself." Her voice hitched. "I thought I could settle for less...but I can't. I won't." Philippa raised her arm to point to his car. "Now go, Matthew! I've said everything there is to say. You and I are over. It's Stuart I need to find now."

Matthew stared at her. He took a tentative step towards but at the fierce look on her face and another imperative gesture towards his car, he obviously gave up.

"Don't think I'll be so willing to take you back, Philippa," he muttered over his shoulder as, scowling, he began to walk in the direction of the MG.

"I won't be asking!" Philippa shouted after him, turning back towards the hangar and squeaking with surprise when Edith stepped out.

"I'm so sorry I overheard all that," Edith apologised. "Philippa, that's your name, isn't it?"

The girl nodded warily.

"It seems we are both looking for Stuart Price."

Philippa flinched. "What?"

Edith cleared her voice. She usually wasn't so diffident. "I didn't mean to eavesdrop, but I rather got the impression you were acquainted with...my boy."

She saw the young woman's forehead crease in puzzlement as she steadied herself as her heels sank into the soft soil. "Your boy?" Her voice was wooden as she repeated the words. Edith wasn't even sure she was even registering.

Edith tried again. "I don't know if Stuart ever

mentioned me—" She took a couple of steps closer, for she really wanted to talk to Philippa— "but my name is Edith Franklin."

It was as if something wondrous happened within the girl, for suddenly her face transformed as if lit up by the profoundest joy.

"Mrs Franklin!" she cried, her cognition and the force of her response balm to Edith's soul. "You're here because you believe in him, *too*?"

And then, to Edith's great astonishment, young Philippa threw herself into her arms and began to cry.

The rawness of her distress aroused a rare protectiveness that Edith hadn't felt since young Gracie had sobbed in her arms a decade earlier, and she began to stroke her hair. It had been a long time since anyone had needed her.

Footsteps sounded nearby, and a generator whirred into life, powering the single light globe in the hangar.

"Excuse me—" Edith began, turning to the mechanic in dirty blue overalls who'd just arrived while Philippa stepped back. "Has Stuart Price's plane been delayed?"

The young man shaded his eyes, then pointed at the mountains. "Bad weather," he said. "Looks like he'll be spending the night in Mokhotlong."

***

PHILIPPA CHECKED into the Maseru Hotel in a room down the corridor from Mrs Franklin and James. She couldn't impose on Elizabeth at such short notice.

Well, of course she could. The guest cottage was always ready for a last-minute visit, and Elizabeth would have been delighted to have shared reminiscences with her childhood friend.

But the inevitability of having to discuss the details of the devastating newspaper article in which Stuart was all but named was too much.

It seemed that it was all anyone could talk about. As she made her way to the dining room for dinner, she was shocked to overhear someone in the passage say that "the pilot" had tried to make a getaway and had stolen an aircraft.

She was just digesting this outrage when someone said to the receptionist, "Terrible business. Captain Price seemed like such a decent fellow. The things people will do when they're desperate for money."

Desperate for money. The words screamed through Philippa's mind as she crossed the dining room floor, tearful as she took a seat opposite this woman she barely knew, before she said, with only the most basic preamble before relating what she'd heard, "Stuart wasn't desperate for money—*I* was."

And now *he* was paying the price for her desperation.

Without feeling the need to go through the usual introductory process, Philippa was ready to bare her heart. Over two shandies, she explained to this kind, attentive woman the instant attraction she'd felt for Stuart when they'd had to ditch their plane into a mealie field. An attraction she'd refused to acknowledge as she'd been determined to marry the young man Mrs Franklin had witnessed trying to pressure her into going ahead with the wedding.

"But how can I do that when I love Stuart?" Philippa now asked, feeling again the threatening convulsive sobs rising up in her throat.

"You can't marry Stuart if he's already married," Mrs Franklin reminded her gently, diffidently asking for details, which Philippa related with her unashamedly biased perspective.

"I thought I had time!" she added, on a hiccuping sob, angrily wiping away fresh tears with a furtive look to ensure no one she knew was in the vicinity. "And now his wife, Lizzie, is working as a nurse at a clinic in Mapolaneng while I'm here, and I *need* to see Stuart because I have to return the money he gave me. But now I don't know where he is."

Mrs Franklin put her hand over Philippa's. "She and Stuart must love each other if they were only married a few weeks ago," she said.

Philippa shook her head. "Not as much as he loves me," she declared. "He told me does only a few days ago. He married Lizzie on the rebound when I stupidly told him I was going to marry Matthew. When I thought I had time to change my mind right up until the last moment," Philippa wept. "I was so blinded by how much Stuart loved me...And now he says his duty is towards Lizzie."

"And so it is," said Mrs Franklin, with no trace of censure and a great deal of sympathy. "Perhaps it would be easier if you gave the money to someone else to hand to him so that you wouldn't have to see him again."

Philippa's eyes widened. "Not see him again? When I owe everything to him?" She shook her head. "I have to give him the money, and I have to explain to Daddy that Stuart is only in trouble because of me." She began to cry again. "But I don't know how I'm going to do that. I can't think of that now, but please will you come to Mokhotlong with me tomorrow? I'll get a message to Daddy ahead of time, but we often have guests staying in the guest rondavel since the Packhorse Inn burnt down. He won't mind. And—" she added with a sniff, "please will you tell me everything about what Stuart was like when he was growing up?"

CHAPTER

FORTY-FOUR

MASERU

Stuart wasn't sure if he was glad that an unexpected break in the weather offered him a window to fly back to Maseru, just as the sun went down.

He'd seen the newspaper late that afternoon, and, although he hadn't been identified, he knew the photograph looked suspicious enough that the authorities would be knocking at his door sooner rather than later.

He certainly hadn't expected it to be as early as 5.30 AM the following morning!

Blearily, he registered the time on the clock on his bedside table at the sound of insistent pounding on his door.

Charles was probably worried he'd do a runner before he was brought in for questioning.

"Coming, coming," he muttered as the pounding came again, more urgent this time. So, this was it.

Pulling on a sweater over his pyjamas, he padded barefoot to the door of their small room at Mrs Henderson's boarding house, opening it without checking who was on the other side.

"Good God, it's you!" Stuart stared, not quick enough to close the door before a black boot wedged itself in the crack.

"Captain Price?" Piet van Wyk's voice was low. "We need to talk."

Stuart's breath caught in his throat. He glanced back at the bed, thankful Lizzie wasn't in it, then back at Piet, who stood in the shadows. Instead of the slick businessman's attire from last time, he was dressed in work clothes, his dark hair hidden beneath a wool cap.

"What the hell are you doing here?" Stuart whispered, reluctantly stepping out when Piet wrenched open the door.

"Business, Captain. Urgent business." Piet's voice carried an edge of barely controlled desperation. "We need to take a little flight this morning."

"I told you—I'm not doing it."

"See, that's where you're wrong." Piet stepped closer, and Stuart caught a whiff of stale cigarettes and nervous sweat. "You don't get to decide when you're out. Not when there's unfinished business."

Stuart crossed his arms, trying hard to work through the logistics of how best to reel Piet in to the authorities. Was Charles in Maseru or Mokhotlong? If Stuart could apprehend Piet, maybe he'd be the hero and not the villain.

He knew the DC would have made plans to get back to his official district at the earliest. Mokhotlong had jurisdiction for Letseng-la-Terai and Chief Thabo's village where, Stuart had heard, the investigation into the chief's role in the last two medicine murders had turned up important new evidence.

"Sorry, Piet, my business with you is finished," he said, more firmly this time.

Piet shook his head. "Not with impatient creditors breathing down my neck, it's not." Piet sent a hunted look toward the stairs, then back to Stuart. "My associates have given me until noon today to deliver something special from Letseng-la-Terai. After that..." For a moment he looked cold and focused, but Stuart could see panic at the edges.

It gave Stuart the courage to say in a tone steadier than he felt, "That's your problem, not mine."

"Wrong." Piet's hand moved to his jacket pocket, and Stuart caught the outline of something that suddenly made this conversation so much more dangerous. "You see, my associates have done their research. They were delighted by the outcome of our previous arrangement, and they're very keen to ensure our continued cooperation."

Cold sweat beaded Stuart's hairline. Piet was clearly a desperate man. Carefully, he drew in a breath. He needed to keep a cool head, but he needed Piet to know that he would not budge. He knew also that Mrs Henderson herself might have her ear pressed to the door. Lowering his voice, he said, "Do you know how dangerous it is to land when the winds are not in our favour? At eleven thousand feet, with gusts coming from the wrong direction, and an airstrip barely long enough to land—even when the winds are coming from the right direction—we could both end up dead."

"Don't make this harder than it needs to be." Piet's smile was grim. "The outcome of our previous flights to Letseng-la-Terai made my associates very happy. Just do what you did before. Who doesn't love a big, beautiful diamond?" He paused, studying Stuart's face, then said in a more wheedling tone, "Don't you want to please your lovely girlfriend who clearly needed that money so desperately?"

"Quiet!" Stuart cautioned, shooting a meaningful glance at his door, but Piet just laughed. "I know your wife is in the mountains. Does she know, Captain Price? Does she know about the gorgeous Tremain creature you paid so much money to when last we met?"

Stuart tried to appear unmoved, but his heart beat like a jackhammer against his ribs. In a slightly louder tone—for the benefit of anyone else who might be listening—he said, "You must have the wrong man. I don't know what you're talking about?"

"Ah, Captain, please don't insult my intelligence or try to pretend it didn't happen just because you're afraid of others hearing. You know I'm referring to the meeting at Rand Airport. The envelope of cash you handed to Miss Tremain."

"You're making this up. You have no evidence. Only your word against—"

"I have evidence." Piet reached into his other pocket and withdrew a small photograph. Even in the dim corridor light, Stuart could see it clearly—himself and Philippa at the airport, the moment he'd given her the money. His throat went dry as he tried to assimilate the potential damage.

"Did you think I was alone?" Piet asked. "No, I knew to find you at the plane—and just as I was going to introduce my associate, you answered all my dreams when you whipped out your little bag of cash, counted out the notes, and handed them to Miss Tremain. Couldn't believe it!" He bent his face closer to the photograph and marvelled, "Even managed to get that hungry look in your eyes as your hand closed over hers."

Stuart's world tilted on its axis while his brain whirred with the implications. What was today's date—? Still a few days before Philippa's wedding— Lizzie was safe at the clinic— Charles was in the mountains—

He felt cold, clammy sweat bathe his body while he explored every ramification. If he could only play his cards right, they'd all remain unhurt by his actions.

Piet gave a short laugh. "My associates are very thorough. They like to know exactly who they're dealing with. Which should be a further warning to you they are men who are not to be messed around with." He pocketed the photograph. "Now, I'm sure the very upstanding local District Commissioner would love to see evidence of his daughter's... financial difficulties. Especially so close to her wedding to young Myburgh."

Stuart tried to steady his breathing. He didn't know what to say except for a lame, "You bastard."

"Business, Captain. Nothing personal." Piet checked his watch—an expensive piece that hadn't been on his wrist during their previous encounters. "We leave as soon as you're dressed. Dawn's the perfect time for a supply run to the mountains. A stop at the diamond diggings, of course. Completely legitimate, nothing suspicious about it."

"I can't just—"

"You can and you will." Piet's hand emerged from his jacket pocket now, revealing the snub-nosed pistol Stuart had glimpsed earlier. He kept it low, casual, but the barrel was pointed directly at Stuart's chest. "Because if you don't, I guarantee you that by this afternoon, everyone—and not just in Cape Town society—will know the kind of dubious financial business Miss Tremain is mixed up in while consorting with a married man. How disappointed the District Commissioner will be learn of his daughter's—affair." He chuckled. "Believe me, I make it my business to know these things." His lips curled in a rictus of a smile. "The wedding will be called off, her reputation destroyed."

Stuart stared at the gun, his mind racing. In the distance, he could hear the boarding house beginning to stir—footsteps in other rooms, the sound of running water. Normal people beginning normal days, unaware of the drama playing out in their corridor. He had to try everything he could to avoid meekly accompanying Piet on this latest illegal jaunt.

"What makes you think I won't go to the authorities?"

"Because you're not stupid." Piet's voice was matter-of-fact. "My associates have people everywhere, Captain. Police, government offices, even the DC's own staff. You make one move against me, and Miss Tremain's photographs will be all over the Cape Town social pages before sunset."

Stuart's throat felt thick. But even though he believed Piet was bluffing, he asked, soft and low, "So, tell me exactly what you want and when there'll be an end to it?"

"One flight. Letseng-la-Terai and back. There's a miner up there who's found something extraordinary. Already they're calling it The Lesotho Diamond because it's bigger than anything found before. He hasn't registered it yet, which gives us a small window of opportunity."

Stuart shook his head. "The security has been upgraded."

"Not yet, it hasn't. We're talking about a donkey track and a couple of police troopers up there who know and trust you. But we need to move fast. I saw yesterday's newspaper, but these *okes* at the diggings won't have heard the news just yet." Piet checked his watch again. "We don't have long, and my associates have given me until noon. Now let's go!"

Stuart thought of Lizzie, far away at the vaccination clinic, nursing the children she loved, and her hurt at his disloyalty. Would she believe he'd never been unfaithful?

He thought of Philippa, probably choosing flowers for a wedding that was only days away; thought of Charles Tremain's trust, his own carefully constructed life, the inevitable investigation into van Wyk's activities that would certainly come home to roost with Stuart's complicity—unless he could somehow apprehend the diamond thief and hand him to the authorities.

The thought gave him at least a modicum of hope. "And after this flight?"

"After this flight, we never see each other again. You get your quiet life back, Miss Tremain gets her society wedding, and everyone's happy." Piet's smile was razor-thin. "Especially my associates."

Stuart tried to keep his voice steady. If he flew Piet to Letseng-la-Terai, how could he alert Charles beforehand? Stuart would not be Piet's comrade-in-arms. He'd be the man responsible for delivering Piet to face justice. He felt a prickle of hope. This would solve everything—wouldn't it?

"How do I know you'll keep your word?"

"You don't. But you know what will happen if you refuse." Piet tucked the gun back into his jacket. "We need to be airborne at the crack of dawn, Captain, and before anyone else is at the airport. I'm sure you don't need to file a flight plan or do anything other than turn on the engine. If you have to, make some excuse for why you have to leave so early—medical supplies, mail delivery, whatever story you prefer. I'm sure you mountain pilots do these things every day."

Stuart looked toward his door, imagining Lizzie, who would have been still sleeping inside, so relieved she was in the remote mountains far away.

His first responsibility was to her. "If anything happens to my wife—"

"Nothing will happen to anyone if you do exactly as I say. And as your wife is away, I'm coming inside to keep an eye on you." Piet nodded towards Stuart's door, then followed him inside. "Get dressed. Then we can both go to the airfield." His nostrils flared. "I'm sure I don't need to warn you about trying to be clever. My associates are very good at holding grudges, and I don't intend to be in their crosshairs."

What could he do? Stuart dressed quickly while Piet leaned against the wall, his hands in his pockets, the outline of the gun fully visible.

Outside, the first pale light was beginning to touch the mountain peaks.

"Ready? Good. Let's go." Piet hustled him outside, along the corridor and down the stairs, towards his Land Rover.

CHAPTER
FORTY-FIVE

PHILIPPA, MRS FRANKLIN, AND JAMES GOT THE LAST THREE SEATS on a flight leaving for Mokhotlong at 8am, having ascertained that the DC was back at home and that Stuart was *not* in Maseru.

Their pilot, Roger—a man of few words—flew them up through the morning mist that shrouded her familiar, beloved mountains. When Philippa asked if he knew where Stuart was as they disembarked, he shrugged. "That's what everyone wants to know, miss. That, and where AHJ, Drakensberg Air's newest Cessna, is."

Philippa's mouth dropped open. So, what she'd overheard was true? And yet, Stuart wouldn't have taken unlawful possession of a plane unless he...was forced.

Suddenly she was even more frightened. Had her urgent need for money placed Stuart in an even more desperate situation than she could have imagined?

Philippa stood tentatively with her hand on the iron gate, willing herself to open it and walk from the airfield through the garden to the house.

It was possible that her father was at the administrative

offices. Or perhaps he was at Letseng-la-Terai, getting a firsthand description of the rogue pilot who had supposedly cheated those poor miners.

Only, Stuart wasn't to blame. It had been that awful Afrikaner. That Piet van Wyk, who'd used his leverage over Stuart, who hadn't done anything wrong, other than borrow—for a really short while, too—from Mrs Oosthuizen.

Surely there was no more to it than that? Except...that was bad enough.

"Philippa?" The surprise in her father's voice when she stepped into the living room where he was sorting through files on the dining room table was to be expected. But the pleasure in his expression nearly undid her as he opened his arms for a hug, saying, "I got your message about half an hour ago." Stepping back, he smiled at Mrs Franklin, adding, "And you are very welcome, too."

Philippa waited tensely as the proper introductions were made. In a few minutes his disappointment would be crushing. Would he be tight-lipped? Would he insist Stuart must bear all the blame because Philippa was above recrimination?

"Any friend of Philippa's is a friend of mine," he declared before calling Francina in from the kitchen to ask her to make a tray of tea.

His pleasure at seeing her bolstered Philippa's courage before his inevitable question, asked with a worried frown, "But, my dear girl, what are you doing here when you've got a wedding to prepare for in less than six days? Or should I be cancelling my flight to Cape Town on Thursday?"

Philippa reddened as she gave a slight nod. "I'm so sorry, Daddy," she whispered. "I know it's late notice but

—" she sucked in a sharp breath, hoping she wasn't going to exhale on another sob— "but I called off the wedding. I don't want to marry Matthew anymore." She glanced at Mrs Franklin, who was now seated on the sofa by the window. James was playing with a toy train that Francina had brought through with the tea, happily oblivious to the strain in the room. "I've told Mrs Franklin the full story, so you can say whatever you want to." She gave a short, bitter laugh. "Matthew's mother certainly didn't hold back. She thinks I'm making the biggest mistake of my life not marrying her perfect son. Not to mention the inconvenience and embarrassment, which she regards as a bigger issue than my lifetime's happiness."

"Pre-wedding jitters?"

Of course, her father asked the obvious question, but Philippa was prepared. With a nervous glance at Mrs Franklin, she said, "Daddy, there's something I need to tell you. About Stuart Price."

Her father's hand stilled on the teacup. The look he sent her was suspicious. But then, hadn't she once told him about her feelings for the pilot he clearly saw as bringing the administration into disrepute?

"Stuart?"

Philippa nodded. "I saw yesterday's newspaper, but I was already on my way here to explain to you— Stuart's in trouble because of *me*." The words felt like stepping off a cliff, but she rushed on, not wanting him to interrupt. "Yes, me! I asked him for money. I needed it urgently, and before you ask why, just accept that I got myself into a...terrible scrape and I was too ashamed to tell you, so when I bumped into Stuart I told him that my future with Matthew...my very *life*... depended a sum of money... *urgently*—"

"Philippa!"

"You see! That's how you'd have responded if I had asked *you* for money!" Philippa knew she sounded defensive. God, this was hard. "I was too ashamed, Daddy. Please don't ask me what it was about. Anyway, it's all worked out now, and I've learned my lesson and will never be so foolish." Of course, this was minimising it, but she had to if her father was to take a less dim view of Stuart. "When I saw Stuart and...and poured my heart out...and told him *how* urgent it was, he...he borrowed money, which he handed to me in an envelope at Rand Airport. But then—" She was trembling now, wishing for it all to be out in the open but desperately afraid of diminishing herself in her father's opinion. Or diminishing Stuart. "There was this awful van Wyk man who took a photo of...of us...and Stuart handing me the money, and he blackmailed Stuart to fly him to Letseng-la-Terai."

Charles, who had been pouring himself a second cup of tea—probably so he could look anywhere other than his daughter—set down the teacup with careful deliberation and repeated quietly, "You asked Stuart for money— urgently? He gave it to you, and then he was blackmailed?" He paused. It seemed the seconds ticked by. Philippa could only hear the *choo-choo* noises of the train James was playing with.

Philippa nodded.

"So, you're saying this situation of your making compromised Stuart? Which leads me to ask—" He glanced at Mrs Franklin before checking himself, so it was Philippa who burst out, "I was in love with Stuart. He wanted to marry me but...but stupidly I said no. I chose Matthew after he made that ridiculous, public proposal when suddenly I had stars in my eyes again, and thought I wanted the life he could offer me. But when I realised I didn't, and that all I really wanted was Stuart...it was too late!" She ran the back of her hand across her eyes. "He'd married that...that nurse, Lizzie Cameron. And I know you won't ask—but just so you never think it—no! Stuart was *never* unfaithful. I wanted him so badly, but he was only ever the most decent of husbands to Lizzie. Even though he doesn't love her! But now I'm here because Stuart is in terrible trouble only because of me. And Mrs Franklin is here because she read about it in the newspaper, and she knew it *couldn't* be true because she and her husband looked after Stuart like a son for six years during the war and—"

Charles set his cup down with a sharp clatter. "Forgive me, but *you* are the widow of Ernest Franklin? The Pretoria QC?" he asked. "A truly brilliant man. And Stuart... Stuart lived in *your* home?"

Mrs Franklin nodded. "He did, and he was as close to me as my own son, Michael, who was at boarding school. I didn't know Stuart had come back to South Africa—or rather, here—until I read the newspaper, and then I had to come straight to Basutoland because...because I know my boy is not a criminal," she finished softly.

Philippa watched her father carefully, her trepidation growing as seconds of silence ticked by. "Please, Daddy, you—"

The radio on her father's desk crackled to life, cutting through her words. The voice that emerged was tense, urgent.

"Mokhotlong Base, this is Maseru Control. Reported suspicious activity with aircraft en route to Letseng-la-Terai, Alpha Hotel Juliet. Pilot cited a medical supply run, but there have been no reports of a medical emergency."

Charles was on his feet instantly, reaching for the radio handset. Philippa watched the blood drain from his face.

"Maseru Control, this is Mokhotlong Base. No medical emergency reported to this office, and all flights to Letseng-la-Terai suspended as of yesterday. What's the pilot's status?"

"Aircraft is now maintaining radio silence despite repeated attempts at contact. Pilot identified as Stuart Price. ETA Letseng-la-Terai approximately five minutes."

The handset trembled in Charles's grip. "Copy that, Maseru. Maintain surveillance and report any developments."

He set down the radio and turned to Philippa, his expression grim. "Stuart's flying to the diamond fields right now. Unauthorised, radio silent, under false pretences."

"Oh, my God." Philippa felt the world tilt around her. "Van Wyk must have forced him. Daddy, you have to help him—"

"I have to stop him." Charles was already moving, grabbing his jacket from the coat stand. "Whatever's happening up there, Stuart's walking into a situation that could annihilate him. Now, I thought I didn't care, but after what you've told me—"

"Daddy! Let me come with you!"

"Absolutely not." He swung round. "You've done enough damage already, haven't you?"

The words were like a slap. Philippa watched her father stride toward the door, then pause with his hand on the handle.

"Philippa," he said without turning around, his voice heavy with disappointment, "I hope whatever Stuart did for you was worth destroying a good man's life."

The door slammed behind him, leaving Philippa alone

with the radio's static and the crushing weight of what she'd set in motion. Through the window, she could see the Police Land Rover mobilising, her father orchestrating whatever response he could manage from this remote outpost.

Somewhere in the sky above the mountains, Stuart was flying toward a confrontation that could destroy them all. And she was the one who had sent him there, as surely as if she'd held a gun to his head.

The envelope of money lay forgotten in her handbag. All those blood-stained bills that had cost Stuart everything and solved nothing at all.

CHAPTER
FORTY-SIX

ROMA MISSION SCHOOL

Outside, the thunder rumbled, and the wind blew across the noonday sun as Mpho cowered in the corner, trying to be as unobtrusive as possible while the tall young men around him grew louder. The concerns they had brought to this meeting in an unused schoolroom at Mapolaneng mission had sounded reasonable at first. Cheats and greed should not go unpunished. But then the biggest and meanest of them all, Moses, the student who had been in Russia, stood up on one of the desks and started shouting that while it was the job of the police to bring justice for the Basotho people, the Basotho people themselves must make the police realise what kind of justice was needed.

Such talk frightened quiet, law-abiding Mpho, who wanted only to be left in peace to study so he could get a good job in the government and make his mother proud.

He suspected Moses had had too much sorghum beer with his friends. Mpho could smell it on them, and he knew this meant trouble. Men who drank too much sorghum beer with troubles on their minds often used their fists if their words didn't work.

Moses had called the meeting in a hurry. With angry shouts, he'd shepherded the students into the schoolroom, saying he'd heard a message on the radio that the two white men who had committed a terrible crime and cheated the miners of Letseng-la-Terai were on their way back there. No doubt they were going to try to cheat and steal once more.

Horrified, the faithful acolytes were waving their fists and picks in anger.

Now Moses punched his own fist in the air as he balanced on a school desk. "The Afrikaner who has cheated my uncle thinks he is above justice. He thinks he can travel whenever he likes, using false money to buy his diamonds. Why?" shouted Moses. "Because his friend is a pilot. A man with a plane like a donkey that goes wherever and whenever this man wants. The white pilot will take him to the diamond fields so together they can cheat another Mosotho miner of the diamonds he has toiled to find."

Mpho wanted to say that just because the pilot had taken the Afrikaner in his plane did not make the pilot guilty of illegal diamond buying or cheating. The pilot, Captain Price, had been good to him, once showing him the levers and buttons in his plane and, on another magical occasion, taking him on a flight. But Mpho was not ready to say anything with all those angry boys egging each other on. They would turn on him, he knew it. Far better to remain quietly in the corner and hope no one noticed him. He was small and rarely spoke. They never noticed him at the best of times.

At first, the students, who were aged from twelve to

their early twenties, sat obediently as they listened to Moses shout and wave his fists.

Then one of the less bold boys spoke up suddenly. Wide-eyed and with a voice shaking with fear, Jacob Mbogeni rose and said, "It is the wife of this pilot we speak of who injects the children of our parents, our own brothers and sisters at the clinic with the poison of the white man. That is what my father says."

A milder voice interrupted to say this was the measles vaccination programme that his mother said kept them safe, but he was shouted down as the original speaker, joined by a growing cacophony of voices, started arguing its dangers. Jacob Mbogeni's bloodshot eyes reminded Mpho of two poached eggs as he cried, "But this time is it not measles medicine, it is a different poison that is injected into the veins of the babies to make them weak and always the white man's servant."

A lot of shouting erupted at this until Moses, who seemed to see this as an opportunity to build upon, thundered over the crowd, "And so we understand their plan. The white pilot also wants the Mosotho as his slave so he can cheat him of his diamonds while his wife comes up here to put the poison in the children's veins that will make them slaves."

Mpho could smell the sweat that came off the angry, pacing and more placid bodies. He could feel the palpable rise of tension in the room, and he was terrified. Almost too terrified to move, only he knew that if he did not somehow manage to slip away and take his chances he would be a coward and unable to face his mother ever again because terrible things would happen which he'd done nothing to stop.

Slowly, carefully, inch by inch, he shuffled his small

body closer to the door at the very back of the room. Everyone was facing the front, except the orator, whose bloodshot eyes roamed over the audience. Moses was building himself up on the rising tide of feeling, feeding on the enthusiasm of the boys near the front. Foam caked the corner of his lips, and spittle flew from his mouth when he cried out the last words Mpho heard, "And where is this White Witch now? In the clinic poisoning our brothers and sisters so that they will become slaves of the white man!"

With trembling hands, Mpho carefully and quietly turned the doorknob. The crowd were now on their feet and surging towards Jacob, and Mpho had to believe they'd not notice him, just so he could galvanise the courage to thrust himself out of the room. If they caught him, they would beat him. He could feel the anger like a living beast.

A beast with murder in its veins.

The door made a clunking noise when it closed behind him and as he gulped in a mouthful of air that was not tainted with sweat and violence his head cleared and he knew he had done the only decent and courageous thing he could, even though his terror was almost too great to bear. For he truly feared they would kill him if they saw him running.

But run was all he could do. Fast and furiously down the hill, not to the mission where it was too risky he would be detained by the brothers too long while he was questioned, but towards the trading store where he knew they had a two-way radio and where Mrs Mack was always kind to him and gave him boiled sweets and had always believed him in the past.

CHAPTER
FORTY-SEVEN

It was still cold when, mid-morning, Lizzie took her tea onto the small *stoep* and gazed at the magnificence that surrounded her.

At least up here, she could feel some peace and calm. She didn't know how she could return to the lowlands to resume her married life knowing that her husband didn't love her.

Or—worse—that he was trying to love her ...except that she would always be second best.

She'd accepted the truth now. When Stuart had accidentally pulled out a photograph of Philippa Tremain from his wallet, he'd explained it away. She'd believed him because she wanted to.

And because he did a convincing job of pretending to her that he was a newlywed in love. Besides, a party with alcohol involved may well result in a photograph of couples who were not romantically involved embracing in the moment.

But there was no way of explaining the photograph the Afrikaner mechanic Piet van Wyk had deliberately dropped on the table—obviously for Lizzie to see but to make a point to Stuart.

Again, a photograph of Stuart and Philippa Tremain.

What had hurt so much had been the look on Stuart's face in that photograph. She'd never seen such adoration.

Certainly not directed at her.

So, not only did Stuart not love her, he was now apparently wanted in connection with illegal diamond trading. How had it come to this?

Gripping the tin mug with both hands, she forced a smile for a couple of Basotho mothers who were sitting on the steps a few feet away, their sleeping babies strapped to their backs in the traditional colourful Basotho woollen blankets.

The cherubic faces of the tiny tots made her heart clench. But not with the desire to have her own baby—though that had been very real until recently. Until she'd realised that having a child with a man who was in love with someone else would trap them all in a prison of resentment and lies.

"Nurse Cameron, it appears we're running low on surgical spirit." Dr Molapo stepped out of the clinic. "Someone must go to Roma to replenish our stock. But perhaps you need a rest from here and would like to be that one?"

Lizzie raised her eyes towards the sun before turning back to the young doctor. She shook her head. "I'm perfectly content to stay here and attend to the patients and the children."

And she was. She didn't know when she'd be ready to leave, though of course, she'd have to soon.

But what would happen to Stuart? She imagined everyone would be talking about the photograph that identified him in the newspaper, standing next to his plane and the Mosotho miner who'd been cheated.

She swallowed painfully. Charles had warned her to leave him—though of course, that was before he knew she was married to the man he was about to bring in for questioning.

And then what?

Did she have the fortitude to stay?

But how could she not? She was married and that bound her inexorably to Stuart Price—until death...

Which would be bearable if he only loved her.

Stifling a sob, she rose stiffly. If only she could stay up here in the mountains forever. Here, she mattered. But what awaited her back in Maseru? A husband who saw her as a consolation prize?

A husband who was not only a liar and a cheat...but a criminal?

Tossing the dregs of her lukewarm tea onto the barren earth, Lizzie gazed up at the mountains. This would have to be her solace. Beautiful, majestic sights like this.

The tears that had been gathering behind her eyes now spilled down her cheeks. How wonderful it would have been if the man who had pledged his future to her had truly wanted to marry *her* above all others.

If she at least had the comfort of knowing that, she'd have done anything for him—even with the knowledge that he was a criminal.

FORTY-EIGHT

STUART HAD NEARLY ABORTED THE LANDING BECAUSE OF THE gusting winds, but with a gun levelled at him, he'd gritted his teeth and thumped the Cessna onto the dirt runway. The aircraft bucked and shuddered as crosswinds tried to lift its wings, but Stuart fought the controls, knowing that a missed approach could mean a bullet in his skull.

It seemed Piet didn't care about the danger—perhaps he was as frightened of his Johannesburg overlords as Stuart was of the Afrikaner pressed against his shoulder, reeking of sweat and desperation.

As long as they made it down alive, that's all that mattered to Piet. That, and the transaction itself, which he conducted with remarkable speed by Basutoland standards. Gone was the leisurely haggling Stuart had witnessed before. This time, Piet was a bully with a tight deadline, panic radiating from him like heat from sun-baked stone.

Stuart watched with disgust as the miner—a weathered man with calloused hands—hesitated over his diamond find. He hadn't wanted to hand it over at first. He hadn't liked Piet's hectoring tone.

But when Piet had put his face up to his and shouted at him, before whipping out a wad of bank notes, the diamond had finally changed hands and, with a muttered thanks, Piet had saluted him and his band of concerned friends, and marched away.

"You're a bloody criminal," Stuart muttered. He'd tried to stop the transaction. But Piet was too desperate and impatient to fulfil a promise he'd obviously made to the men who had ordered him to complete this final operation.

And he had a gun in his pocket.

"Now we will both be rich." Piet visibly relaxed as they climbed into the cockpit, Stuart's hands moving automatically through the pre-flight checks while his passenger buckled himself in. Piet fingered the stone one last time, rolling it between his thumb and forefinger like a talisman, before returning it to its hiding place inside his jacket.

"I don't want a penny of it," Stuart said through gritted teeth as the plane accelerated down the runway, winds buffeting the small aircraft like a child's toy.

They were airborne, climbing into the thin mountain air, when the radio crackled to life.

"Alpha Hotel Juliet, come in, Alpha Hotel Juliet, can you hear me?"

Piet's head snapped around, his eyes wild. He pressed the pistol barrel against Stuart's temple, the metal cold through his hair. "Ignore it!"

Stuart frowned, trying to identify the voice through the static while maintaining level flight. "I have to respond—"

"I have a very nice little stone in my pocket that will set me up for life," Piet hissed, his breath hot against Stuart's ear. "We are so close to getting away with this. I will kill you if I have to."

"When did you get your pilot's license?" Stuart asked grimly. "Because if you shoot me, we both die."

Piet gave a nasty laugh. "Reckon I could fly this thing well enough to save my own skin. Don't test me, Captain."

The radio sparked again, the voice crackling through the airwaves more urgent now. "Alpha Hotel Juliet, you are instructed to return to Mokhotlong immediately. Do you copy? Return to Mokhotlong immediately."

Piet raised his eyebrows, peering out at the landscape rolling beneath them—endless mountains cut by deep gorges. "News travels faster from the mountaintops than I'd expected." The anxiety that had gripped him earlier seemed to dissipate as he settled back in his seat. He grinned. "In twenty minutes we'll be putting her down across the border. And you, of course, will come with me."

Stuart reached for the radio controls, but Piet smacked his knuckles hard enough to make his eyes water.

"Alpha Hotel Juliet, this is an emergency." The voice was clearer now, more desperate. "A mob is advancing on the clinic at Mapolaneng. You are instructed to turn around and land in Mokhotlong to pick up police troopers and then continue to Mapolaneng immediately. Do you copy?"

Mapolaneng? The words slammed through Stuart... Lizzie was at Mapolaneng.

Stuart turned in panic. "My wife is at that clinic," he said, his voice hoarse. A mob—Christ, what had the radio said about a mob? His hands shook on the controls as he digested the implications. "They're targeting Lizzie to get back at me. You saw the newspaper, didn't you? They didn't need to print my name—everyone knows it was me flying you to Letseng-la-Terai."

He banked the aircraft, but Piet clipped him sharply across the ear, his lip twitching in amusement when Stuart yelped with pain.

"It's a ruse, you fool. They're trying to trick you into landing where they'll be waiting with handcuffs." He gave a short, ugly laugh. "Besides, I thought you couldn't wait to be rid of her, Captain. Now you can have it off with that fancy piece of yours—the DC's daughter—without looking over your shoulder."

White-hot rage exploded behind Stuart's eyes. "You bastard—"

The gun butt caught him across the temple, stars bursting in his vision. Pain roared through his skull, but he managed to keep the plane level.

"Just enough damage so you understand I mean business," Piet said, though his bravado couldn't quite mask the fear creeping into his voice. "Now maintain heading and don't be a fool. It's obviously a trap—can't you see? Once we're across the border, you'll be my guest for twenty-four hours. Insurance, you understand. You're in as deep as I am, but if you try to betray me, I'll make sure the authorities know exactly who flew me to every diamond deal." He gestured toward the radio with the gun barrel. "Ignore them. Follow where I'm pointing."

With the pistol pressed against his skull and his vision still blurred from the blow, Stuart felt he had no choice. Below them, Lizzie faced an angry mob seeking someone to blame for his crimes. And here he was, flying in the opposite direction, a prisoner of his own cowardice.

The landing strip Piet directed him to was nothing more than a straight stretch of dirt road carved between vast fields of maize. Stuart slammed the Cessna down harder than necessary, his fury making him reckless, and taxied toward two massive gum trees marking a bend in the road.

"Turn off the engine," Piet commanded when Stuart hoped he might discharge his passenger and escape.

Stuart shook his head. "Let me go back. You'll have hours to disappear. My wife is about to be lynched because of what we did at Letseng-la-Terai."

"Should have thought of that before you started playing around with the DC's daughter," Piet sneered. "Turn off the engine and get out." He vaulted from his seat, circling to Stuart's side with the pistol trained on him. "Out! Now!"

A warning shot split the air, sending a startled cloud of birds bursting from the nearby trees. "I've got a king's ransom in my pocket—enough to disappear forever. I'm not a murderer, Price, but I'll kill you if you force my hand."

Faced with the desperate man's wild eyes and the gun barrel inches from his face, Stuart shut down the engine and climbed out. Immediately Piet advanced on him, pulling a length of rope from his pocket.

"Hands out."

The words had barely left his mouth when Stuart struck, his right leg sweeping up in a vicious arc. The pistol flew through the air, both men diving after it, landing hard on the thorny ground.

They grappled desperately, rolling over broken branches and stones. Stuart's mind raced—Lizzie's life, Philippa's reputation, his own honour—everything depended on the next few seconds. His hand closed around what felt like the gun grip, only to find Piet's fingers beneath his own.

With all his strength, Stuart twisted on top of the Afrikaner, driving his knee down to pin Piet's gun hand. But

Piet was wiry and desperate, whipping his arm free just as Stuart lunged again.

The shot seemed to echo forever across the maize fields. Stuart felt the impact before the pain—a sledgehammer blow to his chest that drove him to his knees. When he looked down, blood was already soaking through his shirt where his shoulder met his torso.

Through a haze of agony, he watched Piet scramble toward the gum trees, retrieving a hidden bag from their base. The man turned back, waving his gun almost apologetically.

"I wish it hadn't come to this, Captain," he called out, already backing toward the maize field. "You made some very stupid decisions! At least I don't have to kill you—! I don't think you'll be going anywhere soon!"

And then he was gone, swallowed by the tall green stalks, leaving Stuart bleeding in the African dirt with his wife's life hanging in the balance hundreds of miles away.

Stuart pressed his fingers to the burn in his left shoulder. The round had ploughed a hot groove high across the deltoid. It was bleeding, but seeping rather than spurting.

He drew a careful breath.

The pain was sharp but there was no wet rattle, no bubbling at the wound.

Testing his reflexes, he opened his hand, then closed it.

The grip held.

Carefully, he lifted his elbow—and felt fire along the muscle, but it obeyed. With an effort, he removed his jacket, tore a strip from his shirt, packed and cinched it tight, then raised the arm to slow the bleed.

The world narrowed, tilted—then steadied as the black at the edges ebbed. He could fly. Not comfortably.

But he could fly—

And that was what Lizzie needed from him.

CHAPTER

FORTY-NINE

Out in the bitter wind, Charles acknowledged each police trooper who'd reported for duty in the urgent minutes since the call had gone out. "Sergeant Letse. Sergeant Jacob. Sergeant George." Three good men, led by the burly, competent Mosotho, Sergeant George—a man Charles would choose as his right hand any day.

The tense wait had stretched like a wire about to snap before they'd finally abandoned hope that Stuart would respond to their repeated pleas to turn back to Mokhotlong. Even after Charles had hinted at leniency, only static crackled through the airways.

Yes, even with his wife's life hanging in the balance, Stuart refused to acknowledge the peril.

Stuart's *wife*—innocent Nurse Lizzie Cameron. Charles's jaw clenched, disgust and despair warring in his chest over what Philippa had revealed. She was integral to what was happening now, the specifics too vague to process, leaving Charles to act on pure instinct and adrenaline to avert a potential bloodbath.

The troopers shifted restlessly by the airstrip, excitement and agitation crackling between them like electricity. Drakensberg Air's Chief Pilot Dan Greene had been their last resort after Stuart's silence. Roger, who'd flown Philippa up earlier, was stranded on the other side of the country. In Roma, a contingent of troopers was making its way across the mountain on horseback—but Charles knew they'd never reach Mapolaneng in time.

His watch ticked mercilessly. Adrenaline surged through his veins as his mind churned with images of Lizzie at the mercy of Moses Shakane's mob. The fiery agitator, driven by grievance and Russian ideology, would show no mercy now he knew the criminal pilot's wife was within reach.

Especially since he'd just made another illegal trip to the diamond diggings.

Why had Charles not seen this coming? The inevitable explosion when Moses learned the DC was prosecuting his uncle Thabo while the perpetrators of crimes against his uncle Tumelo walked free.

Lizzie had become their scapegoat, their symbol of colonial injustice.

The guilt was crushing. He could picture Shakane now, megaphone raised, fist pumping, rallying his supporters for blood.

The wait stretched endlessly until—

"There!" A speck appeared in the distance. "It's Dan."

"Get ready to jump in!" Charles barked as the plane levelled with the landing strip, nose dropping, touching down in a cloud of dust and taxiing toward the gate.

"Good God! *Stuart*?" Through the windshield, Charles recognised the pilot's haggard face. "Why didn't you answer the radio?" he demanded, yanking open the door and shepherding the troopers past the still-rotating propellers.

"Stuart!"

Charles spun. Philippa burst through the gate, running toward the plane with desperate urgency. Mrs Franklin followed, clutching young James's hand.

"Stuart!" The anguish in her repeated cry cut through the engine noise.

Charles tried to be dispassionate as he watched Stuart lean out to take his daughter briefly in his arms, before Sergeant George shouted to the troopers and the doors were slammed and the plane was taxiing once more across the tarmac, nosing upwards and, thank God, they were on their way to save Lizzie.

Philippa stumbled backwards as Stuart slammed his door, a cruel and cold barrier to replace the brief cathartic warmth of his embrace. She'd had so many words for him, but all her love, regret and fear could not be said in less than five seconds, so she'd said nothing. The look in his eye, though, had spoken volumes and the strength of feeling that swept through her during their fleeting touch confirmed that she was, as ever, a slave to this man's ability to make her feel in a way no one else could.

And then, glancing down at the front of her white blouse, she staggered back in horror.

Mrs Franklin was by the garden gate, shading her eyes as she watched the Cessna disappear towards the sun.

She came running.

"Stuart's been shot!" Philippa cried. Her breath came in staccato gasps of panic as she pointed to the red stain on her blouse. "I didn't see the blood on his brown jacket." She touched the sticky patch. "It's blood! Oh God, it's all my fault, and Daddy wants to kill him for it." She put her hands to her face and began to sob.

CHAPTER
FIFTY

IN THE DISTANCE, BARE, RUGGED MOUNTAINS DISAPPEARED INTO the horizon as the plane passed over great gorges and valleys. Charles directed a dispassionate glance at Stuart. The young pilot's mouth was pulled into a grim, taut line, and Charles could see the tension in his strained tendons as he gripped the controls.

Now was not the time for the hows and whys, thought Charles as he leant over the seat to shout instructions, but —irrespective of Philippa's involvement— Stuart had flown a diamond thief on several unauthorised flights to the diggings. "It's a north-south runway. Tricky in a crosswind. Look out for it at the top of the hill. A disused cricket pitch about 800 yards from the clinic."

"I know," Stuart muttered.

Charles leant back to shout over his shoulder to Sergeant George. "Wait for instructions from me on how to proceed. The trouble might have blown over by the time we get there, and we don't want to exacerbate the situation. Father O'Rourke may already have talked sense into the lads. Caution might be better exercised. I won't know until we get there."

No, he really had no idea what to expect until he got there. That was the cursed truth of it.

He flicked a glance to his left. Stuart looked very pale; his forehead sheened with sweat. The pilot must have heard him, for he muttered, "I pray to God that's the case."

"Pity you didn't think of that before you and van Wyk got into illegal diamonds," Charles couldn't help responding.

"I didn't get into anything with van Wyk other than fly him when he had one over me."

Charles snorted. "That'll be for a more objective examiner than me to decide. You've treated your wife abominably. You don't deserve Lizzie."

"I don't," Stuart agreed as he stared grimly through the window, assessing the weather and looking below him.

He dropped to five hundred feet as the runway came into sight. To the east, Charles could see the little fibro and tin clinic perched on top of a treeless hill, at the base of which the handsome sandstone mission rose up in God's glory, a beautiful anachronism amidst the bleak but impressive county surrounding it.

"Right, let's do this," muttered Charles, scanning the landscape, his horrified gaze fixing on a dark, slow-moving mass in the distance.

It was heading towards the clinic. Dear God, it was almost on the doorstep of the clinic.

CHAPTER

FIFTY-ONE

MAPOLANENG CLINIC

"Do you hear that noise?" Lizzie had just finished vaccinating the tenth child that morning when she raised her head and called out to Dr Molapo who was preparing for minor surgery in the next room.

Outside, the line-up of mothers waiting patiently, kept growing. Many had walked great distances, and in all weather, with their babies sleeping on their backs secured with the ubiquitous blanket tied beneath their breasts.

"It might be thunder," the doctor called out, and Lizzie agreed as she went to put the kettle on. She'd been working without a break for nearly two hours since that brief tea break. Taking any sort of rest made her feel guilty when there was so much demand. But the women were so patient; so understanding and grateful, and there was never any sense of disgruntlement. Lizzie thought she'd like to work here her whole life.

During her first week at the clinic, she'd concentrated only on getting through as many vaccinations as she could, but then mothers had brought children with ailments Lizzie could see were easily remedied with the right advice.

She'd then set aside an hour at the end of each day for an informal session where mothers and babies were offered tea and biscuits while Lizzie discussed general healthcare, with Dr Molapo translating.

"Kettle's boiled!" Lizzie called, managing a smile as Dr Molapo came through and took a chair at the small table opposite her. She had to stop thinking of Stuart or she'd go mad with worry. "Shall we take five minutes?"

Dr Molapo sat down, his brow furrowed in thought. The young man was such a diligent worker he never seemed to fully relax.

"When your husband sees the important work you've been doing here, he will be proud of your interest in the good people of Lesotho. Your husband is a fine man."

Lizzie accepted the compliment with a nod, though her chest tightened. She pushed the plate of biscuits towards him, and Dr Molapo dunked his biscuit into his tea. He seemed hesitant to continue, then managed awkwardly, "Captain Price has always shown respect to the Basotho people." He didn't look at her. "Some Basotho prefer not to fly with the other pilots, for they feel they are not respected, even though they have money to pay."

"I...I'm glad you think he's a good man," Lizzie replied, her voice catching slightly as she wondered if the doctor had heard the rumours and was trying to reassure her. The knot in her stomach tightened. Very soon, she and Stuart would need all the allies they could get.

She glanced through the window, and up at the blue skies, frowning as unease prickled at her. "If it's not thunder, I wonder what that noise could be."

Dr Molapo cocked his head. "It sounds like chanting."

"Not the religious chanting I'm used to hearing," Lizzie commented as she stood up and walked towards the door, her pulse quickening.

She had just put her hand on the knob when the doctor, coming up behind her, let out a shout, pushing her aside as he hastily shot the bolt.

Terror shot through Lizzie at his uncharacteristic behaviour. She pressed herself against the sink, her heart hammering as she turned her gaze towards the window in the direction Dr Molapo pointed, her throat going dry as she saw the mob advancing up the hill.

"What is it?" she whispered, her voice barely audible, but the doctor just shook his head, his expression as shocked as her own.

The chanting that had been growing louder was now a terrifying cacophony of sound as the group, some armed with knobkerries, she saw, others shaking their fists, encircled the clinic.

Fear clawed at her chest. "What do they want?" Remembering the group of Basotho women and babies waiting in the reception annexe, Lizzie ran to open the door that separated them from the clinic, her hands shaking.

They crowded in, eyes large with fear and confusion which matched Lizzie's own, babies whimpering as they picked up on their mothers' anxiety; and Lizzie heard all around her the common question, asked in Sesotho: "What do these boys want?"

The chanting stopped, and a loud voice, carried via a megaphone, cut across the short distance that separated Lizzie and the terrified occupants of the clinic: "This is a message for the pilot's wife. Come out now!"

STUART BROUGHT the plane down on the dilapidated cricket pitch with a hefty bump that jolted all their teeth.

The five men piled out of the Cessna, grabbing their weapons before heading for the clinic at a run.

With an oily rag stuffed against his wound beneath his jacket, Stuart brought up the rear, unable to keep up the pace as the DC raced across the stony ground flanked by Sergeant George. The Mosotho policeman was an impressive figure as he confronted the agitated crowd, his stern ascetic profile and his towering bulk having an immediately dampening effect on the mob's restless enthusiasm after he'd pushed to the front and stood on a boulder to address them.

Glancing over his right shoulder, Stuart could see Lizzie's terrified face at the window, and his gut clenched with self-disgust.

His head throbbed, and it was hard to stand up.

Charles had moved to stand shoulder to shoulder with Sergeant George. Raising their own battery-powered electric megaphone, he now spoke to the mob in a voice louder and more imperative than Stuart had ever heard him use: "Violence is not the way to air your grievances. If you have a complaint, there are formal procedures for addressing it."

The mob, which consisted mainly of boys aged in their late teens, shifted uncomfortably. He could see the uncertainty on individual faces in the face of authority; the dissipation of their purpose now that they were on the cusp of achieving it—whatever 'it' was. Perhaps they didn't know for it only took a charismatic agitator to bend malleable minds to his will.

And here he was. Moses Shakane, the tallest and oldest of the group identified himself, whipping up outrage with his carefully choreographed actions and words.

Stuart had sunk to his knees, lacking the energy to continue. And as he supported himself upon a rock, the scene swimming before his eyes, he thought that this boy had the look of an angry dog. Perhaps one that is used to being kicked by those higher in the pecking order but which has now discovered its power as the head of a new pack, he thought whimsically, as he felt the energy ebb from his body.

But if he couldn't bring himself to do anything, he could still hear, and, as he clung to the rock, he heard the ringleader cry out, "You prosecute my uncle for *diretlo*, but you will not prosecute the pilot for IDB," he said, turning to point an accusing finger at Stuart. "Why? Because he is white. The Basotho people want justice for all."

Charles made a sweeping gesture with his arm to encompass all the young men before he put his mouth to the megaphone. "Where there is evidence to convict, we will prosecute," he said.

Stuart felt the words like a lash to his weakened frame, though the DC's tone was calm. He watched the wary looks of the mob while he sagged with pain on the sidelines. Some of the boys looked unsure; others, more belligerent. Resignation that he had much to answer for mingled with the fear he felt on Lizzie's behalf.

Had the boys not recognised Stuart? Why were they not setting upon *him* with their knobkerries?

Why go after Lizzie, unprotected in her remote clinic? Clearly, the mob had left their place of congregation and were acting upon the single-minded orders of their organiser.

He glanced at the fiery orator—clearly a young idealist indoctrinated by his own version of the truth and unable to change course.

Lizzie was an innocent woman, trapped in a mountain clinic doing good work for the Basotho people.

But Stuart was right here. If he were a real man, he should offer himself up as a sacrifice.

Yet he could barely stand up.

Sergeant George thrust his chin forward and his eyes bulged as he scanned the crowd before he returned his gaze to the oldest boy.

"Moses Shakane! You have come just now from Russia."

Moses, who looked proud and haughty, inclined his head.

Sergeant George stabbed his finger. "These Russian ideas are not the ideas we Basotho want for our new democracy. Do the Russians preach violence as the means of seeking justice?" He looked at a smaller boy in the front row who dropped his eyes. "Do they teach you in school that violence will solve a man's problems?"

There were a few mutterings as the group shifted, some scuffing their feet, others staring into the middle distance rather than face the police trooper's contempt.

Charles's authoritative voice cut through the silence. The mob was quite quiet now. "I will not ask what you were planning to do," he said with a pointed look at their knobkerries. "And for those of you who disperse now, there will be no repercussions, other than a closer scrutiny of how you conduct yourselves in your classrooms."

He made a gesture back to the convent, his voice cold and warning. "You are all free to leave."

Moses pulled his shoulders back and took a step forward. Stuart felt the change in mood, the shift in uncertainty as the boys weighed up the power of their leader against the power of the white administrator.

Behind the fiery young man, the mountains rose in harsh, jagged peaks.

Stuart had grown up on the history of this vast and violent land—at school as a young boy and from the stories of Mrs Franklin. His Aunt Edith.

And for the first time since he'd been shot, a new thought that wasn't about Philippa, Lizzie, Charles, or IDB, nudged into his brain. A thought he'd barely been able to process.

Was that Mrs Franklin he'd seen standing by the gate in Mokhotlong? His foster mother?

The woman standing behind Philippa when she'd thrown her arms about him had looked so much like her.

Wishful thinking perhaps, he acknowledged, as his body weakened and cognition dulled. But a thought that was infinitely calming and pleasurable.

He blinked open his eyes once more. He could feel the last of his energy draining away, but he must try to remain conscious long enough to ensure that Charles prevailed over this restless mob so that he could be reassured that Lizzie was safe.

Poor Lizzie. She was so deserving, and he'd treated her so badly—

"You think you can make us leave with empty promises of justice?"

Stuart jerked back into the present as Moses jerked his chin up and angrily thrust his knobkerrie in the air.

He held his breath.

He understood that Moses was one of the new generation of youth, impatient with his elders and their willingness to move in step with the administration. He wanted change, but he wasn't prepared to wait for a lawful transition. Democracy had been promised, but a date had not been set. In order to achieve change now, he wanted to implement his own agenda. Or rather, that of his mentors.

And now, buoyed up by the money his Russian backers supplied him, he was brimming with confidence.

Stuart understood all this and wished he had the strength to do something. Anything.

He was on his knees now at the back of the crowd and his vision was swimming but he realised that now was when the normally law-abiding schoolboys who'd chosen to follow Moses an hour ago would have to decide between the law and their testosterone-fuelled impatience and desire to prove themselves in an unlawful forum.

He saw Moses swing around, one fist clenched, the other shaking his long stick, appealing to the crowd.

But suddenly his compatriots were not interested in staying when the DC had offered them a reprieve. They shuffled away, giving Moses a wide berth, while Sergeant George said quietly, "Moses Shakane, we wish to ask you some questions at the Mokhotlong Police Station. Please come with me."

Stuart didn't know if he did or not. He was vaguely aware of the sound of boots on stones, shouted commands, the cry of a bird overhead and then his own name being uttered by Charles in tones of great contempt. Three times.

Until the tone changed and the sound of boots on gravel grew louder, deafening.

A pair of strong arms—Sergeant George's, he thought—wrapped around him from behind and hoisted him from the ground.

The last thing he was conscious of was the feel of such excruciating pain as he'd never experienced before his world went black.

Lizzie, who'd had her face pressed to the window throughout the dramatic back and forth, felt her knees suddenly go weak as Charles's clear, loud tones had the desired effect and the crowds turned and melted away. When the door opened and a familiar voice cried out her name, she stumbled forward.

"What did they want with us?" she asked, staring at Charles, the police troopers standing behind him.

"They wanted Stuart, but they found you. Lizzie, we have to get back to Mokhotlong, but first we need medical assistance for Stuart." His tone was urgent. "He's been shot."

"Shot?" She jerked backward, her hands to her cheeks. "How? The boys had *guns*?"

Dependable Dr Molapo, who had been calmly directing the mothers and children, came forward as two police troopers carried her unconscious husband inside.

"Lizzie, are you up to this?" asked Charles, and without answering, she turned, wanting more than anything to show him the professional she was. She nodded, leading the way to the annexe with its makeshift operating table. "Dr Molapo, I shall prepare for surgery. Tell me what you need me to do and I promise I won't faint." Turning, with a wry smile, she said, more for Charles's benefit, "It doesn't matter who this man is when he's injured and in need of medical help."

CHAPTER

FIFTY-TWO

Hours passed.

There was nothing Philippa and Mrs Franklin could do but wait, while Francina brought in seemingly endless pots of tea before Philippa decided something stronger was needed.

Putting down her gin and tonic, she rose and paced back and forth in front of the large windows that over-looked the magnificent mountains, straining her eyes for some sign of a plane.

"Daddy was so angry," she said, not for the first time, shaking her head. "But he didn't know Stuart was injured. He just shouted at him to fly them to the clinic. What if Stuart lost consciousness and—"

She'd refused to change her blouse, for the red blood-stain on its front was a symbol of her defiant championing of the pilot whose fall from grace she accepted as her own responsibility.

"Stuart has the will and resources to do what he has to do, Philippa, and right now he has to rescue his wife from an advancing mob," Mrs Franklin said gently, putting her hand on Philippa's shoulder.

"Oh God, I hate her! And I'm terrified for her! And I hate myself for my part in this mess," Philippa said, allowing herself to be comforted as Mrs Franklin drew her into her embrace.

This practical woman she'd only met yesterday was so different from her mother—and so different from Mrs Myburgh—yet her common sense and her refusal to judge either Stuart or Philippa was what she needed right now.

"Stuart's injury mightn't be as bad as you fear, Philippa," Mrs Franklin reassured her. "And his wife is a nurse. By the time they get back here, all will hopefully be well."

But Philippa heard the doubt in her voice and realised she was as worried as she was.

"I hear the plane overhead! It's them!" Philippa broke away and ran to the other window, pointing, before making for the verandah steps.

Behind her, she heard Mrs Franklin following with James, who'd leapt up at the promise of more plane spotting.

Yes, it was the same plane, but Dan was flying, and as his passengers stepped out, with no sign of Stuart, fear crashed over Philippa. Out of the back door came the three local troopers, dispersing towards the government Land Rover, while her father jumped out of the right-hand seat before going round to help out the final passenger.

Lizzie Cameron.

The stab of jealous hatred that speared Philippa was so strong and surprising, she had to turn away before manners

—and a final, reluctant acceptance of the situation—came to her rescue, and she stepped forward, saying simply, "I'm sorry for what you went through."

Her father was at Lizzie's side. He put his hand on the young woman's shoulder and said, "Lizzie was very brave. She didn't lose her nerve. Not when the mob was on her doorstep and not when she had to—"

He broke off suddenly, staring at the bloodstain on Philippa's blouse. But Lizzie had already seen it, and as she raised her eyes to Philippa's, Philippa felt shame and embarrassment stain her cheeks.

"I was wishing your husband Godspeed before he flew off to rescue you," Philippa mumbled. "It was only then I realised he'd been injured. I was so fearful he might crash because Daddy didn't know he'd been...shot!..and was pushing him on."

"You knew he'd been shot, Philippa?" her father asked, not waiting for an answer before he went on, "Stuart rose to the occasion. As did Lizzie."

There was something unusually proud and almost proprietorial in her father's tone, but Philippa cut him off.

"What about Stuart? Why isn't he here? Please tell me he's going to be all right." What did it matter that her trembling voice and intensity gave her away? She was in an agony of suspense, whereas Lizzie was clearly unscathed.

"Dr Molapo operated to remove the bullet, which had lodged beneath his shoulder." Lizzie's voice was calm and dispassionate. She did not sound like Philippa thought she should: in an agony of fear for the man she loved...or was supposed to love. It took all Philippa's resources not to charge her with her lack of feeling.

Lizzie smiled. "Don't worry, Philippa. Stuart's going to be fine, and will be transferred to Maseru hospital."

"Why didn't you go with him?" Philippa demanded. "You're his wife!"

"Philippa. Stop."

It was Mrs Franklin who spoke, her tone gentle but forceful. She nodded at Lizzie. "I am Mrs Franklin, and Stuart and his sister were evacuees from London who became part of our family for six years during the war." She paused, her voice breaking, and Philippa sent her a suspicious look for it seemed Mrs Franklin wasn't as self-possessed as she made out.

Philippa was about to suggest they go to the house, but the older woman went on, "When I saw the newspaper report that seemed to implicate Stuart, I immediately came here, even though I haven't seen Stuart for years. But I came because I know he's spent his life trying to distance himself from the dubious activities that his father was involved in back in England and that, of all the honourable and good-hearted men I know, Stuart is a king among them. So, if it's true he really is involved in these diamond thefts, there must be more to the story. That's why I came."

She was now looking at Philippa's father, who met her level stare with a contemplative look.

"I now acknowledge there is far more to the story, too," he conceded, looking at his daughter. "But please let's go into the house. I need to be close to the telephone for updates on the situation. Stuart has given us a good indication of where van Wyk was last seen, and I have notified the police across the border in the Orange Free State. I think they have as much of a motivation to act quickly," he added, his tone ironic, "and no doubt they'll want to claim credit."

Five minutes later, they were all seated on the linen sofas in the light-filled sitting room. Philippa still hadn't changed her blouse, for there was so much news to catch up on, but she noticed Lizzie's glance drawn to it, and, again, embarrassment clutched at her.

What did Lizzie know about Philippa and Stuart? Certainly not everything. But did she know Stuart had wanted to marry Philippa before he'd asked Lizzie? Surely, that would be a bitter pill to swallow.

Just as it was for Philippa to stare across at Lizzie and acknowledge who had actually won this war. Not for his affections—so perhaps *that* was the bitter pill—but for the right to a future with him.

Finally, it seemed, Lizzie found the courage to address Philippa directly. "Philippa I know that—" she began, her tone clear and decisive.

The telephone rang shrilly, cutting her off, and Philippa's father, who was waiting tensely, seized the bakelite receiver.

Everyone craned forward, waiting for news on Stuart's condition, or van Wyk's whereabouts. Could he have been apprehended so soon?

Stuart was supposed to make a full recovery, but what if his condition deteriorated unexpectedly? These things happened. Philippa was shocked that Lizzie was not at his bedside. *She* certainly would have been. She'd have stayed there all night, watching over him to make sure—

"I'm sorry—you're wanting Mrs Price, you say? Yes, yes, can you repeat that? The line isn't very clear. Please don't cry. Yes, I can hand you over— Yes, yes, I can hear you— Good Lord, what—?"

Mrs Price. A poisonous fury filled Philippa's veins, replaced almost instantly by terror over the reasons the caller wanted to speak to Mrs Price and why her father was looking so concerned.

Please, Lord, don't let him die! Her heart was beating so hard she wondered if everyone else in the room could hear. She sent an accusatory look at Lizzie. Of course, the hospital would want to speak to her. She was his wife, after all. She had all the authority now.

Lizzie leaned forward expectantly, her expression fearful, her hand outstretched, only now Philippa's father was talking again.

Philippa studied Lizzie's face as she clearly tried to overhear what was being said on the line. Did she look concerned enough? Why was she not hysterical? Philippa was doing everything in her power to contain her own emotions. Where was Lizzie's grave fear for Stuart's welfare? Where was her pride in her husband, who'd risked his life to expose the nefarious dealings of this infamous diamond thief, van Wyk?

Yes, yes, Philippa silently conceded, her own role was not insignificant, but she'd owned it when spilling out her confession to her father, and it would be dissected, and she'd tell the truth—though her father wouldn't need to know *why* she needed money in such a hurry.

"I'm sorry, Lizzie."

Philippa jerked her head around to her father as he put down the phone.

"Daddy! No!" Leaping up, Philippa ran across the room and gripped his shoulder. "What did they say? Please God, he's going to be all right, isn't he? It isn't terrible news, is it?"

She knew she was becoming hysterical, and it was Mrs Franklin who rose and drew her back, saying, "Let your father speak, Philippa. Remember, the hospital has news for Stuart's *wife*."

Briefly, Philippa covered her face with her hands as she

nodded, her shoulders slumping with resignation. "Of course they would want to speak to Stuart's wife," she repeated bitterly.

"It wasn't the hospital."

Philippa jerked her head up at her father's tone. He was looking at Lizzie, a strange, uncertain, puzzled look on his face.

"What is it, Charles?"

Charles? This usurper, *Mrs Price,* was now calling her father *Charles*?

"The line was very bad, and the caller was afraid it would drop out before you got to hear what she's apparently been trying to call you about for some time."

Lizzie's face had gone very pale, and as Charles moved from the telephone towards her, as if to comfort her, she suddenly stood up and gripped his hands. "It's not about Stuart? Then...is it my mother? Has something happened to her?"

"No, nothing like that at all." An odd smile was now turning up her father's lips that Philippa couldn't interpret at all.

Lizzie tried again. "Please, Charles, tell me—"

"I will, I will. I'm just trying to...make sense of it," he added, as if his mind truly was spinning over a million different ramifications.

"Daddy!"

Philippa's hysterical tone seemed to jerk him back into the present for, looking very intensely into Lizzie's eyes, he said, "It was Clodagh Brennan from the Magistrate's Office in Pietermaritzburg, regarding your marriage to Stuart a month ago."

Tensely, Philippa waited. She saw Lizzie hold her breath.

"The young woman has tried repeatedly to get in touch with you—"

"She was crying, you said, Daddy? Why was she crying?"

"Please, Philippa, let me finish." Her father turned back to Lizzie. "Miss Brennan is hugely apologetic and deeply embarrassed by the discovery, that upon trying to register your marriage, the age verification uncovered that one of the witnesses to your marriage was—" he swallowed, bit his lip as if he truly needed to digest the implications of whatever he was about to say, before imparting the news — "was underage."

"Underage?"

Philippa wasn't sure who repeated the word with the greatest shock: herself or Lizzie.

"Underage? What does that mean?" Lizzie asked carefully.

Equally carefully, her father said, "Miss Brennan was anxious to reassure you that it's easily rectified and that such matters do occur from time to time. However, technically, a witness who is under eighteen means that your marriage isn't..." He hesitated, shaking his head, before saying slowly, "legal."

"Our marriage isn't legal?" Lizzie repeated, her tone wooden as if she hadn't understood.

Philippa watched as her father nodded. "Miss Brennan assured me that no one needs to know, however she said that you and Stuart will need to appear at the Magistrate's Office to go through the legalities once more, as soon as possible, so she can submit the paperwork by month's end with no harm done."

Philippa felt a buzzing sound in her head. She saw the same confusion on Lizzie's face, and observed, from a strange other universe, the diffident way her father put both his hands on Lizzie's shoulders as if to comfort her, and said, "Did you hear that, Lizzie? " The Magistrate's Office is telling you that you are not, in fact, legally married to Stuart."

And then Lizzie did the most out of character thing Philippa could have imagined. That insipid wife of Stuart's, who'd thought she'd won the day, put her head back, covered her face briefly with her hands, and laughed.

She laughed, with no shame, rocking back and forth.

Then, she dropped her hands, directed a meaningful look at the blood stain on Philippa's blouse, and said in tones of the greatest solidarity, "Well, Philippa, I think you and I have just had the best news we could have wished for." She glanced at Charles, smiled, then returned her attention to Philippa to add, "And I think you'd better get yourself down to Maseru Hospital so you can tell Stuart he has an appointment at Pietermaritzburg Magistrate's court —" she raised her eyebrows, shook her head in wonderment, and added—"with *you!*"

STUART OPENED his eyes to the sharp smell of surgical spirit and the sight of three women at the foot of his bed, and felt the crushing weight of disappointment. He'd truly thought he'd make it through this; that Piet's bullet hadn't torn through a vital artery and that he'd get a chance to atone to those whose lives had been affected by his actions. But clearly he was dead. And the three women to whom he owed the most for the good parts of the life he had lived: Aunt Edith and Philippa—and Lizzie, to whom he owed the greatest apology—were all looking at him, waiting for the necessary words before he moved through to the next sphere of judgement.

They were all here with one noticeable exception.

"Where's Gracie?" he croaked.

He was happily aware that the moment he'd opened his eyes, Philippa had darted forward and was now holding his hand. He squeezed it. Ah, but it was good he'd been allowed to see her one last time.

"Gracie?" Aunt Edith appeared on the other side of his bed. She bent closer and said, softly and slowly—in the same tone she'd used when he'd been a small boy—"You know why she's not here, Stuart."

He sighed. "Will I see her soon? In the next world—? No…" He answered his own question with sadness, closing his eyes. "I'm not going there. I failed her. She's in heaven."

He heard Lizzie at the end of the bed—notably, the only one who hadn't moved closer—say, "Nurse, what drugs have been administered to Captain Price?"

Aunt Edith kissed his cheek and then stood back, still holding his hand. "You were a wonderful brother to Gracie. You didn't fail her," she said.

"I killed her." Stuart stared up into that good woman's face, drinking in the kindness that radiated from her. "I crashed the car and she died."

"Gracie was already dead, Stuart."

"You don't know that." He had just enough to argue that point. It was the truth and he shouldn't be given a reprieve.

"I read the coroner's report, Stuart. Gracie was like my own daughter, just as you're like my own son." She squeezed his hand. "Of course, I made sure I understood everything. I just wish I'd known where to find you so we could have shared the grief together."

"But you did find me." Stuart blinked a few times. A strange sense of wonderment was coursing through him. A nurse propped him up on pillows and he winced at the pain, then coughed as he drank the concoction she gave him. He managed to smile. "I'm so glad to see you."

He felt moisture in the corner of his eyes, and as the mist cleared, it slowly dawned on him that, actually, he wasn't on his way to the afterlife; he was lying in a bed in Maseru Hospital. And if he didn't believe it, a plaque on the wall proclaimed it so. Shaking himself into greater clarity, he struggled up further onto his elbows, stifling the cry of pain this caused him—and which also caused Philippa to drop his hand and cup his face and place a kiss upon his brow.

"Lizzie—" he began as a strange cocktail of emotions— not limited to shame and red hot desire plus an undertone of regret—threatened to swamp him.

"It's all right, Stuart," Lizzie said, still looking at him from the end of the bed. "I'm not your wife. You're free to love who you want." There was the ghost of a smile about her lips, but it was her lack of emotion that struck him most.

"I don't understand—"

Philippa squeezed his hand again, and as he looked up into her face, he was overcome by her glorious radiance so that he barely registered Lizzie's words when she said, backing away towards the door, "I'll leave it to Philippa to tell you."

EPILOGUE

JOHANNESBURG AIRPORT

Philippa shaded her eyes against the glare of the afternoon sun and waved as Stuart emerged from the terminal in his crisp South African Airways uniform, freshly minted wings pinned to his chest. Her heart still gave that familiar flutter whenever she saw him, and she wondered if it would always be like this.

"You look frightfully official," she said, kissing him lightly, breathing in the familiar scent of his aftershave mingled with the lingering traces of aircraft fuel.

"I feel frightfully official," he murmured, his arm tightening around her waist. "In twenty-four hours, I'll be making my first border crossing with a cabin full of passengers and no room for error."

"Or cheeky pranks like cutting the engine mid-air?"

Stuart grinned that boyish smile that had first undone her. "I'm glad that didn't come up during the interview."

They laughed, and Philippa tucked her arm through his as they walked to the car, savouring the solid warmth of him beside her. Johannesburg shimmered with summer heat, the tarmac wavering in the distance, and the promise of a new life stretched before them like the endless African sky.

"By the way, Daddy sends his regards, and says he thought you'd be interested to know that they've finally wrapped up the van Wyk case. Piet slipped up trying to sell an uncut stone to an undercover policeman in Maseru. Daddy coordinated the sting operation."

"I'm glad he finally had that satisfaction after Chief Thabo's acquittal," Stuart said with a grimace, opening the car door to help Philippa in, his hand lingering protectively on her back before climbing in the other side. "Actually, he rang me first to fill me in on the details and happened to mention, along the way, that he and Lizzie are holidaying in Knysna."

Philippa smiled, a warmth spreading through her chest that had nothing to do with the summer heat. "Well, I'm happy for both of them because, at least she's not holidaying in Knysna with *you*. But did Daddy mention Piet's handlers? He always tells you more than he tells me."

"All rounded up. A criminal syndicate based in Johannesburg—ex-de Beers employees, would you believe?"

"My goodness! I did hear that it all started after Piet boasted in some bar about knowing a pilot in Basutoland and having 'something over him'—meaning a sure thing to get an under-the-radar trip to Letseng-la-Terai." She didn't want to voice the details further. That had the potential to conjure up something that was still too painful, the memories still sharp enough to catch her breath. But with a smile, she added, "Serves him right! Swaggering talk like that nearly destroyed us both."

Stuart leaned across to take her in his arms, his touch gentle but urgent. "Well, swaggering boasts about diamonds don't always end badly," he said with a pointed look at the genuine 3-carat stone catching fire in the afternoon light on Philippa's left hand. "Though it wasn't so long ago, you were flashing around a fake stone and boasting to Piet's brother that we were married when we weren't."

Philippa pretended exaggerated hurt, placing her free hand dramatically over her heart. "I know! What a liar Granny was, telling me her diamond ring was real when it was just a clever phony!" She kissed him softly, tasting the salt of perspiration on his lips and the sweetness of their shared relief. "At least this time, everything's genuine. Now," she added, changing the subject, "are we going straight to Aunt Edith's for dinner tonight or home first? Apparently, Margaret and James will be there, and James won't stop talking about his flying lesson with you and how he wants to be a pilot."

"Philippa, Philippa, what do you think?" Stuart asked, shaking his head with mock despair, before adding with a lewd wink that sent heat spiralling through her, "I haven't seen my wife for twenty-four hours. Of course we're going home first!"

THE END

WINDS OVER MAPOLONENG (BOOK 4)

Basutoland, 1964. Lizzie runs a remote vaccination clinic in the Maluti Mountains—reachable only by pony or by a light aircraft brave enough to land on a brutal high-altitude strip.

When German pilot Elias Voss arrives, Lizzie expects trouble. Elias expects only a job—and distance from a past he refuses to name. Instead, he finds a woman who challenges him... and an attraction he can't control.

On the eve of Basutoland's first elections, Moses Shakane returns, turning people against Lizzie's clinic. With foreign money behind him—and diamonds as the prize—violence climbs the mountain paths.

Then storms and snow cut Mapolaneng off from the world. Lizzie and her patients are trapped, and the only way to reach them is a flight through cloud and deadly downdrafts to a landing with no second chances.

In the Malutis, survival is never guaranteed—and love even less so.

Coming Soon!

AUTHOR'S NOTE ABOUT
IDB AND DIRETLO

I spent my earliest years in Mokhotlong in the African mountain kingdom of Lesotho, near the top of the Sani Pass that features so prominently in this novel.

My first memories are of my Mosotho nanny, Francina, and playing with her children—Mpho, Moeketsi, and "Anne-Bubba"—all of whom appear in these pages. The airfield really was at the bottom of our garden at the District Commissioner's residence, and those small planes were indeed our lifeline to the outside world.

The Lesotho Diamond in its novel form was born from twelve years of helping my father, Spencer "Ted" Nettelton, craft his memoirs of his time serving as a district commissioner in Lesotho during the early to mid-1960s. During those years helping him with his manuscript, *Working in the Colonial Service in Lesotho in the 1960s*, I absorbed not just the dramatic events he recorded—complete with newspaper clippings and official correspondence—but the smaller details that bring an era to life.

He investigated the crimes that form the backbone of this novel—illegal diamond buying and medicine murder

—before becoming Private Secretary to Lesotho's first democratically elected Prime Minister, Chief Leabua Jonathan.

Our family's connection to the region, however, began long before my father's posting. We were children of Africa, our roots running deep through generations—Dad was born in Botswana, and his father was born in Lesotho before the family moved during the Boer War (1899-1901) so his own father could head the newly established Bechuanaland Police Force on Chief Khama III's recommendation. In many ways, Dad's posting back to Lesotho was a homecoming.

He often spoke of those fraught yet exhilarating years leading to Lesotho's democracy in 1966, a time when he organised the independence celebrations and navigated the complex tribal and political tensions of a changing Africa.

The Lesotho Diamond is my tribute to both my parents and to the remarkable people of Lesotho who, in embracing our family, gave me not just memories but a legacy to be proud of.

The fact I feature a pilot in my Wings over Africa novels is a tribute to my wonderful husband, Eivind Eikli, a handsome Norwegian bush pilot I met when I was a safari hostess in the Okavango Delta.

A NOTE ON THE HISTORY BEHIND THE FICTION

While the characters and their story are my own, the world they inhabit is grounded in a complex historical reality. For readers interested in the factual background of the novel's central themes, the following notes may be of interest.

DIAMONDS

A Note on the History of Letseng-la-Terai

The story of Letseng-la-Terai, one of the highest diamond mines in the world at over 3,100 meters (10,000 feet), began in 1957 with the official discovery of its kimberlite pipes by British geologist Peter Nixon. This discovery confirmed the theories of prospectors like South Africa's Colonel Jack Scott, who believed diamonds found in the Orange River must have originated in the high Maluti Mountains. Scott's company was granted a prospecting concession by the Paramount Chieftainess 'Mantšebo in the 1950s, and his early expeditions in 1958 proved the mountain held diamonds.

This news, combined with the site being declared a "government digging" in 1959, ignited a massive diamond rush. Throughout the 1960s, this remote, freezing, and inaccessible area was transformed into a "Wild West" frontier as thousands of local Basotho diggers flocked to the site. They endured primitive conditions, working small, individual plots with basic hand tools. By 1967, this chaotic period of artisanal mining, which involved up to 6,000 diggers, produced one of the world's most famous gems: the 601-carat Lesotho Brown, found by a local Mosotho woman, Ernestine Ramaboa.

This era of independent diggers was the one my father administered, grappling with the subsequent rise in illicit diamond buying (IDB). This period soon gave way to corporate interests, with companies like Rio Tinto and De Beers exploring the pipes with mixed success before the mine was closed in 1982. Reopened in 2004, Letseng is now legendary not for the *quantity* of its diamonds, but for their *extraordinary size and quality*, having produced some of the largest and most valuable stones ever found, including the Lesotho Promise and the Lesotho Legend.

DIRETLO (MEDICINE MURDER)

Just as the diamond trade represented a struggle for Lesotho's economic soul, the chilling phenomenon of *diretlo* spoke to its spiritual and political tensions. Often translated as medicine murder, it represents a dark undercurrent in the region's history, a practice entirely distinct from murder committed in anger or for simple gain. Its core belief is that human body parts, harvested from a living victim to capture their vitality, can be used by a traditional doctor (*ngaka*) to create powerful medicines (*muti*) that imbue the user with strength, protection, and success.

Historically, and during the period of the 1960s, these horrific acts were often tied to traditional structures of power—a chief seeking to fortify his village against rivals, to ensure bountiful harvests, or to win a land dispute.

I hope you have enjoyed this journey into the world of *The Lesotho Diamond*, where the promise of love and riches is set against the backdrop of this potent and complex history. For more stories and behind-the-scenes adventures, please visit my blog at https://beverleysbooks.com/en-au/blogs/my-adventures.

WINGS OVER AFRICA SERIES

From the snow-dusted peaks of 1960s Lesotho to the lion-haunted floodplains of 1980s Botswana, the *Wings over Africa* series tells sweeping, emotionally charged stories of love, danger, murder, and survival beneath vast African skies.

WHISPERS IN THE KALAHARI (Book 1)

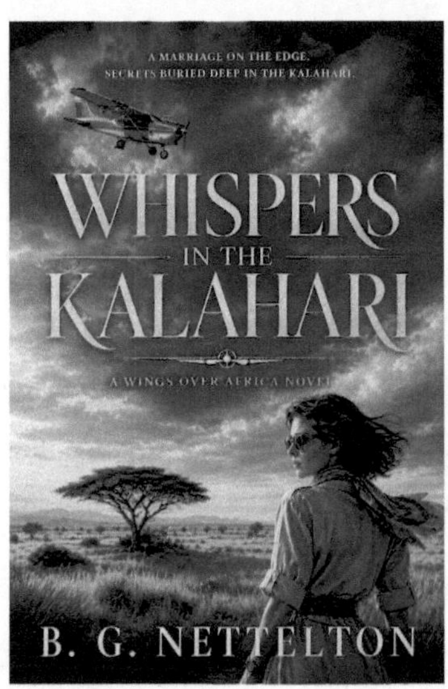

In **_Whispers in the Kalahari_** (1989, Botswana), a bush pilot's wife, adrift after an airline dispute shatters her life, must confront a fractured marriage, a long-buried death on a remote safari camp, and the brutal shadow of a poaching ring before she can reclaim herself.

Perfect for readers who love atmospheric, Africa-set fiction where the wilderness is as powerful and unpredictable as the human heart.

WINGS OVER THE OKAVANGO (Book 2)

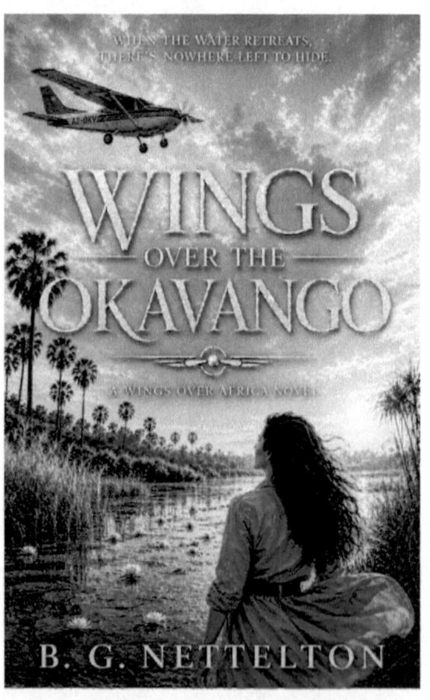

1996, Botswana

Six years after discovering who her father really is, Angie returns to Maun with a broken heart and no intention of staying. But when a wealthy hunter dies and suspicion falls on her father, Starky Willis, she is drawn into a dangerous web of secrets, betrayal, and old wounds.

And when the bush pilot she once loved steps back into her life,

Angie must decide whether to trust her heart before the truth turns deadly.

THE LESOTHO DIAMOND (Book 3)

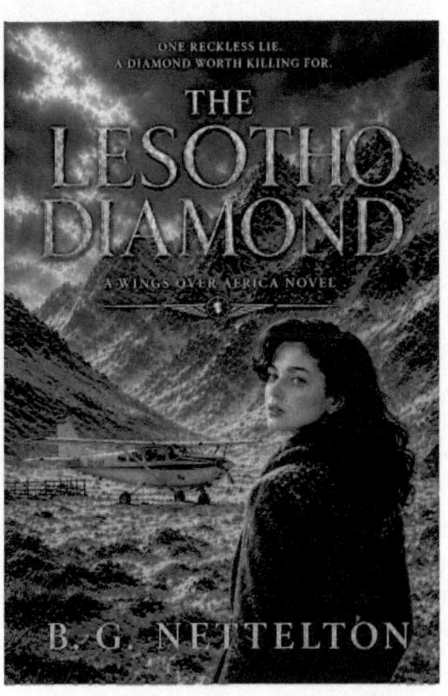

In **The Lesotho Diamond** (1962, Lesotho), a forced landing, a reckless lie about a marriage, and a cache of illicit diamonds entangle a District Commissioner's daughter and a bush pilot in a deadly web of blackmail and forbidden love in an African mountain kingdom on the brink of change.

Perfect for readers of Wilbur Smith's epic African adventures and Kate Quinn's character-driven historical sagas.

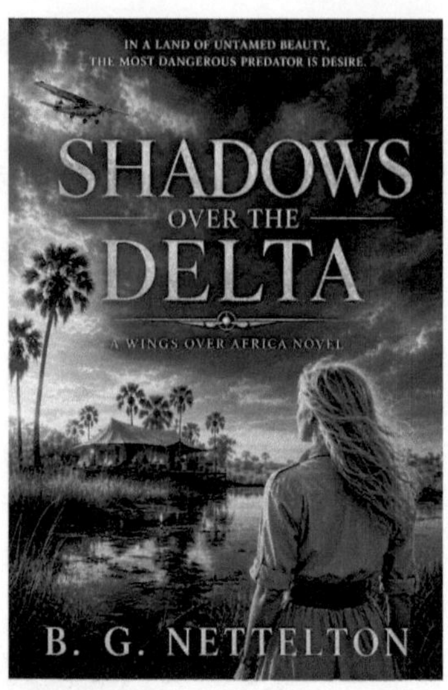

The mystery of Starky Willis began long before the Kalahari.

At a remote safari lodge in the Okavango Delta, Lucy Brennan falls under the spell of a man haunted by rumours of poaching, scandal, and a fifteen-year-old death.

Read **Shadows over the Delta**, the irresistible prequel to **Whispers in the Kalahari**.

Drawn from the author's own real-life experiences managing a luxury safari lodge in Botswana's Okavango Delta.

THE MEMOIRS THAT INSPIRED THE FICTION

THE NOVELS IN THE 'WINGS OVER AFRICA' SAGA ARE FICTION, BUT they are deeply rooted in incredible true events.

They were directly inspired by the real-life memoirs of my father, S.E. "Ted" Nettelton, who grew up in Botswana in the 1930s and 40s, and served as a District Commissioner in colonial Lesotho in the 1960s. For readers who wish to dive deeper into the true history, here are the original memoirs that inspired it all.

GROWING UP IN BOTSWANA IN THE 1930S AND 40S (TALES OF ADVENTURE IN COLONIAL AFRICA BOOK 1)

by Spencer 'Ted' Nettelton

Spencer 'Ted' Nettelton grew up in Botswana during the 1930s and 40s when herds of wildebeest stretched across the horizon and locally shot game was part of the staple diet.

In Volume I of his memoirs, Ted describes the daily life of an adventurous boy living in the bush, and the impact on his family when caught in the spotlight of international events.

From the banishment of Botswana's King Seretse Khama - later elected Botswana's first president - to the birth of a new African nation - Lesotho - Ted and his family played integral roles.

Educated in Cape Town, Ted followed his father into

the British Colonial Service, was posted to the mountains of Lesotho in the 1950s, organised the country's Independence Celebrations a decade later, and then served as Secretary to Lesotho's first democratically elected Prime Minister, Leabua Jonathan, with whom he enjoyed an enduring friendship.

Paperback (Colour) ISBN: 978-0-6486221-9-2

Case Laminate hardcover ISBN: 978-0-6486506-0-7

WORKING IN THE COLONIAL SERVICE IN LESOTHO (1952-69) : TALES OF ADVENTURE IN COLONIAL AFRICA

by Spencer 'Ted' Nettelton

Book 2: Tales of Adventure in Colonial Africa

During the 1960s, Lesotho gained its independence and the Basotho people elected their first Prime Minister

In Volume 2 of his memoirs, Spencer 'Ted' Nettelton reflects on the momentous changes he witnessed during nineteen years working in Lesotho as a District Commissioner in the British Colonial service. In 1966, he organised Lesotho's Independence Celebrations before serving as Secretary to the country's first democratically elected Prime Minister Chief Leabua Jonathan.

Accompanying Leabua to the US where the prime minister delivered his first address to the United Nations General Assembly, Ted and the PM were guests of President Lyndon Johnston at the White House during a hugely successful tour of the country.

Supported by dozens of contemporary newspaper clippings, Ted describes the masterful juggling act of an astute prime minister at the helm of a newly independent African nation landlocked by apartheid South Africa.

From Constitutional crisis on the eve of Independence to the machinations employed by Russia, China and South Africa to gain influence in the strategically positioned country, Ted's memoir provides a snapshot of daily life and a broader picture of a bygone era punctuated by medicine murder and illegal diamond buying overlaid by the irrepressible spirit and strength of the Basotho people amongst whom he had many good friends.

Paperback (Colour) ISBN: 9780648650614
Case Laminate (Hardcover) ISBN: 978064840599

ESCAPE BACK TO THE OKAVANGO WITH A FREE PREQUEL

Escape to the Okavango Delta, where love, danger, and secrets stalk the night.

Join my readers' list and get a free copy of **Shadows**

over the Okavango— the prequel to *Whispers in the Kala-hari*—delivered straight to your inbox.

Meet Lucy, a woman running from the wrong man into the arms of a dangerously charismatic hunter, and discover the truth about Starky Willis long before Verity ever sets foot in Botswana. If you enjoy emotional, Africa-set romantic suspense with bush planes, campfires, and lions in the dark, this one's for you.

ACKNOWLEDGEMENTS

I grew up amidst the Maluti Mountains—in Mokhotlong at above ten thousand feet—that form the backdrop for Philippa's story. However, it was in the beautiful wetlands of Botswana's Okavango Delta that I met my husband, a handsome Norwegian bush pilot who'd been flying there for some years.

When I handed my darling Eivind Eikli—now my husband of more than thirty years—my first attempt at a novel (on a floppy disk, no less!), we were preparing to part ways. After working as a safari hostess, I was supposed to be returning home to South Australia to marry my boyfriend of eight years. Instead, Eivind became my rock, the unwavering support, and the greatest champion of my writing ambitions I could ever have wished for.

Standing aboard the *Achille Lauro* as we left the docks at Cape Town watching Table Mountain grow smaller, I thought of the Maluti Mountains of my childhood, and the beginnings of this book began to germinate. This surprise 'practice honeymoon' that Eivind had secretly arranged was a nostalgic reminder of what it's like to live with majestic mountains in view, for there are no mountains where we live in Melbourne, Australia.

As a side-note, the *Achille Lauro*—already notorious for being hijacked by terrorists in 1985—sank on on the next leg of its voyage, just after we disembarked, a tragedy that resulted in several casualties.

I also want to acknowledge my critique partners and wonderful writers in their own right—Lexi Greene and N. D. Campbell—whose keen eyes for story structure and talent for honing the elements of romance and suspense played such an important role in shaping *The Lesotho Diamond*.

Writer friends from The Saturday Ladies Bridge Club were also stalwart in their encouragement and belief in this book.

My editor, Carla Molino (writing as Cathless Ross), did an amazing job highlighting the story's deficiencies while celebrating the parts that worked. She sent me into my final rewrite with genuine enthusiasm—a wonderful counter-point to the despair I felt fifteen years ago during a research trip to Lesotho in 2010, when I lost 30,000 words forever. My iPad, in the back of a Land Rover going up the Sani Pass, had something heavy placed on it, causing every jolt to delete a few more paragraphs.

And if you've read *The Lesotho Diamond*, you'll know there are many jolts involved in that nine-kilometre jour-ney, which, in 1962, took four hours to reach the 2,876-metre (9,436-foot) summit on the Lesotho border.

There are so many others whose belief in this story and in me as a writer have infused the project with joy, but my greatest inspiration were my parents, Gail and Ted Nettel-ton. Their extraordinary lives in Mokhotlong—the British

Empire's remotest outpost—became the blueprint for my own adventurous life.

Mum's stories of 1950s parties and university balls, of zipping around Pretoria in a cream Austin Healey Sprite before she met Dad with his British Racing Green MG, were a great inspiration for the life Philippa, in this book, aspired to.

Mum's car was later replaced by a Land Rover when they married and she followed him to Lesotho to embrace a dramatically different life. Dad served as District Commissioner in both Maseru and Mokhotlong during the early 1960s, and the meticulously documented details from his memoirs, *Working in the Colonial Service in Lesotho (1952-1969)*, underpin my fictional attempt to capture the contrasting worlds of their lives.

Great storytellers and adventurers both, they gave me not only the DNA for adventure but the happy elixir that has coloured my entire life. *The Lesotho Diamond* is, in part, my attempt to thank them for this extraordinary gift.

About Whispers in the Kalahari

CHAPTER ONE

Maun, Botswana, 1989

Susan sat alone at the bar, nursing her third vodka and lime, wondering what madness had brought her to this Wild West saloon in the middle of Botswana.

It wasn't because she'd seen the writing on the wall at her dreary copywriting job in Johannesburg when James had mentioned there was a position going here.

There were far more salubrious places to further a career than this dorp, with its perpetual dust, its heat haze shimmering above battered Land Cruisers and pickups, and the smell of spilled beer, sweat and avgas drifting in whenever the door swung open.

Catching the appreciative eye of a khaki-clad stranger jostling through the crowd with a handful of Castle Lagers, she sent him a sultry look as she adjusted her cleavage. He wasn't bad-looking. Mid-thirties, perhaps—a little older than herself—dressed in the ubiquitous bush gear that failed to distinguish hunters from safari guides, or the pilots servicing the safari boom, shuttling tourists between camps in the flooded Okavango Delta like a taxi service.

She watched him dispense his alcoholic burden. Sweat darkened the cloth between his shoulder blades. Two days' stubble. Floppy, dirty-blond hair. Funny how she was always attracted to the same type.

She ought to have learned by now.

"Susan?"

She swung around, disappointed. Hunter Dude had looked as though he was heading her way, but someone else had cut in.

"James!" Of course she'd known she'd bump into her cousin within a day of arriving, but his timing was less than perfect. "What a surprise!"

"What are you doing here, Susan? You should have let Verity and me know you were coming!"

"Oh, I'm not visiting. I'm here for good." Susan curved her lips into a secretive smile, not just for James' benefit, for she could still see Hunter Dude from the corner of her eye. And he definitely had his eye on her too.

"The job on the *Okavango Observer* you told me about," she clarified at James's questioning look. "I was already sick of life in the big smoke, and when you mentioned the reporter's job, I acted on a wing and a prayer and decided to come home."

"Impulsive as ever. But Maun has never been home, has it? Not after we were kids in Serowe?"

"No, I meant Botswana in general. I'm a bush girl at heart." Susan picked up her vodka and drained it. "I'm hoping I'll feel the same in a month."

"You and me both. And, of course, I hope so much that Verity will feel the same, soon, too!" said James, looking momentarily stricken as he signalled to the barman for another vodka for her and three beers for himself.

"It'll come back quick smart for you. You grew up here," Susan said. "Verity might be a harder nut to crack. Especially after what happened to Saskia. I wondered if they'd both be on the first plane back to Australia after that ghastly attack. Sorry, I should have asked how Saskia is. God, I'm hopeless." She took another sip, then added, "Though I did know she's okay, otherwise Angie would have told me. I gather the cousins have become firm friends at St Anne's. Of all the coincidences. Who'd have thought?"

"And who'd have thought you were old enough to have a fifteen-year-old daughter at all, much less one going to the same boarding school as Saskia." James looked about to say more when a shout from the back of the bar pulled his attention away. "Sorry, Susan, I've got to get these to the thirsty throng. You okay on your own for now? Waiting for someone?"

Susan smiled. "Always waiting," she said, dressing up the painful truth with a flippant laugh.

Like maybe Hunter Dude next, she thought, as James disappeared into the crowd.

But Hunter Dude had vanished into the jostling mass, so her gaze roamed over what other possibilities this frontier saloon might yield. Overall, the prospects were far more to her liking than the suits who congregated at the bars she used to frequent in Jo'burg.

Her eye settled on the khaki-clad back of a man of decent height, broad-shouldered, sleeves rolled to reveal biceps that made her insides quiver. Dirty-blond hair. No, not Hunter Dude, but—

"Lady's bounty!"

She stilled, poised for him to turn, ready with her best

smile. But he was making a play for some ridiculously young blonde backpacker by the look of her—yes, you could spot them a mile away—brandishing a carved elephant he'd no doubt picked up for a song from one of the traders. In answer to the girl's unintelligible question, as she squealed with delight, he said, "Yes, of course I carved it," accompanying the lie with a theatrical wink.

She should have known it was him by the performance, if not by the words themselves.

Heat flooded her body. Red-hot rage. Shame.

Every emotion under the sun except any that were good.

Goddamn womaniser, Starky Willis.

She should have known she'd bump into him on her first day in this godforsaken dump.

It was why she'd come here, after all.

Not on impulse.

Not on a wing and a prayer.

No.

She'd come here for something far more calculated.

Vengeance.

Get it HERE!

ABOUT THE AUTHOR

Planes and books are amongst Beverley Oakley's great passions. Her earliest memories are of the single-engine Cessna 206 that flew her to medical appointments from the bottom of her garden located at 10,000 feet in the African mountain kingdom of Lesotho.

So perhaps it wasn't surprising that she married the handsome Norwegian bush pilot she met while managing a luxury safari lodge in Botswana's beautiful Okavango Delta several decades later.

Trading her job as a journalist on a South Australian metropolitan daily — the safari hostessing had been a side-line adventure — meant life was never the same again as she and her husband worked in aviation across twelve countries and many more towns and cities.

It was here that Beverley's childhood dream of becoming a writer found its genesis. Arriving in a new town or country can be lonely, and it was also lonely, at times, being the only female crew member in Namibia, Greenland, or French Guiana — until she started to create her own worlds and cast of characters.

With 40 historical romances to her name, Beverley now divides her time between "Wuthering Heights," the dog-friendly South Australian bed and breakfast and farmstay she runs with her two sisters, and her Melbourne home, where she enjoys her husband's company—when he's not flying the world.

She also makes regular trips to Norway, where their two daughters are studying.

Beverley crafts Africa-set romantic suspense under her maiden name, B. G. Nettelton, romance under her pen name Beverley Oakley, and non-fiction under her married name, Beverley Eikli.

You can read more at www.beverleysbooks.com, or:

Visit her website, see her full range of books

Or say hi on her Facebook page or at https://www.insta gram.com/bgnettelton_author/

If you enjoyed this story, a rating or review would be very appreciated. It helps the author by making the book visible to others.

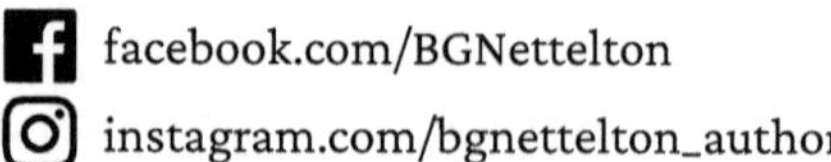

facebook.com/BGNettelton

instagram.com/bgnettelton_author

www.ingramcontent.com/pod-product-compliance
Lightning Source LLC
Chambersburg PA
CBHW050946210726
48287CB00004B/1160